Evelynish

Brian B. Hawthorne

INCLUDES

"CAGE KITTENS OF HYPERSPACE!"
AND "DAYBREAK"

LitPrime Solutions
21250 Hawthorne Blvd
Suite 500, Torrance, CA 90503
www.litprime.com
Phone: 1-800-981-9893

Published by LitPrime Solutions   09/26/2022

ISBN: 979-8-88703-053-1(sc)
ISBN: 979-8-88703-054-8(hc)
ISBN: 979-8-88703-055-5(e)

Library of Congress Control Number: 2022916838

Contents

Evelynish

Brian B. Hawthorne

Doctor Tenerife Brandon observed the animation closely. There was a clue here if she could just figure it out.

"What are you studying, Mom?"

Dr. Brandon sat back, relaxing for a moment. She looked to her left, where her daughter stood just a small step away. As usual, Evelyn was only half dressed, if even that.

Evelyn was wearing sandals and a painting smock. She looked like an under-dressed house elf, for the smock came only to the middle of her bare buttocks. Reaching out, "Ten" brought her daughter into a hug, tenderly caressing that little bare butt.

"This is an animated version of a time-lapse demonstration of wound healing. When you speed it up like this, it looks as though wounds disappear in a miraculously short period of time."

Ten noticed that Evelyn was bouncing on the balls of her feet. Moving her hand up a bit, she felt the artfully linked metal band of Evelyn's favorite ornamentation, a thong garment without fabric, around the girl's diminutive waist, which held a cute little smiley-face in position over her primary sexual characteristic.

Evelyn had been a tightly strung bundle of nerves growing up. As she was approaching sevenish, she had been at sixes and sevens. She had been like a taut and vibrating harp string, full of energy and nervous tension. Doctor Brandon recognized, now, that this behavior had been triggered after the divorce. She knew intimately the effects that the separation had had on her, but the way it had affected Evelyn was as if she had fallen off a cliff. Initially, the child was patient and calm. Slowly, that changed.

As the absence of a male parent became an increasing factor in their small family's relationship, the child needed more and more attention and understanding, at a time when the new doctor's schedule was stretched unnaturally tight. Being a young mother, with little experience to guide her, Tenerife had struggled. Enriching the child's environment, the recommended procedure, could only do so much. Toys and books, new clothing and entertainments, provided merely a momentary respite from the little girl's requirement for guidance and companionship. A sibling or replacement husband was out of the question.

Doctor Brandon had become quite desperate to find some way to either calm her only daughter somehow, or to harness her overabundant energy. Finally, in a quiet celebration, Ten had given her a tiny instrument to help harness and focus her intensity.

It was, if truth should be known, a dildo. Most children would not be ready for such perversions, but Evelyn had caught her mother using one, and no explanation short of experimentation would satisfy the child that it was not pain she had seen on her mother's face.

Every few months, Ten would update and resize the insertable device. By now, she was on the fourth generation, and was very nearly ready for devices of a more standard size. The slow accommodation had allowed Evelyn to grow into her "calming" exercise without stress or discomfort. Being a doctor prevents one from making ordinary excuses. Unfortunately, it also opens unconventional paths to vexing problems.

Ten sighed. "You are so full of bounce."

Evelyn looked over at her mother, and let her eyes roll up in their sockets as if she were about to pass out.

Ten leaned over and kissed the girl on the lips, holding the kiss and bending her backward as if in romantic conquest.

Evelyn smiled, perfectly at ease to be held off-balance like this. Her mother had shared with her a special and wonderful joy, and she trusted her to never cause harm.

"I feel very alive, Mother."

"I'll bet you do. You bounce all over the house. I'll wager there's not an ounce of fat on you anywhere." She reached under the smock with her right hand and moved it gently over the taut skin of the girl's belly, tickling her.

Evelyn giggled and straightened up. "I wouldn't have anyplace to put it, Mom. I can barely bend into the right dance positions now."

Ten laughed. "You bend in ways I can only envy! I'm glad you're keeping up with the dancing."

Evelyn smiled again.

Dr. Brandon turned back to her screen, still moving her hand along Evelyn's side from her leg to her ribs. The girl craved affection, and thrived in its presence. "I'm trying to determine a correlation between robotic surgery and the rate of wound healing."

Evelyn watched the animation as it looped once again. "Robots can heal their wounds?"

"What? No." Dr. Brandon said. "Robots don't heal. The robots are the surgeons doing the surgery. Then the patients have to heal from the cuts that are made, but they don't heal as fast as they sometimes do from natural injuries. It's that difference that I'm studying."

"Oh, too bad. I'll bet if robots could heal, they could do it even faster than that." She nodded toward the screen, where the time-lapse effect was showing the healing occurring at a prodigious rate.

"I suppose. I guess it's something to think about." Dr. Brandon looked again at her daughter. "Besides that, are you trying to tell me that it's time to come to dinner?"

Evelyn nodded. "Yep. Rosita said come whenever you're ready."

"Well, that means that it's time to come now. Let's go eat!" Dr. Brandon shut down the program, saving it for later perusal. Her daughter's observations had been interesting too.

Rosita smiled to see them arrive for dinner, with an undercurrent of disapproval at Evelyn's casual state of dress. She had previously spotted the smiley face in its inappropriate place that Evelyn wore constantly. She thought the expression on it looked a little devilish.

Luckily, she had never said anything to Evelyn about it, or the spunky girl might have tried to find a way to make the device even more apparent. At least Rosita had no idea how devilishly involved the little face was being.

In a household of only women, however, her concern gained little traction.

Rosita worked from seven o'clock to three in the afternoon, which gave her time to do the necessary cleaning, laundry, and the meal preparations for breakfast and dinner.

Her presence also permitted Doctor Brandon to continue her medical career of consulting and advising on various boards around the State, without having a problem with the fact that Evelyn was being home-schooled.

Many afternoons, and even the entirety of some weekends, Evelyn never saw her mother at all. Doctor Brandon considered it a precarious situation, but it was the best arrangement that she had been able to contrive, and she worked hard to keep her family life very private.

For reasons such as these, Evelyn had discovered that she could get away with some surprisingly mischievous behavior. Still, in her own opinion at least, she was a very sweet and mannerly girl. Even she admitted, however, that her fashion sense was disturbingly twisted.

But she got away with it anyway.

After dinner, Rosita cleaned up and said her goodbyes.

Evelyn went back to her studio, and her current "art" project.

And Ten went back to her program, although she sat in silence for a long time thinking about how robots could be made to heal. Evelyn's observations were often more helpful than even the other adults in her research groups. Intellectually, the child seemed more mature than most adults.

Chapter Two

Doctor Brandon was trying a different approach to her study. She had already looked at speeding up time-flow as a means of comparative analysis. Now she was using scale, physical size, as a magnifying factor.

It had come out of Evelyn's casual query about robots being able to heal. Like many scientists, Ten considered the current crop of robots to be little more that overgrown metal insects.

So she was imagining insects and what they do when trying to heal.

Essentially, they can't. Insects have a very primitive form of self-repair and immune response. If robots were to incorporate "healing", they would have to become more like colonies or hives of large numbers of individual components.

Necessarily, each component would have to be flexible enough to become whatever it needed to be to satisfy that section's requirements for accomplishing the robot tasks.

If, for example, the robot had the general task of checking for bombs, and something happened to its drive mechanism, then rather than having a robot stuck in a doorway, or on a stairway landing, or if some bad guy took a pot-shot at it, that robot would simply collect up the damaged components like a hive of honeybees, and send in replacements to take over and restore function in the specific area or purpose.

The robot would fix its track mechanism, repair its motor, and seal up its fuel tank, by … well, let's call it "healing".

Ten had seen videos and presentations about robot "teams" working together for overcoming obstacles and such, but this was on an entirely different size and numbers dimension. It was almost the equivalent of nanometer scale robots and other hypothetical medical devices.

Rather than think about the programming of such tiny things, Ten considered how their interlinkages might work. Obviously, like ant-colonies in the rainforest, the hordes of tiny robots would have to "link arms" together. More likely they would use something like crab pincers or insect appendages.

And the robot itself would have to have a standard design, with programming coming in only after it had been constructed and assigned to a task. That meant that programming, at which she was only minimally competent, was the last consideration of how to build such a thing.

The first part would be the robot individual component, essentially a shrunken hive insect executed in metal and silicon. These things would be *tiny*, and able to link together like living chains, or to assemble into rods or sheets of material, perhaps even closely enough to contain liquids, or form long strands of high strength steel wire, even binding into cables!

But because each had the ability to change its own shape minutely, the whole assortment of them would be able to move, to pull on the cable, or wrap around an object, and to grow or re-grow the physical structure of a part that had been damaged.

Then; she realized, *then* the robot would be able to heal.

In her after-dinner reverie, Ten was very nearly dozing, picturing the minuscule crab-like shapes plugging themselves together like a self-assembling jigsaw puzzle, forming sheets and towers, and connecting them with cables of moving, squirming, discrete components.

The crab would jiggle its protrusion into its neighbor, then stuff an arm in to lock the connection together. Each one had an addressing mode telling it where in the total structure it was, so that after so many iterations of sheet building they would begin to form a tower.

Each one would have integer counters set into it, presumably in the near equivalent of quantum computers, for counting positions, iterations, directions, and durations. Each individual one would have its own identification, and these numbers would be huge.

The skin of each one would have panels of transparent gem scales, in ever-thinner layers, so that a particular color could be developed on the upper or lower surface of each individual. Each would be a single pixel for the overall structure, and the high-definition would be as large as she might care to assemble it.

They would *tile* themselves! The overall structure could take on any appearance characteristic she chose!

Ten thought about how such a huge amount of individuals could be programmed and addressed, and how wonderful it would be if this cage of flexible structure could simply open itself up to a collection of biological cells like an on-board pilot, so that messages could be sent to the neighbors and down-stream as the organism/structure formed. No, not pilots but passengers, each to its own storage bin so that biologically produced chemicals could be brought directly and sequentially to the surface they were working on.

Doctor Brandon startled herself awake, but the images and the overall concept remained fixed in her memory, as if she had been visited by an epiphany.

She started an entirely new program, while the imagery was fresh in her mind. Her computer program, which incorporated elements of game theory and structure, was very helpful in getting the shapes right so that they could interlock and connect facing optical surfaces so that program messages could be passed along throughout the entire structure.

Her tiny robots would be able to form any structure, and all of it would be addressable, but the real elegance would come from being able to send the light in different directions, for communications processing as well as camouflage and surveillance.

The trick was going to be selecting the right construction materials and techniques, and designing the switching optical processors on the appropriate scale. That would depend on the materials available, and how she could design tiny robots with sufficient power to cut and weld with chemicals and light, and to make more copies of themselves so that once started, the end result would be only days away!

Only robots working on this scale of size could build other robots of such tiny dimensions. More research would be needed to decide the final configuration, but then the problem would be the classic chicken-and-egg situation. She would have to build an interface to build the next-scale interface, and so forth.

But, my oh my, this was an exciting idea!

Evelyn had resumed her painting project. She was painting an imaginary garden of fantasy flowers, including pitcher plants, which were watering other plants already growing in potted containers, while tiny butterflies were exiting blossoms like school-children out for a playground adventure.

Vines were pulling on bell-shaped flowers, as if the garden itself was playing music.

Evelyn's painting smock was becoming an art project itself, catching small dabs of red and yellow as she danced merrily in front of the canvas, putting her energy into the picture as if her joy was the brush she used.

She was nearing completion, but she realized that the last few minutes had been a kind of nervous dancing that one saw in small children just before they would show a panicked expression.

She had to go to the bathroom!

Scurrying in to the closest bathroom, Evelyn tossed off her painting smock and sandals, and quickly divested herself of her little smiling friend.

A few minutes later, when she was more comfortable, Evelyn elected to take a quick shower. She had gotten into the habit of showering several times a day. This was one of the reasons she kept her hair rather short and used a pixie hairstyle. It simply required no time at all!

Cleaning and reinserting her dildo appliance, Evelyn wrapped the towel around herself and went in search of her mother.

As before, Evelyn approached her mother soundlessly and studied what she was doing before announcing her presence. She toweled her hair once more before laying the towel over the back of the recliner.

Brushing her hair down with her fingers, Evelyn moved up to where she could see the screen over her mother's shoulder.

She stood there for a few moments sorting out the images she was seeing.

"Is that some kind of taxicab you're building?"

Ten looked over her shoulder. Reaching out, she beckoned the child to approach, and pulled her up on her lap.

"You're going to get cold walking around like that." She said, rubbing Evelyn's arms a bit. "You should be wearing something warmer."

"Yeah, but then I wouldn't get to sit in your lap."

"Good thinking." Ten kissed her. "No, it's not a taxicab. It's a new style of robot. It's supposed to be able to connect together like a train car, and form robotic structures to be able to do different tasks."

"Oh, robots. They look kinda cute."

"How can they look cute? They don't even have a face."

"Well, it's sorta a face, if you think about those two humps there as eyebrows, and this thing at the bottom as a tongue sticking out. Who's going to make them?" Evelyn snuggled down more while Ten rubbed her hip and thigh.

"Oh, I don't know. I thought I might."

"Really? Cool! What will you be able to do with them?"

"I'm not sure. If I get it right, there may not be much I *can't* do with them, but that will depend on being able to build them in the first place, and then figuring out how to control them."

"I'll help you. I know you can make all kinds of things, and I like the things you make."

"All right. The first thing we need to figure out is how big, or actually how small, to make them, and then how the first robots can make more of them."

"Remember to put a stop switch in, so they'll know when to stop."

Ten stopped moving her hand. "That's a good idea." She looked at the girl. "It's a *very* good idea."

"Well, sure. Everybody knows how monsters happen." Evelyn looked up at her.

"True. I would be a very bad doctor if I made a new cancer."

"Well, you're a good doctor. You may be a mad scientist, but you're a good doctor."

"Why would you say I'm a mad scientist?" Ten looked at the girl in surprise.

Evelyn said nothing, but slowly raised her hand and pointed downward.

"Ah, yes. Good point. We shouldn't talk about that, though."

Evelyn zipped her fingers across her mouth and smiled.

Doctor Brandon looked back at her computer screen. If she scrunched up her eyes a little, she could almost see a face.

"How big will they be?"

Ten raised her eyebrows. "Not sure. Somewhere between too small to see, and bigger than a buckyball."

"Oh. That is tiny then." Evelyn looked up. "Are you going to use them inside people, to do operations?"

"Hmm. I could, maybe. What kind of operations?" Ten smiled.

"The kind of operations that only mad scientists do, obviously." Evelyn said with conviction. "Maybe you could use them to help people heal."

Doctor Brandon looked at her daughter in frank incredulity. "That is a fantastic idea! How in the world did you come up with that!"

"Sheesh! It's obvious, isn't it? You were talking about wound healing, how long it takes, then we talked about 'healing robots', and now you're going to make them. What else would you do with something too small to see except use it in an operation?"

Ten hugged her daughter, and then set her upright. "All right, go get your pajamas on, or go to bed. It's still wintertime, and you can't run around naked in the wintertime."

"But mom! I'm not naked; I'm wearing a smile!" She smiled, and put on her brightest, cutest expression.

Ten looked at her again. She was standing there without a stitch of clothes on, even if you counted the smiley-face dildo. Technically, she was wearing two smiles. By lexicographers construed, that meant that she was almost fully dressed.

Ten hugged her once more, gently fondling that little bare bottom. "Go and get dressed, before I spank that little butt to warm it up."

"Ooh, kinky!" Evelyn said while wriggling her eyebrows, but she scurried off. A bare-butt spanking was something to be avoided, after all.

Smiling, Doctor Brandon turned back to her program. This would complicate things, she was sure. Trying to figure out how these little robots could work in a biological medium was going to take even more analysis. Let's see; the manipulators would have to be able to cleave along the cell wall barrier, separating cells like shelling corn from a cob. But that would mean that certain chemicals or coatings would have to be applied from a storage location inside the little medi-bot. That might mean that they would have to be a few nanometers bigger, and clearly on a scale with individual cells.

Maybe cells could be taken internally within the device, carried somewhere else, and then re-deposited in the proper position to work in the new area. For that, though, she would need the equivalent of cell glue to hold them in place …

Chapter Three

"Doc! Hey, Doc!" The earnest young man was looking strangely at her. "You kinda faded out there. Are you giving up on me?"

Doctor Tenerife Brandon focused again on her surroundings. "I'm sorry, Mr. Littlefield. I was just following a chain of conclusions and evidentiary findings to a rather remote possibility. That's usually the sign of a researcher getting a little too personally invested in a procedure. I'd like to think that I was just trying to check off some research avenues that might be unproductive. We all do have to pick and choose, you know."

"Yeah, well that's what worries me. In the picking and the choosing, I might get tossed back into the cold reality of cold reality."

"Not quite yet. I have a few more tests and procedures I want to set up, if you're willing to be our guinea pig for just a little while longer."

"Not a problem at all, Doc. Go ahead and stick me with all the needles you want. It's better than anything else I've got lined up." The young man essayed his practiced fetching smile again, but Doctor Brandon gave it her usual neutral response.

In truth, he was a fine looking man in his early twenties. But Dr. Brandon knew what he had done to get incarcerated in the first place, and she knew the depths to which he could sink if he thought he could get away with it.

Her carefully neutral expression thoroughly masked, she hoped, some of the ideas she had rattling around in her thinking process. These next few weeks were going to require some very careful choreography, and some administrative details as well.

She returned to filling out the forms in front of her. These requests, unimpressive and mundane as they appeared, still constituted a bit of a Rubicon for her. This was a commitment assuredly, if not an impending disaster.

She smiled at him in her professional manner. "We'll see you again next week, Mr. Littlefield. Thank you for coming in."

Ten looked over at the rows of packaged items on the far wall of her sanctum sanctorum, her mad scientist's laboratory. One might be forgiven for thinking that it looked like an operating room, but one would never have been allowed to see it.

Six feet below the garage floor, a secret room had been constructed. She had, at the time, thought that it could perhaps serve as a "panic room" or emergency storm shelter in the case of an impending tornado or other natural calamity.

Maybe it simply represented a portion of her insecurity after her husband Gordon, Evelyn's father, had decided to leave her. The separation was moderately amicable. He was willing to give her almost anything to get out of their relationship, but it was painful at the time and still was. She had been a good wife, dammit! And Evelyn had been only three years old! She fumed mentally for a moment.

Ten took a few calming breaths. What she was committed to now had nothing to do with him; nothing to do with men in general, even if it might look like she had some score to settle. But of course, one would never be allowed to see that either.

Six feet below that level was an even more secret and secure facility. One might think it would make a fine prison, but only for those allowed to see it. Even when she was building it, she wasn't sure how she might ever find a use for it. Times change, they say.

This was science; cutting edge science, at that. She looked at the operating table. The cutting would be done there. A lot of cutting, as it turned out. Mr. Littlefield might not appreciate it, but this was, in addition to being science, a rescue operation.

Better that he take his chances on her experimental procedures than on the certainty of his likely fate in another twenty years of incarceration. He had been fortunate to avoid general population before, but that would no longer be the case.

Most sensible people would choose death over that possibility. Littlefield's crimes had been of the particularly unforgivable sort, especially among prisoners whose macho bravado was like a skin of armor.

However, Doctor Brandon was offering something a little better than death. Maybe. Disfigurement and captivity might not appeal to him, but it should be preferable to death.

She shook off her musings and concentrated once again on the procedure. A monitor was cycling, again, through a kind of time-lapse scenario: a before and after, if you will.

The actual surgery would involve disassembling and then reassembling a large portion of his lower anatomy, with tissues realigned and nerve connections carefully repositioned. It was microsurgery on a tremendous scale, with entire organ structures being fabricated, while others were discarded.

Everything within the limits from his nose to his toes was going to change. And that was just the first step, mere cosmetics. The rest of the procedure would be … monstrous.

"So, you remember some time ago, when I gave you a very special present?"

Evelyn smiled, jiggled herself energetically for a moment while standing in place, and said, "Yes! Yes, I do remember that!" Her eyes became a little unfocused for a moment, but her smile was quite enduring.

"Well, I have tried to come up with something better for your advancing maturity." Ten waited a moment for the meaning of that to sink in.

"*Better?*" Evelyn's eyes grew very large indeed. "What could be better than *that?*"

"I've brought you a pet." She could see immediately the disappointment in the girl's eyes. "Let me take you down and show you, but you can't play with him yet. You'll have to wait for your birthday, for that."

"What kind of a pet?" Evelyn did not sound very enthusiastic.

"Let me show you." They approached the secret lair together, activating the code that summoned the elevator.

Standing together in the thin tube, they were slowly lowered into the most secret part of the house, below even the laboratory with its medical devices.

"Close your eyes, and try to be quiet," Ten told the girl.

"All right, Mom." Evelyn closed her eyes and leaned back against her mother. The elevator stopped and Doctor Brandon moved them forward out of it.

"Open your eyes now."

Evelyn opened her eyes. Strapped securely onto a low cot was a handsome young man, perhaps in his twenties. A few remaining connections of intravenous tubing were flowing into his arms, and a connection on his forehead looked like an EEG attachment.

He had wavy brown hair, and wide shoulders. Elsewhere, his skin appeared to be entirely devoid of hair, and he was absolutely, gloriously, naked.

Not only that, but he was sporting a lovely, beautiful, full-engorgement erection, even with his eyes closed.

"Shhh! He's still healing from the surgery, and he's as asleep as I can make him. But I wanted you to see your birthday present, anyway, so that you will know what to do with him."

"Oh, he's just beautiful, Mom! Can I touch him?"

"Yes, but only very gently. I think two more days of healing will make him strong enough for us, but we should still go very slowly about introducing him to what we want to do with him. And we'll have to work up to it a bit ourselves as well. I have to admit, I'm a little out of practice."

"You said, 'What we want to do with him'. Well, what are we going to do with him?"

"What do you *want* to do with him? What do you want to do with your birthday present?"

Evelyn's eyes got big. "I want to … Ooh, I want to … Can I touch him? Oh I can't believe he's real!"

"Touch him, then. But be gentle, please."

Evelyn stepped forward. She walked over and looked at his face and smiled, then strolled down to stare at the magnificent penis. She reached out and touched the skin of his stomach. He did not react.

Evelyn stroked his skin and watched him. He lay very still.

"He is so still … but at least he's warm." She stared at the penis. "Wow!"

"Go ahead and touch it."

Evelyn reached out. Her hand delicately traced along the smooth skin of the penis. It moved slightly as she pushed against it. She wrapped her hand around it and traced her fingers up and down. It felt so different from an un-living dildo. It was so warm and nice!

"Will I be able to … " she looked at her mother. "Will I be able to put that inside me?"

"Yes, eventually. Not right away. I know you want to. I want to! But we'll have to make sure that everything is working properly first. I had to make a lot of changes."

Ten stepped closer. "Your new pet is nothing like any other man, or anything like what he was before."

"Appearances aside, he doesn't have what it takes to be a man. He no longer has the ability to make a woman pregnant, but more importantly, he no longer has the urge to try."

"It was probably that urge that got him in trouble with the law, for he forced himself on two little girls, raping them, and making them very hurt and very afraid for a long time. They may never be normal again. But he will never be normal again, either."

"He looks normal." Evelyn said.

"No." Ten smiled, "You haven't seen a man naked before. Normally, if you saw a sleeping man, even naked, he wouldn't have an erection like this. I have given your pet a *permanent* erection. It will never go down."

"Most men, if you play with their penis, it will rise up like this, and they will want to put it inside you, wriggle it around a lot, and then it's just like they're blowing their nose inside you. It feels better than that, but it's just as messy."

"And then, just after they've done that, they and their happy little friend lose all interest in you, and they're usually both ready to go back to sleep."

Ten placed an arm on Evelyn's shoulder. "But your pet is not going to be like that. His penis won't go up or down. It will just stay up. That means we can play with it, and play with him, for as long as we want. Go ahead and rub it some more."

"Be gentle, of course, but try to be stimulating. The penis is exquisitely sensitive, and I hope for his sake that I didn't damage anything that would take away from his pleasure. One of the things that will make him want to be nice to us is that we can bring him a lot of pleasure. That should make him be gentle and kind with us."

"Something you probably wouldn't have noticed is that his testicles have been removed. They're gone. Men are very sensitive about that, because it's easy to hurt them. Men have baby-making organs *outside* their bodies, and they hurt like the dickens when something hits them. Getting 'kicked in the nuts' is enough to knock a man down."

"He won't have to worry about that now. He can't be hurt like that anymore, and I've smoothed out his skin down there as if they never existed."

"You should be noticing that some slippery stuff is starting to come up out of the penis. That's a good thing! When we're moving up and down on him, he's going to keep us lubricated so that our movement feels really good! And don't forget that we can keep on moving as long as we want to! No matter how good it feels, we can still keep having more and more fun, until we decide to stop. Now that's a birthday present!"

Evelyn found that by now, the stuff was very apparent. It had begun to flow out and down along the penis and over her hand as well. It was warm and slippery, but she had no reason to think that it was nasty.

Her mother had explained about how the slipperiness would make everything better.

"There are still a few other things you are going to want to know, Sweetheart." Ten continued. "First off, taste that juice that's on your hand."

Evelyn licked her hand. It was sweet and even a bit minty. "Wow! That's like candy!"

"Yes, it is. That worked out even better than I thought it would, but I can tell you, a lot of science went into it!" She went over and brought a sample of the fluid to her own lips.

"The human body can put out a lot of different chemicals, mostly on the skin and as part of sweating. The trick was to get the parts that have a good flavor, and put them together in a new system to make the lollipop taste better!" She bent over the penis and began licking it.

"It's a lollipop?" Evelyn squealed.

"Try it!" Her mother encouraged her. "That's another way that we're going to make your birthday present glad to be your pet instead of being beaten up somewhere else. It gives him even more reason to be nice to us, because we can be really, really nice to him. And don't forget, he's attracted to little girls, so when you are, yeah, when you are doing *that*, he's going to *really* like *you!*"

"Now, one more thing. He's being kept asleep right now through hypnosis and chemicals to keep him knocked out. On your birthday, he'll wake up, and that's when you can come and play with him. We have to find out then how he feels, and whether he's hurting anywhere. That will be your job. I'll be monitoring remotely, but it's your birthday party, and you can let your party last as long as you want to."

"But he will also still be under a very strong hypnotic compulsion. I didn't want to take any chances with our safety, so anything you tell him to do, he will feel compelled to do. He won't be able to resist it. Whatever you tell him to do, he must do it! So don't tell him to do anything stupid, and especially don't tell him to hurt you, or *let* him hurt you."

"Wow! I can tell him what to do, and he'll have to do it! I have POWER!" Evelyn exulted.

"Yes. But you also have a new pet. Let me tell you about house-training your new pet."

And so they continued making preparations for the big day …

Chapter Four

alcolm Littlefield woke slowly in a room he had never been in before. "Crap!" he thought, "I've stuffed it."

The room itself was pleasant enough. Bright light, presumably daylight, filtered through the window on his right. A clock on the wall showed nine-thirty. It felt like morning. A calendar with removable pages showed the date as July seventh of 2018. Hell! It had been still June the last he remembered!

It looked a little bit like a hospital room, and a little like a bedroom. But his bed was anything but normal. It only supported him where his body rested, like a stripped-down recliner. It was as skinny as he was.

The clue that he was in trouble though, came from his arm positions. His arms were raised over his head and strapped into tubes like big plastic plumbing pipes. He wasn't handcuffed, but he couldn't move his arms or extract them.

His legs were similarly strapped down and trapped. Whoever had put him here would have to be the one to help him out.

A light cover was drawn over his torso, strangely elevated as if hoops of some kind were holding the fabric aloft. Was he a burn patient?

He felt … different. A little bit sore, but just generally. He could not place the pain or irritation in a specific spot. Maybe he had been operated on. Malcolm began to sweat mentally a bit. There was only one operation that might have been performed on him without getting his permission and understanding first.

Once more he began cursing his impetuous and foolhardy nature. His sexual fantasies and appetites had gotten him in trouble before he had figured out a way to avoid getting caught. As far as he was concerned, any pain or fright to others was their problem; his was having left too clear a trail.

He had already served three years for his crimes, out of a possible and expected twenty or more. Luckily, he had been selected for a program to "reprogram" his aberrant tendencies, and had spent more than a year working within that program to change himself into a more stable citizen.

Obviously, it hadn't worked. He had tried. He had co-operated. But they were scanning his brain in various ways while stimulating him in others. He had been chemically dosed, hypnotized, and PET-scanned until it seemed as though they had just decided to give up on him and ship him back. They knew his brain and how it worked, or didn't work, better than he did.

Malcolm hadn't wanted to go back, but he could not change what he was. Hell, he didn't know how to change! If the Doctors couldn't do it, how would he?

One doctor in particular seemed reluctant to surrender the concept of brain reprogramming, but even she had appeared downcast and defeated during their last interview. In fact, that was the last thing he remembered.

A movement caught his eye. In the corner of the room, a clear cylinder, which he had thought was a design element, was showing the descent of a circular platform. He saw feet coming into view. Feminine feet.

In astonishment, Malcolm watched as the rest of the girl came into view. She was naked!

The platform stopped, and the clear plastic rotated to allow the girl to step out. She smiled at him, and he realized that she was not *completely* naked. She wore sandals and a glittering golden bracelet on each wrist, and she had what might charitably be called a thong-style "G" string, made of a smooth linked metal band in a color about halfway between that of her skin and her hair. It concealed nothing, and the spot over her pubic region had a face design on it, like a cross between a Guy Fawkes mask and a smiley face, done in cream and a chocolate brown.

"Hello Uncle Huggy!" she smiled again, completely unconcerned about her state of dress. "I'm Evelyn."

"Do I know you?" Malcolm asked.

"No, not yet. You know my mother, though. She's a genius, and she's been your doctor for about a year. She's Doctor Tenerife Brandon."

"Where is she?"

Evelyn stood still and let her smile fade. "She's presenting a paper on the results of her recent study, and why it was such a colossal failure."

"Her recent study," Malcolm bit his lip. "That would be me."

Evelyn stepped closer. "Yep. Let me give you a rundown. Your program was terminated almost a month ago. You were having your results interview at the end of it, when you became violent, assaulted her, robbed her, and said you were heading for San Francisco."

"That didn't happen." Malcolm said. "I don't even know anybody in San Francisco."

"That's why they won't be able to find you there. It's a matter of record by now. You have disappeared from public view, but the police are looking for you."

Malcolm struggled lightly against his bonds. He was still very securely entrapped.

"I don't get it," he said.

Evelyn smiled and raised her arms to encompass the room they were in, "It's Plan B!" she said.

He simply watched and waited.

"You've been getting operations, pretty much around the clock, for almost the last month. A week ago, you were finished, and allowed to heal." She stepped up beside him, placing a hand on his forehead. "How do you feel?"

"Operations?" his eyes went frantic.

Evelyn nodded, smiling all the while. "Mom decided that the attempted procedures were inadequate. You were 'too far gone' in what motivated your deviant behavior."

Malcolm spoke softly, "Deviant behavior?" allowing himself the slightest glance down at Evelyn's nudity.

"Yes," she smiled, "that specifically. You are not very good at recognizing and observing the rules of civilized society."

"And you are?" Malcolm said with some bitterness.

"Oh, no, no, no!" Evelyn moved her hand to his shoulder, rubbing down to his chest. "This is what we meant by 'Plan B'; if you can't behave in your world, you can come and *misbehave* in ours."

She carefully drew off the light cover that concealed the rest of his body, casually removing and stowing the flexible hoops that had held it up over his lower torso, then folding the material and placing it on a shelf below his cot-like bed.

Malcolm looked down. Clearly visible at his crotch was a respectable erection. As he looked more closely, he realized that he had been thoroughly shaved.

He looked at the girl.

Watching his eyes, Evelyn spoke casually, "It's permanent."

"What's permanent?" Malcolm said with a catch in his voice.

"Everything! Your erection, your smooth hairless skin, your ability to have unlimited sex. It's all permanent!"

He shook his head in disbelief. "That's not possible! It isn't … you had no right."

"Snap out of it! You think you would have been better off back in prison for the next twenty years? Mom's got too much time invested in you to let you get flushed away like that. She's the one, the *only* one, who could have saved you from it. What you've given up is nothing compared to her effort in your behalf."

Malcolm rattled his bindings. They were still secure. "Wait, given up? What did I give up?"

"Well, there's good news and bad news, I guess. You won't have to worry about making anyone pregnant, and you won't ever have to shave again, *any*where. You also won't have to worry about getting kicked in the testicles again either. They're gone."

"They're gone? Wait, my *testicles* are gone?"

"Yeah. It's easier for you to stay calm now, and it's easier to keep your hair under control. You're going to be our pretty boy toy, so you need to be pretty, don't you?"

"Pretty? You're kidding, right?"

"Not at all. Mom said it a long time ago, just not to you. When she decided to steal you and modify you for our purposes, your being pretty for us was a big factor."

"I'm glad you found me suitable," Malcolm said bitterly.

Evelyn was rubbing his smooth, hairless skin from his shoulders to just above his knee. She smiled, "You'll like it better as you become more familiar with the benefits. It's better than being in prison."

Malcolm fell back. "Yeah, I guess so."

"How many times were you raped in prison?" Evelyn asked with quiet interest.

He glared at her.

"You're going to lose count of how many times *we* do it," she pointed out, as she continued stroking his skin in a possessive manner.

He looked at her. "You're going to rape me?"

"You're bound," she smiled. "I'm determined. Why not?"

He smiled ironically. "I don't think it means … what you think it means."

"You'll see." She said calmly. "Close your eyes."

Malcolm closed his eyes.

"Why did you do that? Why did you close your eyes?" Evelyn asked.

"You told me to," he responded.

"Do you always do what little girls tell you to do? Have you ever before?"

"No," Malcolm said slowly. "Why *did* I close my eyes?"

"Because you've been subjected to electro-hypnotic conditioning. When either my mother or I tell you to do something, you *will* do it. You can't *not* do it. It's a conditioned compulsion, almost as strong as the reflex that makes you draw back from a hot surface."

"Interesting," Malcolm observed, but not through using his eyes.

"Oh, yes. I think you will find it most interesting." Evelyn was moving her hand down Malcolm's chest, gently stroking the smooth skin and making circles all the way down to his hips.

She moved closer still, stroking his chest, abdomen, and inner legs with a smooth, delicate touch. "How does this feel?"

Malcolm moved gently, wriggling from the ticklish pleasure. "It feels good. I'm ticklish, I suppose. But it also feels … um, erotic I guess is the word. Are you sure you know what you're doing?"

"Hold still," she commanded, "I'm testing you."

He stopped moving, but tensed visibly.

Evelyn leaned down and licked his penis. It throbbed visibly as he responded.

She licked it again, pushing her tongue against it as if it were an ice cream cone. Malcolm arched upward.

Delighted to see him responding in such a positive fashion, Evelyn grinned as she began singing mentally to herself, 'Lollipop, lollipop …' She continued torturing him gently in this fun and delicious way.

Soon Evelyn placed her whole mouth over his penis, smoothly swallowing down as far as she could, moving her tongue and her lips as she bobbed up and down on it.

Unable to contain himself, Malcolm ejaculated into the girl's mouth. She began swallowed his offering as if she were slurping up a milk shake.

After a moment, she pulled away, keeping one hand on his still throbbing shaft.

Malcolm felt her lips on his, kissing him with the wetness she had extracted.

"Open your eyes," she said.

Malcolm opened his eyes.

"What does it taste like?" She asked.

He licked his lips. "It's sweet … minty. My God! Did that come out of me?"

Evelyn smiled, stroking his penis again to push out a dollop of creamy fluid. She brought this also to his lips to let him taste it.

"That's … that's impossible!" Malcolm blinked.

"I told you. My mom's a genius." She smiled. "Sweet boy, you are now our toy!"

He simply stared at her.

"Mom told me to be gentle with you. I know that sounds funny, you being a hardened criminal and all …" Suddenly her eyes opened wide and she started giggling. "I mean, um, I didn't hurt you, did I?"

"No. I'm not in any pain. I just can't figure it all out. Basically, I just woke up, after I was expecting to go back to prison, and I find that I've lost about a month."

He looked up. "Now you tell me that I've lost much more than that. I don't have body hair, permanently you say?"

She nodded. "No more shaving for you, and no more 'short and curlies', either. That's what Mom called them." She moved her hand around the base of his penis, where his skin was very smooth and hairless.

Malcolm looked slightly taken aback. This girl, though obviously quite young, was surprisingly blunt and plainspoken.

"And you really mean it about the testicles, too? I can't see them from this angle."

She nodded again, reaching under his penis to where testicles would have been, and stroking the smooth skin that replaced his former 'baggage'.

He closed his eyes again for a moment. "God that feels weird."

"I think you'll get used to it." She shrugged, gently trailing her fingers up from between his legs, along the base of his penis, and twirling them around its top.

Malcolm watched as it throbbed and responded to her touch. "You aren't very shy, are you?"

Evelyn smiled.

"What else was it you said? That I was going to be a 'pretty boy toy' for you and your mom?"

"Uh-huh, and that we were going to rape you repeatedly. I'd start now," the girl looked very intently into his eyes, "… but Mom told me that I had to be sure you were completely healed first."

"Aren't you a little …" he swallowed. "Well, you look kinda sexy and disturbingly aware, but do you really know what you're talking about? Oh, and thanks for the oral, um … thanks, anyway."

She studied him for a moment and then backed up. "A year or so ago mom gave me a special present, as therapy for being overly tense. She gave me SEX!"

Evelyn released a connection on the mask-face and extracted the thing that was connected to it. Slowly she pulled out from her interior a relatively large dildo, which she had been wearing internally all this time. Malcolm realized that it was fully as large as his own real equipment.

Evelyn shook the dildo, and then placed it against him.

Malcolm was shocked to feel it *vibrating!*

"Mom started giving me these over a year ago. They were much smaller then. It's kinda like getting braces on your teeth. Little by little, it changes the shape of your smile, and I guess having a vibrating dildo that gets wound up every time you bounce will do the same thing!" She giggled. "I get a lot of exercise too!"

"So now I'm big enough inside to let *you* inside me," She looked at him rather intensely as she placed the dildo near his erection for comparison. "*You're* my birthday present this year. Are you ready?"

Malcolm's eyebrows shot upward. He couldn't think of anything to say.

Evelyn put the dildo aside. "Mom changed you inside so that you would have a permanent erection. She had read a book that described such a person. Among other things, she used micro-surgical robotic techniques to give you modified internal organs, which produce that fluid as if you were producing seminal fluid. We'll look at some of the diagrams in a little while."

Evelyn looked intently into his eyes again. "You might think she acted as if she owned you." She smiled. "That's probably the best way to look at it."

She began stroking and caressing his groin area again, not embarrassed at all about being so intimate and familiar with him. "Are you sure you don't feel any pain?"

"I'm fine. You were saying …"

"So that means we can rape you as much and as often as we want to." She smiled at him as she tickled his stomach. "And you will be producing this fluid so we stay all smooth and liquidy."

Gently her tickling fingers stroked along his penis.

Malcolm stared at this phenomenon, perplexed that his erection was still fully engorged, and that it seemed almost ready to … He shivered, and looked back into her eyes.

She could feel him tensing again, and she reached over to press a button on her wrist bracelet.

Malcolm felt *himself* begin vibrating! The sensation was indescribable!

"Mom put that circuit in there too. It's like the device I wear, getting its energy from your daily motions."

That she could speak so calmly while this *fury* of delight was engulfing him only told Malcolm that her ability to actually *rape* him repeatedly was no idle boast.

Chapter Five

Evelyn finally released him from his captivity. Malcolm glanced over at the clock to note with astonishment that the time was still nine-thirty! Even the daylight coming in the window was indicating early morning!

Evelyn saw his glance and look of surprise. "This chamber is part of a time-stasis field. Since I'm celebrating my birthday, I've decided to celebrate it for maybe a week or a month or two. It's going to stay my birthday morning until I get tired of raping you."

Malcolm just looked at her in astonishment.

"All right, then. Over here is the bathroom. Let me show you something."

"You will no longer stand up to pee. Mom switched your inner workings around so that the pee goes down and the juice goes up." She smiled.

"Here, let me show you."

She activated a computer monitor and accessed a display. "This is the normal routing diagram of a man's penis. You'll notice that it is in a flaccid state."

"You'll also notice that the tube connecting the urinary bladder has to travel a long, long way to get to the tip of the penis. Well, we didn't want your pee to mix with your sweet juices, so Mom cut the tube *here*, and redirected it *down here*. A lot of your less-important sex organs had to be redesigned, reassigned, and realigned, but you won't have to think about any of it."

"You've got a new opening between the base of your penis and your butt-hole, where the pee can come out. All you have to do is sit down, and use the same muscles you always used when you want to pee. One thing that's different is that you'll have to do what we girls do, and wipe yourself off afterwards. That's cleaner anyway, and it keeps you from dripping like a slobbery dog." She led him into the bathroom and positioned him in front of the toilet.

Malcolm was standing there in total confusion.

"Sit down, Uncle Huggy," Evelyn said.

Malcolm sat.

"Now pee," she said, "you know you have to."

Malcolm stared down at his erect penis. At the same time, he could hear the unmistakable sound of water splashing below him.

Evelyn knelt before him and kissed his penis a time or two, giving it a lick as well.

"Now do you understand?" she said.

"Yes, thank you. Now I understand."

"Good." She responded. "Now wipe yourself and flush the toilet." She shook her head. "Boys, my god."

Malcolm chuckled and smiled at her. "You're still kinda short stuff, you know."

Evelyn looked up at him. "I can take *you*." She grinned.

"Now I want you to give me a bath, a very thorough bath. And I want you to get yourself clean as well."

Malcolm led her to the tub/shower unit and began his preparations.

"Mostly we're going to keep you naked, you know." Evelyn said casually.

Malcolm looked at her.

"Well, think about it. It would be … hard to cover up certain aspects of your shape, wouldn't it? Besides, when we want to rape you, we don't want any delay getting in our way."

Malcolm moved them into the warm water and began a thorough cleaning procedure. "So you think your mother is going to get into having her way with me too?"

"Most definitely. You're the way you are because she made you that way, and that's the way she wants you, wants you, wants you." She smiled. "I'm going to be watching you do it."

Malcolm got a puzzled but goofy look on his face.

"Maybe I'll hit the button when the time is right," Evelyn said.

"Ack!" Malcolm acted as if he had gotten some water down the wrong pipe.

Evelyn laughed.

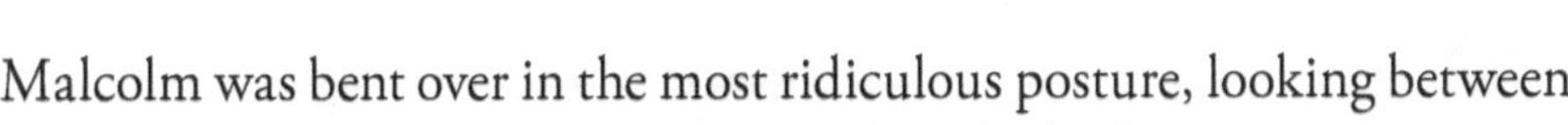

Malcolm was bent over in the most ridiculous posture, looking between his legs at the reflection of his rear end in the bathroom mirror.

Evelyn inspected his openings. "That's pretty clean, but you can probably do better. Don't make yourself sore though. Just soak it a bit longer, and then you can give it a good scrubbing."

He looked again at the base of his penis, where he had once had a scrotal sack, with occupants. There was now no evidence that it had ever been there. The skin below his penis was as smooth and featureless as that above. The entire area was devoid of hair.

She looked at his face, which was turning red. "You'll want to be as pretty as you can make yourself, you know, especially when Mom gets you for the first time."

"Are you going to be watching that one?"

"Maybe. I'll ask Mom about it; see what she wants." She looked at him. "Are you good at making love with grown-up women?"

Malcolm turned and sat on the bathroom floor. *"What?"*

"You got in trouble for going after little girls. It's a legitimate question."

"I thought we were friends."

"We *can* be friends. You're a criminal, Uncle Huggy."

"Hmph. I *was* a criminal." He looked thoughtful. "I got fixed." He looked at her.

Evelyn raised her eyebrows in surprise, and then they both burst into laughter.

"You know, I thought I'd miss them." Malcolm said.

"Your testicles?"

"Yeah. But now I don't have to be careful sitting down. I'm not going to hurt myself."

"You're less likely to hurt us, too. Do you feel more calm?"

"Maybe. It's kinda hard to tell. I don't get to meet a lot of people."

"Well, whose fault is that? You're just stuck up!"

Malcolm laughed and picked her up. He strolled with her into yet one more room in this place, which seemed to be a kitchen.

"You know, it occurs to me that I might have missed a meal or two."

They relaxed in the kitchen, snacking and each getting used to being naked in the presence of the other. It was surprisingly easy to do.

"So you've been wearing that gizmo most of the time for over a year?"

"Yeah. It's derived from something called Ben Wa balls. They're little things that women can stuff inside themselves and have moving around in there. We tried them, but I couldn't get the hang of it. Mom came up with the idea of a 'training dildo', and she put the vibration thing in it."

"Hard to think about her worrying about me being weird. My doctor."

"My doctor too. But you got in trouble for hurting people. That's different from just being weird; it's being mean."

"Yeah. I know." He got a distant look on his face. "Maybe these damn chemical things should be better controlled."

"Yes, they should be, but that's *your* job. As a man, you're supposed to figure out how to use the strength they give you, without hurting other people. Maybe we could teach *that* better."

"I guess some people do." He shrugged. "I'm glad I met you."

"We'll work things out. You're still in prison, you know."

"Yeah, in a way. Not a bad prison, though, as prisons go."

They were silent for a moment. Malcolm turned sideways, and looked down at himself.

"It's ugly, isn't it?" he said softly.

"What? No! Do you think boobies are ugly?"

"God, no! Breasts are beautiful … no offense, mind you."

She laughed. "Men are beautiful in a different way. They have sleek muscles and strength that appeals to a woman because she thinks they can protect her. Your penis is like a little machine, designed to do a job. It has a kind of elegance in its design, that a thumb or finger doesn't have." She looked into his face, "and let's not even mention *toes*."

He laughed.

Chapter Six

They moved the restraining cot out of the way, and brought in a proper bed. It was a small bed, but Evelyn and her mother had always intended the occupants to be cozy in it. Evelyn figured that all three of them could fit in it if they were being friendly, and she intended to be friendly.

"So what do we do now?" Malcolm asked.

"It's my birthday. What are you going to give me?"

"How about a happy face?"

Evelyn looked puzzled, then delighted. She collected her smiling dildo, and presented it to Malcolm.

He examined it, exclaiming over its fine construction. He noted that the connection that went up between her butt cheeks to a flat triangular plate, was a cable covered by a smooth vinyl tube for comfort. Then he took it into the bathroom to wash it off. The entire visible surface area was smaller than a hand print.

Coming back into the room, Malcolm held up the gleaming trophy.

"It works better with some juice on it," Evelyn said. "Come over here."

Without a negative thought in the matter, Malcolm moved closer.

Evelyn grasped his proffered appendage and stroked it gently. Malcolm stood still, continuing to be under the thrall of her command. He realized that whatever had been done to him made him ready for sex even without much preparation. He didn't have to 'get into the mood'; he was *always* already in it. Soon a bit of fluid was oozing out of his upright penis. Evelyn moved the dildo around along Malcolm's penis, bathing it in his juice.

"Okay, now. You can put it inside me. Slowly, if you please." Evelyn lay back on the bed with her eyes closed, and spreading her legs apart in a pose that would fuel his fantasies for weeks to come.

Malcolm knelt down and eased the rounded end of the device into Evelyn's tiny opening, letting the lubricant and stimulation work slowly to get it started.

Slowly, slowly, the gentle protuberances worked along her constricted interior. She shivered with delight, clearly enjoying the gentle technique.

Malcolm attached the metal band to the device, securing the closure as he had seen Evelyn release it. Then he gently continued stroking her delightfully smooth skin, rubbing her in places that would have been rude had they not been such close personal friends.

Evelyn slowly stood up in front of him as if in a trance. Then she opened her eyes, gave him a kiss, and began to dance.

After a few steps of silent motion, Evelyn pressed a button on her wrist bracelet. Music began playing from hidden speakers as she danced.

For twenty minutes she performed for him, building in intensity, as he knew she was feeling the vibrations initiated by her motions. Standing still, the girl was lovely, but in her practiced and graceful motions she was incredibly beautiful.

At the end, he was watching her breathing hard, with tears in his eyes.

She came to him then, and pushed him backwards, telling him not to move. Grabbing his penis, she licked it and stroked it, moving her mouth over it again and again as it began flowing in response.

Her intensity of stimulus surprised him, but his body seemed to know what to do. As the pressure built, he felt the orgasm beginning, and that's when she stepped up the pace!

He could not move away from her. He was under her compulsion to *not* move. But the pressure mounted again and again, as if he were under some chemical stimulant that boosted his responsiveness. He ejaculated his sweet spicy flavor, and then began building up for yet another eruption, and then another.

Eventually, he passed out. It's possible that men are not really wired for multiple orgasms. Like a rabbit, he lost consciousness.

When he awoke, she was gone from his chambers. It was still morning, and the clock had not yet moved. He struggled to orient himself better on the bed, and then collapsed again.

When next he awoke, nothing had changed. He looked at the clock and the calendar, and neither was any different. He could not believe it, but Evelyn's mother had worked other miracles. Who knew what the truth was?

He felt good. He felt energized.

Malcolm got up and did a few rudimentary exercises. He knew little about getting into shape, but he thought that some conditioning would be helpful for his new avocation.

After a few more minutes of pointless activity, he took a shower.

That's where Evelyn found him. Without hesitation, she stepped in to join him.

They began soaping and washing each other, not really needing either introductions or instructions. Like puppies or kittens playing with each other, each knew precisely what to do.

"Happy Birthday, Evelyn!" Malcolm said, giving her freshly rinsed face a kiss.

"Thanks for remembering!" Evelyn smiled up at him.

"I was looking at my face in the mirror, but I don't even need a shave!" Malcolm exclaimed in surprise.

"You never will! Mom took care of all of that extra nonsense while she had you in surgery. She said that was some of the most time-consuming of your medical treatments. You don't even have hairy armpits any more!"

"I'm almost surprised that she left my ears on; she seemed to be snipping and trimming everything else!"

Evelyn laughed.

After drying off and having a quick meal, Evelyn pushed Malcolm back to the bed.

"What now?" he said.

"It's still my birthday. Do you know anything about foreplay?"

"Foreplay?"

"You don't know what it is? I can teach you." Evelyn smiled at him wickedly.

"I know what it is, little miss. I'm surprised that you think you need it, since you have a Mexican Jumping bean in your little pee-hole!"

She laughed again. "I don't *need* it, I just *want* it! So let's get started!"

Malcolm wasn't sure whether she realized that by saying things in that way, she was leaving him no choice, but in any case he had no choice. He began stroking and caressing her gently.

Soon Evelyn pushed him down and clambered on top of him. Slowly and gently she lowered herself onto him as if she were installing her dildo.

On the bed, they experimented with various positions and speeds. Under compulsion, he could not relent until she commanded him to do so. She was not telling him to stop or even slow down. It occurred to Malcolm that he had simply wasted his time trying to get exercise this morning.

After a time, Evelyn called a temporary halt, and bade Malcolm to wash her and feed her. As if she were a doll or a baby, he did exactly that.

"How do you feel now? You aren't sore or hurting, are you?" Evelyn seemed very concerned that she might damage her mother's Frankenstein sex toy.

"No, I'm not hurting. Everything's fine, except that I think I may be living in some dream or nightmare place."

"Nightmare?" Evelyn looked concerned. "I'll have to be even more gentle as I rape you."

"Yes, please." Malcolm said softly.

Evelyn smiled and instructed Malcolm to resume once the break was behind them.

Having at least a small amount of choice in the matter, Malcolm set a slow pace.

That may not have been quite the balm they needed though, as the bouts seemed to take even longer.

Finally Evelyn acknowledged that he had satisfied her criteria, and she commanded Malcolm to lie down and sleep.

He collapsed immediately and knew nothing further of anything that might have happened around him.

Chapter Seven

alcolm awoke to the morning of July seventh, at nine-thirty, again.

In the back of his mind, it briefly flashed through his consciousness that this would make an effective Hell.

Strangely, though he knew that he had been exhausted, he felt fine once more. The only possible explanation he could think of was that his doctor had put something in him to help him recuperate incredibly fast. He could only hope that Evelyn had the same capability, or did he? A day of relative rest would not be unwelcome!

It was not to be. Evelyn showed up, well at nine-thirty. It was her birthday, or so she said. She brought books.

Arranging him in the bed, Evelyn placed a couple of books around, and made him raise his knees.

Then she climbed up, faced his feet, and folded herself down onto his still (of course) erect penis. She wriggled a bit to get settled properly, and then picked up a book and started reading, leaning forward against his legs.

Malcolm observed the delectable body perched on his lap. She was so small, but circumstances being what they were, he found her rather attractive. All that he could see of her was bare, naked flesh, and the back of her head.

He reached out and placed his hands on her shoulders, and began caressing her, gently stroking down along her ribs and out along her thighs.

Evelyn took in a big breath of air and slowly released it in a satisfied sigh. She seemed to relax a little, so Malcolm continued stroking her.

This went on for … well, the clock was useless. He continued caressing her, enjoying that as much as he was enjoying the gentle swaying movements of his penis inside her. He knew that he was pushing fluid up into her, and that it was probably flowing back down and leaking out, but he really didn't care about it. This was nice.

After a timeless interval, Malcolm saw the platform rise up without anyone on it. Then it came back down with Doctor Brandon standing on it. She was fully dressed, though not in her professional clothes.

Malcolm knew that Evelyn had seen the motion, but she had not moved other than to turn another page.

The Doc stepped out of the elevator and smiled. She walked over and gave the little girl a kiss, without having said a word. Then she came to stand beside him.

"Good Morning, Malcolm. Would you like to have me call you something else? Evelyn says that she calls you Uncle Huggy. We think that it would be a good idea to not use your name too much, in case one of us accidentally should mention it somewhere else. Evelyn is not supposed to know you, after all."

Malcolm had been trying to relax from his fright, but it was almost all he could do to not faint in this situation.

A calm discussion was out of the question. He tore his eyes away from the girl's mother and resumed gently stroking the back of the little girl in front of him.

"Awkward situation, isn't it? I'll forgive you if you don't get up." She smiled.

"How do you feel? Any tenderness or soreness? Any muscle pain or stiffness … other than, well, you know." She laughed.

"No." Malcolm swallowed. "No, no pain. I feel … I feel really good, actually. I know I had operations, but I don't feel any pain at all. Most of the time I feel great."

She reached out and stroked his face. "It saves you a lot of time in the morning not having to shave, doesn't it? It's always important to be on time for your date."

Malcolm essayed a tentative smile. "No, I wouldn't want to be late for that."

Evelyn closed her book and set it aside. Then she arched back, way back until her face was right in front of his face. She kissed him and then relaxed on his chest, still having his penis up inside her.

Malcolm moved his hands around to her front and began stroking her gently there as well, moving his hands from her chest down over her stomach and upper legs.

Evelyn sighed again. "This is a nice birthday present, Mom. You're the best mom ever!"

"You look very comfortable, Sweetheart. Will I be able to examine my patient any time soon?"

Evelyn placed her hands on Malcolm's hands and moved them around again on her own stomach. "Hold that thought, Uncle Huggy. I have to go pee anyway." She pushed his hands aside and slid upward off his erection, to stand upright with a graceful move, rising vertically in a maneuver that neither Malcolm nor Doctor Brandon could even attempt. Using his knees as a steadying platform, Evelyn climbed down from the bed.

Before she went into the bathroom, Evelyn collected the books and set them on a cabinet. "He's all yours, Mom." She said as she went into the bathroom.

Doctor Brandon turned to her patient, or victim. "You're looking much better than when I last saw you."

"I've lost a little weight."

She laughed. "You seem to be in good spirits. I was worried that you might resent being the victim of a terrible prank."

"Prank? I don't think prank quite covers it, Doc. What the hell have you done?"

Ten recoiled just a little, her smile faltering. "I … well, yes, I guess I should have discussed it with you, gotten your permission, that sort of thing. You realize that I couldn't do that, don't you? I couldn't take the chance that my plans might be discovered." She braced herself. "You wouldn't have liked that either."

He looked away. "That's true." After a moment he continued. "I've had time to think about it; about all of it. You've probably done me a favor." He looked at her. "It seems you were doing yourself a favor too, but that shouldn't make any difference to me. I may have been a criminal, but you made yourself one too."

"You and I," Doctor Brandon looked just slightly haunted, "criminals yes. By odd coincidence, virtually the same crime too."

Malcolm seemed taken aback by the comparison. "I know I'm a bad guy. I never thought of you that way."

Ten reached out and stroked his cheek again. "I never thought of you as a bad guy either, even though I knew you had hurt people. I guess I was just willfully deceiving myself. Now we've fallen into criminal enterprise together, I suppose."

"Yeah," he said, looking into her eyes, "strange bedfellows."

Ten smiled again. "You can say that? Are you really mad at me?"

"I wasn't." He looked down. "I'm not. I respected you. I kinda hoped you'd be able to find a cure for me, something that could put me back on the street and living a normal life." He looked around. "This isn't normal, but it isn't bad."

Evelyn had come back into the room. "Oh yes it *is* bad! We be bad, mister. Have you kept count, how many times you've been raped? Do you know what the number is?"

"What?" Malcolm looked confused. "Raped? No, I wasn't … I mean, no I didn't keep count."

"See? I toldja you wouldn't be able to count how many times we did it. *That's* how bad we are!"

Malcolm smiled at her. "I love you."

"Of course you do." Turning to her mother, Evelyn continued, "Classic Stockholm Syndrome, don't you agree?"

"Well, I love you too." Ten said.

"Naturally!" Evelyn smiled and struck a pose, "Who could resist?"

Malcolm turned to the mother. "Stockholm Syndrome?"

"The captive comes to sympathize with his kidnappers. I don't think it quite compares." She smiled, "But it shows that my daughter is quite well-read and intelligent."

"Yeah. I couldn't help but notice that she's a lot smarter than I am. Most people are."

"Actually, you're more intelligent than you think you are. You need a bit of training up, maybe." Ten observed.

"I agree," Evelyn said.

"Thanks," Malcolm looked at the girl. "I still love you, though."

"Just proves you're smart." Evelyn said. "Mom, you haven't even touched him yet. What kind of examination is that?"

"I've touched him!" Ten said defensively, "I stroked his cheek. I like that it is smooth."

"*All* of him is smooth. You should touch more of him."

Ten rolled her eyes. "Do you mind?" she looked at Malcolm.

"I like being touched," he said softly, "go right ahead."

Tentatively, she reached out and moved her hand across his chest. He looked rather like a male photography model; one who shaves his chest hair. His skin was smooth.

She moved her hand down along his flank, and across his thigh.

"Take your clothes off, Mom." Evelyn said.

"What?"

"Take. Your. Clothes. Off." Evelyn repeated. "The rest of this could get a little messy, so take off your clothes." She shrugged.

"I'd like to see what you look like." Malcolm said. "You were my prettiest doctor, you know."

"Not even Willard Barnett?"

"The guy with the goatee? No, you're prettier than he is. Go ahead, I'd like to see if my imagination was right."

Ten shrugged, and began disrobing. At thirty-seven, she was still rather shapely, and took the time to exercise as often as she could. Tending to forget about eating probably helped keep the weight down too.

She stood up straight, knowing that she was presenting herself to be ogled.

"Nice! Much better than I expected." Malcolm said with a smile.

"May I kiss you?" Ten said hesitantly.

"You may do … anything you want to do." Malcolm said softly.

"*Anything?*" Evelyn emphasized.

"Oh, yes. Absolutely anything. I am in your hands." He responded. "Looking forward to it, actually."

Ten leaned over, placing a hand on his chest again, and kissed him.

"You have a lovely body," Malcolm said softly, "may I?" He raised a hand.

"Yes of course," Ten responded, "Thank you. Your body is amazing too. You're just gorgeous!"

He reached out and placed his hand on her breast, cupping it gently. He smiled. "Oh, how I wish I had been able to do that months ago!"

"That would have been entirely inappropriate at the time, Mr. Littlefield, but I think the rules will be different now." She reached out and grasped his erection, squeezing it and rubbing her thumb over its top.

Malcolm wriggled pleasantly.

"This rape would go much faster if we were still using the confinement cot." Evelyn said.

Ten raised her eyebrows.

"There's no hurry. Take your time." Malcolm said.

"He likes being raped, Mom. Go for it."

"No pain or discomfort?" Ten asked.

"I'm fine. You did a good job. Feel free to take a test ride."

Ten looked over at her daughter, uncertain.

Evelyn put her hands on her hips, such as they were, and glared at her mother. "Get. On!" she said in a low threatening voice.

Shrugging her shoulders, Ten reached over and stroked Malcolm's very erect penis delicately, assuring herself that it was well lubricated. Taking a bit of that lubricant with two fingers, she reached down to her own vaginal opening and spread it there.

Then she climbed awkwardly up on the small bed with him and positioned herself carefully.

Like an aircraft carrier deck attendant, Malcolm reached up with both hands to hold her breasts as if helping her to align herself, and to guide her in for a landing position.

Slowly, with a little side-to-side wriggling, Doctor Brandon conducted an in-depth interview with the patient, pulling herself upright at the end to smile in triumph.

"Goal!" Malcolm said with enthusiasm.

"Kind of a tight fit, actually." Ten looked over at her daughter speculatively.

Evelyn stepped closer. "It works for me. I like to wriggle."

"I like it when you wriggle too. But this is pretty nice as well. At least I don't think I'm going to break someone." Malcolm was still caressing the breasts as if tuning in a distant channel.

"Yeah, it gives you something to play with, too, doesn't it?" Evelyn leaned against the bed and reached up to help Malcolm caress her mother's breast.

"It's kind of a fun game, way different than anything else I've ever done." Malcolm grinned. "I used to have to worry about timing, and reacting too soon, and yeah, foreplay as well, Miss Beany-Butt. Since I got fixed, though, I have all the time in the world." He looked over at Evelyn and smiled. "It's like it's always the same day, every day!"

"Oh, yes! Happy Birthday, Evelyn!" Ten said, with a little catch in her voice.

Chapter Eight

Evelyn woke up sharing the bed with Malcolm. She studied his face for a while. They were even covered by a thin blanket, although both were naked.

"Hey!" Evelyn said softly.

Malcolm's eyes opened, fluttered, and looked around. Eventually his gaze settled on her, and he smiled.

"What kind of perverty perv would stick me naked in a bed with a notorious criminal like yourself, Mister Criminy Criminal?"

"That would be your mother."

"Oh, yes, the mad scientist. Yep, she would certainly do that, all right."

"I'm your birthday present, remember? I'm just trying to figure out what I did so deserving that I got a present as nice as you. It isn't even my birthday."

Evelyn smiled. "Not deserving, *perverted*. All us perverts gotta stick together."

"Okay, in that case, may I fondle and caress you? I've discovered that I like holding you and petting you."

"All right. Let's see how that goes for a while. It ought to wake me up at least."

Malcolm reached out and gently pulled the girl closer, rubbing her smooth skin tenderly; stroking her as one might a kitten.

Evelyn lay still and studied her own reactions to this. It seemed this might be some of that "boyfriends and girlfriends" stuff she'd heard about.

Hmm. She yawned and stretched. Malcolm continued stroking her. This was nice, but it wasn't getting them anywhere. "All right; enough of this. Since you want to rub me, just take me in the bathroom and give me a bath."

Malcolm stopped immediately. He picked her up and carried her into the bathroom. Holding her, he started the water running, waited a moment, and then he placed her in the tub.

"You moron!" Evelyn said, glaring at him.

"Your mother said I'm more intelligent than I think I am."

"What does that mean?" Evelyn asked.

"I don't know." He admitted.

"Moron. Did you have to be so clumsy?"

"You told me what to do!"

"Fine, then. Be as clumsy as you want!"

Malcolm sat back. "I'm sorry, Evelyn. Don't be mad at me, please."

She looked up at him. "Hey, what happened to my big, bad criminal?"

Malcolm looked down. "I'm not a big, bad criminal. I'm just a stupid kid who got big and got in trouble for not knowing what to do with being big. I wish I was like you."

Evelyn stared at him.

"Like me, how?" she asked softly.

"Small, innocent …" he looked up, "… someone that someone loves."

He looked up and then looked away again. He seemed on the verge of tears.

"Wow." Evelyn studied him.

He sat there.

"Hey!" Evelyn said. "I want you to …" she stopped. This had to be worded properly. "Don't …" she stopped again and closed her eyes.

"What else would you wish for?"

Malcolm looked up. "I wish I had never hurt anyone."

Evelyn smiled. "We're okay so far. You want to get a bath with me?"

"Yeah. That would be fun."

She started to say come on in, but then she stopped, looked at him, and zipped her fingers across her lips.

Malcolm climbed in and washed her and washed himself as well. They had fun.

After a while they ate some breakfast and sat at the table quietly.

"Did you ever come up with a name?" Evelyn asked.

"What do you mean?"

"I feel silly calling you Uncle Huggy. And Mom wants to forget about that other name."

He smiled. "I didn't like that name anyway." He chewed another bite of toast. "How about a nice strong name, like Stone?"

"You want to be called Stone?" Evelyn grinned, and then rose forward, looking over the table as if trying to peek at his crotch. "You mean like Rocky Stone?"

Malcolm smiled. "No, not Rocky. How about ... Mark. Mark Stone."

Evelyn shaped her lips around it. "I like it! Pleased to meet you, Mark Stone!"

"Thanks! Now if I just weren't a moron."

Evelyn grinned again. "Now that I can fix!" She stared into his eyes for a moment. "Be smarter! Be smarter! Be smarter!"

Mal ... Mark looked at her for a moment. In the back of his mind he realized what she was trying to do. That hypnotic compulsion that had gotten him in trouble this morning was powerful stuff.

But maybe it could work in his favor. He had done some powerfully stupid things in his life up to now. Maybe he could somehow ride a compulsion to be smarter. He thought about the smartest thing he could do right now. And then he smiled.

Mark leaned over the table and gave Evelyn a kiss. "I love you!" he said.

———— ✦✦✦✦✦ ————

"I know you've already showed me what normal looks like. Can you show me the changes she actually made?"

"I'm pretty sure that's in here too. Let me look." Evelyn was peering into the surgery procedure manifest. After a few minutes she displayed a very graphic picture on the screen, with a compiled list of actions to be taken and the order in which to take them.

They studied the plan.

"Here you go. The first step is a complete depilation. This looks rather extreme. She used radiation, chemicals, lasers, and even topical hormone treatments. I think she was in a hurry."

She looked over at him. "According to this, with estrogen soaking into your skin like that, you should have had goose bumps all over you, maybe with little tiny nipples on them."

"*What?*" Mark reacted.

Evelyn grinned. "It's a joke; estrogen on your skin; tiny little booby bumps."

"I don't know if I'm any smarter, but I'm smart enough to know that's a dumb joke."

She stuck her tongue out at him. "Well it worked. You don't have any hair on your body. I like that, by the way." She rubbed his leg, which was as smooth as her own.

Mark smiled. "Yeah, it worked, but we already knew about that. What came next?"

"Hmm. Actually it was taking place at the same time. She had harvested tissues from all over your body and started cell cultures with them. Ah, here it is. She used a scaffold tissue system to build multiple versions of your seminal vesicles. That's what gives you the volume to be able to respond the way you do. It looks as though she tied the feed-streams into your lymph system. You are never going to run out of juice!"

"That's good to know. The way the women line up waiting for me, that could have been a problem."

"It's good to know that I don't have to worry about my lollipop supply."

Mark put on a rather goofy expression. "Somewhere in there she tied the right nerves together. That lollipop business is a lot more fun for me that it likely is for you."

"I'll try to keep that in mind."

"What else?"

"One thing that's apparent is that she has divorced your prostate gland from its normal positioning and operation. Her notes say that will prevent you from having problems when you get to be an old man." Evelyn read out from the surgery preparation notes. She looked over at him.

"I wasn't looking that far ahead, but thanks to your mom anyway." Evelyn nodded.

"Ah, here's the meat of it, if you don't mind my using that expression. She used scaffolding again, as well as a lot of cartilage structure, to build up and replace the normal way a penis gets bigger. Just keeping the blood in there for too long is dangerous, as people have discovered by overdosing on so-called 'male enhancement' pills. Evidently, surgery in the way my mom did it is the only safe course; that and mechanical pump systems."

"I've heard of those, but one thing that would permit is that a guy could go back to normal after a while."

"You'd want to be able to go back to normal?" Evelyn looked at him.

"Well, I don't think I'm going to get my testicles back, but I could maybe wear normal clothes again."

"Wear clothes?" Evelyn tilted her head, "We're not going to give you any clothes, Dobby."

Mark looked puzzled, and then realized the meaning. "Yeah, 'cause then Dobby would be *free!*"

"The cops are still looking for you, Dobby. Your freedom could be short-lived."

"Oh, yeah." Mark looked a little depressed. "I guess I'd better stick around."

"Don't worry. We'll keep you busy. You won't get bored."

"Heh," Mark looked over. "You might, though."

Evelyn looked startled, "Wow! A lascivious and salacious inference! You aren't feeling 'horny', are you?"

"You even know those words?"

"I study for spelling contests." Evelyn said primly.

"That or you read the wrong kind of books." Mark watched her.

"Nothing my mother wouldn't approve, I assure you."

Mark grinned. "Isn't she about due back? She's put a lot of work into her 'project', I'd say."

"She'll be back." Evelyn studied him. "You really don't know how to take any of this, do you?"

"I don't know what you and your mother talked about, but nothing prepared *me* for this situation. I feel like some rich guy with a harem, except that I'm the harem for a couple of rich chicks."

"Rich chicks." She smiled.

"Yeah," he responded, "beautiful too."

Evelyn smiled. "You're nice to us; complimentary, too."

Mark shrugged. "That's easy enough."

"All right, where were we?"

"Naked together, I have an erection." He shrugged, "I'm not sure what comes next."

"Right then. So the penis has a cartilage base structure like the ear or the nose. It was also set up with a plentiful blood supply, or the existing supply was not reduced. Mom's notes say that she was concerned that heat loss might make you feel uncomfortable." Evelyn was referring back to the medical notes. "Hmm. It says she boosted your thyroid levels a little. That's supposed to give you a faster metabolism."

"That's why the temperature feels so high in here?"

She glanced over at him. "The temperature *is* high in here. It's one of the reasons I usually show up like this."

"I thought you were just being nice to me." Mark said.

Evelyn smiled, but did not look away again. "There's also a note here that says you might need a good blood supply to promote healing."

Mark raised his eyebrow. "That sounds ambitious."

"I hope you're up for it," Evelyn said softly.

Mark laughed. "Now who's making dirty remarks?"

"Lascivious and salacious, if you please, sir. There is the matter of proper decorum to be considered, you know."

"I know that just hanging around you is going to make me smarter," Mark said. "Thanks!" he added.

She smiled again. "Then there's a note here that I don't quite understand. It says that as a result of the surgery and modifications, you may be a candidate for eventual colonization by medical nanometer scale repair devices."

"What the hell is … excuse me, what the *heck* is that?"

"Tiny little robots; some people call them nanites or nanobots. My mom is working on building some."

"What would they have to do with me?"

"General maintenance, restructuring inside your body in case something isn't designed right or working right. It gives a chance to correct mistakes without taking everything apart again."

"So as long as I'm okay, I shouldn't need that?"

"Yes, except for two things, which is why I'm uncertain about it. First, I think she was getting carried away with the whole 'redesign' possibility, and she may have wanted to keep her options open. Like it or not, you *are* her guinea pig for medical interventions, and maybe for a good reason; if you get sick or injured, you won't be able to go to the hospital."

Mark looked at her. "Crap! I just remembered! When you said guinea pig, I remembered that I was talking with Doc before the surgeries, and I told her to go ahead and treat me as her guinea pig." He blinked. "I told her I didn't have anything better to do."

Evelyn put her hand on his arm. "Don't worry about it. She's not going to hurt you. She likes you, you know."

Mark looked at her. "She likes you too. But she changed you anyway."

Evelyn stared at him. It was true!

"I guess I was right to call her a mad scientist."

"You know that only leaves us one course of action, don't you, Pinky? What do you want to do tonight?"

Evelyn smiled, "The same as every night, of course! We have to take over the World!"

Chapter Nine

octor Brandon looked in on her daughter, who was asleep for a wonder, in her own bed. She sat down on the side of the bed and moved Evelyn's hair out of her eyes.

"Hi, Mom." Evelyn said sleepily.

"Are you tired, sweetie?"

"We only talked, Mom."

"Really," Ten asked mildly, "why is that?"

"It's your turn?" Evelyn looked at her. "No, really. We just wanted to talk. I think Mark wants to get into studying more seriously."

"Mark?"

Evelyn nodded. "He chose a name. He wants to be called Mark Stone. I think that's a good choice. Almost anything someone else tries to make out of that, we can keep our secret."

"Yes," Ten said, "I agree that's a good name."

"I think you should set up another computer down there. We could work side-by-side, but he could set his own pace, the same way I do. He's way behind, but I think he can catch up quickly."

"You're both quite serious about this, aren't you?"

"Well, sure. He's part of the family now, even if you might want to shoot him up with nanobots in a few months." Evelyn said, rolling over and yawning.

"What? Where did you get that idea?"

"From your medical notes. Mark is very curious."

"Well, I guess he has a right to be. A whole mountain of strange has fallen on him."

"I think some of it bothers him, Mom. He said he wished that he could be like me."

"What do you think he meant by that?" Ten asked slowly.

"He said he wished he could be innocent; maybe even small. I think what he really wants is to feel like part of a family. I told him he was."

"That sounds right. I think you're good for him." Ten looked at her curiously. "Do you think you're ready for a brother?"

Evelyn stared. "No more than you are ready for a son! Have you forgotten what we *do* with him? I'm going to be doing it again tomorrow, and you should probably go down there right now and have at him very thoroughly. Make it an all-nighter if you want to."

"Really?" Ten rocked back just a little. This was more forceful than she had expected.

"I *don't* want to think of him like a … *brother*. I want to think of him as what he is. I *like* thinking of him as what he is. What *you* made him. I want to use him, a lot, and order him around and have a servant and have a toy and a birthday present in his *birthday* suit and all of it." She paused for a moment.

"But I also want to study with him and talk with him and … sleep with him. I think I'm starting to like him a little, but I don't even know what that means. I think he'll be good for me and my school work, and I'll probably be good for his." She looked up. "I want to go down there tomorrow and have a lollipop with him … and let him rub me all over."

Ten sat quietly for a moment. "You know," she said, "You know, that sounds like a very good plan; a very mature plan." She leaned down and kissed her daughter. "Good night, sweetheart. You're going to have a busy day tomorrow."

Evelyn smiled and closed her eyes.

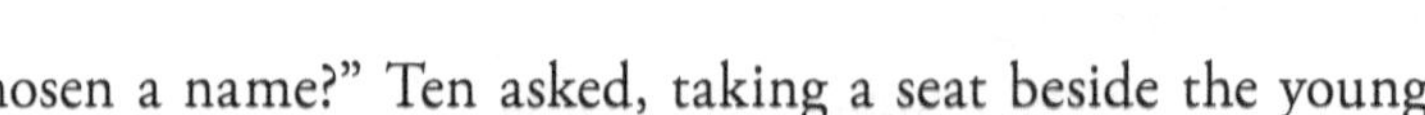

"You've chosen a name?" Ten asked, taking a seat beside the young man on the bed.

"I'd like to be called Mark Stone, if that's all right with you, ma'am?"

Doctor Brandon raised an eyebrow at the formality of the request.

"Very well. I approve the name. Call me Doc, by the way. How are you feeling today?"

"I feel great! I was asking about you earlier."

"Evelyn mentioned that. She seemed to think you needed some exercise, and that maybe I did too."

"I like spending time with her, with whatever she wants to do. She's nice."

"I'm pleased to hear you say that. She seems fond of you too." She stood up. "Would you mind helping me out of these garments? It's starting to feel warm in here."

"It will be my very great pleasure to assist you, Doc." Mark swung his legs around and stood up beside her.

She let him remove her garments and put them away. And then she let him move his hands over her, awakening her, and caressing her, and bringing her to life!

And then she let him take her into the bed. Her considered opinion later on, was that he was in excellent health, and that they both had gotten a very good amount of exercise.

Evelyn found him sleeping. She checked around, but everything looked neat and tidy. Evidently they had cleaned up afterward. Or he had. M ... Mark couldn't really find a sleep schedule, with the way he was constantly interrupted, and stuck in a time warp, anyway.

She guessed that *that* joke had run its course. He was already mightily impressed with her mother's science credentials. So was Doctor Ten's daughter, for that matter.

They could, and probably should, bring him back onto a moving time frame. Put a decent clock and calendar in, at least. Then he could go to class, and take tests, and all that rot.

But it was needed. He really was going to be a part of the family; maybe the adopted Frankenstein monster part, but part of it anyway.

If he really was intelligent, and he had nothing else to do all day except study, and to be used for sex by his insatiable captors, which didn't take all that long actually; well, then maybe he could really help Doc with some of the research work. No matter how well you theorized and put experiments together, there was always data to record and transcribe, and information to be either filed away or looked up.

Yeah, he could be useful, for getting work done and for taking breaks from it as well.

'Training up', she had called it. He needed training up. Evelyn took down the clock and calendar, and put them in the out bin along with other trash and used-up stuff. Somebody had to keep things orderly down here, and the prisoner couldn't be trusted to take the garbage out.

"You know what your mom said?"

Evelyn looked around. Mark had been watching her for a few minutes. She shook her head.

"She said we're going to be classmates. We're going to study together."

Evelyn nodded. "I asked her to get you your own computer to work at. You've got some catching up to do, and we can't be proper minions to the evil scientist if we don't keep up our lessons."

He smiled. "It's been a while since I was in school."

"Well, home-schooling is different. Of course, in your case it's going to be the-prisoner-in-his-cage schooling. We may even start beating you."

Mark smiled.

"Okay, yeah, *that* would be a bad idea. No whips then."

"Oh, I wouldn't hurt *you*. That would be like hurting a piece of cake or a bit of fruit by not eating it. I *like* having fun with you, and I can't think of anything you might want to do with me, that I wouldn't think was fun!"

"Pervert!" she said contemptuously.

He nodded his head, smiling at her with a leering expression.

Evelyn got up on the bed with him.

Mark pulled her close and began caressing her in ways he knew she liked.

"See! I said you were a pervert."

"I think your mother knew what she was doing, maybe." Mark said slowly. "She's a very capable psychologist, as well as unbelievably skilled as a surgeon, but I think she realized that the best motivation she could find for me, to make me pliable and cooperative, was … well, someone like you." He moved his hands over her, bringing thrills up her spine.

"And at the same time, she knew that you wanted something really, really exotic out of life … not that I'm all that special, mind you, but …"

"She knew that I was sexually precocious, you mean." Evelyn said, stretching her limbs out and relaxing. "She knew that I wanted to take a short cut to finding … the pleasure that romance is supposed to bring."

Mark leaned over and kissed her tenderly. "I'll try to bring you a little romance too." He smiled. "I never really had much of it myself, so maybe I'm just catching up with my lessons there, too."

"Yeah, sure." Evelyn said softly, "You just want to feel me up."

"Like this, you mean?" Mark lightly moved his hand over her chest and stomach, stroking and gliding gently as if she were some sleek animal being groomed.

Evelyn closed her eyes and quivered as if suddenly chilled. "Yeah … kinda like that …"

Mark kissed her again. "I love you," he said softly, "I love you very much."

As he studied her eyes, it looked as though a tear were forming in the corner of each, ready to trickle down at any moment.

"Do you tell Mother that?" Evelyn asked in a whisper.

"Yes," he said, "sometimes, when I think she wants to hear it. I mean it, too."

"How can you love us both?" she said haltingly.

"How can I not?" He gently moved his hand along her flank, and her hip, and her thigh, and then he nuzzled her neck with his lips. "I love you," he said softly, "I love you so much. Please … believe me." He held her close and lay still with her.

They slept together for a time, and then awakened. Evelyn rolled him over and rose up on one elbow to study his face. She stroked the muscles of his chest, and let her hand glide down across his stomach.

She grasped his penis, and moved closer to it. It was a fountain of sweetness. She began licking it like an ice cream cone. She did not want its melting to let the sweetness slip away.

She licked at it, as if she wanted to lick it all the way to emptiness.

Mark put his hands under his head, and lay very still. He could not sleep, like this, but he lay very still.

Evelyn pulled away and used her hand to stroke the machine of sweetness. A syrupy flow trickled down from the top of it. She climbed over him, bending her knees to align herself, and to sink into position over the mooring post. She settled into position and began a rhythmic motion as if riding a horse. She sat up straight and looked at a spot on the wall.

She rode. She closed her eyes and moved in rhythm as if taking a long journey.

Mark moved his hands out to the sides of the bed, breathing deeper and feeling tension as the motion continued. He lay still, except for the trembling of his hands as they gripped the bedclothes.

He felt the release as its warmth and fluid pressure moved through their contact. He did not move at all, simply waiting, and feeling the motion; the motion, and the joy.

Evelyn looked down at the man's face. He was not smiling, but focusing on what they were doing. She began tensing her muscles internally, a game she had invented for herself.

Her muscles inside could grip and release the object she had learned to carry and hold like a baby in her arms. She could squeeze it, and let go. She could squeeze it, and pull against it, as if trying not to slip from her mount.

She had never been able to play this game this way before, combining the motions and the exercise into one activity. This game felt ... very intense. It felt very nice.

Mark felt balanced between torture and delight. He dare not move, but the sensations flooding him were like a current of electricity through his body! He felt as though every muscle in his entire body were thrumming like a guitar string!

She could feel it when it happened, of course, each time it happened. It was like hitting a piece of bumpy road, yet she knew that he was feeling an intensity of pleasure that was most unusual in happening again and again. Whatever Doc had done to make him their slave, this condition, and conditioning were going to make him a salivating poodle of slavish and loving devotion.

Evelyn was okay with that. This was the journey she had been preparing for, with the years of muscle training, dance, and unending activity. This was the purpose of her effort, and the conquest she had sought.

"Did you break him?" Doctor Brandon asked quietly.

Evelyn looked up. "Is he broken?"

"Well, no. He's not broken, I don't think," Ten looked at her daughter appraisingly, "but he acts like he's gotten a lot of mileage put on him recently, and I know it wasn't me."

"So long as he knows who's boss," Evelyn said calmly, "I guess everything is all right."

"I'll keep that in mind." Ten said softly.

"Are you going to set up the other computer?" Evelyn asked.

Ten nodded.

"We need a clock too. Maybe we should have a printer down there, so we can print out tests and stuff. I want to study with him, and show him how smart I am!"

"I think he's scared of you already!"

Evelyn smiled. "We have a plan, you know. We're going to help you take over the world!"

"How do you plan to do that?"

"Don't know yet!" Evelyn said, "But we need to train and learn as much as we can in the meantime."

"Well, I can't argue with that," Ten said, "but take it easy on the boy for a while, would you? I can't tell you how embarrassing it would be for him to put in a request for transfer back to the prison." She looked very sternly at her daughter with this statement.

Evelyn looked up at her and blinked. "Yes, Mother, I understand."

Chapter Ten

"What's this stuff?" Evelyn was looking at a patch of material lying innocently on the counter near the computer workstations.

"Your mother left it," Mark said. "It's what she called a proof of concept."

Evelyn picked up a hexagonal piece of fabric about eight inches in diameter. It had wires attached to it, and a small battery pack with buttons.

The thin material was very flexible. Evelyn tried stretching it, but it wouldn't stretch at all. She tried tearing it. It would not tear.

She smoothed out the fabric again, and pressed a button on the battery pack. Immediately, the fabric seemed to almost be sucked down flat against the surface.

Mark was watching. "Don't touch it!" He cautioned her. "Wicked Mad Scientist, remember?"

Evelyn nodded. She picked up a notepad and pushed it against the fabric. It slid over to the edge of the counter and stuck out stiffly like a piece of flat metal. Cautiously, Evelyn picked up the fabric as if it were a pizza cutter without a handle. She pushed it against the paper pad, and it went an inch and a half into the edge of the pad.

Evelyn dropped the fabric and paper back on the surface. It fell into a sort of tripod, with the paper pad still being cleaved by the fabric.

She carefully selected a different button to press. As soon as she did, the fabric began rolling up like a window blind, severing the corner from the paper pad and turning into a square tube about two inches on a side.

"Whatever that is, it's sharp!" Mark warned.

Evelyn nodded. She pushed one more button, and the fabric relaxed again. She picked it up, and it was once more just flexible fabric.

She set it off into the corner. "Do not touch that!" she commanded. "You could lose a finger!"

Mark nodded grimly. "What do you think it is?"

"Mad scientist, remember?" Evelyn said mildly. "Wait, wicked?"

Mark nodded, "Wicked mad; can you doubt me?"

"Ah," Evelyn said. "Good point." She stared at it. "What's with the batteries?" She looked at Mark.

He shrugged. "Control panel?"

"Hmm." Evelyn picked up the shredded corner of the paper pad and examined the cut marks. She had never seen evidence of a sharper blade.

"I think it might be some kind of nanotech." She looked over at him to see his reaction; another shrug.

"I think Mom built the robot shells for nanometer scale robots, but without any brains in them, just the tiny manipulators; proof of concept of how they can link together." She looked over at the fabric. "It's brilliant!"

"It's dangerous!" Mark reminded her.

"Look, those things are too small to see," Evelyn said, "so they're all linked together like a chain link fence. You can roll up a chain link fence, but when it's stretched out, it's a barrier."

"You should be able to see through it," Mark suggested.

"Maybe, maybe not. Mom had a picture of something that looked a little like a crab, about as big as a flea's freckle, but they could sit side-by-side, and link arms to form ..." she looked over at the innocent-looking scrap of fabric, "... that."

"Okay, Mom, explain," Evelyn said, "and keep in mind, it's a miracle I didn't cut my fingers off just playing around with it."

"All right." Doctor Brandon said, "You're right. That could be something dangerous to leave lying around." She looked more sharply at her daughter, "Wait, you didn't hurt yourself, did you?"

"No, Mom, we're fine." Evelyn assured her. "Just explain, please."

"Fine. You know I'm researching this. This part of it may be the trickiest hurdle of them all, the basic configuration that links everything together. I needed to figure this part out first. I think I have."

"Okay, what is it?"

"It's a mesh of linked nanobots, a kind of fabric that can define its own form. Tightly linked, it's like metal plate, although thin. More loosely joined, it feels like a piece of fabric. If I can control the angle of joining, I can make a sieve for gases and liquids."

Evelyn was nodding. Mark was staring without moving.

"With the rest of the interface, I can send light signals through the mesh. With proper sequentially cascading addressing, I could set up a display system."

"Try not to get too far ahead, Mom. Why the battery control system?"

"Ah, well. Basically, what I've done is build the equivalent of armor for ants. Without the ants inside them, the shells can't do much."

"So you've got a machine that knits robot shells together, and you can then do some of the things you want to be able to program them to do?"

"That's it!" Ten exulted. "Now all we have to do is program them!"

"Cool! How do we do that?"

"I don't know."

Evelyn looked at her mother. "What will you be able to do with it when you can program them?"

"I'm not sure."

"Is someone going to make you, make us, incredibly filthy rich for working this out?"

"Um, not likely. Some of the ideas I've simply lifted from some other bright minds, and my best shot at a programming structure is still being worked out but will be owned by the Defense Department."

"So is there a little piece of it that you could sell and make some money?"

"No, not yet."

Evelyn waited.

She looked at her mother.

She looked at Mark.

He shrugged.

She looked back at her mother. "So what's your plan?"

Doctor Brandon grinned. "I'm planning to steal the program structure from the Defense Department, swindle the nanotech production interface procedure out of the Medical Research Lab, hornswoggle the graduate student quantum computing team, and build a secret production facility to make nanobots!"

Evelyn stared at her mother.

Mark let his mouth gape open like a fish.

Ten grinned at them.

Evelyn smiled. "Well, all right then. Let's get started!"

Five months went by.

Rosita had been replaced by Giselde Brunner, a German immigrant who was working in the college cafeteria, but staying with Doctor Brandon in an alleged au pair relationship which did not bear even the most remote scrutiny.

She lived in the guest room, studied, practiced English, helped with cooking and cleaning, and did not ask questions.

Evelyn did not go to school. She was still ostensibly home-schooled. Her test rankings at the moment placed her as a sophomore in high school. Possibly in two more years she might "graduate".

The police had not yet captured the escaped convict and parole-jumper Malcolm Littlefield. His whereabouts remained unknown, but Doctor Brandon always became very upset whenever his name was mentioned. She preferred to not discuss her department's most prominent breakdown in public relations, and was apparently still living in fear of the man's violent history.

Evelyn felt like a queen. As evidence of her royal status, she wore a crown.

Okay, it was a tiara, but it was jeweled. Could she at least be considered a princess?

She felt like a princess. Virtually the entirety of the house responded to her commands.

Doctor Brandon had struck again. Evelyn now sported an unseen link into the house's electronic communication system. Although she had nothing at all wrong with her hearing, Evelyn had radio-linked hearing implants on each side of her head.

The tiara had an uplink through the radio link that fed a camera view from her tiara down to the crypt, where Mark could view it at any time. He spied on her constantly, watching everything she watched, and very inconsiderately commented through her hearing implants on what he saw.

Evelyn sometimes thought he got a better deal out of it than she did.

He got to watch cartoons or movies when she did. He got to see her naked reflection in the bathroom mirror when she bathed.

Evelyn had actually raised this point, and had been roundly laughed at by both Mark and her own loving mother. The fact that she routinely went naked in Mark's presence seemed to diminish the legitimacy of her complaint. Privately, Evelyn had to agree with the assessment because she usually left the tiara on the counter, facing the tub, while she bathed just so Mark *could* watch her doing it.

In fact, Mark's complaint in this regard was that she still had no boobs worth looking at, so he had no reason to stare at her anyway.

Evelyn threatened to stomp on his testicles, if they could be found somewhere. Mark kissed her and hugged her and invited her to try.

She still wore the strap-in device when going about her daily activities, but even that most personal of considerations had now been sullied. Another radio link into her dildo could be activated by Mark, at times of his choosing presumably, and she would be gifted with an unexpected orgasm at occasionally inconvenient times.

This development had actually sponsored a kind of war between them, with her goosing him at odd times using her bracelet, and with him getting even with her at others.

Oh, sure, she could simply have not worn the device. His voice in her head she could not turn off in any way. But Mark liked to think he was doing her a favor, normally only sending the signal when she had been productive, amusing, or generally having behaved in an exemplary fashion. Then, according to him, she deserved a reward.

At first, it had been jarringly stimulating, a delightful surprise that made her jump and squeal. But after a period of time, she had come to almost expect it, even when it was totally unexpected, and she had developed the ability to evince no outward indication at all that she had been secretly stimulated. This actually pleased her a great deal, because rather than cause a sudden embarrassment, what it actually meant was that she got even more of the pleasurable stimulations than she had been getting.

True revenge is a dish best served in the most rewarding and delightful manner. Evelyn was now known to smile serenely and sweetly at even the oddest of moments.

"Are you coming down for a visit?" Mark asked.

"Um-hum" Evelyn hummed softly. The implant sent this inaudible response out to the tiara, which sent it on to Mark's console. With simple yes or no responses, Evelyn could hold an entire conversation with her unseen companion, and no one in her presence would be aware of it.

The fact that she never got a chance to use it did not keep them from practicing.

"Could you bring some ice cream?" Mark sounded hopeful.

Evelyn tilted her head slightly.

"I know, I know. You're worried that I'm getting too many calories. I promise I'll work it off. Ice cream, please?"

"Hmm." Evelyn's non-committal response was good enough for him. Of course, for her, his working it off meant a casual marathon sex session at her earliest convenience. She was still trying to figure out whether she got more out of it than he did, or vice versa.

Oh well, the experiment was ongoing. Evelyn got some ice cream and went through the normal security protocols; making sure the house was secure, the telephone patched through, and all lines of communication set to their proper destinations.

She went down to the lab first. There she checked the settings and alarms again, and then proceeded on to the really secret location where Mark lived.

First they shared ice cream.

"How's the simulation going?" Evelyn asked.

Mark smiled; eating and plotting went together well. "The basic form is almost complete. We've known the cage works from the beginning. What gives us trouble is having to smooth out the jaggies using addressing modes instead of being able to switch up to say 128 positions instead of 16." He took a moment to swallow more ice cream.

"But with sixty-four functions to control, it just slows things down too much to try to have fine control of movements and angles, when just shoving the motion down the line works as well, and four times faster." He ate again.

"I'm thinking this iteration will prove to be fast enough and capable enough to go with a burn. I know your mom is eager to have a trial."

"You know we have to be patient. These simulations can be shoved out three times a day. But our first burn is going to take six weeks to produce enough nanites to conduct a decent test. It's better to have the procedure nailed down than to have to scrap it again after all that effort."

"I know. I'm just getting antsy." He looked up hopefully. "Do you think your mom is going to tell us what the first project task is going to be?"

"I know she wants to, but I also know that as a psychologist she's not going to let us get our hopes up to the extent of messing up the schedule by skipping something. With nanites, you just don't mess around. There may be billions of them, but every single one of them has to be built right, and programmed like an unstoppable tank. You only get one chance to do it right."

He leaned back. "I think we're getting close. Whatever she wants to build, the capability is in it. These buggers will be able to cover any shape, make it damn near bulletproof, pick it up and move it if necessary, and even pretend to be something else while it's all going on! If you wanted to rob a bank, these guys could do it with their eyes closed!"

"They don't have eyes, Mark." Evelyn said reasonably.

He waved it off. "Each one is an eye if it wants to be. That's their power! They're just like an army, and just as unstoppable as an army too."

"Power? Are you kidding? It would take ten million of them to move a book!"

Mark grinned. "That's true. But if you wanted to move a bookcase, all you'd have to do is multiply that by a million!"

"Ten million million? Ten trillion?" Evelyn looked thoughtful. "Yeah, that might work. How long does it take to make that many?"

Their conversation was interrupted by the arrival of Doctor Tenerife Brandon, Mark's abductor and butcher, and Evelyn's mother.

"Hey, kids! How is everything today?"

"Hi, Mom!" "Hi, Doc!" She was greeted.

"Mark is getting impatient, Mom. He thinks the latest iteration is ready to go, but neither one of us knows what the test is going to be."

"Sorry kids, but no impatience. I will tell you this; the first test is going to be the final test. We're going for broke with this, and we can't afford to be wrong by one atom." She looked at them very sternly.

"Told you!" Evelyn said.

"Let's take a look at it, shall we?" Ten said. "Roll it, Mark!"

Mark activated the simulation.

They watched as waves of tiny figures went through their paces, marching, climbing, absorbing energy, transmitting energy, collecting electricity and sending it down the line, and receiving beams of light of various frequencies and intensities only to separate it in various ways to either be reflected, absorbed, or retransmitted after processing.

The focus went in, to show how individuals interacted, locking together in different ways, using their connections to bend and shape the mass of robots and the light that was transmitted through them or reflected from them. Each one had dozens of manipulators, each under individual control that could move around in various ways, and an integrated "quantum processor" which received instructions, checked their addressing, and either acted on them or sent them along in the appropriate direction or did both as needed.

It was the programming that defined the utility of the robot. Even a low-tech bulldozer had its uses. These robots had brains, and they could combine their brainpower in various ways to solve tasks on the fly, even though they weren't using transistors or printed circuits at all. Each processor was mechanical in function, much like simplified versions of Charles Babbage's original Difference Engine, but being so tiny that miniscule motions could take place faster than electrons could migrate.

These were robots that were built from sheaths and stems of atomic scale structures; buckytubes and compounds that could bend and move under electrostatic compression; plastic muscles and atomic-force pincers to grip and rend. These robots could build, or they could disassemble objects. It all depended on the programming.

Doctor Brandon wore a serious expression. "We're not ready."

Mark raised an eyebrow.

"What more do we need, Mom?"

"I think our system could work, but I'm concerned about security. The top end is wide open. I think there's a danger that our whole program could be Shanghai'd."

"Well, you're probably the expert on that," Mark said acerbically.

"I've had some practice stealing things," Ten admitted, leaning over to kiss Mark in recognition, "but we need to be able to *prevent* this stuff from being stolen. It's a different perspective."

"What do you think we need to do?" Evelyn asked, biting at her lip.

"Among other things, we need to make sure our top-end only listens to us. The programming is so simple, necessarily because it's mechanical and basic, that any security protocols will have to be designed into the receiver link. I want all of us to concentrate on how we can make our nanobots answer only to us, no matter who tries to horn in."

Mark looked thoughtful. "You know how our address function and iteration count protocol has to deal with huge numbers? Is there a way we can piggyback on that to put in an uncrackable cipher?"

"What do you mean?" Ten asked hopefully.

"We send the program command down the line, until it reaches the insignificant PFC in his pup tent on the battlefield. He compares the cipher code to his preset, and sends it either to the trash can or on to the Command Center."

"I get it! And we could stack that up a few times, just to make sure no one else ever figures it out." Evelyn suggested.

"Sure. You could even break it up into smaller pieces, and reverse a couple of them. That's how DNA likes to shuffle genes around to make sure everyone gets a random mix." Mark added.

"Except that our message has to match the other strand of DNA which is buried inside the nanobots coding! And since the address can be reset with every command string, no one will be able to intercept it and hijack the robots. Brilliant!" Doctor Brandon grabbed Mark and kissed him passionately, bending him backwards on the stool to make a thorough job of it.

"Hmm. I don't know if I want to be next to kiss him, or next to be kissed," Evelyn said curiously.

"I'll start," Ten said. She moved her attention over to her daughter, kissing her just as thoroughly and passionately as she had their mutual lover.

"You two can sort it out after that. That is a brilliant idea, Mark! I hope we can make it work like that. I've been worrying about this idea all day."

Evelyn sat up, her mind whirling. Being kissed passionately by her mother was a new experience, much akin to being kissed passionately by anyone. Passion was still a bit of a foreign and unfamiliar concept to her, since she lacked the pheromones and hormones to make such activities reach the excitement levels they perhaps could. She quietly theorized that this might be the kind of filtering process the nanobots might be using to prevent signals from disturbing their purposes and goals.

This entire thought process then totally evaporated when Mark came over and began kissing and caressing her into a complete confusion about where she was and what they had been talking about. She did not find this to be disturbing at all, however, accepting it as precisely what a princess deserved.

They broke for dinner anyway. The security protocols could be revamped and tested with the next simulator runs. For now it was time for pizza, and maybe some sex.

"Let me get this straight. You want me to help you make the presentation when you introduce the nanobots to the challenge. It's in San Diego. And we're taking a trip out there for the procedure. Am I right?"

"Except that Mark will be staying here and manning the base, yes." Ten glanced over toward Mark to see if he noticed anything about her wording. He mouthed the word "Nuts!" in her direction and grinned. Technically and scientifically, Mark was no longer a man. He had been converted into a eunuch with an artificial and permanently erect penis. This sad state of affairs did not seem to trouble him.

"Cool!" Evelyn beamed. "Now I get to pick out a beautiful new outfit!"

"Whoa! Back off there, sister! This will be a scientific conference. To achieve maximum effect, I'm thinking about having you make the presentation naked." Doctor Brandon calmly looked down at her fingernails to see if they were in need of trimming.

Evelyn stared at her mother aghast for a moment, and then took a breath to calm down.

"Oh, okay. I had kinda forgotten that we were operating on a budget." She made a cute curtsy as if practicing for her presentation. "Of course, Mother. Whatever you say to make the event successful. I'm sure I'll be able to handle it."

Ten pulled her daughter into a rough-and-tumble hug, and kissed her. "You're so cool! You didn't bat an eyelash!" She kissed her again. "What I meant was that I was planning on having you wear the nanobots themselves as a costume, and then we'll just pull off a portion to have them work on the challenge. What better way to show that they have the flexibility to do *anything?*"

"Wear nanobots as a costume?" Evelyn looked surprised, "Ooh, that's kinda sexy! I like it!"

"You'll be beautiful, I know it. You're beautiful already, and having you walk out there with our nanobots all over you like a beekeeper's beard will prove how safe and controllable they are!"

Mark started working on the idea right away. He almost envied the tiny robots in getting an opportunity to get up close and very personal with the sweet girl.

But then he had an epiphany. He would design as well, her next iteration in the smiley-faced intruder in the dildo line, and it would be made entirely of nanobots!

He worked on the costume ceaselessly, collecting measurements and designing robotic analogues of cloth and soft, comfortable fabric, as well as durable and flexible materials for shoe leather and stretchy belts for Evelyn's very special thong underwear.

It was a labor of love, indisputably.

Doctor Brandon's facility had been working overtime producing nanobots. They had about ninety pounds of tiny robots, but for this function would only need about thirty-two pounds.

Evelyn would wear her accustomed princess tiara, her strap-in dildo, some delightfully fashionable boots, with matching wrist bracelets and arm bracelets, a soft pink sleeveless top with glittering white shorts and a white leather belt. Thirty-two pounds of clothes would be a lot for a little girl. She only weighed about eighty pounds herself.

But the crowning achievement of all of this design work would be that every tiny bit of it would be made of nanobots! Her tiara would duplicate the electronic ability of the physical one, and even the secret dildo would have the new radio capability so that she could be gifted with a reward when the time seemed appropriate.

It wasn't a secret. Evelyn had even been very cooperative in getting the information collected. They had used scanning cameras, motion capture, regular scans of her former dildos, and a variety of other techniques. But the level of detail in the computer's memory was astonishing!

Mark had even used an animation program to display the memory information as an active person inside the computer display. It was simply amazing.

Along with the fabric definitions and clothing descriptions, the personal data was downloaded into the nanobot's reference library. When the programming information went out to the nanobots, they would have a clear picture of exactly who and what shape the girl they were enfolding happened to be.

Mark also made sure that the library information included what was currently known about a young person's internal arrangements, including all biological systems; coronary, circulatory, bone structure and joints, and other pertinent and even embarrassing details.

It was actually easier to set up and transfer almost unlimited information on chemistry, pharmacology, strengths of materials, electronics, architectural details, and everything else than it was to choose a way to select in advance what would be needed. Doc had unrestricted access to an incredible array of medical and scientific disciplines, and they simply opened the floodgates to duplicate it in the most compact form that had ever existed.

The nanobot reference library was astonishingly compendious, considering they were using essentially physical analogues of detail information. A virtual memory of sorts described the world to the tiniest imaginable entities. A homunculus of Evelyn resided in their memory, and every way she could bend and fold was in there too.

Mark's next challenge, although of course he was not working alone, was to prepare the database and the robots for an unknown challenge. Rumor had it that the contestants would have fifteen minutes or so to collect information and transfer it once the challenge was announced. After that, the competing contestant programs would be on their own.

They practiced assigning tasks in to the simulators to see how "ideal" nanobots would react to the challenges. The results were mixed. Some tasks seemed almost trivially easy, even though without nanometer scale technology it would all be impossible.

Other tasks, which seemed straightforward, were hopelessly mired in inscrutable details the nanometer-scale machines simply could not unravel.

Mark looked exceedingly frustrated. "Doc, I want you to take a gun with you, and if someone throws out a knitted sweater for the nanobots to reproduce, I want you to shoot that person right there on the spot!"

Ten gave him a hug. "Don't worry about it, Mark. That's not going to be the challenge. We already know how to make knitted sweaters in factories. It's going to be something we can't currently do, trust me."

He relaxed. "Well, that's it then. That's all I can do. I couldn't figure out driving a nail with a hammer right now. I'm played out."

"Okay, that will have to do, then." Ten looked around. "I don't even know whether we will *have* competition, but there's nothing more we can do about it either way. Let's just relax for the rest of the weekend and take it from there."

In the morning, Evelyn tried on the tiara. Although it was made of nanobots, it felt like the same thing she'd had before.

Mark claimed that the screen resolution suffered somewhat, but he was mollified to learn that the tiara as well as the nanobot dildo had incorporated cell phone technology, so that their range was virtually unlimited.

For Evelyn, a unique difference surfaced right away. She discovered that she could communicate directly with the nanobots through her tiara. The voice sounded unusual, as if it had to circle the world a few times, and the cadence and timing were a bit strange, but being able to chat directly with the nanobots put her on an equal basis with Mark and his keyboard.

She was able to update precise fit and comfort information to the robots as soon as she put on the rest of the outfit. They were very accommodating, almost as if she were wearing magic resizing robes from the Harry Potter universe.

An especially pleasant surprise was her smiley-faced companion. Not only did it fit well, but it also had the unique property of being able to reshape itself as if alive inside her. She found that she could relay information through the tiara down to the dildo, and have it conform itself with her wishes. Prudently, Evelyn decided to say nothing to anyone about this option.

Evelyn played with the capabilities. She found that she could robe or disrobe at a whim, allowing the nanobots to swarm into her hidden crevices and onto her bracelets, or out of them, in a curiously rapid stream that only took a couple of eye-blinks to complete. Wearing nanobots was the equivalent of wearing an entire wardrobe, or of wearing nothing at all.

Of this capability she also said nothing.

The capacity of the robot swarm seemed to multiply the longer she wore it. Her verbalizations, preparatory to speaking, seemed almost enough already to initiate the requested action. It only required verbal confirmation to begin the procedure. Meanwhile, the nanobots were mapping out the territory she occupied in their own inimitable fashion, by stationing linked units at periodic intervals. The links of their chain-link were very open, indeed. But by using a form of phased-array signal production and wave reception, the whole structure being mapped became the memory array for it.

Essentially, the tiny robots were turning her body surface into the equivalent of a wrinkled brain surface, where signals and information processing could be mapped and promulgated. Evelyn had become the processor for the program that was Evelyn.

Her whole outfit could communicate with any portion of it. Evelyn had the notion that she could walk out on the stage right now and compete with whoever else was out there, and still win the competition. The nanobots listened to her, apparently recognizing her voice from within their own core as an appropriate and authorized speaker. They were incorporated and affixed to their own database. The nanobots understood and accepted her commands.

This newfound power was, in a word, heady. Evelyn did not tell anyone else.

Doctor Brandon had enough on her mind already. Arranging for transportation, checking to see that Mark's communication was secure, and remembering her own clothes and the scripts she had prepared kept her in rather a tizzy.

Mark too was experiencing anxiety. He would be trying to control things from a remote location. If communication broke down, he would likely be tearing out by the roots what little hair he had left.

Evelyn just smiled at everyone.

The hotel was buzzing. This was the new technology, and everyone wanted the story.

"Don't talk to any of them, Dear. You're with me, and that's all. Just smile and keep walking."

Mark was annoyed. His view, being situated at the top of Evelyn's head, was still head and shoulders *below* a typical man's viewpoint. All he saw was chaos.

"Can't you get higher?" Mark complained.

"Mom, Mark wants a better view. How about if I go up on that balcony?"

Ten looked around. "All right, dear. Stay in view up there, and I'll be watching you. The presentation is at eleven, so all we have to do is keep it together until then. Be careful!"

Evelyn scooted out from the throng, ducked under a velvet rope, and ascended the curving stair to the balcony. Leaning over the rail, she had a perfect view of the whole setup. It still looked like chaos.

"Much better, thanks." Mark said.

"Ola!" said another voice. Evelyn looked around. A young man, about twenty, dark-haired and with a thin mustache, was wearing a serape and smiling at her.

Evelyn looked around, but there was no one behind her. He was talking to her.

"Oh, hi!" Evelyn said. "It's kinda crowded down there."

"Si," said the young man with a smile, "that's why I came North."

Evelyn smiled. "Are you here for the science convention?"

"Yes, my uncle. He is very interested in production using 3-D printing."

"That sounds very interesting."

"We hope to make a lot of money." He said.

"That would be a good thing." Evelyn said, "Good luck with it!" She noticed that even up here the noise was still quite a presence.

"Gracias!" he said, "You aren't here alone are you?"

"I don't like this guy," Mark said. "Mmm." Responded Evelyn.

"No, I'm here with Doctor Brandon. We'll be presenting in a little while."

"My name is Carlos Sanchez. Let me get you some punch." He looked over his shoulder at a companion who had quickly and silently materialized. The companion had a waiter's tray with two drinks on it. Carlos picked up the drinks and turned to face her with a smile.

"Don't drink that!" Mark said. "Something's going on."

Carlos handed her the drink.

Evelyn sniffed it and set it carefully on the handrail. "I'd like to know what's in it," she asked softly.

"It's just punch," Carlos replied.

Evelyn formulated instructions to her wrist device, commanding the robots to check her drink. She watched as the tiniest tendril of thread crept out and dipped into the liquid.

The tiny devices, working together, formulated a response; 'Your drink has a carbonated beverage, some port wine, chloral hydrate, and Rohypnol. If you drank it, you would become unconscious.' This was delivered through her hearing implants and inaudible to her companions.

"You are very kind to me, Mister Carlos." Evelyn smiled, batting her eyelashes at the young man. "Where is your girlfriend? I hope she won't get jealous."

Carlos looked slightly confused. This was going in a direction he had not expected. He smiled, "Ah, sadly, I do not have a girlfriend. Perhaps that is why I am being so daring, to even speak to someone so lovely as you are." He bowed in a gracious manner.

"I hope you're not falling for this load of Mexican baloney," Mark said in her ear. "This guy has got to be working for the competition."

"Oh, gosh, I'm sorry, Mister Carlos, but I just got the I-want-you-right-here-right-now signal. I've got to go. See you later!" She spun away and disappeared down the stairs.

Two minutes later, Evelyn appeared at her mother's side. Ten smiled at her, "And this is my daughter, Evelyn. She has worked on my project with me, and she will be making our presentation!"

"A pleasure to meet you, Young Miss. I'm always happy to meet young scientists." The distinguished elder gentleman smiled at her and nodded politely.

"I just had an adventure, Mom." Evelyn said, watching the older man move to the next conversant.

"Already? You work fast! Oh, we can move to our table now."

Evelyn decided to tell her mother about Carlos later. Maybe she would just let Mark tell her. She looked around, but there was no sign of the young man.

Despite the confusion and noise, events somehow managed to roll along at a good pace. Opening remarks were kept blissfully short, in consideration perhaps of more informative speeches after the contest.

Soon Evelyn and her mother learned of what the contest was to be. Their nanobot friends would be challenged to build a ship in a bottle, right in front of the assembled crowd.

One contestant on the right side of the stage was already attempting to set up, and complaining volubly about the inadequate conditions under which he had to work.

Evelyn got up from the table, after Mark gave her the go-ahead, and walked around to a plain table set up at the front of the stage. A clear empty gallon bottle was resting on its side in a wooden stand, with the lid open. Beside it was a pile of small components.

Evelyn smiled and curtsied to the audience, removed her tiara to place it just beside the bottle, and walked back to her seat.

She could not hear Mark's commands to the nanobots, but she presumed it was on the order of build us a ship in a bottle that looks like this picture. Evelyn had no idea what the picture would look like.

She looked up at the railing of the balcony. The glass she had been offered had disappeared. Evelyn wondered what would have happened if she had drunk from it.

In twenty minutes it could easily be seen that something was happening in the bottle. Slowly the pile was getting smaller, and something was taking shape inside the bottle.

A TV camera had moved closer to focus on the bottle. As far as she could tell, theirs was the only project showing progress.

Time was called at forty-five minutes. Most of some kind of a ship was clearly visible, and some form of mast with a small sail could be seen at the top. The pile of material had gone down about two thirds.

The other teams had either not shown, or made no progress at all. Evelyn, after being prompted once more, calmly went up, picked up her tiara and placed it on her head, curtsied once more, and returned to her seat.

There was thunderous applause.

The Master of Ceremonies stepped forward and immediately called Doctor Tenerife Brandon up to speak to the crowd. Again applause was thunderous.

Evelyn was applauding as loudly as anyone when suddenly the lights went out. A cloth bag had been placed over her head and pulled tight, forcing a sodden bit of cloth against her mouth with a sickly odor to it.

Rough hands grabbed her and pulled her backwards, and soon she knew nothing more.

Ten smiled and nodded, raising her hand to the crowd and looking around. The MC was handing her a microphone and trying to say something she could not hear.

Finally she thanked everyone and turned to call Evelyn out to stand with her. She looked back at the table and Evelyn was gone.

Pandemonium reigned. The two gentlemen who had been seated nearest to the ladies seats appeared to need medical attention. Voices were calling out that two, three, or even four men in dark clothing had appeared, grabbed the girl and assaulted others, and disappeared. No one even had any idea where they had gone.

Mark was more than ready to panic. His breath was coming fast as if he had run a thousand yards at top speed. He knew something had happened but he was nearly as much in the dark as Evelyn.

He was ahead of the game by one factor only; he knew that she had been abducted. He had one face and a likely made up name, but probably some kind of Hispanic drug gang.

Mark sat again and typed commands into the nanobot hierarchy itself. He also spoke over the voice channel that he used to talk to Evelyn. "This is Mark. Listen to me! I know you can hear me because you're sending my voice in to Evelyn. While you're there, you can help her! She is not responding to me and I have to assume that she has been knocked out, either physically or with some chemical. This is Mark. Please respond in some manner. I need to track your location. Can you send a signal to show your location?"

Mark stared at the display board in frustration. Why hadn't they considered this need? Damn! Where was Doc? She should be able to call him. Damn!

"Mark"

He looked up. Nothing had changed. Was he hearing things? Did something actually call his name?

"Mark"

"Yes, this is Mark!"

"Mark, this is … clothing. Evelyn is not speaking."

"I didn't know you could talk!"

"Evelyn talked to us. She is part of us. She is inside of us. We are inside of her. She is part of us. You are not part of us."

"I am not part of you, but I am part of Evelyn. I will help her. I will help you. Tell me where Evelyn is. Tell me how Evelyn is. Is she breathing? Give her clean fresh air to breath."

Time went by.

"Listen to me," Mark repeated, "Fix her! Get in there and do something! Help her breathe. Wake her up. Make her strong. Don't let her slip away!"

"Chemicals have been moved. Evelyn is breathing."

"Thank you!"

"Evelyn is breathing. Evelyn does not speak."

"She may need time. Check her heartbeat and respiration. Use your medical database. Make her healthy. Make her strong. Help her breathe, and help her see. FIX HER for me! MAKE HER STRONG AND FIX HER!"

"We proceed."

Time went by. For nearly an hour Mark kept calling out, telling the tiny robots to fix whatever was wrong with Evelyn, to make her strong and help her with what she needed.

Damn!

Time went by.

"Unnh."

"Evelyn!"

"M … Mark? Ow, my head hurts."

"Sweetheart! I'm glad you're alive. Are you okay?"

"Can't see. I think it's dark. My hands are … my hands are … taped together I think."

"Can you talk to the guys? Can you talk to the nanobots?"

"Oh, yeah. I forgot about that. Hang on."

Mark waited.

"Crap! I had a bag over my head. The guys are chewing through the duct tape. I should be free in a minute. Ow! What did they hit me with? I've got a headache."

"They probably used chemicals. Try not to be too loud. They may be very close to you. Where are you? Any idea?"

"Chemicals, yeah, probably. That sounds like their style. Hey, I think I'm on a boat!"

"Look, when you get free, you're only halfway there. They can't hear me, but you'll need to keep your voice down. They may be coming to check on you shortly. You're going to need to be ready for them."

"Mark, I'm scared!"

"I understand. You're in the position I was a year ago. You're about to be sent back to prison and maybe killed. That's a scary position. But you're not alone. I may not be able to do anything except cheer, from here, but you've got an army with you."

"What are you talking about?" she whispered.

"How well can you talk to your little buddies there? They got you out of your bindings. What else will they do for you?"

"I had them changing my outfit before."

"That may help. You're not dressed properly for the present social situation. Tell your little friends to fix your dress for you. You need a suit of armor."

"A suit of armor?"

"Armor for ants, remember? Only now you're the ant. Get dressed!"

Evelyn wished she had a phone in her hand so she could stare at it. Mark was making no sense.

Then her hands were freed. Suddenly she understood what he meant. The nanobots were waiting for her to give them their marching orders. She didn't need to make a ship in a bottle; she needed to do what a girl does best, go shopping!

Evelyn sent out her requests; rebuild my clothes with dark material, cover me up completely, make my clothes hard where they don't need to bend, and put a cover over my head to protect it too, but make it so I can see out of it.

Her confusing set of orders had them scurrying, but step by step she got closer to what she needed. If she had time, she would be able to … well, what?

To think, maybe … Evelyn moved over to what seemed to be the door. It was locked. Okay, she couldn't get out; let's lock them out.

Evelyn asked her guys to jam the door closed.

"Mark, what next? I've changed to my Ninja outfit." She whispered.

"Good! How about weapons? Are you still in the dark?"

"There's a little bit of light. I think we're moving out of the port."

"We're running out of time. I think they're trying to get you out of the country. That would be bad. If I were there, I'd try to take over the boat. But I'm not there. What do you want to do?"

What did she want to do? Evelyn remembered how she got into this mess in the first place and instructed some of her workers to fix up her mask to keep out more chemicals.

She looked at her hand and flexed it. With the dark uniform, it looked intimidating.

"I'm going to turn this boat around."

"Good, be careful!"

"Yeah."

Evelyn thought about it. She had thirty-two pounds of nanobots. At present she was using about five.

"All right, guys, time to go to work. Put some muscle on this suit, we're going to kick ass." Evelyn pushed the nanobots out to reform the suit again, making cable connections to move the arms and legs, and twisting them into muscle mass to pull against the cables.

She could picture it in her mind, and what she described to them, they executed. On the fly, out of most of the material she'd been carrying around under a smile, she was forming an exo-suit to multiply her strength. Under this suit, she was naked. Her blouse, shorts, belt, bracelets, tiara, and even the thong hardware went into the suit.

After five more minutes, the eighty pound eleven year old had put on twenty-five pounds of something about a hundred times stronger than muscle. She took a few tentative steps around in the confined space, testing her movements and agility.

There was even a mirror. She looked at her reflection. It looked muscular, but sleek. It didn't look at all feminine. But it did look menacing.

Showtime. The curtain was going up. The operating room is ready, Doctor Evelyn.

She could feel the fear, the trepidation. It was a physical presence. She had the butterflies in her stomach all right; hell, she had robots in her, well nearly her stomach, anyway.

Evelyn took a deep breath. She gritted her teeth, and she steeled her resolve. It was time to move. It was time to dance.

Chapter Twelve

Evelyn instructed the nanobots to clear the blockage and unlock the door. Locked from the other side meant nothing to nanobots.

She opened the door and checked the passage. Clear.

She listened for voices. Someone talking in a radio room seemed unlikely. They were running, and every eye would be watching for pursuers.

She headed left, toward the rear of the boat. It was a bigger boat than she had thought.

The hatch, leading out into the night, was open. She moved silently and stealthily toward the opening. Lounging at the rear of the boat was a man with a cigarette stuck in his mouth and a large gun dangling from the crook of his arm. He was watching the coast recede in the distance.

Looking around as carefully as possible, Evelyn saw no one else. When the man drew on his cigarette, she moved out like a cat. Close enough to strike, Evelyn hit him with great force with the armored side of her left hand just under the jaw-line. She felt and heard bones crunch.

The man dropped where he was. Evelyn caught his gun. She laid it down carefully and picked up the fallen cigarette, tossing it over the stern. She looked quickly toward the bow, and then turned to study his face. This man was unknown to her, but he had been one of those to take her, to threaten her. She could not move on with his threat uncertain behind her. She checked his pockets, removing a smart phone and wallet.

Evelyn placed his wallet and phone on the deck. There was only one way to neutralize the threat he posed. With one arm and her multiplied strength, she picked up the man and watched as he tumbled overboard, receding into the silent depths.

The boat moved on. She turned around and studied the scene in front of her.

She moved forward toward the control cabin. There were two men inside. One looked like the waiter who had brought her spiked drink. The other was Carlos.

Between the entry and where the two men were was only about six feet. Both men appeared to be armed.

In the stealth provided by what were effectively her stocking feet, Evelyn made a running start, penetrating the control cabin at a dead run, and sliding up to the two men. She struck the waiter in the throat with stiffened fingers, and brought the side of her hand up against Carlos' head with a firm strike.

The waiter collapsed, choking. Carlos also fell, dropping a knife onto the deck. Evelyn looked down. Carlos had attempted to stab her, but the knife did not penetrate her suit. She might possibly have a bruise there in the morning. For now she felt nothing.

The waiter expired on the scene. He never got a hand on his weapon. Evelyn picked up the knife and put it in a tool cupboard.

Carlos was still alive. Evelyn bound his mouth with a strip of nanobot fabric, wrapping it around his head like duct tape. Then she bound his arms and hands behind him the same way.

She went through the pockets of these men too. Two more phones and wallets joined her collection.

Evelyn stopped the motors, leaving the engine idling. She went very carefully through the rest of the boat, finding no one else aboard. She had been quite fearful that these men might have had another woman on board. She would not have known what to do about that. She pulled her mask away and stretched it over the back of her head. It was nice to breathe fresh air again.

She returned to the control cabin, turned the boat, and headed back toward the coast. Somewhere she needed to find a safe place to put in and hide her booty. Piracy was such difficult work.

Dragging the two bodies down to her previous quarters and locking them in, Evelyn again made contact with Mark, telling him precisely what she had done, and asking for guidance on what to do next.

Mark was very upset about her having dumped one guy into the ocean. She reminded him that she had a second body also but that she didn't want to get rid of it just yet.

Neither knew what to do about Carlos. Doc was going to have to make some decisions pretty soon.

"I said I want you to figure out a way to help me keep the boat, and that I want you to bring Mark with you."

Doc was upset, and justifiably so. But this was no time to panic. Taking over the world beckoned, and things had to be done in the proper order.

Evelyn still wore her Ninja outfit. She felt a lot safer and was more confident while wearing it. So far, she hadn't had to go to the bathroom, but that was probably when she would choose to change costumes again.

Speaking of costumes, Mark was an absolute delight as an overweight jogger. He needed a bit of extra padding to pull it off, but it was still night when they got together.

It was a long night though, and dawn was on the rise. Doc wasn't going to like this part of the plan either.

"Why did you insist that I bring Mark out? And what are you trying to start other than a life of crime?" Doctor Tenerife Brandon hissed in fury.

"Hello Mother, hello Mark." Evelyn kissed both of them. "Mark, hold out your hands." Evelyn placed some oversized mittens on Mark's hands.

"And now let me borrow your face for a little bit too." Evelyn put a mask of sorts on Mark's face. All of the items were made of nanobots.

Mark stoically bore the indignities, actually exulting in finally getting out for a bit of fresh air, though frightened by all the violence.

"Mother, tonight a lot of terrible things have happened. But out of tragedy can sometime fall a blessing." Evelyn looked around, again making sure that their conversation could not be overheard in the remote area, but lowering her voice anyway.

"I still have one more corpse to dispose of, and Mark is still wanted by the police for his former indiscretions. I propose to turn my extra corpse into Mark's old identity, and arrange to kill two jailbirds while saving one Stone in the process." While speaking, she removed Mark's gloves and mask, and took them back to her new boat.

The dead man had been brought out to the corridor, so that his fate would be unknown to Carlos if he managed to survive the night as well. Trailed by her mother and Mark, Evelyn put the gloves and the mask on the body, and stood up.

"Questions?" she asked.

"You're doing what?" Doc said. Mark stood mute.

"I'm transferring Mark's fingerprints and face to my extra corpse. Of course the nanobots are doing the work. All we have to do now is dump this guy in an alley somewhere, and the cops will find him, identify him as their long-lost friend, and Mark's case will be closed." She smiled at them.

"Oh, one more thing; at some point, we'll have to get Mark some new fingerprints. Okay, that's it."

Doc and Mark just looked at each other, completely flummoxed.

Evelyn picked up the corpse, flinging it over her shoulder like a sack of marshmallows, and said, "Well, have you got some room in the SUV or not? Let's go!"

They drove around for a short time, looking for the perfect spot to get rid of a body. They finally settled on an area a few blocks from the hospital where no surveillance cameras could be spotted. Evelyn pulled her hood over her face again and dropped the body artfully in the alley, leaving it propped against the wall like a drunk.

"You really think that will work?" Mark said.

"Why not? The body has no identification; they'll run the prints, find out he's a wanted felon, and presto! Another closed case! Why wouldn't it work?"

"He doesn't even look like me."

"Who cares? We only need his fingerprints to look like yours, and that for just a short while. Just forget it. You'll see."

"Let's get back to the boat and the other prisoner. What are we going to do with him?" Doctor Brandon was looking in all directions as she drove. She was, naturally, the only one licensed, and therefore the only one who could drive because Evelyn was not yet even twelve years old, and Mark had just officially passed away, or very nearly so.

It had been a very stressful day.

"What happened at the hotel after I disappeared from it?" Evelyn asked, leaning forward from the back seat.

Ten glared at the girl, knowing she wanted to scold her for not wearing her seat belt, but also knowing that priorities dictated that more important matters be dealt with first.

"Well, I was a wreck, I'll have to admit. Hotel staff and security were getting on my nerves no end, what with constantly trying to reassure me that everything would be fine while at the same time obviously having no clue what was even going on."

"I finally found a quieter room where police personnel were taking statements and organizing a time and flowchart of information. They shortly had a few names and blurry photos posted and were sending out search parties and organizing communications."

"It was about that time that I finally got through to Mark. We had a devil of a time trying to pass information to each other without giving away too much. The clincher for me was when he told me you were going to try to turn the boat around. I had been ready to faint for hours by then, and with that fainting sounded like a good idea!"

"I was in almost the same situation," Mark continued, "possibly made worse by being alone and not being able to go anywhere. I have to say, you were the calmest head out there, Evelyn! You helped us more than we helped you!"

They had arrived back at the boat. "Why don't we just dump this character down near the hotel and go home for some sleep?" Doctor Brandon suggested.

"Hah. You don't know how tempted I was to leave him out there in the middle of the ocean."

"Not the middle of the ocean, dear. You were still quite close to shore."

"Yeah, I know. There's a possibility he might have survived out there." Evelyn admitted. "Still, I think we need to interrogate him before we let him go. If we give him to the police, they'll have him isolated for weeks while we're biting our fingernails."

Mark looked at her hands, still covered with a black surface of unknown constitution. "I don't think you could bite those fingernails with a chisel."

Evelyn looked at her body, which was admittedly a strange modification from what she had looked like only hours earlier. The rising daylight made her dark appearance increasingly out of place.

"All right, all right. I'll change on the boat. What do we do with Carlos?"

"Wait a minute. I've seen that face." Doc rummaged through her purse, coming up with her smart phone. "The cops had some pictures posted. I don't know where they got them. This guy was on that wall."

"He said his name was Carlos Sanchez. Mark was listening."

"I took a picture of his picture. Here it is. Take a look. His name is Carlos Mendoza."

Evelyn shrugged. "So who is that?"

"The cops said that he was a part of one of the big drug outfits south of the border." Doc was biting her lip. "Now you know how they can afford this big boat." She looked up.

"We need to get rid of this guy, and we need to get you clear of anything that happened out there." Doc was thinking furiously. "We'll leave him tied up here, and you'll wake up over there, just coming out of your drug haze and calling for help. You don't know what happened or who did it. Got it?"

"I can't keep my boat?" Evelyn pouted.

"Before, they only thought about kidnapping or killing you. If they find out you're the one who messed them up, they're going to want to *hurt* you."

Evelyn nodded. "All right, but we're cleaning out all the money we can find, and I've collected all the weapons, too. I'll put them in the SUV."

Ten nodded, "Let's clean up the scene. We have to take away any evidence that you were moving about on your own. That will include any nanobot evidence."

"We'll have to change his bindings then. We can't leave those straps." Mark suggested.

"They used duct tape. There should be more." Evelyn said.

"Wait! Get some surgical gloves out of the SUV. We can't leave fingerprints on the boat. Mark, you get the gloves and tape up Carlos like a Christmas present. Evelyn, as soon as you can, change your costume back and make your way out into the civilian area. You're going to come out of a drug-induced sleep and not know where you are."

Doc looked around after a few minutes. "Nothing but you and your costume was on the boat. We're not leaving any nanobots on it." She looked at Evelyn. "You don't know what happened. You blacked out at the hotel, and you're just now coming out of it. You're scared and you want your mommy, got it?"

"I got it. Are you sure there isn't somebody else I have to kill first?" Doc glared at her.

"All right, all right, just kidding." Evelyn began putting her costume back together the way it had been at the hotel. This included her welcome internal presence, and the costume's functional jewelry. She put her boots, shorts, belt, and blouse back on, and her "underwear", of course. It was amazing that the Ninja suit, so capable and transforming, could simply evaporate into such apparently harmless clothes!

Doc and Mark got back into the vehicle. Carlos was secured with duct tape in the prisoner cabin, and the door was locked. As far as they could tell, he had never regained consciousness, and they didn't care if he did.

All the weapons had been salvaged, and the phones of the missing minions had been thoroughly smashed and the bits scattered. Their wallets were with the weapons and other booty looted from the boat. All told, it looked like a haul of about fifty thousand dollars, most of the money coming from a cabinet in the master suite.

"Mark and I will head back to the house. We'll secure all the contraband and wait to be contacted by the police. Give us a little time to make our way, sweetie. I haven't had a wink of sleep last night worrying about you. I'm going to look just terrible for the cameras."

Evelyn grinned and kissed her mother good-bye. She watched as the vehicle drove away.

She watched the sun rise in the early morning calm. It was beautiful. Slowly, she wandered up into the more civilized and stirring parts of the little industrial cove where she had tied up.

Smiling, she activated the connection between her tiara and the concealed dildo. She gave herself a stimulation or two, jumping as it vibrated inside her.

Carrying the weight without having it boost her strength, Evelyn struggled up the hill, finally feeling the weariness. "Listen, guys. It helped a lot when you were making me stronger. Maybe you can do more of that somehow? As long as it makes me pretty and nothing else changes, please help me."

She listened for a response but did not hear any. Something was happening to the clothing she wore. Perhaps it was adjusting in size again. The hill seemed to level off a bit and the going got a little easier. She signaled the dildo again thinking that such a stimulus would help her stay awake. Groggy and staggering, almost unfocused on her surroundings, she found her way into a working-class morning restaurant.

Chapter Thirteen

"Honey, are you all right?" the waitress asked with a look of concern.

"I think I'll be alright now." Evelyn responded. She sighed. "I don't have any money, but what I mainly need right now is if you can call the police for me."

"What's wrong, sweetheart? What do you need the police for?"

"I think I've just been abducted. Somehow I got away, but I need to call my mom and the cops."

"I'll call for you. You just sit here and rest. What's your name?"

"Evelyn Brandon."

The first patrol car arrived in about four minutes while Evelyn was still on her first cup of tea. Within fifteen minutes, they had six more patrol cars.

Evelyn told them that she thought she had been held on a boat, for she was walking away from that boat when she came to awareness. They found the boat.

She gave them her home address and phone number. They called Doctor Brandon, who was near fainting with worry and sleeplessness. They offered to provide her a driver. She declined. She would meet them at the hospital near the hotel.

The police found Carlos. He was removed in an ambulance. Whether he was talking or not could not be determined from this distance, but he was guarded in transit.

They were searching the boat, and they were tracing its ownership.

They told Evelyn that they would be taking her to the hospital, where a police medical examiner would check her out; a female doctor, of course.

Evelyn had a moment of panic. She had dressed for this trip, and re-dressed after her adventures, in the same way she gallivanted about at home. But she was about to be examined by a doctor, and she was wearing a dildo!

Quickly, bearing a very subdued attitude, Evelyn gave instructions to her nanobots. -- Dissolve the dildo and make it disappear. You can make the bracelets bigger, or add to the boots, but make all of the thong and its mechanism dissolve and disappear.

Evelyn was very concerned that she may have escaped from a criminal enterprise only to have her mother face the wrath of a misunderstanding police department.

How could Doc explain a dildo in her daughter? That she was being treated for Hysteria?

Evelyn spent her time being transported concentrating on sending the message to make the dildo disappear. It felt as though the message had been received, but it was difficult to be sure.

Programming within the nanobots was, if not equally upset, at least equally at cross-purposes. They had the commands entered from the master controller, which followed the proper coding sequence and command structure. They had voice commands from internal structure and program memory requiring them to reconfigure all that was internal.

They had requirements to make the Evelyn stronger, to fix her, to help her breathe, to make her healthy, and to help her see better, regardless of light conditions. There was also a command to make her pretty and let nothing change. They had the resources to re-deploy several tens of millions of nanobot structure in order to accomplish the above lists of requirements. Arrayed in this manner, all of the tasks were in alignment with each other and the resources available.

Placing the lists in parallel rankings of importance and procedural priorities, they set to work. The dildo was dissolved, its components going internal in the Evelyn to build a matrix of bone-strengthening sheaths around the long bones of the Evelyn, and to harden the joint surfaces of the knees, hips, shoulders, elbows, and so forth so that extreme stresses would not damage them.

More robotic structure went into making the muscles stronger. The tendons and attachments were very underdeveloped, and required considerable reinforcement to prevent damage under quite reasonable stress loads such as had already been experienced.

Lungs and eyes required modifications to their interface structures. Lungs could work better by trapping carbon dioxide in nanobot cages rather than tie up hemoglobin. Those same cages of robotic structure could store oxygen beforehand so that efficiency would be maximized.

The only changes needed to the eyes involved multiplying the sensitivity of the receptors at the retina. With these changes, the Evelyn would be able to see under any conditions including total darkness, because her eyes would be able to see the infrared energy being output by her own body.

With a few million extra nanobots still free for various purposes, all blood vessels were cleaned and polished to reduce the back-pressure of the flowing blood, and surface capillaries had deposits of quick-reacting chemicals to block blood loss from abrasion. Tiny ligaments of connected nanobots would then pull the skin back together and make it whole again. Evelyn had learned how to heal, and to heal very quickly.

A survey was begun of the most basic programming within the Evelyn program and database. Squads of nanobots were assigned to analyze the DNA information inside individual cells, which comprised every organ and tissue, and to store the results in nanobot shared memory for reference. Repairs could then be made to those cells where information was no longer accurate, based on comparisons with the stored and verified information. This process would take an exceedingly long time to complete, but it had to be done at a low activity level to prevent interference with the normal functioning of the Evelyn program.

To secure the Evelyn against additional damage a rigorous error-checking program was begun to monitor growth, which might indicate pre-cancerous development. Accordingly, all growth chemicals were restricted to repairs for observed damage. The form that Evelyn occupied at the present moment, in the world and in the nanobot shared memory, was now fixed and invariable. It was at that point that the Evelyn stopped growing older, unless by her own command and design she wanted it to happen.

Evelyn, by her own request, at least until further notice, which backed up the program directions irrevocably ordered by Mark, was now locked into permanently being an eleven-year old girl.

One embarrassing detail had evidently escaped Evelyn's consideration. When the police lady doctor examined her, she wasn't wearing any panties.

It was a minor foible. At least she had no evidence of a harness, or much indication of long-term familiarity with adult entertainments.

But the doctor did comment that it was easy to determine Evelyn's current physical development state, because it wouldn't be long before she learned the practical reasons for wearing underwear, and for keeping tampons nearby as well.

Evelyn handled the situation by appearing to be very embarrassed.

After not too much longer, Evelyn and her mother were released, and they were able to go home. It wasn't as though Evelyn could recall any of her ordeal, after all. She had met Carlos only briefly just before the dust-up, but she had never seen the face of any of her kidnappers.

Her mother had seen even less.

The police were not worried, however. Sufficient evidence of the girl's imprisonment on the boat was there, and the boat had many intriguing cubbyholes with traces of interesting materials. Carlos would not be going anywhere for a long time, and neither would the boat.

As soon as Evelyn got home, she went straight to bed, and slept nearly around the clock. During that time, nanobots inside her were scurrying about, cleaning up, restructuring, fixing up, and generally doing a restoration of the Evelyn's health and structural permanency that would withstand almost any challenge. Even the material from the arm bracelets was absorbed back into the girl's body to complete the ordered modifications.

Inside her, the migrating nanobots utilized practically empty areas of sinus cavities and lymph passages to move about and organize their presence and new functionality. Of the thirty-two pounds of nanobots that Evelyn had started with, only fourteen pounds could be accounted for in the weight of her blouse, tiara, shorts, and shoes. These things were heavier than they had needed to be, but they were simply conveyance devices for the maximum weight of nanobots that she could carry.

Everything else had been absorbed into the girl's body, much of it surrounding and infiltrating her brain, neck, and upper thoracic area.

From fingertips to pre-frontal cortex, the newly made pathways and transfer sites for messages had the effect of making the girl's thoughts and sensory impressions move through that space at an accelerated pace, much of it traveling as functional radio waves rather than neuronal synaptic chemistry. Her thoughts came more quickly and cleanly than ever before. Her reaction speed was astonishingly fast and her movements graceful.

Oddly, even with all the recent changes, and many more to come, her body shape had not changed. It would take several years before that fact became inarguably and continuingly apparent.

✦✦✦✦✦✦✦

Evelyn woke up feeling very energized, and very hungry. She made her way to the kitchen and began wolfing down cereal, fruit, and a large glass of orange juice.

"That hungry, are you?"

Evelyn looked around. "Mom! You're home?"

"Yes, of course!' Ten smiled. "Considering what we went through, a few days off seems warranted, don't you think?"

Evelyn smiled. "Yeah, I guess. So we won, huh? What did we win?"

Doc laughed. "For all we went through, we should have won a million dollars! But no; No, I could have sold my research, probably for that amount. But I'm not ready to surrender it quite yet." She smiled. "We'll just have to get by on what we can scrape together for a while."

Evelyn drew out some additional nanobot material, and set up a dark figure in the lower level. She was wearing only her old thong harness and smiley face, and a pair of sandals.

Mark was sitting at the table watching her. To his eyes, her naked innocence and playful activity were like a calming medicine. "Where are your wrist bracelets, Evelyn?"

She smiled at him, holding her arms open and embracing her free nature. "I've recycled all of it. We could always make more, but I wanted to try some new ideas with the nanobots."

Ten rode down in the elevator, dressed for no discernible reason in scrubs. She came out into the activity area and gave Mark and Evelyn each a kiss. She placed a hand along Evelyn's jaw, looking at her clinically, "You seem a bit warm, Sweetie, are you feeling okay?"

"I'm feeling fine, Mom. I have a lot of energy, which is good, because I ate a lot of food!"

They walked together over to the dining area. Ten slid her hand down to Evelyn's stomach. "Well, it hasn't gone to your waist yet, dear. You're as thin as a young doe."

"I *am* a young doe, ready to run and scamper through the forest!" Evelyn stretched her arms over her head, twining them together with her fingers interlaced.

Taking a seat at the table, Doc moved her hands gently over the taut flesh as Evelyn stood still for her, lightly tracing up to the forearms, and then from the arms down the ribcage, and over the gently curving rump to the upper thighs. "A doe would envy you your smooth, supple skin, darling! I am amazed that you have no injuries at all from your adventure."

Evelyn crawled into her mother's lap. "This is the second time in two days that I have put myself in the hands of a Doctor." She smiled.

"It's probably a good thing I didn't have my little friend with me the first time."

Mark watched with interest as Doc reached down to Evelyn's crotch and gently prodded the smiling face of the internal dildo.

Evelyn smiled as she did this, looking slightly distant.

"Yes, I'm very glad you thought to make that disappear before your examination. That saved me an abundance of very awkward questions." Doc admitted.

"Do you think you were being a bad mother?" Evelyn adopted a very serious expression and tone of voice.

"I suppose I could make all kinds of excuses." Ten looked over at Mark. "I know I've done some frankly reprehensible things to both of you." She hugged Evelyn. "That was a very bad time in my life. It's when I was building this space, you know, trying to work out my frustrations with physical work." She looked into Evelyn's eyes. "I guess I thought you needed something similar for your … therapy, when it came time for it."

"Without having much social contact, it struck me that taking a short-cut to maturity would be good for you. It would allow you to evaluate what being an adult in adult relationships would be worth to you, without going into the sacrifice of time and effort that such things normally require."

"You wouldn't be meeting very many people, because that's the path I had set for myself as well. Actually, I was being selfish, even while I was making the excuse that it was all for you." Ten looked into the little girl's eyes with a touch of sadness. "I guess I was trying to make you grow up too soon."

Evelyn gently laid her hand on her mother's cheek. "I had to grow up much too soon just a day or so ago, Mother. It's a good thing I'd had some practice beforehand. Being kidnapped and taken hostage from your party was … could have been, the worst experiences of each of our lives."

Ten nodded her head.

"I thought about what they wanted me for. They had put a lot of effort into getting me, first with the drugged drink, and then the outright public abduction…"

"Wait a minute," Ten said, "what drugged drink?"

"Oh, you didn't hear about that?" Evelyn looked up. "When Carlos introduced himself to me up on the balcony, he tried to get me to drink some 'punch'. It had wine, chloral hydrate, and Rohypnol. I didn't drink it, of course. But if I had, they would probably have taken me from the balcony. I'm not sure why they put me on the boat, but I think trying to get out of the country before anything else is a clue to what the 'anything else' would have been."

"What do you think it would have been?" Mark asked quietly.

Evelyn studied him. The length of her silence became awkward.

"I think Carlos wanted *me*. He was kinda short, still a little young to be winning girls on his own, and able to use his family's connections and drug money to do things most teenagers could only fantasize about. I think he wanted me to be his personal plaything, something he could use any way he wanted, without having to learn all the social niceties required to do it the right way. He was in a hurry."

Mark looked down. Now would be a good time for the subject to change.

"That may not have been all he wanted to do, but it would be a start. Then they might try for some kind of ransom, possibly related to the kind of money they thought might be involved in our cutting-edge science. Even if he couldn't get ransom, after he had his fun, he could just sell me to another sick pervert, or a whole string of them. It didn't look good."

Evelyn looked at her mother. "You're probably wondering how I could have worked up the nerve to take on those guys, to beat them at their own game, and to become the physical nightmare they thought *they* were." She smiled grimly. "That's how! I could almost read their minds, and I decided to change their minds for them, whatever it took. Dumping that one guy overboard was easy, once I had a clear picture of what they were about."

Doctor Brandon had a look of absolute horror on her face. "The cops said … they were about drugs."

Evelyn put on a wry expression. "Yeah, drugs all right, and then the thing that comes after drugs. For some people, being able to take what you want, that's a bigger high than any drug can bring."

"Oh, honey! I was so frightened! But even I couldn't have imagined anything as bad as that!"

"She's right though," Mark said. "I didn't see many like that in my prison experience, but she's got them down on what they were thinking and planning." He looked at Evelyn. "You did the world a favor, lover."

"Mark never fantasized about doing things like that to me," Evelyn said, shaking her head slowly. "He didn't have to." She looked up. "I got to him first."

"She's awesome, you know?" Mark looked at Doc. "Just absolutely awesome!" He stepped over to the little mini-kitchen and started putting together a breakfast for the Doc.

Evelyn slowly separated from her mother and went back to the mass of nanobots.

"What are you doing over there?" Doctor Brandon looked at the dark figure.

"This is a copy of my exo-suit, the outfit I wore to fight with the bad guys. Basically, it's something I could put on, but its bones and muscles would be surrounding mine. It worked, but you can see how ugly it was."

"I can see how intimidating it was, and how effective it was. You took down all three of those guys by yourself!" Mark commented.

"Well, they ruined my party." She looked at him for a moment.

He held up his hands to show that he got the point. *Nobody* messes with Evelyn's party.

"What are you going to do with it? I would imagine I could use it to become a feared and powerful minion myself." He grinned at her.

Evelyn studied the figure. She didn't want to wear it, but it couldn't do much on its own. She thought about it for a few minutes and then began moving her hands around in the air as if modeling clay from across the room.

The figure began writhing and reshaping itself.

"It's been a while since I played with dolls. I think I'm going to make myself a doll to play with." She continued moving her hands. The figure took on a more and more human shape.

"How are you doing that?" Mark was staring, incredulous. Doctor Brandon simply stared, unable to speak. Mark set the food in front of her, and she began eating without having said anything.

Evelyn pointed to her head. "I've got nanobots all through me. I can hear them and talk to them. They said I'm the Evelyn program that is the core of what they are. I think I'm the hardware that their program runs on."

She studied her hands. They seemed completely normal. "Apparently you were ordering them to fix me and help me, and I was yelling at them to help me and fix me, and so that's what they did."

She smiled. "Then when I tell them what I want they can send out messages to these other guys. All I have to do is show it to them in my imagination, and they just put it together."

"You mean you can program them and command them just by talking to them?" Doc asked.

"Just by *thinking at them*, actually," she smiled wistfully, turning back to the figure.

Mark and Doctor Brandon watched as the figure redefined itself, standing up straight and bearing a remarkable similarity to Evelyn's shape. The skin tone had changed from black to a healthily tanned flesh tone. The figure was naked, and bald.

"This is the shape they surrounded. It's what I looked like under the armor." Evelyn looked more closely. "The face doesn't look right."

Mark came around. "That's not the face you see in the mirror. That's the face you *wear*. Everybody has little differences from one side of the face to the other. The prettier you are, the less difference you see."

Evelyn was nodding, until the last part of what he said hit home. "Wait a minute! What was that last bit?"

"I'm sorry. I didn't mean it like that. You're absolutely gorgeous."

Evelyn glared at him, and then looked at her mannequin again. She practiced switching it from mirror image to straight image a few times to see the slight distortion that had always been in her own face.

Ordinarily, this would have been something to just shrug off and forget. But in this case, with nanobots available …

She gestured slightly, and the figure in front of her smoothed its appearance, muting the minor differences from one side of the face to the other. It was a little hard to tell, and even more difficult to admit, but the face *was* prettier when smoothed like this.

Evelyn sent a command into her own structure; adjust my face to be prettier by smoothing the differences from left to right, but only do it while I'm sleeping. She received a kind of hollow echo, which she had learned to interpret as acknowledgment.

'Do you still have Mark's face in your memory?' she asked her robotic retinue.

With confirmation, she commanded that the figure in front of her have a properly sized, age-reduced depiction of Mark's face on it, with the facial features smoothed like hers. Then she watched as the face transformed.

Oddly, with nothing else changing but the face, the figure now looked remarkably like a boy!

Evelyn tilted her head, looking at it in surprise. Then she commanded that the figure be given hair like a boy, generically just brown and wavy, and medium length.

Now the figure definitely looked like a boy. 'All right, let's go all the way. Make this figure look like a boy of this age and size, using the data from your knowledge base.'

Slowly, the figure changed, broadening the shoulders slightly, and narrowing the hips. At the groin, a small penis and scrotum appeared, and the legs grew skinny. Other than on the head, the body had no hair.

Observing the penis, Evelyn made a wry face. "Oh yeah, I forgot about that." She walked around the figure. With just a slight gesture, the posterior lifted into a more appealing curve, and the legs grew slightly more muscular.

One more tweak of the lad's shoulder and arm muscles, and he looked stronger and more athletic. He was also surprisingly beautiful.

'Now give me piercingly blue eyes, set in a friendly smiling face.'

In a few seconds, the face opened its eyes, and smiled.

"How do you like it?" Evelyn asked.

Mark stared. "I like it … possibly a little more than I *should* like it. He's so beautiful, I almost want to kiss him!"

"Androgynous, I think is the word you're looking for. Maybe you should try to think of him as your son." Doc looked at Mark for a moment.

"Way better looking than me," Mark muttered.

"Hmm. He's based on you. Maybe it's just the eyes." Evelyn said.

"Yeah, sure. All right, now you've got your doll. What are you going to do with him?"

Evelyn pulled up a chair and sat on it. "You know," she said, "that is a really good question."

Ten was looking at the figure. "So it's like a picture, then."

Evelyn nodded, and then shook her head. "Well, there's no brain inside, but there are bones and muscles."

"What good are bones and muscles without a brain?" Doc said with a smile.

"It worked okay on the boat." Evelyn said with a wicked grin.

"If you wanted to give it a brain," Doc said with a curious expression, "what kind of brain would you give it?"

Evelyn pulled up her left leg and hugged it. Being naked, and very flexible, this was an easy posture for her, but her mother scowled faintly at the indecorous pose.

"All of it is made up of robots, so I'd guess it should have a robot brain." Evelyn said, "Too bad we don't have any brains handy."

"It's just a matter of defining it." Ten said, "A little while ago you didn't have bones and muscles."

Mark cleaned up the breakfast items. Then he went over and lounged on the bed. He had a hunch he would end up there sooner or later anyway.

"The bones are just a kind of crystalline structure, held firmly in place. The muscles are simply nanobot cables with a knot of tangled cables designed to pull tension on the limbs, the same way ours do. I'm estimating this figure will be about a hundred times stronger than a man." Evelyn was pulling on her lip. "I could control it, if I concentrated, but to make a brain would be beyond my knowledge level. Isn't that more like programming?" She looked over at Mark.

"You'd have to have signal lines going into the muscles, and then routing back to the brain. You would also need many sensory devices scattered all over the skin, as well as inside, so that the robot could feel what it's touching, and how it's moving."

Doc nodded with a smile. "You guys are good! I wish I had talented people working with me in the hospitals like you two!"

Evelyn looked over. "We *are* working with you. So how do we make a brain?"

Doc shrugged. "Let the nanobots organize it. Just explain that you want the sensory inputs to go in and be processed to reach conclusions and exhibit behaviors, and then come back out to have the muscles take the appropriate action. Make sure your instructions include a way to have feedback on the actions, so there can be a learning curve, and then let the brain learn the same way a baby does, by playing and doing things, and sometimes even making mistakes."

Evelyn looked at the figure.

"But don't forget to have control over it." Her mother reminded her, "When you yell 'stop!' you definitely want something that powerful to stop right away!"

Evelyn nodded.

Marc added, "Don't forget how much learning takes place based on vision. Those pretty eyes need to see and understand what they're seeing. Then, what it's seeing needs to be reported to the brain so that the robot can think about what it's seeing, and decide whether to take an action or not."

"Okay, we'll need eyes and ears, that's obvious. I think I'll make the ears be able to hear on radio frequencies too." Evelyn mused. She looked up at her companions, "Because that's *so* handy, of course."

"I recall reading some articles about how the miniaturization in some weapons systems provided the ability to sense positions even without reference to satellite data and such. One of those devices could help your robot with keeping its balance. Acceleration and force-stress monitors and ring-laser gyros could take the place of our inner ear, and the sense of how your limbs are moving."

"It sounds like my robot is going to have all kinds of input channels. I hope they won't be confusing."

"You know," pondered Doc, "that organization into hierarchies may be what gives us the ability to think. Otherwise, we'd be distracted by every slight sound or motion. ... Oh, look! Shiny!"

Evelyn went to her mother and smiled. "You like my robot, don't you?"

Ten hugged her daughter and rubbed Evelyn's bare bottom with large circular motions. "I have a hunch your new puppy is going to make messes. But it will be your job to clean up after him."

"I will, Mom." Evelyn promised.

Ten stood up and stretched, watching Evelyn clear the activity area. Then she looked over at Mark and smiled. She began taking off her blouse as he moved over in the bed.

Evelyn saw what was happening and simply smiled. She had a new toy to play with anyway.

While Ten and Mark were busy depleting their energies, Evelyn thought about the energy system for her robot. Anything she came up with would be child's play to put together using the nanobots. And she was a child, so that all fit, of course.

Evelyn took up a position near the workspace she shared with Mark. Her recent studies had propelled her into more and more advanced research for things like robots and manufacturing processes. To help visualize and easily interact with the information displays and virtual access panels, she was sitting very erect on a stool, her legs entwined with the stool's bottom rungs while her arms and upper body were free to move like a conductor's baton.

On her face was a pair of high technology goggles, similar to safety glasses, but displaying at an apparent focus a multitude of synthetic colorful screens with active and interactive displays.

She could grab images and expand them, rotate them and flip them, set them aside or follow electronic trails to even more detailed schematics and diagrams. This was an engineer's playhouse, and to see the young girl sitting naked and silent on the stool, with her arms waving around to an unseen orchestra, you could be forgiven for thinking she was avidly listening to her favorite music.

But she was pulling ideas, material designs, and execution diagrams from the thin air in front of her, like a magician pulling out streams of cloth of various colors. She was intuitively interacting with the computer system in much the same way she controlled the nanobots. Perhaps this was partly because the nanobots were helping her translate her gestures and commands into values the computer system could handle.

She would be able to bury a small internal combustion engine inside the robot somewhere; after all it would have to have organs of *some* type. That would then fit together with needing to breathe, and having energy so that it could feel warm to the touch. Properly designed, the power plant could help make the robot appear rather human in its physical characteristics.

Evelyn had focused on a ceramic rotary design engine, which would burn alcohol or vegetable oil, and run silently. Meanwhile its heat would go into warming the otherwise cold robotic body, making it a fit companion for the sofa, or even a small bed.

The engine could provide power as if for power steering as well as electrical power for the nanobots. A hydraulic pump could pressurize a reservoir and make a sound at the same time like a heart beating. Hydraulic muscles could supplement the nanobot muscles to smooth their operation and appearance, and flowing hydraulic fluid of some kind could seep under the skin to keep the body's surface warm, with a rosy color coming from the fluid itself. Then should the skin be damaged somehow, the robot would bleed like any other individual.

The robot would breathe in and out, of course. Warm breath coming out would have the telltale biological product of carbon dioxide, and the oxygen going in would combust with the alcohol or vegetable oil.

Evelyn loved how the plans were coming together for her newest toy. At the same time, her mother was watching the girl and her choreographic antics from the other side of the room. They were *both* very happy ladies.

Chapter Fourteen

Doc and Mark collaborated on developing the brain for the robot. Evelyn had showed them the power-plant design and they could not suppress their delight for the thoroughness of her project.

In the months following the ordeal, Doc flung her heart into making Evelyn's robot a work of art to rival the success of the nanobot project. Doc's notion of using stacked processing hierarchies seemed to bear fruit almost immediately. They were able to simulate many motion and sensory parameters into a kind of memory base, which allowed memory algorithms to process movement as a mathematical expression, subject to known rules for extracting further information from it.

Mark set up the robot vision system, using multifocal processing algorithms to extract movement detected by advanced cameras as if they were physical objects to track and target. Edge detection and shadow analysis, combined with the equivalent of ray-tracing comparisons to derive an almost intuitive understanding of the nature of the object observed. After all, if the robot brain could dream up an object that would move like the one seen, then the one seen was quite likely to be identical to the one imagined. This meant that the robot vision system could identify objects by sight alone.

These algorithms reported in hierarchies, so that simple movement was not a distraction. Instead, it triggered analysis, path orientation, and threat potential even before it was reported to the robot situational parameter base.

Mark was using Evelyn's display goggles, or actually using his own version, since he could not quite get the level of fine control that she was already manifesting, and since she was also using her goggles and would not share them. Like the nanobot iterations, the brain program was being built in virtual memory, where its capabilities could be measured and tested.

Mark turned from his corner of the former study area, which was now more of a production area for advanced technology, as long as "production" could be defined as imaginary, and looked at Evelyn, again comfortably perched upon her favorite stool. She appeared to be surveying her kingdom, or princess-dom, with quiet satisfaction. For this morning's session, and not for the first time, Evelyn had foregone even the most limited form of clothing, her thong "underwear". She had come to work with the computer clad only in sandals, and they were currently lying discarded on the floor.

She was naked, yes; as naked as she could possibly be, except for the display goggles on her head, and the casual and customary smile on her face.

He was actually looking at her through the transparent viewing portion of the display goggles. No overlays were operational at this viewing angle. Viewing angel – Mark visualized a halo circling the girl's head and began searching for overlays that might show how the computer interface affected her appearance. She was always an angel in his eyes.

Using a projection designed to map electrical and magnetic fields around conductors, to show how proximity and shielding affected them, Mark was surprised to see that Evelyn had, as far as the computer was concerned, a field surrounding her entire upper body. Not only that, but it was active. As she moved her hands, flicking and sliding over imaginary display surfaces, blue and gold auroral clouds flickered and dashed from her fingertips and around her head.

Curious, he watched her interacting with her computer station. What could explain the way the computer was showing these flashes?

The answer came to him, nanobots. Evelyn had said that she had nanobots all through her, and that she could hear them and interact with them. She had said that they could respond to her visualizations and her imagination.

That meant that the nanobots were circulating through her brain, and reading her mind! A shiver went through him as he realized that this could have been disastrous! They had unwittingly exposed this innocent girl … um, scratch that, this young girl to a nanobot infestation, with no idea how it could have turned out.

But how had it turned out? Mark thought about Evelyn's recent behavior, particularly her academic and mental behaviors. Certainly it would only derail his thoughts to consider her sexual behavior – the girl had been a whirlwind of energetic intensity whenever they had gotten together – anyway, her mind had clearly also been boosted in its speed and general cognitive ability. Mark frowned; it appeared that the thought he'd just had could apply to him as well. Had he been infested with nanites too?

He struggled back to the original matter. Just how much smarter might the girl be now? She had already almost finished her ordinary education and was currently working on the equivalent of post-graduate projects and analysis. Could she test out of her home schooling and graduate officially?

Evelyn was looking at him.

"What you lookin' at, you perverty perv?" she asked in a friendly manner.

"Ah," he acknowledged the rudeness of his staring, "I was just admiring the activity level of your magnificent brain."

She tilted her head. Sitting there, with her sandals kicked off, and her only concession to even the concept of clothing her display goggles, she looked indescribably delectable. "You can see that?" she asked.

"It's the electro-magnetic field overlay. You have a cloud of nanobot gnat-messengers buzzing around your head."

Evelyn held up her hand toward him. A bright flash appeared around the tips of her fingers, and simultaneously, his penis began vibrating, as if she had used the special button on her wrist transmitter. But she wasn't wearing her wrist transmitter, and hadn't for months.

Mark stared as she released the signal. Evelyn could send out radio signals with no more effort than giving it a thought!

"Pretty cool, huh?" Evelyn grinned at him.

"Wow! No wonder you stopped wearing your bracelets! What about the music?"

Evelyn turned both hands upward. A blue glow emanated from her hands, and the background music started playing at a soft volume.

"That is amazing! Can I kiss you?"

"You may worship me in any way you choose, my loyal subject." Evelyn took off her goggles and set them on the work surface.

Mark also removed his goggles. He approached the girl respectfully and picked her up from the stool. She came willingly into his arms and looked up at him.

"You are the most amazing, beautiful, sexy, and joyful bundle of loveliness it has ever been my pleasure to look at, much less to touch and hold." Mark said with all sincerity.

Evelyn smiled at him. "That's exactly what you told my mother last night."

"No," Mark answered, "not exactly. It was something similar, but not precisely the same. I know I didn't call her a bundle of loveliness."

"Very well. For those kind words then, you may kiss me."

He smiled and murmured to himself, "Let me see now; I have a thoroughly naked nymph in my arms. What shall I do with her?" Mark gently deposited her on the bed.

He looked at her face for a moment in stunned appreciation. "You are absolutely the most gorgeous person alive."

She smiled back at him, and he kissed her most tenderly. She smelled delicious and felt wonderful. Mark used his lips and his gentle hands to caress her and in his own way to worship her.

"This way? You want me to do it this way? I'm afraid that I might hurt you." Her splayed limbs were so inviting, but he really did love the girl. He would not harm her for the world, even though in the back of his mind both his innate desires and his hypnotic conditioning made him want to proceed with unaccustomed vigor.

"I'm tougher than I look." Evelyn smiled at him, "I'd like to get the full effect."

Mark let his weight come down somewhat on her, introducing his most prominent feature gently as she wriggled to accommodate him. Even from the first thrust, he could tell that this was different and more intense than ever before.

It went on and on. With long, practiced strokes, Mark glided into and out of the girl's well-conditioned sexuality. He watched her face, to see how she concentrated and grew more intense as the session wore on.

For Evelyn, this was an entirely new experience; she was getting additional feedback even as the procedure continued. It seemed that her nerves were being grown and multiplying to give more and more of the signals of pleasure even without changing anything in the intensity or pressure of each stroke. She realized that her busy little associates were assisting in her growing appreciation of the activity. Why would they do that? Were her nanobots nano-pervs as well? She smiled, but that gesture was inundated by the other expressions shifting and changing on her lovely new face.

In any case, this session of lovemaking with Mark was the most rewarding she could recall, and she had worn him out a number of times in their long association.

Eventually, she allowed him to relent, and he withdrew and collapsed beside her.

Presently she sat up and looked around. Her mother was sitting at the table, watching her. Doc gestured to the seat beside her, where a teacup waited.

Holding up a finger, Evelyn slid off the bed and went into the bathroom. Showering quickly, she came out of the bath still drying her hair, and then placed the towel where it could dry while she simply shook her head to let the hair fall into its accustomed pixie hairstyle.

Evelyn smiled at her mother.

Ten tilted her head. Glancing over at Mark, who was clearly exhausted, she raised an eyebrow. "I was a little concerned when I first saw you two. He's got a few pounds on you. He's not too heavy?"

Evelyn grinned. "He didn't feel heavy at all. I gave him a good workout, didn't I? I can see why you like that technique."

"I honestly never expected to see you using it. It was a little much to see, as a mother I guess."

Evelyn shrugged. "Mark's butt isn't that ugly." She smiled.

"Wasn't what I meant." Ten looked her daughter over. "Have you been cutting your own hair?"

Evelyn sipped on her tea. "No, why?"

"I've just realized that I haven't taken you to the beauty parlor for a hair trim in months. I know we've been occupied, but it's just been slipping my mind. Why isn't your hair longer?"

"I don't want it to be longer."

Ten smiled, "Ordinarily, just wanting doesn't make things happen."

Evelyn looked at her mother. Then she raised her hand and turned it face up. The background music stopped.

Ten looked around.

Evelyn gestured, sweeping casually outward with her arm. The lights faded and dimmed. Then she raised her hand again, and the music came back on.

"It does for me." Evelyn said with a smile.

Ten stared at her.

"Your hair has stopped growing?" Doc said with incredulity.

"Not stopped, I guess. It just doesn't get any longer unless I tell it to. It saves a lot of trouble."

"And the music, the lights," Ten stared.

"Mark said he could see electricity moving around me with his goggles." Evelyn said. "He described my brain as magnificent."

"Nanobots," Ten said.

"Nanobots," Evelyn agreed.

"So all this research, the work you've been doing?" Ten looked at her.

"Me and my buddies are curious, and they know a lot of stuff." Evelyn replied evenly.

"All that data that Mark downloaded into the nanite core ..."

"*I'm* the nanite core." Evelyn said levelly. "I've got a science library in my head, and it's growing every day. They call me *the Evelyn*."

Ten shook her head. She reached out and placed her hand against her daughter's cheek. "What else have you noticed?"

"It's like flying a fighter plane. I can set up a heads-up cockpit display to interface with the nanobots. I have a clock and a direction display. For them I don't even need those goggles." She gestured toward the goggles lying discarded at the workstation. "I only need them when I'm working with the other computers."

She looked at her mother. "If I could fly, I would *be* a fighter plane."

Ten looked at her strangely.

"I'm faster. I think I'm stronger. I don't know how to test myself." She looked over at Mark, asleep after his long session. "He was worried about maybe hurting me. I don't think he *could* hurt me, and not just because of hypnotic conditioning. I'm pretty sure that I could pick him up and carry him the way he carries me. *I'd* probably hurt *him* though; my hands are too small."

"He weighs more than twice as much as you," Ten said, "and he's male."

"Not any more. You fixed him, remember?" She grinned, "He's either a hyper-male, or a useful eunuch."

Ten shook her head. "You're incorrigible."

Evelyn smiled.

"Want to go to a party?" Ten asked.

"Sure!" the girl responded immediately, "What are we celebrating?"

"We should be celebrating another birthday for you, but you don't seem to be getting any older. I'd almost forgotten how close it is. How can we give you a twelfth birthday party if you're still just eleven?"

"I'm content to be eleven for a little while longer; it's just about perfect for me. Forget about the birthday. What's the other thing?"

"We got an award for the nanobot presentation. No money involved, because I wouldn't sell my work, but we won the contest. So they're giving us an award to recognize our achievement and the milestone it represents."

"Cool! When is it?"

"Next Saturday."

"So I get to pick an outfit? Unless you want me to go naked again," Evelyn looked down at her body. "I'm ready, in that case."

"You *are* incorrigible."

"I bet you think I'd be too embarrassed."

"No, but I would be." Ten smiled, "I don't think you'd be bothered by *anything.*"

"That's because I wouldn't be." Evelyn looked over at Mark. "Too bad Mark won't be able to go."

Ten nodded in agreement. "Too bad your robot won't be ready. That would be something to display."

Evelyn looked over in the corner, where the robot leaned nonchalantly and forlornly. Still naked, but now with his eyes closed, he seemed almost to be napping.

"Well, if we rushed it, we could put together a skeleton and musculature. Obviously the skin is ready. My power system is complete in design. We could do something with the eyes easily enough. What we're missing is a brain. I don't think we can push that. It isn't ready, and won't be for a few months."

"It would be nice if we could show it off. But we don't even have a control interface." Ten said.

"What would you do with that?"

"Oh, just make him walk around. If we told people it was a robot, they wouldn't expect much from it."

"You'd almost need some brain power even to do that." Evelyn said, "You could operate it by remote control, maybe." She looked over at the robot again, and grew thoughtful.

Ten watched her. "What?"

Evelyn looked over at Mark. "I was thinking about a control interface."

"To let Mark control it?" Doc asked, puzzled.

"To let Mark *be* it!" Evelyn said with a grin. She looked back and forth between Mark and the robot, obviously coming up with yet another mad scheme.

"All right, explain then." Ten suggested.

"We can power the robot. It will look right. But it needs a brain.

Suppose we put Mark in a full-body motion capture suit, with vision displays like those goggles. All he has to do is walk around, talk to people, shake hands and stuff, all by remote control! He wouldn't really be leaving here, but it would feel like it. He'll get to go out, to go with us to the party, and we'll just introduce him as our new robot!"

"If we did that, he wouldn't look like a robot. He'd look like another human being. Why should we introduce him as a robot?" Ten looked over at the robot. "Why not say he's your cousin from out of town?"

Evelyn looked toward Mark. "I think Mark would really get a kick out of that. I might even be able to get him to dance with me!"

"I don't think you'd want a robot stepping on your feet." Doc chided her.

"I'm tougher, remember? Besides, this robot will only weigh about forty pounds. He's going to have a lot of hollow space inside."

"Really?" Doc said, "How will you do that?"

Evelyn ticked off the items, "Carbon fiber bones, hydraulic muscles, a ceramic engine, nanobot skin, advanced camera optics, and about eight different cell-phone links to carry the data. It could all fit in a cardboard box."

"Well, I thought we were going to walk him in."

"Sure. That would be easier," Evelyn admitted, "but if he steps on my toes, I'm going to throw him through a window."

They laughed.

Mark built the skeleton and the hydraulic muscles. These were simply flexible muscle shapes attached to the skeleton and able to expand in the middle when filled with hydraulic fluid. A strong fiber woven around the shape allowed it to stretch in volume by shrinking in length. It looked like human muscles in action, and was controlled by simply monitoring what Mark would be doing in the suit.

The suit would be holding him up so that his legs could walk without moving him, and his arms could move while he pretended to shake hands, and everything else he needed to do to operate the robot by remote control.

Mark would see what the robot saw, and the robot would do what Mark did.

Evelyn built the power system. She made a small rotary engine, designed in this instance to run on pure alcohol. Such a fuel had less chemical energy, but it was easier to mask its combustion as a normal biological process. The engine would power the muscles; the heat would seem normal; and only water and carbon dioxide would exit the "lungs".

This assembly was fitted into the robot's chest, where the steady thump of the hydraulic pump would sound like, were anyone close enough to hear it, a human heart.

The enclosure would be insulated for sound and heat. The engine could be shut down as needed if the robot body got too warm, and the abundant electrical charge in the batteries would be able to power it for short periods.

The "heart" was not designed to change speeds, but no need was seen for this during a short outing.

Doc had the responsibility for acquiring several phones and the needed accounts to use them as a remote robotic communications system. Mark would have binocular vision, even being able to focus a bit to see longer distances should the need arise.

Everything else that the robot touched would be reported back to Mark, suspended in a full-body suit that gave him pressure sensations for each point of contact the robot made.

Evelyn designed the body suit to mimic the robot's actions. If the robot should begin to fall forward, Mark would be tilted forward, prompting him to try to recover his "balance" by pressing more with his toes.

The whole system, as complex and convoluted as it was, was a good compromise for not having a more autonomous robot. At least this way, Mark would have every sensation of being at the party, from walking in the door and shaking hands with people, to actually holding Evelyn in his arms and dancing with her.

But he wouldn't be able to eat anything!

It was enough to drive a robot to drink.

Doc also had to get the clothing arranged for the party. The robot wasn't quite ready to go out shopping for clothes or to be fitted for a suit, so a few compromises were necessary in this area as well.

"You want me to do what?" Evelyn protested.

"To be fitted for a suit." Ten said. "We're getting you a nice gown. We need to get your date set up with a matching dress suit. And since you're both exactly the same size for some reason …"

"My *date?*" Evelyn stared at her mother. "You're kidding, right?"

"You mentioned dancing with him." Doc said reasonably, "Isn't that a date?"

Evelyn looked over at the robot, now attired in boy's underwear and a tee shirt. He was starting to look just a little bit evil. Still cute, though.

She sighed. "Oh, the things I do for world domination!"

Ten smiled. "Yeah, and you claimed you'd be ready to go to the party naked."

Evelyn glared at her mother. "Naked is one thing, sexual confusion is another," she said confidently.

Ten leaned down and kissed her daughter on the mouth, bending her backward and holding her to keep the girl from falling. She held the kiss until she felt Evelyn's resistance melt away.

They both straightened up.

"Now that we've got *that* settled, when do we go shopping?" Evelyn said.

Mark had been watching them. "Do you want to try the gown out on Nathan?"

Evelyn looked over. "Nathan?"

"It's better than calling him 'nothing'." Mark suggested casually, "Nathan Stone."

Evelyn mouthed the words. She looked at her mother, who shrugged.

"Okay, Nathan then." Evelyn said, "Say what?"

"Do you want to try the gown out on Nathan?"

"If you keep going the way you're going, I'm going to try kicking you in the testicles again."

"Go for it, little girl." Mark grinned.

"All right, you two." Ten said, "We'll go shopping tomorrow. Due to time constraints, we'll have to buy Nathan's suit off the rack. I guess that means you'll have to try something on a few times."

"… world domination." Evelyn said softly, shaking her head.

"I could go with you, and help you change in the dressing room." Mark suggested.

"Pervert." Evelyn said. Then she walked over and stood in front of him. "Kneel down." She commanded him.

Without argument, Mark got on his knees in front of her.

Evelyn stepped up to him, putting her feet wide apart to get close, wrapped her arms around his neck, and kissed him.

Then while holding the kiss, she slowly lowered herself onto his as always upright penis, gently wriggling to get seated properly. Once in position, Evelyn looked into his eyes and smiled.

"You behave yourself now, or I'll be stepping on your toes when we dance."

"You can kick *him* in the testicles if you want. It won't bother me." Mark grinned.

"Good point." Evelyn kissed him again, and began wriggling once more.

"I love you, you know," Mark said, staring intently at the girl.

"I let you, sometimes," Evelyn responded.

"Get a room, you two," Doc commented.

"This *is* my room," Mark said without breaking eye contact.

Evelyn smiled, and wriggled some more.

"So my twin brother needs a suit but he can't come out for the fitting. That's why I'm standing in for him." Evelyn stated firmly and for the record.

"It's okay with me, honey, I just work here," the lady sales clerk said in a bored voice.

Evelyn took the suit into the changing room and began getting dressed in it.

Doc looked over at the clerk. "She tells that story all the time. I think she's a little self-conscious about it."

The clerk made no response, but she seemed less bored as the transactions went on.

When Evelyn came out in the suit, she looked entirely different. Perhaps the addition of the tweed newsboy cap with matching vest completed the look somehow.

"Oh, honey, you're going to love that suit. You look very stylish!" the clerk rambled excitedly.

Evelyn narrowed her eyes at the woman, but turned and looked in the mirror again. "Do you like it, Mom?"

"It looks very nice on you, sweetheart." Ten said.

Evelyn turned her head slowly. "Fine. We'll take it, and that's the end of trying things on. I think I need to find a bathroom."

With a nod from her mother, Evelyn went back in to the dressing room to remove the suit.

After the girl came back out, Ten handed the clerk two shirts to go with the suit, and they waited quietly for the purchases to be rung up.

"What was wrong with her, Mom? Did she forget that I said it was for my twin brother?"

"I told her you made that story up." Ten admitted.

Evelyn looked at her, attempting to convey a haughty disdain, but ultimately failing by beginning to snicker in laughter.

"You did look very sweet and stylish, my dear." Her mother said.

"World domination," Evelyn said softly, "World domination."

"We have to get some shoes too." Doc mentioned.

"This had better go quickly, or I'm just going to change the size of his feet." Evelyn said acidly.

Ten laughed and tousled Evelyn's hair. Evelyn shook it out again.

"Look on the bright side, sweetie," Doctor Brandon said, "Carlos would be very pleased to see the good use you're making of his money."

Evelyn grinned. "Did he ever get out of the hospital?"

"I heard that he had, but no one's seen him again." Doc said, "I'm not sure what that means."

Evelyn shrugged. "I think it means he won't be crashing any more parties."

"Especially yours, most likely."

Evelyn nodded.

Chapter Fifteen

The robot lay on the surgery table in the Sanctum Sanctorum. All the dark bones were attached together, and the plumbing for the hydraulic muscles snaked its way through to the manifold inside the chest. The power plant, such as it was, had been secured in the chest cavity where lungs would normally be stuffed. Several slightly dismantled cell phones were interfaced together and tied into the control circuitry.

The eyes looked strangest of all, being completely naked of eyelids at the moment. Their control cables ran down to the nest of phones to tie in there as well, and an air-cushioned solenoid was ready to provide blinks. A mechanism to track the eyes together united them, but there was no provision for changing the pupil diameter. Nathan version two would have to incorporate those things.

One thing though, that any version of Nathan would require of course, was lubrication. Evelyn filled that tank too, while Doc was checking the electronics outside the body.

Doc and Evelyn made the last connections, filled up the fuel tank, and started the engine.

"Oh, my, that's too loud!" Doc said over the noise.

"Still a bit of sound muffling to go on, Mom, and then we close it up." Evelyn placed a fiber pad over the engine compartment, and leaned back.

With a gesture, purely for showmanship, Evelyn beckoned the open skin of Nathan Stone to close up. The scalp tissue crept down the face, covering the eyes and forming the mouth, and then down to the neck, where it met tissue coming around from each side of the chest.

Further down, all the flesh came back into position, including the genitalia, still hairless, and still rather unexpectedly small.

Finally, the entire body was complete.

"Time to wake him up, Mom." Evelyn said.

Ten spoke into her phone. "All right, Mark, make your connections."

They watched in fascination as Nathan Stone came to life. "It's alive! Alive!" Evelyn exclaimed, her eyes very bright.

First he sat up. Slowly, he began testing the movement of his arms and head, looking left and right, up and down. He moved his hands together and apart, closed the fingers together one at a time, and began to make tentative mouth movements.

Looking, for the first time, at the women in turn, Nathan spoke. "How do I look?"

Doc shook her head, and adjusted a control on her phone. "Try that again."

"How do I look?"

She adjusted it once more. "One more time."

"How do I look?" the little boy's voice came out, moving in synchronization with the lips and chest motions.

Doc looked at Evelyn.

Evelyn nodded in affirmation.

"You're doing well, M … Nathan. Your voice sounds normal now. Let's try standing up, okay?"

Nathan slid carefully to the edge of the table, and then allowed his legs to come slowly down to the floor. Still leaning against the table, he let his weight settle on his feet. He even wriggled his toes.

"You're doing fine! Now let Evelyn steady you as you try to walk."

Evelyn stepped up to take his hand and elbow.

The boy looked at her. "Wow!" he said, "You're big!" Then he looked down along his front. "And I'm … do I even *have* a penis?"

"Yeah, it's there, Romeo. Now stand up."

Nathan looked at Evelyn again and smiled. She smiled back.

"Hey, even that works!" He looked down again and moved forward.

Evelyn gripped his arm. He looked at it. "Don't squeeze too hard, sweetheart. I can feel that."

Evelyn realized that the force she was putting into holding him was being transferred through their links into how the motion suit was squeezing Mark's arm. Still keeping a good grip, she backed off the pressure.

Nathan pushed off from the table, and wobbled a bit. Evelyn steadied him.

"Whoa! I hope the signal delay won't get too bad. That's tricky."

They practiced walking him around for a while. Then they got him dressed.

"Okay, it's still early yet. We're going to ask you to sit here now, and just take a nap. Close your eyes, please, Nathan." The boy sat in the chair, closed his eyes, and stopped moving.

Evelyn looked up at her mother. "That's a little weird to see, even when I know what's going on."

"I get a lot of that," Doc said. "All right, let's go down and have dinner with Mark. He's about to have a long evening."

They put Nathan in the SUV, fastening his seatbelt, and then went back into the house for one last check of everything. Their garments were fine, the house was secured, communications checked, and it was time to depart.

"A party in your honor, Mom, and you still managed to make an adventure out of it."

Doctor Brandon smiled. "The story of my life." She looked at Evelyn. "Are you ready?"

"I'm ready. I've got a date to go dancing!"

The ladies went out to the vehicle, and began their evening.

Nathan sat quietly for the most part. Out on the highway, he found the window control and rolled down the window. Sticking his arm out the window, like a … well, like a kid, he found that although he could not feel the air, he could feel its pressure as it pushed against his hand.

He grinned and looked at Doctor Brandon.

"Nathan, sweetie, I know you're having fun. But it's wintertime, and the air is chilly."

"Oh, sorry. I haven't been out for a while." Nathan put the window back up.

Evelyn was simply looking at him. Nathan version two, she was thinking; temperature sensitivity.

The venue for this event was slightly more upscale. It was a country club in the hills, with understated elegance, where liveried parking attendants helped them from the vehicle and toward the front entrance. Evelyn kept a steadying hand on Nathan's arm as they took their time ascending the steps.

"Doctor Forrestal, thank you for the invitation."

"Doctor Brandon, our Guest of Honor, thank you so much for coming."

"You'll recognize my daughter and research assistant, Evelyn Brandon, of course. This is my nephew Nathan Stone, who is staying with us for a short time while he recuperates from a bit of a fall recently. He's still getting his land-legs."

"Welcome aboard, Mister Stone. I know how that can be. I spent a few trips on the high seas myself, and had to recuperate from a fall or two as well. Come in; come in! Miss Brandon, it is quite wonderful to see you again! You are of course looking more lovely than ever. I do wish I had such fine research assistants in my work, I assure you."

Evelyn had met Forrestal before, perhaps when she was eight or so. Still, he was flattering, and maybe he did remember her from the hotel. They had seen quite a few people from the stage, and been seen by more.

The lights and the music were in full panoply for the occasion. To have so many turn out to honor her mother was very flattering. Nathan seemed to be enjoying himself immensely, but did have some difficulty navigating.

Evelyn suggested to her mother that they find some seats as soon as they could.

In a moment, Doc had gotten them situated where they could watch and listen, without having to worry about being trampled. Nathan was grinning like the Cheshire Cat.

Doctor Brandon continued to circulate, while the organizers rather vainly tried to bring order to the conclave. Evelyn was pleased to observe her mother in her proper element, the upper class of society, where the educated and the influential rubbed shoulders. She smiled to see how well the mad scientist fit in.

Finally, the hosts were able to get people generally settled down, as some of the first speakers simply began talking, using the amplification of the public address system to give weight to their forgettable words.

In this manner the audience learned of the history and influence of this well-established country club and its heralded membership, and the many ways that both had contributed to the society at large.

After this soporific introduction, the real meat and potatoes of speeches began.

Doctor Forrestal had a real stem-winder going, talking about the many ways Doctor Tenerife Brandon had alighted like a golden-winged angel in the medical advisory community, bridging the gaps between the islands of expertise in such diverse fields as public health, criminology and psychological services, immunology practices and disease vector analysis, and many other categories designed to showcase Doctor Brandon's varied and valuable talents.

Evelyn and Nathan managed to subtly slip out of the main hall during this, and take a stroll out on the softly lit back patio. The tables and chairs for poolside dining had been put away, and above the quiet setting a blaze of stars was visible.

Arm in arm, Evelyn and Nathan strolled, she to be seen with the handsome lad in her lovely gown, and he to practice walking as well as to enjoy the freedom it permitted.

"It's hard to walk and enjoy the stars at the same time." Nathan said.

Evelyn marveled at how convincing it was to hear the little boy voice coming, as she knew, from Mark's voice, miles away, over a telephone channel, and then adjusted in frequency to have the right sound in the throat of a charming robot.

"You don't get out much, do you?" Evelyn teased.

"No more than you, actually." He responded. "You look very lovely tonight."

"I owed it to my handsome date to do him proud." She said, "You cut quite the handsome figure yourself. The ladies find your eyes particularly striking."

Nathan smiled, looking down at the patio. "You finally got a chance to play with your doll, doll. Are you having fun?"

"It's a little soon to tell," Evelyn said, turning to face him and tilting his head up. "How are you at kissing?"

Nathan blinked twice in succession. "I haven't the remotest idea."

"Let's find out, shall we?" Evelyn tilted her head and pressed in to make contact.

Nathan wrapped his arms around her and closed his eyes. Back in the bunker, Mark could feel the pressure, and could tell that he was holding the girl, but the moment lacked the intimacy he might have wished for.

Nathan opened his eyes again. The expression on the girl's face was unreadable. "Well?"

"My mother kisses me better than that," Evelyn said with a smile. "At least you don't have bad breath!"

Nathan smiled. "Your mother kisses me better than that, too."

Evelyn grinned at him. "Well, we might as well find out how badly you suck at dancing while we're at it. It'd be a shame to get all dressed up for nothing."

Nathan held her arm out, pulled her body closer to his, and attempted to move in what should have been a simple box step. The results were … not encouraging.

"About what I figured," Evelyn said. "Let me try something." She backed away from him, and raised her arms in a graceful ballet fifth position. There was some faint background music playing on the patio music speakers. Evelyn danced in the dim light under the stars, as if she truly felt the joy of young love with her handsome prince.

After about two minutes of this, when Nathan was wondering if his circuitry might allow him to weep for her in tribute, a soft hand of applause was heard near the entrance to the main hall. Doctor Forrestal had found them.

"You dance divinely, Miss Evelyn. I have long been an admirer of your beauty, but I had no idea that you were so talented in other ways. Do forgive me, but your mother is about to receive her award. I think you will want to be there."

"Thank you, Doctor Forrestal. My mother thinks very highly of you as well."

He nodded, and moved back into the hall.

Evelyn came to Nathan again, and took his arm. "Coming, cousin?"

"I wouldn't miss being with you for anything in the world!" They strolled arm in arm back into the main hall, leaving the quiet serenity of the patio to the serenading of the nocturnal insects.

"… and despite that harrowing experience, our Good Doctor has continued to work for the betterment of our community even though her accomplishments already would allow her to rest on those laurels for a very long and well-deserved reward and relaxation. Ladies and Gentlemen, I present to you, Doctor Tenerife Brandon, winner of the Southern California Scientific Achievement of the Year Award."

In the midst of the applause, a background chant of "Ten, Ten, Ten, Ten," could be heard.

Doc stepped up and accepted the microphone, bowing several times in acknowledgment of the honor conveyed. Straightening up, she looked around to see where Evelyn was, and watched her for a moment to be sure she stayed in place.

Evelyn smiled, raising her hand joined with Nathan's hand as a victory symbol.

"Thank you, everyone. It is very flattering to realize that a girl can get such recognition simply by going to work regularly. You may think that I have been most dedicated or something, to have become familiar to so many of you, but I have to tell you, that was simply where all the interesting stuff was happening! How could I stay away?"

Doctor Forrestal stepped up once more, to shake her hand, to hand her the engraved plaque certifying her achievement, and to give her a big hug as well.

It was late in the evening when they finally managed to tear themselves away from the partygoers and well-wishers. Evelyn again held Nathan's arm to steady him as they descended the entrance stairs once more, although she tried to make it look as though *he* were helping *her*.

The SUV was brought around for them, and they all climbed in, Evelyn helping Nathan, of course. They waved as they pulled around the circular drive and stopped at the entrance.

And they all caught their breath when one of the liveried parking attendants opened the passenger side door and slipped inside. He was pointing a gun at Doc.

Chapter Sixteen

"Turn right and drive." The man said. He held the gun in a steady, unwavering hand.

Nathan could be damaged, of course, but not hurt in any way. Evelyn was confident that she could move quickly and possibly defend herself.

But Doc was completely vulnerable, and she was directly in the line of fire for whatever might happen. They had little choice.

Doc turned toward the right, and pulled out onto the road.

"Keep driving until I tell you where to turn. None of you move otherwise."

The man did not seem nervous or overly excited. He seemed almost bored. It might even appear that he had done this many times. That he was a professional.

None of this was comforting in any way.

"Turn here, on the right." He did not gesture with the gun. It was held rock-steady.

Doc turned the SUV. They drove on for a while.

"Stop up there around the curve. Then turn off the lights and the motor and drop the keys."

There were a few trees at this curve, tending to block the sky and make a puddle of darkness. A vehicle was parked on the side of the road, a van. It had no markings of any kind. There was no visible license plate.

Doc pulled over behind the vehicle. She looked at the man. Then she powered down the vehicle and removed the keys. They were in darkness except for the courtesy lights.

Ten let the keys fall on the floor.

Nothing happened for a minute. Then several men surrounded them, dressed in dark clothing and with hoods pulled up. They opened the car doors and pointed more guns at them.

"Everybody get out and take off all your clothes. Put your clothes in the vehicle. Move."

Doc stepped out and looked back at the children. They were moving as commanded. She took off her clothes, tossing them carelessly in on the driver's seat.

The first man grinned, showing white teeth in the relative darkness. "Shoes and underwear too. All of it. Strip!"

Evelyn was first to be naked. She saw that Nathan was having trouble, so she moved to help him, saying, "He's a little clumsy and needs help."

The men watched her closely but did not prevent her from assisting the boy. Soon all of them were naked, standing barefoot on the sharp gravel, and each covered by at least two guns.

"Now get into the van, on the passenger side." The first man said.

Slowly and mincingly they moved across the stones, and around to the hidden side of the vehicle.

Behind them they heard the doors close on the SUV. It was being abandoned.

Doc thought about this. They didn't want the vehicle. They wanted the people. They wanted the people thoroughly helpless, naked and defenseless.

They got into the van, and were gestured to sit on its floor together, while two men took up seats across from them, and the doors were closed.

This portion of the vehicle had no access to the front. Likely it was locked from the outside. Even if they overpowered the two armed men, they were still trapped. They all sat very still.

The rest of the ride went on in silence.

No chances were taken with them when they reached their destination. They were escorted into a solid looking building through a solid looking door, and down several flights of stairs.

One by one, they were all taken into a large underground room, where each, still naked, was chained in an X pattern to a wall. Nathan was chained to the wall on the left. Doc was fastened to the end wall. Evelyn went to the wall on the right. Then they were left alone there.

They could see each other, and they could see in their minds what was going to happen.

Evelyn examined her binding chain. It had been wrapped around her wrist in a double-loop before being secured with a small padlock. Each ankle was the same. The room was concrete, and chilly. The floor was damp and stained. It had the smell of a slaughterhouse.

"You look beautiful, Evelyn. I've never seen you more lovely." Doc said.

"You look quite beautiful yourself, Mom. You have a striking figure."

Evelyn turned to Nathan. "I hope they don't hurt your testicles, Nathan."

He smiled. "Okay, here's my plan …"

They all laughed.

The door opened. "Well, I never expected to hear laughter in here. Other than my own, of course." The man closed the door, locking it, and walked boldly into the room, looking triumphantly at his victims.

He wore what looked like a toreador's outfit; a puffy white blouse and tight pants. He walked over to a cabinet and opened it, taking out things and placing them on the table; knives, whips, other things looking sharp and painful, and likely not even having names at all.

It was Carlos.

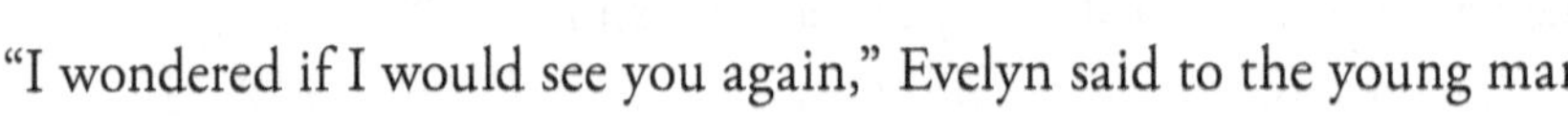

"I wondered if I would see you again," Evelyn said to the young man.

He looked at her with a blank expression.

"Aren't you going to offer me wine again? I was wondering what would have happened if I had been able to share that drink with you." She smiled at him.

"You would have passed out." He said indifferently.

"From *wine?*" she laughed. "I've had wine before. A little wine never hurt anyone."

Carlos was somewhat intrigued. Just how stupid was this girl? He picked up a small wooden chair and walked closer.

"It wasn't just wine. It would have knocked you out in about a minute. Then we would have carried you out and taken you away."

"Why would you do that?" Evelyn looked at him as if he had said he wanted to eat flowers.

Carlos looked at her bonds. Her wrists and ankles were tightly chained in place. She could not move more than an inch or two, even if she drew blood trying. He looked quickly at the others. They too were well-secured and made no effort to even try to move.

He brought his gaze back to the girl. He placed the chair in front of her and sat down.

She was looking at him in complete innocence, as if unaware that she was naked and helpless in front of him.

He leered at her. This stupid runty bitch did not have sense enough to realize the situation she was in. Even more than putty in his hands, she was *flesh* in his hands! He could do anything he wanted to do!

"Why would I do that?" He grinned at her, "Why, so I could do this!" He reached out and placed his hand on her chest, orienting his palm on her left breast, and moving his hand around possessively.

"Did you think I wouldn't let you do that? I thought you were kinda handsome, you know. I was wondering what it might be like to kiss you." Evelyn's eyes got big as she seemed to realize how embarrassing that admission was.

Carlos laughed at her. He let his hands play on her, stroking and caressing her chest and stomach, her legs and inner thighs. "Would you let me do that?"

He leaned forward and kissed her, smothering her mouth roughly with his lips, while his hands sought their own pleasures on her helpless body.

He pulled back to look at her. "Would you let me do this?" He leaned in again, roughly mashing his lips against hers while moving his hands around her rump and across her pubic mound, searching for and seeking …

He plunged his fingers into her vaginal opening, twisting and turning them. Prodding and pushing, he looked again at her face to see if she was crying yet, or showing the shocked face of fear and pain.

She was watching him.

He stared.

She looked at him, and twisted her head slightly in mild curiosity. He did not see fear or pain on her face.

"What …" Carlos moved back, kicking the chair away from behind him. He straightened up, and backed away from the strange girl.

Carlos wiped at his mouth with his sleeve, and wiped his other hand on his pants.

"What did you … Did you have drugs or something?" He looked at his hands, and wiped them on his pants again.

He ran to the table, looking for a weapon. Picking up a savage looking knife, he began stumbling back toward Evelyn. After two steps, he stopped again, dropping the knife and pushing down on his matador pants.

He pulled his pants and shoes off and stood straight again, looking down and screaming in agony. He ripped his shirt off and threw it away from him.

He was bleeding at the crotch. He looked at his hands, trying to figure out what had gotten on them. He screamed again.

His penis and his testicles fell off.

He stared at the pathetic pieces of flesh lying on the floor like a spilled breakfast. Then his crotch began to heal over, forming smooth flesh where once he had sexual features.

He looked up, toward Evelyn, only to notice that his hair was falling out, as if some crazed lawnmower had just buzzed over his scalp. In seconds every hair that had been on his body had fallen around him like leaves in autumn.

Again he looked toward the girl. As he prepared to step in her direction, his right hand detached, leaving only a bare nub of flesh where the wrist ended.

Then his left hand fell off.

He fell over. Looking down at his legs, he realized why he had fallen over. He had no feet. They too had simply separated, and were sitting where he last stood, like a pair of discarded sneakers.

Evelyn stepped away from the wall, letting the chains and locks fall to the floor.

She walked over to the pathetic nebbish creature and stared down at him. He writhed and wriggled, trying to move away from her.

Turning her attention to Nathan, she watched as he too walked away from his bindings. Nathan went over to Doctor Brandon, and let most of his outer skin fall off.

The carpet of what looked like flesh wriggled its way, somewhat more effectively than Carlos, over to Doctor Brandon.

She looked at it with some apprehension as it rose up and covered her nakedness.

In a moment Doc also walked away from her captivity, but she was covered in a smooth, armored carapace of flesh and bulging muscle. She looked like an Olympic bodybuilder, of undetermined sex, with a helmet also of bronze.

She approached Evelyn, still standing near Carlos' discarded flesh.

Doc gave Evelyn a hug, and some of her bronze flesh moved over to Evelyn, clothing her nakedness as well.

Evelyn did not display the bulging muscles that her mother did. She was simply arrayed in a form-fitting uniform and helmet of bronze, which truthfully looked quite striking.

They turned, needing no discussion in the matter, and began walking toward the door.

"Wait! What about me!" Carlos wailed, still trembling in fear and pain.

"What about you?" Evelyn said, "We're never going to see you again."

They walked out, locking the door behind them.

"Now, Mom," Evelyn said, "we're not done here yet. My plan is to go through this building and leave no one else alive. Do you have a problem with that?"

Doc stopped and put her head down for a moment. "No, dear. I don't think I do. Lead on."

"Okay. We're not bulletproof, so we need a battle plan. There should be a way, somewhere in here, to turn off all the power. Then we'll move through and engage. Mom, I want you to go outside. You'll be stronger and faster and hard to see, but don't let them shoot you. Check for lookouts, and deal with them as you see fit. You can let them live if you have doubt. Try to spot which vehicles are the gang's. We'll need at least one of them, but the rest can be destroyed. We don't want anyone leaving the building, so you might want to acquire a gun out there and be prepared to shoot them as they make a run for it."

She looked at her mother, or her mother's armored figure. "Now's the time to deal a mortal blow, and I mean that in every sense of the word. We don't want to have to worry about these people any more. Period. Are we clear on this?"

Doc nodded. Nathan, who looked horrible, also nodded.

"All right. I'm going to turn out the lights in two minutes. Nathan, you're with me. If anyone shoots at me, you need to be the target or draw their fire, while I turn Ninja and sneak up on them. Ready? Let's move out!"

They moved out.

Doc went out the door into the night. Evelyn moved through the building, using her sensitivity to things electrical to guide her to the breaker panel. She counted down the time and shut off all power in the building.

Circling out from that point, Evelyn and Nathan patrolled the building. On each level, there were about ten people. No one looked innocent or appeared to be another captive, so all were put down in as quiet and quick a manner as possible.

On the third floor, they faced armed opposition for the first time. Perhaps in this interior area the gunshots could not be heard outside. It would not do to have the police arrive too early. Nathan kept the gang members pinned down; using a confiscated weapon sparingly, while

Evelyn went up through a suspended ceiling. It was dark up there, but she hadn't been bothered by darkness for some time, and no longer even took notice of it.

From overhead, she spotted three figures. She dropped on two of them, and then shot the third with another weapon taken from the person under her.

Evelyn found that she had to strike with all her strength, as she was working only with the augmented muscles she had been able to fit on her slender eleven-year old frame. Using the advantage of surprise, and gravity, that strength was sufficient.

In about a half-hour to forty-five minutes, silence reigned. Evelyn and Nathan swept though again, collecting a few choice weapons wrapped in a blanket, as much bundled cash as could be stuffed into Nathan's abdominal cavity, and some potentially useful biometric information and wallets. Nathan had quite a pronounced limp, as he had taken about six rounds through his body, with only three actually striking something solid.

No one, save the possibility of pitiful Carlos, remained alive in the building.

Nathan was first to go outside. Mom might be nervous, after all.

She approached. "I've got the van we came in. There was a guy inside it, but he's, uh, sleeping it off now. Two others will have really serious headaches, and I didn't see anyone else. You kids okay?"

"I'm fine, Mom. Nobody even laid a glove on me. Clumsy here, though, will need some patching up."

They checked the van. It seemed serviceable, and they prepared to depart.

"Still no police response yet, even with the gunfire." Doc said.

"Bad neighborhood, I guess. Your 'sleeper' has a cell phone. Let's dial 9-1-1 just before we leave and leave the phone here. If the cops want to do their job, they'll have plenty to do. There's money and drugs all over the place. I kinda want to go home and get a shower."

"I'll help you." Nathan suggested.

Evelyn looked at him. "Well, I might let you, in a manner of speaking."

Holding out the cell phone, Evelyn said, "Here, you do it. Tell them, shots fired, people down, and then we'll lay the phone down."

Then Evelyn helped Nathan into the van and they departed.

"Mom, turn the lights on. We don't want to attract attention."

"Oh, I didn't realize they were off." Doc said.

"You're still wearing your Ninja suit. Take this next left. I've got a map up on display."

"You must still be wearing *your* Ninja suit, too." Ten said.

"I always am, Mom. I always am." Evelyn smiled into the darkness.

Chapter Seventeen

"Worked up a theory yet, Doc?" Detective Lieutenant Henry Muller inquired, popping a stick of gum in his mouth and pocketing the wrapper.

Lead Medical Examiner Dr. Frank Holtzmann nodded. "Looks like a hit from the competition; very professional. No evidence left behind; the only gunfire confined to the money room, and quiet but deadly force used elsewhere. Are you sure it wasn't some of your boys?"

Hank snorted. "I could wish it was my boys. They don't have the training for this kind of hit. It would be a good way to supplement our budget though. We didn't find much cash left behind. It's like they brought a vacuum cleaner."

"Well, no witnesses here," Doctor Frank put away yet another pair of disposable gloves.

"I do have a live one for you, Doc. We found him in a locked room. Very strange condition, in my non-medical opinion."

Doctor Holtzmann looked into Muller's eyes, his concern evident. The Golden Hour of medical care applied to gang violence too.

"He'll keep, Doc. He's stable at the moment. You'll see what I mean. I would caution you, though, to be very careful exactly what you say and how you write it up. This one's pretty out there."

* * *

The patient was nearly catatonic. Despite the injuries sustained, he was, as the Detective had stated, stable. Medically stable, that is.

Psychologically, Frank wouldn't give you a snowball's chance that he'd have anything useful to report.

The experienced M.E. looked up at his old friend. Pulling out his recording device, he began speaking in a calm and clinical voice. "The patient shows evidence of having been tortured, perhaps in an aggressive interrogation. His hands and feet have been amputated, and his genitals have been severed. This procedure has been followed by an as-yet undetermined manner of wound closure similar to cauterization, although no evidence of thermal damage appears. The patient will require corrective surgery as soon as possible to permit elimination of body wastes and drainage from the injury sites. He will be transported immediately to the emergency ward of the nearest hospital. No interrogation of the patient will be permitted until he has been properly stabilized."

The Medical Examiner looked once more at the unbelievable sight. The man remained naked at the moment, although looking at his groin was similar in perception to looking at the joining of two fingers on the hand. He had been thoroughly neutered, without even leaving evidence that he had ever been male, or female for that matter. Surgery would have to be scheduled within hours, for there was no way at the moment for his urinary bladder, if it still remained, to find an exit for its waste.

"I'm dead." The man groaned.

"We'll take care of you, lad. You'll be transported right away." The doctor signaled for the paramedics to place the patient on a stretcher and carry him out to their ambulance. Armed officers would also escort them.

"I'm dead." The man said again. "I'm a dead … thing. I'm dead." He collapsed back down, more in dismay than apparent exhaustion.

Frank looked over again at the Detective. He shook his head. The Detective shrugged and moved away to oversee the rest of the long day's evidence collection.

Doc had driven them back to the scene of the abduction. Her vehicle was still parked in the same place. In the early morning dark, they got out and began resuming their normal appearances.

Doc sloughed off the armor, watching it crawl away like a living thing to begin wrapping itself around Nathan again. As miraculous as the phenomenon was to witness, it was also chillingly creepy. She put her clothes back on and tried to make herself look presentable.

Evelyn let her skin-tight uniform peel itself off her to join the material enfolding the robot. She put her arms up and began dancing around on the road.

"Naked dancing in the middle of the road is probably not a very good idea, my dear. You should get dressed again so we can go home."

Evelyn grinned. "But I feel so good! I want to celebrate!"

Ten smiled. "Very well. You can have the first turn at helping Mark to work out his kinks after being confined in his cellar. But first we'll have to get back home."

Nathan was limping around, looking particularly helpless. His flesh had covered him again like a warm comforter, but his clothes and shoes were going to be a challenge.

Doc gave him a hand sorting out and putting on his new clothes for the second time.

After twenty minutes or so, they were ready to rejoin civilization, and they turned around on the narrow road to go back in the opposite direction. The van they had appropriated was left on the side of the road.

Doc headed into the house for a long hot shower and then some comfortable scrubs.

Evelyn too went to her own bedroom, carrying Nathan's clothes as well as her own. Not certain what else to do, Evelyn hung his clothes in her own closet. She took a shower, and then still naked, carried Nathan's body down to the lair.

Mark was waiting for her, welcoming everyone back to the security of his underground hideout.

After Evelyn released the nanobots from being Nathan's skin, a small stack of what looked like oven mitts went to the computer work area, and then they put a box full of shimmering fabric in a storage cabinet.

Nathan's skinless torso was lying on the confinement cot, looking like a smashed trash container filled with stacks of currency. His dark limbs splayed out like a squashed bug.

"Well, Pinky, what do you want to do tonight?" Mark looked over at the resilient heroine.

"The same as always, of course!" She leaped into his arms and began kissing him. "First a lot of hugs and kisses, and *then* we'll count the money!"

Mark spun her around, holding her tight and kissing her as if he hadn't seen her for a year. "You danced divinely, Beany-Butt! Both at the country club and out in the street as well."

"I did pretty well at the gang hideout too. I was kicking butt and taking names!"

He pulled back to look in her eyes. "That you did!"

"You want to see the names I got? I have an idea!" She slid down from his arms, avoiding getting hung up for the moment. She pulled out a handful of wallets from Nathan's derelict torso.

Spreading the wallets out on the work surface, Evelyn began reading the names inside, and removing the cash as well. She hopped up on her stool and perched like a little songbird in her cage. She put on her goggles and began searching for a history of the names of some of the gang members.

Doc, through her working relationship with the State Board for Recidivism Analysis and Parole Recommendations, had an authorized communication channel with the national authorities for getting information about suspected criminals.

Evelyn looked around at Mark. "You can start counting the money! I'm curious about that as well."

Mark brought the stacks of bundled bills over to the work surface and began organizing them.

Into this scene Doctor Brandon strolled, one hand casually clutching a bottle.

Mark stopped on his current trip back from Nathan's carcass with a handful of money to lean over and kiss the Doc.

She patted his bare rump fondly and sent him on his way. She continued on to the little kitchen with her bottle of wine. She was looking for glasses.

"Okay, here's what I was looking for; Armando Gutierrez, one of the perps we dealt with tonight, has no Federal or State police record. It's clean. That probably means he has never been arrested, or has not been involved in crime for very long. He's only eighteen years old."

Mark looked over. He grew a little pale. "All of the people whose records you're checking died tonight."

Evelyn turned and looked at him. Like her, he was naked and sitting on a stool. But in front of him there were stacks and stacks of money.

She activated the application he had mentioned a few days ago. Surrounding him in her goggles was a glow of nanobot activity. The mass of nanobots that had surrounded him had left a surface contingent mapped over his skin. There was no indication they had penetrated further.

Evelyn turned and looked at her mother using the same application. Even with scrubs on, Evelyn could see that the nanobot manifestation all over her was greater in degree, especially around the head and eyes.

Doctor Tenerife Brandon had had her Ninja upgrades acted upon. This bore thinking about, but right now Evelyn needed to ground Mark about his role in the activities this night.

"Mark, these were people who came looking for us. They brought trouble *to* us, and for the second time. They knew that bad things were being planned for us, but they didn't care. They had their own priorities, and the lives of innocent people were not going to stop them from taking what they wanted, and *doing* what they wanted."

"The only way to stop them, to stop them from coming after us again and again until we were dead, was to do what we did. We had to stop them, or die."

She watched him breathing deep breaths, trying to calm himself. "You did a great job there, too. I couldn't have done it without you." She smiled at him. "Our reward for doing a good job of stopping them from hurting people, is sitting there in front of you. And we have more to do than just tonight. We need to get ready to do that more, because there are other people out there too; people who need to be helped, and people who need to be stopped from hurting others."

Mark looked up. He remembered that she had used that expression before. He knew that he had been one of the people who went around hurting other people. He had a debt to pay for that, and Evelyn and her mom were helping him to do it. He nodded.

"Remember the boat?" Evelyn watched him. "That was the first time, and the last time, that you were able to leave here. You had a record, and the police were looking for you. That night, we took care of part of your problem; they aren't looking for you anymore."

"But you still can't go out there. They aren't looking for you, but if they find you, you'll still be in trouble." She smiled at him. "We have another opportunity to do something now, that will fix that part of the problem as well."

Doc brought out glasses for Evelyn and Mark. She poured some wine into the glasses and then retrieved her own, raising it in toast. "To our successful exploit tonight! Mischief Managed!"

Mark picked up his glass and sipped it. Then he grinned. He drank to the toast.

Evelyn sniffed the drink. It smelled very similar to the drink Carlos had tried to get her to drink. She looked at her mother questioningly.

"What? You were saying tonight that a little bit of wine wouldn't hurt you. I thought it was about time you learned what you were talking about."

"I'm only eleven, mother." The girl said reprovingly.

"You've got a birthday coming. Remember, we're celebrating!"

Evelyn grinned, "Yeah, but I'm still gonna be just eleven for a while." She took a sip of wine. It was sweet, and biting at the same time. She would need to remember that wine could be potent, when you were small, and unaccustomed to it. Still, one could only become accustomed to it by … she took another sip.

Ten smiled. "So, do we have a count yet?"

"Still working on it, boss." Mark noted.

"Mom, I've checked at least one record search, and I've found an identity which could keep Mark out of trouble with the police. Do you know what I'm talking about?"

Ten looked at her. "Just take it from the top."

"I picked up some wallets from where we were tonight. This one, for example, belongs to a guy who seems to have never been arrested or fingerprinted. If we transferred this guy's fingerprints to Mark's fingers, then he could go back out in the world and not be arrested by the police."

Doc looked from one aspect to another; the wallet on the work surface, the computer with its links, her darling daughter with the genius IQ, and the object she had worked so hard to squirrel away from the influences of the world to be her own private gigolo, Mark the former criminal.

Now Evelyn was talking about arranging his freedom! Taking a moment to think it through, Doc sipped on her wine.

"You mean to tell me that even while we were fighting for our lives, you were looking ahead and plotting to find ways to allow Mark to be able to do more than merely walk around as a robot?"

"Yep! Because even though he did manage to walk around as a robot, he's a really lousy dancer."

"You want to go dancing?"

Evelyn's eyes sparkled. "Dancing under the stars, soft music playing, insects singing to us, and a kiss in the arms of my ..." Evelyn straightened up, and took another sip of wine. "Well, it was a romantic location, anyway."

Ten looked at Mark.

He was staring back at her with a look of dawning horror. "Doc, I can't go out there! I *can't!*"

He got up from the stool and went into the other room, standing over the almost completely stripped carcass of Nathan the robot, as if over a fallen comrade.

Doc approached him, placing her arm around his waist. He was warm, but she knew he was feeling cold and distant. Her pet Frankenstein monster was feeling his inhumanity.

"What I need to do is go back to before I was … before I was wrong, a wrong thing. Before I … hurt people." He looked down at the robot.

"Before I grew up. Back when I was a kid, like … like what I felt like tonight, a little bit; awkward, and strange. Looking at all the wonders in the world, and not having anyone expect anything, because I was a kid, and I was … everything was okay." He turned and looked at her.

"Send me back there, Doc. That's what I need to fix me." He looked back at the broken and still form of Nathan. "That's how I need to be fixed."

Ten leaned over and kissed him. "Everybody expects the doctor to be a miracle worker." She patted his butt again and went back to talk to Evelyn.

Evelyn had swiveled around and was watching her move closer, looking through the goggles as if peering through a microscope at her.

"How's your head, Mom?" Evelyn asked.

"What?"

"How's your head? Do you have a headache?"

"No. I've only had a little bit of wine. I don't have a headache." She looked over her shoulder at the other person in the room. "I think Mark needs some comforting, though. I'll just celebrate in my own fashion."

Evelyn tilted her head left and right, looking at her. "Okay." She looked again at Mark, and then turned around and pulled up more images from the computer, doing programming her way, as if she were coloring in a coloring book. With finger-paints. Naked.

Sure.

After a few minutes Evelyn went over to Mark and took his hand. She led him to a chair and sat him down on it.

She had brought two of the oven mitts with her. She placed one on each of his hands, and then she climbed onto his lap, carefully positioning herself to, uh, prevent falling off.

Evelyn leaned into Mark's neck and began kissing him there, and whispering to him.

"I wanted to dance with you, and kiss you out there, under the stars. You're sort of my first boyfriend, you know. Since that was my first date, you helped make it very special." She kissed him and drew back to look at his face.

He was concentrating, she surmised, because of some things she was doing to distract him. Evelyn had learned a few muscle exercises that she could do when they were sharing this kind of intimate behavior. She enjoyed it, and she knew that he did too.

"Did you have a good time?" Evelyn asked him.

"Yes." He looked at her, moving slightly as she rocked back and forth on him. "For most of the evening, it felt like I was wearing Nathan's body, and holding you in my arms. I liked the way we fit together."

Evelyn jiggled and squirmed. "You mean like this?" She looked over toward the kitchen where she could see her mother watching them with a somewhat detached expression.

"This is nice, but no, not what I meant. I liked being able to look into your eyes. I liked … putting my arms around you." He shook his head. "It didn't last long."

Evelyn pulled herself close again, letting her chin rest on his shoulder. Snuggling her chest against his, she put her arms around him and gently rocked as if rocking a baby.

"I had a good time, too," she said softly.

Mark realized that she had fallen asleep. Idly wondering what had become of those oven mitts, he held her as he rose, and carried her to the bed still wrapped in his embrace. He laid her down carefully, and then lay down beside her, pulling a light cover over them.

She had not woken, and he was asleep in minutes.

A little while later, Doc rode up in the tube, carrying an empty wine bottle with her. It had indeed been a very long day.

Chapter Eighteen

Evelyn woke with a start, not knowing where she was. Seeing Mark's face, and realizing she was safe in the bed of their most secure location, she went back to sleep.

"I've counted the money," Evelyn heard dimly. Mark must have been talking to the Doc. "We have sixty-five bundles of one hundred each, hundred dollar bills. There are thirty-one similar stacks of fifties, over four thousand twenties, and a thousand of smaller bills. We have nearly a million dollars sitting right here. It's precisely … nine hundred twenty-five thousand, nine hundred and fifteen dollars."

Evelyn stretched, pushing her arms and legs out to their full extension on the small bed. Then she relaxed again, looking around with interest but little energy.

Doc looked over. "Well, kitten, it looks as though you've finished your nap. Mark tells me that today we're supposed to start taking over the world."

Evelyn grinned. "We started yesterday. Can't a girl rest?"

"Probably not. I'm sure you have to pee."

Evelyn considered, and then grimaced. "Psychologists! Wicked, evil, mad scientists!" She struggled out of the bed and went into the bathroom.

Doc looked at Mark. "Give her a minute, and then go help her take a shower. I'll start breakfast."

He grinned and gave Doc a kiss. She patted him on his naked rump as he passed her.

Evelyn stopped by the computer workstation on her way to the table. She picked up several of the "oven mitts" and placed the others in the bin with the shiny cloth.

As she walked to the table, the oven mitts seemed to evaporate.

Evelyn took a seat at the table and smiled at her mother.

"Are your hands clean, my daughter?" Doc asked.

"I think it is abundantly obvious that all of me is clean, my dearest mother dear."

"Yes, I suppose it is. Thank you, Mark, for seeing to that odious task."

"It was indeed my pleasure, Ladies."

"And mine as well," said Evelyn, "speaking of which, I hope the two of you have taken care of any mutual needs of the flesh, as the phrase has it. In any case, I am well-rested, and well-bathed, so I am probably ready to be well-energized once more."

"Our Energizer Bunny needs to be energized, Mark. I thought you took care of that already?" Ten said, enjoying the banter and the jocularity after their harrowing experiences the previous day.

"I thought I did too. She was plugged in long enough!"

"Just feed me the hotcakes and eggs and nobody gets hurt." Evelyn said darkly. Then she brightened, "Oh, by the way, I've decided how we can celebrate my birthday. I'd like it if we had a party for my eleventh birthday again. I like being Evelyn at eleven and I want to stay here for a while. Would that be okay?"

"Do you want me to strap your birthday present down again for you?"

Evelyn looked at Mark. "No, I think we can work something out. Anyway, I wanted to talk to you about something else, Mom. Yesterday when that guy pointed a gun at you, you had us really scared."

"What do you mean?" Doc asked as she shoveled scrambled eggs and a small stack of pancakes on Evelyn's plate. "There wasn't much I could do about that at the time."

"Well, I wasn't too concerned about me. I've got surprising speed now, and unexpected strength as well. And Nathan couldn't have been hurt with an RPG," she paused to grab a forkful of scrambled eggs.

After a moment, chewing and composing her thoughts, she spoke again. "But you need protection. I just have to ask your permission before setting it up for you."

"My permission?" Doc raised her eyebrows as she put food on Mark's plate as well.

"Sure. Remember when you modified Mark? He was a little annoyed that you hadn't asked for his approval first, not that we could have, of course. It just seems to be the proper medical procedure, that's all."

"Oh," Doc sat down. "What did you have in mind?"-

"You may not be aware of it fully, yet, but you have already been augmented somewhat. You can see in the dark." Evelyn grabbed a big bite of pancakes.

"I, what?" Doc looked puzzled.

Evelyn looked at her. "You can see in the dark like a cat. When we were leaving in the van, I had to remind you to turn the lights on. It would not have been fun to be stopped by the police while we were driving away from a crime scene, and driving naked at that."

"Oh, yeah," Ten said, a little flustered. That episode seemed like something that had happened to someone else. "I guess I forgot about that."

"Actually, you were wearing armor of a sort at the time, and it gave you enhanced strength too. Need I remind you that you dispatched three of the bad guys yourself while we were inside stealing their money, and we didn't even leave fingerprints?"

Ten looked over at the workstation counter-top, where nearly a million dollars still sat, quietly shouting to not be ignored. They hadn't even discussed what they might be able to do with it.

"But that took some preparation time, since we were caught by surprise. What I propose to do is to put some flexible armor under your skin, like a bulletproof vest, but stronger and hidden, always ready.

And then also boost your strength the way mine is, in case you have to deal with trouble sometime and we're not there to back you up." Evelyn studied her mother's reaction as she went back to eating.

Doc stared at her. "Bulletproof skin?"

"I think you can pull it off. You're bigger than me. It will take a few pounds of nanobots to build up a kind of membrane under your skin – don't worry, it won't hurt. But it's all I can do to use what I already have. Adding more weight would slow me down."

She looked at Doc. "But you're a grown-up. It wouldn't even be noticeable to you, especially once you're stronger. Heck, we can reshape you while we're at it, make you the kind of looker that would have Mark leaking just looking at you."

"Hey, I like the way she looks just fine!"

Evelyn patted his arm. "Good minion." She looked at her mother. "I know you don't have time for proper exercise; who does? But even I want to see you take a little off your waist, and see you stand straighter and prouder, the way you used to a few years ago."

"I think I'm being insulted, Mark." Ten said.

"Probably," Evelyn said slowly, "I suck at this. I'm trying to tempt you, so that I can get you protection, in case some other idiot comes at you with a knife, or fists, or whatever."

"My waist?" Ten said, looking down.

"A change in your body shape, to make you look years younger. Why am I having trouble selling this idea?"

"With little robots, tearing up the landscape and moving mountains around?" Ten scoffed.

"Well, they're *his* favorite mountains," Evelyn nodded toward Mark. "Why don't you ask him? I get by without them somehow."

Mark practically buried his face in his breakfast plate. His flush was evident, though.

"See!" Evelyn pointed with her fork. "He wants you to have bigger boobs!"

"Bulletproof boobs," Doc said softly, as if mesmerized.

"Well, sure." Evelyn looked up. "Once I get done with you, you'd be your own SWAT team, even stark naked." She looked thoughtful,

"Probably better, actually. No bad guy would want to damage such beauty."

"Beauty …" Ten said faintly.

"I guarantee it. I'll even get Mark to sign off on all the improvements. If it doesn't make him salivate from every orifice, I'll do it over until he does."

Mark looked up. "Not to be disrespectful or anything, but I'd kinda like to see that." He looked thoughtful. "It would be a way to get even with you a little bit for what you did to me." He grinned.

Doc looked at him. "You want *her* to make me more beautiful, so *you* can feel better?"

"Absolutely!" He smiled broadly at both of them. "That would make me feel lots better, and much happier too."

"Remember, Mom, he's a *pervert!*" Evelyn said. "You picked a good one." She patted his arm again.

"I'll have to think about this." Doc said.

"You know, if the same situation occurred tonight, we might not come out unscathed a second time." Evelyn said. "No pressure of course."

"Third time," Mark reminded her.

"Mom wasn't in any danger the first time." Evelyn said.

"Except from having a heart attack. Can you protect from that too?"

Evelyn looked thoughtful. "Hmm, maybe. Probably." She tilted her head as she considered it. "Oh, yeah, for sure; Heart attack, poison, drugs, pretty much any physical threat. I don't see why not."

Doc looked at her. "Really? So easy?"

Evelyn smiled. "Arm wrestle me, Mom."

"No."

"I'll do it," Mark said.

They squared off against each other. Mark began pushing at Evelyn's arm, and then harder.

Evelyn picked up her fork and started eating again.

Mark strained visibly but made no progress.

Evelyn drank some milk, and then looked casually at the joined arms before simply pushing Mark's hand down against the table.

"Ow!" he said, rubbing his arm.

"You would be even more impressive, Mom. No one would even suspect it. Keep in mind it's to give *me* peace of mind. I can't be there to protect you twenty-four seven."

Ten rolled her eyes. "All right! I think you've proven your case. What would I have to do?"

"Take your clothes off and let me fondle your boobs." Evelyn answered, looking steadily at her mother.

"What?" Doc stared.

Evelyn shrugged.

"Oh, all right. It's not like any of us has any privacy anyway … or pride, for that matter." Doctor Brandon removed her scrubs in mere seconds and sat down next to Evelyn.

Evelyn moved behind her, slipped her hands around as if hugging her, and placed them on the woman's breasts. Leaning her head down against her mother's neck, Evelyn appeared to concentrate as her hands moved around on the soft and sensitive flesh.

After five minutes, Evelyn straightened up and sat correctly again. "That's about all I have to do right now. The whole process may take several days total." She looked over at Doc. "I could have done the same thing just holding your hands, but I thought this would be funnier."

Doc tilted her head, looking at the girl, and then opened her mouth as if to speak, closed it instead, and simply smiled.

"I'd better start washing dishes," Mark said, getting up.

'By the way, Mom, I'm putting in a circuit to let me speak to you silently, mind to mind.' Evelyn was looking at her mother while sitting quite still without moving her lips or making a sound.

Ten stared at the girl.

'That's right. I put in a mind-link. It isn't really telepathy; it's just brain chemistry and radio emission physics. We should be able to get several miles out of it.'

'… and how do I talk silently to you then?'

'That works just fine. You're a fast learner.' Evelyn smiled.

'You're a fast worker. What comes next?'

'I'm building a nano-circuit memory algorithm of your body shape. Once I've completed that, the nanobots will start strengthening your bones and making attachments for synthetic muscles. These are bio-plastic materials that change shape under a linked command structure with your regular muscles. When you perform work, your signals are sent over to the bio-plastics to activate them as well. Everything you do gets easier, and you get faster and stronger. The bio-plastics get most of their energy by absorbing impacts as you move around. Just walking around the house or the hospital should give you all the power you need, and it keeps your feet from hurting, too.'

'That memory picture works to begin the reshaping as well. I plan to take it slowly, letting you appear at work and other places as the changes work through your system. In two months you'll look like and feel like an entirely different woman.'

"You two are being awfully quiet in there. Is everything okay?" Mark called.

"We're fine, Mark. Mom is getting used to feeling things change inside her, and I'm trying to figure out how and when we're going to get started fixing Nathan again."

Mark looked around. "You think we might be able to go on another excursion?"

"I think we should set our sights really, really low this time. A simple picnic lunch or something." Evelyn said.

"That may sound simple to you, but I would *love* it!" Mark said. "Except for the eating part, of course."

"Yeah, I'd buy you an ice-cream cone, but you don't have a tongue." Evelyn said.

Mark stuck out his tongue at her.

'You tease him a lot.' Doc said on their link.

'In some ways, we really are like siblings.' Evelyn looked around at her mother.

'I need to talk to you about Mark.' She said on the link. 'I think he needs to be changed too.'

Chapter Nineteen

octor Brandon looked at her daughter. Nothing, absolutely nothing surprised her anymore, but this might require some explanation. 'Go on.'

'I think we've got it upside down, or inside-out.' Evelyn responded. 'Mark needs to get out; out from being stuck in this place. He's never going to be normal again if we keep him caged. Even if he weren't crazy before, that would drive him to it.'

Doc pulled at her lip. 'But he's … he's not … suitable to be seen outside. We got away with it once, in the dark, with no one looking at him. To go out in the daylight, with him looking the way he does … that wouldn't work out at all.'

'I know.'

"So, Mom, what say we look at Nathan, and see how much damage we have to repair?" Evelyn urged her mother to get up and walk with her over to the pitiful robot body.

Mark watched them move. They were, after all, both naked. He thought about the idea that he could one day be salivating from all orifices, as Evelyn had said. Doc was a handsome woman, for her age and activity level. But the kind of changes Evelyn had suggested might be possible. Wow! He would have to wait and see that!

'It's easy to picture Nathan's body when his flesh is filled out with nanobots. I've also got a really good picture of Mark's body from having him in the control suit. I'm not sure whether I had a dream about it or not, while I was asleep, but somewhere I got an image of Mark walking around outside in Nathan's body while the robot was in here monitoring the console. I know that doesn't make sense, but I was wondering how Mark would react to being a kid again, and being free to dance and run like a kid again.'

Ten looked at the damaged robot body. He had been useful in the conflict last night, but this was just a robot. Mark hadn't been able to move effectively at all, either to fight or to dance. He had only been permitted a tantalizing hint of what freedom could taste like, and even then he couldn't taste anything at all.

But Mark was a fully-grown man! To shrink him down into something this size would be impossible!

'I think I see a slight wrinkle in your dream possibility, sweetie. Mark is six feet tall, and this ... well, Nathan is no bigger than you. There's no way you could squeeze him down enough to fit into ... well, those clothes we bought for Nathan.'

Evelyn smiled. 'Nathan is precisely my size. Yeah, that would be a squeeze, wouldn't it? There's something else you're forgetting, too. If I brought Mark down to this size, what would happen to Mark's penis? We'd lose all reason to even have our entertaining slave at all.'

'Slave? Don't you think that's a bit extreme?'

Evelyn looked at her mother. 'We changed his fingerprints, you know. I did, anyway. I did it last night. We had already cleared his police record. If we changed his physical appearance back to what it was, he could go out there in normal clothes, get a job, drive a taxi or something, and he could be free. Why don't we talk about doing that? Do we want to do that, or is Mark our slave?'

'Well, I know why I don't want to talk about that. I don't want to do it, that's why! No, I don't want to lose my ... I don't want to lose what I have, what we have. I don't know how he feels about it.' Doc was not entirely rational about this subject, and had probably never been. They all had gotten used to the way things were, that was all.

Evelyn nodded. 'I'm not sure. He wouldn't be happy like that. He would look like a man, but he wouldn't; he couldn't *be* a man. Not like he was, anyway. Don't panic, yet. I've thought about this, too. Suppose I shrank him down to Nathan size, but gave him the ability to do with us what he does now, and he would have control over it. I know that would work for me, he'd be my size, but wow would he be man enough for me even then! But then the question for the shrink would be, how would the shrink be able to deal with a shrunken Frankenstein sex toy, just big enough to be her son?'

Ten looked at the girl. 'This is like your playing with my boobs earlier, when you could have just held my hands, isn't it? You're playing with my mind, you know. That's supposed to be *my* job. And psychologists are never far from mental breakdown anyway. You're presenting to me an Oedipal complex even old Gordian would have thought too naughty!'

'You're losing me, Mom. How would you like to have a son? Remember when you asked the question the other way, me having a brother? I could get used to the arrangement, I think. I could take Nathan with the big blue eyes into my bed to have sex with him. I'm pretty kinky myself by now. But what about you? Would you be prepared to have sex with someone everyone thought was your son? Remember, Nathan has been introduced to society now. He's supposed to be staying with us. Would you want to have him in your bed?'

Ten stared at the broken robot. He looked so sad, so dismal. How would she feel about bedding a child? It sounded sick; more perverted even than anything she had thought about before.

But he wasn't a boy. Mark was in his twenties. It would be like dating a guy who was really short.

He would look like a boy. He would be known in the community as her nephew.

But he would have the attributes of a man. He would know how to satisfy a woman. He would be able to satisfy both her and Evelyn too. They were doing that anyway. They even watched each other do it.

Was it better, more moral or ethical, to keep a sex slave in the basement, or to have a young man romancing your prepubescent daughter, and having sex with both of you?

These questions could not be judged on morality or ethics at all. Neither situation was tolerable or justifiable in any way. But she was not going to surrender what she had fought to achieve and attain. She would keep him. He would service her.

As a kindness to her daughter, she would share him with her. Or perhaps Evelyn would be kind enough to share him with her. Would Mark actually care which it was?

Perhaps it could be boiled down to whether one or the other situation would be more beneficial to him in the long run. How would his mental health fare as a basement captive sex slave, in comparison to a free-to-go young man with the run of the house and neighborhood?

Doc had the idea she knew how he would answer that question. Perhaps he already had. What was it he had said? She strained her memory. He had been so anguished, so emotional; "Before I grew up. Back when I was a kid, … not having anyone expect anything, because I was a kid, and … everything was okay. Send me back there, Doc. That's what I need to fix me."

That's what he had said. He had wanted to be Nathan. Now Evelyn wanted him to be Nathan too.

Did she want a sex slave in her basement, or a lusty teenager in her bed?

She looked at Evelyn, patiently waiting and no doubt wondering just what kind of walkabout her mind had been taking. 'Tell me again about how you could shrink him, and yet not shrink him.'

Chapter Twenty

"Wait! You're going too fast. My head is swimming." Mark complained. "Tell me again what you think you're going to do."

"Mom and I have come up with a plan to grant you your freedom." Evelyn said calmly, "It has some limitations and some ramifications."

"All right, I'm following so far."

"First, you won't have to live down here and stay out of sight. Don't even start asking questions yet, just let me go through the basics."

"Okay, freedom, great!"

"Right. We'll be able to travel around as a family. We can go to parks, theaters, circuses, amusement parks, and other stuff that normal people do."

Mark was frowning a bit; this didn't seem possible. He remained quiet.

"Second, you're still going to be our sex slave, and we plan to wear you out every night if we can. We may not even let you run back and forth between our beds; we might just all sleep in a big bed together."

Mark grinned. This part of the story sounded like a lot of fun.

"Third, most of the time, you won't have a noticeable penis at all. You will have a shrunken pitiful remnant like most other men."

He frowned again.

Evelyn grinned. "Fourth, when we want it to be that way, you will again have the magnificent organ of entertainment that modern science has bestowed upon you, with all the delightful characteristics we have all gotten used to."

"Fifth, you and I are both going to test out of the public education system, and be considered high school graduates, and we are signing up for college."

Mark grinned again. College!

"Sixth, you are going to be Nathan Stone, my cousin and Doc's nephew. You will be living with us and meeting again with some of the people you've already met."

"Seventh, we are going to be starting up a factory, and you and I are going to be employed there, in design and engineering!"

"A factory?"

"Yep! You want to know what we'll be making?" Evelyn's eyes were bright with excitement.

"What?" Mark looked dumbfounded.

"Robots!" Evelyn said. "We'll start with power suits, and move up from there! This is going to be great! We'll have everything we want!"

"But wait, there's something I don't understand!" Mark looked at her, "How can I pretend to be Nathan? He's the size of a kid!"

Evelyn pulled his head down to her face. "That's what I like about him! He's my size! Not too big, not too small; he's just right!"

"But how?"

"Remember how I said Mom was going to get a trim waist, and strong bones and super-speed and strength? That's how you're going to change, too. I'm going to do what my mother did. I'm going to take you in my hands, and mold you and shape you until you are precisely what I want you to be. Are you scared yet?"

Mark looked at her. Yes, she was manic. Yes, her mother was even crazier. Yes, they both had committed crimes and they should all be put in prison forever. But yes he loved her and trusted her, and he didn't care what she wanted to do to him, he wanted her to do it.

"Nope. I'm not scared. You and your mother are both just as crazy as bedbugs, but you're my bedbugs, and I want to have fun with you. Let's do it!"

Evelyn climbed on his lap, and climbed on his hitching post too. He was in for the ride of his life.

Doctor Tenerife Brandon continued with her career, attending medical boards and heading investigative review panels across the lower portion of the state. She seemed unstoppable, filled with a raging energy no three other people could emulate.

She had somehow changed her figure into that of a young movie starlet, reducing her waist and increasing her bust size, yet having a firm tautness competitive track athletes could only envy.

Mark had shrunk seven inches in height. He had seven more to go. He had been losing mass everywhere, but not losing energy. He felt as though he could go all day, and he did.

His eyes were changing color, and even his hips were getting thinner. His entire body shape was changing.

His voice was getting higher in pitch.

So far, he had not lost the ability to entertain his lady-friends. His penis stayed quite erect and ready at all times. It seemed strange that everything else on him was getting smaller, but this adornment remained fixed in size and orientation.

That was a good thing, because he had frequent use of it.

Their houseguest had departed. They no longer made a pretense that Evelyn needed adult supervision, for she had already qualified as a high school graduate and was taking college courses on line.

Mark, or Nathan, did not exist in the system, so no one was looking for him. This meant that the kids had the run of the house, as long as they didn't go outside and couldn't be seen through the windows.

What this meant was that they had a better opportunity to learn proper cooking.

It also meant that the big bed in the big bedroom could hold all of them and it did.

Evelyn finally tied Nathan into the mind-to-mind network, and taught him how to use their secret signaling to be a better sex toy for his ladies. With abundant energy, and an endless supply of what made their adventures fun, Nathan was nothing but cooperative.

Finally the day came when Nathan had gotten small enough to fit into the clothes hanging in Evelyn's closet. His clothes, that is, not hers.

Well, except for one thing. One massive, apparent, and quite substantial thing.

Nathan was still sporting a huge, magnificent penis any man would be proud to display. On a beautiful, blue-eyed child it looked imposing but compellingly inviting.

Evelyn had a plan. Her mother's original construction was based on micro-surgery with artificial organs to supply a constant stream of sweet lubricant whenever his surface sensitivity was stimulated.

As a pretend boy, this organ would have to find a way to be less obtrusive, but available when needed. Accordingly, Evelyn reshaped its mounting structure so that it could slide deep into his pelvis and disappear from sight, leaving only a shrunken foreskin to cover the opening, and two fatty lumps which could be mistaken for testicles.

Nathan's lower torso was an engineering curiosity. His intestinal tract and urinary disposal path were nothing like anyone else's, but they were quite functional. The masquerade was only intended to fool a cursory examination, such as dressing at a locker room for example. They didn't plan to let him be in that situation, but it was best to be prepared.

"So am I done then? Am I really, really done?" Nathan stood in the bedroom of Doctor Tenerife Brandon, while Evelyn Brandon walked around his naked figure, studying it.

His voice had finally climbed into the range of a boy suitable for singing in a boy's choir, and Nathan had been singing to entertain his ladies, as well as playing the guitar. His shrinking fingers nevertheless had great strength, and the guitar was a comfortable instrument for him, as long as his enormous penis was not standing out in the way.

Nathan could make it go down and behave itself, but either of the women could command it to rise. When that happened, he was powerless to prevent its ascension.

The ladies were amused to bring him in to the bedroom, and toy with him as they might choose. Although he pretended to be annoyed by this, he was actually most delighted.

Normally his embarrassment continued to allowing one or both of them to apply their tongues to his protrusion, stimulating him to produce a slippery syrupy substance which varied randomly in flavor, rather than being the same all the time. Evelyn's favorite game with a new flavor was to transfer it in her mouth to his.

Their sex games had reached new heights or depths of perversion. Much was made of Nathan's apparent boyhood and childish innocence. In the back of Nathan's mind, and of Doc's mind as well, was his longing to go back into a period of childhood when he was truly innocent of the things that had gotten him in trouble, but could at the same time work his way through the notion of arriving adolescence without the trappings and mental punishments and pain of guilt in the process.

If a paper were to be written about the psychology of this treatment, the appropriate authorities would no doubt reject it. Even so, Doc had the feeling that the pain and guilt that had plagued him was fading away.

For her own part, Doc was content to let the damage to her psyche accumulate. She was having fun and she felt good and healthy about it. Any possible damage to her daughter or to her kidnap victim, she simply shrugged out of her conscious thoughts.

Evelyn, of course, was completely at ease with the arrangements. She even got the opportunity to be even more openly affectionate with her mother, kissing and fondling her at random intervals during their frequent lovemaking events.

And so, they came together to a somewhat compromised maturity. Sexually, each was comfortable regardless of the theoretically embarrassing situations they found themselves in, and physically, each appeared to be surprisingly youthful and energetic.

Eventually, Evelyn and Nathan appeared to grow older. It was a necessary compromise for their more outgoing social presence. Evelyn delayed the process as much as possible, extending their youthful energies and carefree joys to give all of them time to establish a lifetime of pleasant memories.

And then, of course, there were also the pleasant memories they established in their very long, very joyful private moments and exceptionally extended youthfulness.

They all lived very, very happily ever after.

Cage Kittens of Hyper-Space

Brian B. Hawthorne

Chapter One

Tawney awakened, stiff and uncomfortable. She was also naked and on the floor. Well, that had happened before. Discovering that she was in a cage was not a good sign.

Despite her grogginess, and general ill-feeling, she snapped wide awake. The cage appeared to be sturdily built, and beyond it she could see that she was in a ship's stateroom. A man was sleeping in the bed.

Tawney reviewed her last moments of consciousness. She had gone back to her dressing room after the last performance, and of course secured the door against entry. She hadn't had anything to drink for some time. Her kidnapper must have used some form of knockout dart or gas. As she organized her thoughts and memories, it occurred to her that she could not remember anything beyond taking a shower at the end of the day. Could that have been when she was rendered unconscious? Had someone tampered with the plumbing, or something, to have an anesthetic gas seep in with the warm water? She remembered getting into the stall and scrubbing off her stage makeup and the cares of the day, but could recall nothing beyond that. How cowardly, to attack someone when they could not be any more defenseless!

He must have been very determined, because the security at her theater had been pretty tight. He had likely paid off several people. She reviewed who had been on duty that night. If ever she got a chance to interview them, they had better have good explanations.

She tried the bars of her cage quietly. They were certainly beyond her strength to bend. This was the first obstacle to regaining her freedom however, and she bent her mind to the task. Although the cage seemed quite sturdy, she recognized it as mainly a stage prop. The metal would not yield to her muscles, but perhaps the construction was a point of attack. The front of the cage, where the door was, was strongly fastened. The rear, fortunately, was designed to be disassembled to allow the cage to be stored more easily. There were bolts holding it in place.

If she could remove those bolts, she could slip out of the cage.

It was a big if. By straining at the cage, she was able to reduce the tension on one bolt, and get it turning. Her bare fingers could just nudge it a little at a time.

Finally, it came free. Patiently, she worked at the other fasteners, pushing at the loose corner to stretch, and then release the pressure. Her skin was raw by the time she was finally able to squeeze out of the cage.

When she stood, Tawney realized that she was not entirely naked. Or at least, not naked in the ordinary sense. She was in some kind of stage outfit, like nothing she had ever worn or performed in. Something unusual had been done to her hair, and there was a strange sensation on her back where something had been attached at the base of her spine.

Reaching back to feel, she realized that she had been made to look like a lion, complete with mane and tail! Even her skin had been stained a rich coppery color, and streaked to simulate fur. It was a really good makeup job, considering she had been unconscious during the procedure.

None of this was important at the moment. Tawney moved toward the occupant of the bed. If he awakened, she remained pretty defenseless. Not entirely helpless now, but still only a naked woman.

The man was not unattractive, and he was deep under the influence of a sleep-inducing drug. A med scanner on the bed showed he would not awaken for several more hours, until the ship came out of hyper-drive.

Belatedly, she realized why her vision was so blurry, and her stomach so tied in knots. Hyper-drive disagreed with most people, and most chose to sleep it off. There was nothing to see anyway, even if your eyes could work right in that strange twisting of normal space.

Tawney needed the time though, to turn the tables on her captor. She began to inventory her surroundings.

That was when she discovered Dawn, sleeping soundly, if

uncomfortably, in another cage. She had also been decorated in the same manner, complete with lion's tail. Seeing Dawn made up that way let her realize how much effort had gone into this.

It was an alarming thought. This was not just some rich playboy's prank. She and Dawn had been converted into merchandise, to be sold to a high bidder. Tawney looked again at the occupant of the bed. He had probably gotten used to living well, but had invested poorly, or lived too lavishly. In either case, he was now so desperate for money that he had gone into the slavery trade. Suddenly, she lost any sympathy for him that she might have harbored. He was an enemy, and had to be dealt with.

It would be easy enough to kill him, but she was not ready for that yet. She continued to look around. Seeing a bathroom, Tawney glanced about once more, to be sure nothing would change while she was diverted, and went into the chamber.

It was there that she got a good look at herself. She and Dawn had been made to look like twins. They would probably have been sold that way, even though Dawn was four years younger. The lion's mane surrounded her neck, and itched uncomfortably. The real annoyance, however, was the stupid tail! Tawney tugged at it experimentally. It was very firmly attached. If she pulled it off now, she would lose skin, a lot of skin. She left it alone, and tried to ignore the strange sensation it caused when she walked.

She emptied her bladder, and then tried to wash her hands and face. The make-up didn't yield to ordinary soap. Her lovely face remained hidden beneath Halloween whiskers and an odd shape to the mouth. Oh, well, at least she felt cleaner. Going back out, Tawney turned her mind to the problem of her captor. What was she going to do with him?

Tawney began rummaging around, looking for tools, or keys, to help her get Dawn free, and to find out what else the ship contained.

As she searched, she left items lying loosely on top of countertops and tables. This was not good shipboard procedure, but she was not yet certain which items might be useful. When she came across some snack packages, her stomach reminded her that it had been several hours since she attended to it. She ignored it, but left that cabinet door open.

She thought about her predicament. She would need to gain control of the ship. That would not be easy. Shipboard computers were well protected against such possibilities, and it was more than likely she would arrive at her destination as effectively caged as before.

Tawney felt like growling at the thought, adopting for the moment the personality she physically resembled. How much time did she have, anyway?

She inspected the medicomp at the bedside more closely. The occupant was thoroughly under the influence of a powerful sedative, but it was also one, which had a specific time-signature. A little over five hours remained on the dose. She looked over the device. If she tinkered with it now, some watchguard program might wake up and give him an antidote.

It would be better to get Dawn free also, so that if need be, they could struggle together against their captor. Tawney gathered her tools and went to Dawn's cage. In only minutes, she had the back panel completely removed from the cage, and she rudely dragged a nearly comatose Dawn out of the cage.

This caused her to ponder. What was it that had allowed her to awaken hours before, even though she was likely given the same dosage as Dawn?

Tawney remembered the medical investments she had made at the beginning of her career, when the money had begun rolling in rather steadily. A good investment, as it turned out.

Tawney had taken a wide-spectrum anti-sedative treatment. It was designed to piggyback onto her immune system, causing her to react to knockout gas or black-market sedation as if she had developed a fever. It was somewhat surprising that the stuff they had used on her had worked as well as it did, but it had been some time since her system had been challenged. She had been feeling very safe. Now she grew momentarily angry again. No doubt a part of the bribe to pay off her supposed guardians had been her own savings. Tawney discovered that she was pacing, and stopped. Where had that come from? She had never done that in her life!

Dawn had not had this treatment, and she was still quite under the influence of something. Tawney picked up the unconscious form of Dawn and carried her to an adjoining small stateroom. This would normally not be an easy thing to do considering that her burden was completely limp. Dead weight, Tawney thought savagely.

She placed the girl on the bed gently, and connected her to its medical computer. Soon she had a readout on the drug that had Dawn in a stupor -- Mexcalidene! Well, no surprise there. When you go into a criminal enterprise, you may as well go first class. Now to find a way to administer an antidote. The antidote was known, and it was stocked in the medicomp, but it would be necessary to convince the medicomp to use it, without triggering any kind of alarm response.

She went through the menu items carefully. Finally, she found a low-priority selection, which indicated to the computer that this person was not a guest, but a guest worker, and that she would have the responsibility of preparing the ship for the awakening of its master. Then she entered a time factor, which told it that it was time for the worker to wake up and begin those preparations. She watched as the medicomp carefully checked Dawn's vital signs against her medical condition, then she saw activity showing that the antidote was being administered.

This would probably take a while. Tawney went to the kitchen to prepare some food for them both. She selected only emergency rations, not trusting the integrated computer network to remain stable if she started a regular meal. Every indication was that her abductor had supreme confidence in his plan, and had no back-up or emergency procedures, but she wasn't going to trust her life to it.

During the half-hour it took for Dawn to come around, Tawney had time for more thinking. She realized that Dawn's first questions would be about her nudity, and that of Tawney as well. A thorough search of the rooms in this ship showed that there was nothing to be done about it. There wasn't a stitch of feminine clothing aboard at all.

Tawney went to their kidnapper's closet, and hesitated for a moment.

It was possible there was an alarm device or fail-safe here, as well. She stared at the door handle, and reluctantly stepped away from it.

It almost seemed obvious that the creep would use their femininity against them. She and Dawn would have to remain au naturel for a while longer.

She heard a moan from Dawn, and went to her. Cradling Dawn's head in her lap, Tawney caressed her cheek. Dawn's eyelids fluttered open. She looked around, recognized Tawney, and her eyes closed again.

"Wake up, Dawn! Hey, Rube!"

Dawn opened her eyes again. They stayed open. She looked around once more, taking in everything before trying to move. She looked into Tawney's eyes again, and sat up. "Ooooh! My head! My eyes! Ouch! Everything hurts!"

Tawney hugged her shoulders and then stood in front of her.

Dawn looked up, and smiled. Then her face lost its expression again. She looked closely at Tawney's "Outfit" and stared. Then she looked more closely at her own body.

She stood up too, swaying slightly. "My God! What's happened?"

"We were knocked out, with Mexcalidene, just after the last act. Then someone did some crazy make-up on us, and we were put in cages on a starlighter. I think we were being delivered as slaves to a big shot."

"Oh! ... Oh, my!" she swayed. Tawney reached out to steady her.

It was at this point that Dawn discovered her tail. She twisted to observe it better, and then looked more closely at the equivalent piece on Tawney's backside.

"What the...?" She reached out and tugged gently at Tawney's tail.

"Careful! It's pretty firmly glued on. Pull on your own tail if you don't believe me."

Dawn walked around, almost seeming to be on tiptoe. "This is strange! Normally, I would be sick and puking my guts out in hyperspace, but aside from feeling dizzy and disoriented, I feel pretty good."

She studied Tawney's make-up, as if she were looking in a mirror. Then she smiled. "You look really good, Tawney! And I look just like you! I've always wanted to look more like you!"

Slightly embarrassed, Tawney wrapped her arms around Dawn and hugged her tightly. They were sisters now, whatever else happened.

Dawn shivered, though her skin did not feel cold. "What are we going to do, Tawney?"

Tawney pulled away slightly, and smiled. "That's easy enough! We're going to eat something. I'm hungry!"

Dawn smiled, and Tawney led the way to the kitchen.

Chapter Two

The food was unexpectedly bland. They ate in relative silence.

"How did we get into this mess, Tawney?"

She sighed. "I don't know. All I can tell you is that we were knocked out and kidnapped by that guy sleeping in there, and he's going to wake up in less than four hours. We have to think of something."

"We could tie him up!"

Tawney shook her head. Her mane tossed around like a stiff hairstyle. "No. It won't do any good. We need to seize control of the ship, and that means we have to take control of the computer."

"What have you tried?"

"I've been afraid to try anything. I didn't even dare open his closet, thinking that it might be booby-trapped! I couldn't find anything for us to put on."

Dawn smiled grimly. "As if that mattered to us, anyway." Looking toward the computer interface, she rose and moved closer to it.

"If I could remove this shrouding, I could see what kind of circuitry is in there."

"I found some tools. But that's not the main computer connection, anyway."

Dawn's grin looked slightly feral. "That's what I'm counting on. We can't go at the main computer. It would never work. You absolutely have to have the passwords to be able to control it."

Tawney looked puzzled.

"All these computers, and there are many, even on a ship like this, have to communicate with each other. We'll try to use those communication channels to find the information we need."

Tawney looked at her in surprise. "You know about computers?"

Dawn grinned again, and looked down. "Before these grew in, I trained in appliance repair..." She laughed, "... kitchen appliances!"

Tawney smiled, hope glimmering at last. "I'll get the tools!"

Soon they had the cover removed, and Dawn was peering into the maze of cable connections and flashing data indicators.

Dawn murmured in small satisfaction. "Ah. I think I've found a diagnostic reset switch. If we're in luck, we'll be able to intercept the data with one of the diagnostic tools." She used a small device to operate the switch. The screen on the display indicated a change, and several lines of data.

Straightening up, Dawn reached carefully back into the recesses of the system. She recited the steps, as if giving a lesson. "... Three-button programming, the simplest kind. All we can do is choose from the lists of available options, but if the right options are available..." Her eyes were shining brightly.

The screen information changed. Dawn was moving through menus and sub-menus of diagnostic tools and procedures. She selected one and initiated it. A stream of characters began moving across the top of the screen.

"Help me watch that. We need to intercept the password, if we can get it to respond." She looked at the menus again.

"Can it really be as easy as that?" Tawney asked in astonishment.

Dawn looked at her. "Easy? It took me years to learn these systems. And what if our kidnapper were standing here with a zapper? We wouldn't have time to play with the electronics if we had to fight him for control of the ship."

"Yeah, and we could still be in our cages, too!"

"Cages?" Dawn looked surprised.

"I'll show you later. Keep going with the computer!"

"Right! First things first!" She studied the lists again.

"Hmm. This could work. Synchronization. Watch the screen." She pressed a switch.

Immediately, symbols began appearing along the top row of the screen. "There," Dawn announced. "That string of characters, ten in a row. We need to write them down!"

Tawney found a stylus and pad. They recorded the information.

"Let me try once more. We have to be certain this is the right sequence. We may only get one chance." She went over the choices again.

"This should work, 'Confirm Update'. We should see the same characters again." She operated the switch. In a moment, the identical string of characters appeared.

"All right, I'm satisfied that that is the main password key sequence. Do you want to try it?" Dawn was looking for encouragement.

"You've done great so far, Dawn. If that isn't it, we may be almost out of choices. Let's go for it!"

"Okay..." Dawn led the way into the main navigational cockpit, where incomprehensible instruments displayed unintelligible patterns of data. She sat down at a console indistinguishable from the rest, maneuvering her tail to get it out of the way. "Let's give it a try!"

She operated a sequence on the board, and the display changed. Taking a deep breath, Dawn placed her fingers on the console control board, and made a request.

She was immediately challenged to enter the appropriate password key sequence. Carefully, symbol by symbol, she put the string of characters in. Both girls held their breath.

"Accepted." Whoosh. The girls expelled their breath again.

"All right! We're in! Now what?"

"What do you mean, 'Now what?' Now we take control, and lock up the guy who locked us up!"

"No. That's not what I mean. We have to change the programming of the master computer, all of the secondary computers, delete the former passwords and control procedures, and in general, tell the computer what we want to do." She looked up. "So what do we want to do?"

"Oh, yeah! I see what you mean. Okay, let's get the old command structure out of the way, and we'll share command on the ship. Is that okay with you?"

Dawn smiled, "You bet! Let's set up a voice command system, keyed to our voices, and our voices only. I don't want any mutinies."

"Good idea! Let me go check on our sleeping beauty, and make sure he's still asleep. Maybe I should take a frying pan with me!"

"No, wait! I can take care of that right here." She turned to the console again, and operated some sub-menus. "This is the medical section. I'm going to administer another dose of sedative. How about twelve more hours?"

"Good! That should get us through the period of emerging from hyperspace without interference from...." She stopped. They looked at each other.

"Oh, my goodness!" Dawn finished the thought. "Where are we going?" She turned once more to the board. "First, though, I'll put that sedative to work. She typed in the appropriate commands.

Tawney left quickly, and went to the side of the master stateroom's big bed. She watched as the medicomp adjusted itself and sent the chemicals into the sleeping figure. A warning signal began flashing. "Catheterization necessary ... Proceed?"

Tawney paused for a moment. He had been sleeping for a long time, and now he would sleep for another half-day. His bladder would need to be relieved. She reached over and pressed the Confirm button.

A tentacle extended itself out of the side of the unit, and slithered its way toward the sleeping man's crotch. Tawney moved the bedclothes aside, and watched in fascination as the device tracked and identified the orifice it was seeking. With what appeared to be a combination of suction and a continuing eversion of the tip of the tubule, it entered the opening and penetrated deep into the interior of the man's body. Soon a fluid could be seen moving into the medicomp, as the bladder began to be relieved. There was nothing pleasant or sexual in anything she had seen, and she covered the sleeping man again with a slight shudder.

"I need to not be sympathetic to him." Tawney told herself. "We might even need to shove him out of an airlock!" But she knew she could never bring herself to do that. What would they do with him?

Dawn was still busy with the controls, so Tawney went a little further afield in her searching. When she arrived at the door to the cargo hold, it opened for her.

She looked around at the various items. In some respects, these things would be good for trade. That stack of medical computers over there, securely fastened down, would certainly be for trade.

But look at this! A modern rejuvenation chamber, with cerebro-spinal interface! These were expensive! This was either a gift or bribe to someone, or their kidnapper had plans to use it himself. Tawney looked around a bit more and then returned to see Dawn.

Dawn looked up as she entered. "I want to call him Lucas."

"Who? The guy in the bed? I don't think that's his name."

"No! Who cares about him? I'm talking about the computer. We're putting it on a voice command, so we'll need a name for it."

"Lucas ... I like it. Can we call him Luke, also?"

"I'll set it up." She turned back to the console.

Tawney waited a few minutes. When Dawn seemed less occupied, she said casually, "We have a rejuvenation chamber aboard."

Dawn looked around. Her eyes were wide. "Wow! Those are expensive! I don't think either one of us needs it right now, but that's good to know." She turned away. "I hope we live long enough to need it!"

"It has a cerebro-spinal circuit. I was thinking we could stuff what's-his-name into it."

Dawn smiled at her. "You're thinking to punish him? Or were you planning to try to salvage his personality?"

"I don't want anything to do with his current personality. He's a weasel."

"Well, they say if you go back far enough, almost everyone has a good spirit. Do you really want to take the chance?"

"What choice is there? We could stuff him out the airlock, but I have trouble seeing myself do that to a sleeping person, no matter what he planned for us."

"Yeah. Me too. -- What did he have planned for us? We're going to come out of hyperdrive in a couple of hours, and there could be someone looking to receive a present."

"Can't we go somewhere else?"

Dawn looked at her in surprise. "I thought you knew about hyperdrive! It's like sending a package. Once you put it in the chute, it has to go all the way. If you don't have enough Iridium, you can't go anywhere. You won't even start."

"Hmmm. How much do we have?"

Dawn looked apprehensive. "That's a good question. We may need to scoot out of wherever we land in a hurry. I hope we have plenty! -- Lucas!"

"Yes, Dawn." The calm masculine voice came from a hidden speaker.

"How much hyperspace range will we have when we reach our destination?"

The pause seemed momentary. "Three point six light years, Dawn."

Dawn seemed crushed. Tawney stared. "What's wrong, Dawn?"

She looked up. "Lucas! What is our destination?"

"It is listed as Piggledy. We will arrive above the orbital plane of the primary world named Higgledy-Piggledy."

Dawn looked into Tawney's eyes. "Lucas! How many hyperspace destinations are within four light-years of Piggledy?"

"Four."

"List them, please."

"Closest is point five light years, called Chink. Next is three light years, called Faunelle. Next is three point three light years, called Burnitch. Next is three point nine light years, called Scow."

"Oh, God!" Dawn put her head in her hands.

"What? You recognize those names?" Tawney asked.

"Only that we're in the wrong part of the Galaxy. You study them, and pick the best destination. I'm going to take a bath."

Dawn got up from her command chair, and stretched. Tawney was amused to note that she looked like a sleepy housecat. Dawn walked back to the guest stateroom, which had its own bathroom. Her golden hair cascaded across her shoulders, and her tail swung gracefully back and forth, oscillating with her hips. It was a rather fetching and seductive outfit, Tawney had to admit.

She studied their destination choices. Nothing appeared at all promising. Clearly, they could not remain at the point of emergence. Their arrival would be signaled, and without a doubt, someone with nasty intentions would be standing by to take action if they did not come to port.

What kind of person would purchase human slaves? The kind of person who would live on a place like Piggledy, she supposed. Higgledy-Piggledy had been settled early, by a rough crew of asteroid miners, ships crewmen, convict conscripts, and other factions who tended to ignore most legal authority. After a time, they had begun raiding nearby colonies and shipping. That had been brought to a halt, but the now constituted government of Piggledy was still a virtually outlaw regime, drawing the crooks and misfits from across the galaxy for gambling, drugs, and other illicit entertainments. Eventually, they would have to be shut down, but she didn't have the resources, and she was unlikely to find sanctuary in that place.

Chink was just an outpost of Piggledy, where most of the drug trade appeared to be executed. No help there either.

Faunelle was a faint possibility. Most of the planet was very heavily overgrown with large, leafy vines. The fruit of these vines supported a wide variety of animal life, some of which had grown quite dependent on the vine, the fruit of which was mildly narcotic. Tawney suspected that the human, or sentient, population were involved in harvesting the narcotic elements of the plant life for sale to such people as she was trying to avoid. She did not think they could be trusted, either, but it might be possible to hide in the jungle there for some time.

They wouldn't be able to conceal their spacecraft though. She wasn't real attached to Luke just yet, but he represented their only assets, and she didn't want to risk losing him this soon.

If the math was correct, Scow was outside their range anyway, but she didn't think the ancient trading port offered what they were looking for.

What were they looking for?

Tawney scowled. They needed a place far enough away from any pursuers, and where they could settle in for a time to earn a living, and begin undoing what had been done to them.

Burnitch did not seem to be that place, but it offered the best possibility of concealment, and a vestige of normality. It was an agricultural colony, like many which specialized in certain foods or products, enough to sustain a level of interstellar trade. And like many, it had more than its share of quirky residents and strange beliefs.

Considering that they had no real choice, it would have to suffice. Tawney went to find Dawn.

Chapter Three

Dawn seemed upset. "It's not coming off!" Her skin, beneath the golden color, looked scrubbed and pink. She climbed out of the shower, and began to dry herself.

Tawney took the drier and a brush and began grooming Dawn's lovely hair. "We probably don't have time, anyway. We'll be coming out of hyperdrive soon. If it's any consolation, you have a very pleasant aroma."

Dawn looked a little puzzled. "Strange, I hadn't even used any perfumes. But while we're on the subject, I should politely mention that your aroma is not what I am used to smelling from you."

Tawney reddened in embarrassment. Undoubtedly it was true. She had probably not fully finished with her cleansing ritual, and there were the odors of this strange makeup, and a not too clean cage, which had been added. It was indeed time that she get properly clean again.

She smiled, to show that she was not offended. "Okay, step aside, and I'll take care of that right now! By the way, I think our best bet will be a place called Burnitch, but you might want to check on that. I have no idea how to program for a hyperspace jump."

Dawn made room, but did not leave. She continued with the process of drying and brushing her hair. "The computer can take care of that for us, but you need to know more about hyperspace, if you're going to be co-captain."

Tawney programmed the bath unit for a soaking bath. In a moment, she had a luxurious, sudsy warmth enveloping her. Dawn smiled, "At least you don't mind water, like some cats."

Tawney relaxed, "What is it we need again? Irritatium?"

Dawn sat down, holding the end of her tail in her hands somewhat nervously. "No, it's Iridium, a rare earth element. A few centuries ago, it was discovered, don't ask me how, that when you accelerate to near-lightspeed, you can put Iridium into a special chamber, and excite it with various energy inputs, until you set up a quadripole oscillation."

Tawney looked over at her, and blinked.

Dawn released her tail, "Look, you know that you can only get so close to the speed of light, and then all your propulsion energy goes to increasing the mass of your ship." Tawney nodded, everyone knew that!

"The Iridium oscillation converts the mass-energy into a star-drive, propelling your vessel at ten thousand times the speed of light, but it also converts the Iridium into an element with one-fourth the atomic mass. The quadripole oscillation ends up tearing apart the atoms of Iridium in four different directions! What we have in our star-drive chamber is mostly Titanium."

Tawney drained off the bathwater, and rinsed herself down quickly. She stepped out of the unit and began drying. Momentarily, Dawn took the dryer from her and used it and the brush to shape the slightly unruly mane of hair. When they were finished, Dawn leaned a little closer and breathed the clean, fragrant natural pungency of Tawney's body. She leaned against Tawney and placed her arms around her stomach. "I'm glad you're with me, Tawney. There's no one I'd rather be with through any kind of adventure, and this one is shaping up to be a pip!"

Tawney reached around and pulled their heads closer together gently. "You're very special to me, too, Dawn. You always have been. Let's see if we can find some clothes."

They walked together to the master suite, where the master lay slumbering in his bed. Dawn released a deep, throaty growl, and then stopped, embarrassed.

Tawney chuckled, "I feel the same way! Let's look in the closet."

This was an extreme disappointment. They had not expected to find feminine clothes there, but they had expected to find more than this! Other than three or four shirts, and a few pairs of pants, there was nothing but underwear anywhere in the stateroom. In irritation, they threw all of it into the disposer.

Then they turned their attention to the occupant of the bed.

"Let's put him into the rejuvenation chamber." Dawn suggested.

"For how long? I think it takes a month in the chamber to erase a year of decrepitude. We'd have to take him back thirty years to be able to get rid of all of his bad habits and aberrant mental patterns."

Dawn shrugged. "He's no good to us as a criminal. Who cares how long he stays in there?"

"Not me! But if we get captured, and they bring him out of the chamber, that will be one more enemy we have to deal with."

"Yeah. But by that point, it won't matter if we have a hundred enemies, or a hundred and one. We'd still be in way over our heads, but at least we wouldn't be guilty of murder."

"True." They disconnected the medicomp, and turned down the bedclothes. He looked very helpless, and somewhat innocent, lying in the bed in silk pajamas.

"He looks kinda cute." They stripped the pajamas off the inert body.

"Hah!" Tawney laughed. "Look at him! Paunchy, balding, out of shape. He looks like any of the hundred barflies who used to come in and ogle us."

"Yes, and he was probably one of them, a time or two. I don't recognize him, though. I was just thinking, once we get him tuned up a bit, he won't look so bad."

Tawney grimaced. "That's very likely. But it's his mind I'm concerned about. This is the man who plotted and executed a plan to put us into groveling bondage for the rest of our lives! Whatever his body looks like, I want to eliminate the kind of thinking that would come up with that kind of plan, and I don't care if he has to go back to waddling around in diapers! In fact, I might prefer it, so I could smack his bottom!"

Dawn flipped the helpless body over. His naked buttocks lay exposed like a full moon reflected in a mirror. "You can smack his bottom now! Go ahead!"

They both laughed, as between them they picked the man up like a sleeping child, and carried him to the rejuvenation chamber.

Activating the chamber was simple enough. It responded as soon as they opened the door. They made sure it was able to draw power and nutrients from the ship connections, and Tawney began programming the extent of rejuvenation. To a large degree, what she was doing was unlawful, but at this point, she was not concerned about such niceties.

"I'm programming it to scan for certain thought patterns and brain waves. It's been established that there is a correlation between them and overt criminal actions. Most men learn to control their feelings, integrating them into a worldview where violence against others is controlled by relatively rigid rules. The criminal mind takes a shortcut past these limitations, and there are measurable differences laid down in the memory engrams. The chamber is going to take him backward in time, reliving experiences, and measuring these parameters. As long as he is responding in the negative way, it will reset itself and continue moving backwards.

"These machines were developed to make the body more youthful, but the early units had a tendency to cause memory loss. That was compensated by a circuit, which replays the memory of the event as if it were a dream, thus restoring the memory and personality. We're taking that safeguard out, and we're going to run his mental program back to a stage where he did know wrong from right. I'm also setting up some false memories to reinforce the correct way of thinking. By the time he comes out of this, a couple of years from now, he'll think he's a Boy Scout!

Dawn was staring at her in slack-jawed incredulity.

Tawney laughed. "Um, before these grew out, I trained as a Medical Interventionist. We'll get him started on this, and I'll come back from time to time to check on him."

They closed the door on the now-active rejuvenation chamber. Their kidnapper, when he awakened, would be living in a dream world, and his life would be flashing before his eyes, running backward. He wouldn't even be able to grow alarmed about it, because as soon as his thoughts occurred, they were pushed back to the original impetus. He couldn't form a conclusion, because the conclusion was forced to subsume into its original basic precepts, and then these were replaced again by even older events.

Brain studies had been done on people in such chambers, and the consensus was that thinking was happening, but it was happening in reverse, and no one could remember anything that the machine did not plant again in their brain. It was insidious, and such machines were normally closely monitored to keep them from falling into the wrong hands.

The girls went back to the master stateroom, and cleaned it thoroughly. They also kept an eye on the navigational clock.

"Lucas!" Dawn commanded.

"Yes, Dawn." The calm masculine voice responded.

"When we come out of hyperspace, I want you to immediately set up for another jump. The destination will be Burnitch. Do not announce your presence before doing this, and do not answer any hails, even automatic ones. I want us to be gone before anyone knows that we are there. Is this clear?"

"It is very clear, Dawn. It will be done."

"Thank you, Lucas."

"You are welcome, Dawn."

Apprehensively, as the time approached, they sat together on the master bed, holding hands. The clock clicked down smoothly until -- *lurch!* -- they were back in hyperspace again, but there was an indefinable difference to it, as if the boom had shifted on a sailboat, and the breeze was coming from a new direction.

"Lucas! Were we seen?"

"I detected RADAR sweeps from three different units, but we were exposed for only a third of a second. They would not have been able to identify us from that information."

Dawn tightened her grip on Tawney's hand, and the girls smiled at each other. Success! -- So far...

The jump to Burnitch would occupy a minimum of about three

hours. It was time for another meal, and this time it wouldn't be emergency rations.

Tawney sat back, completely sated with food. For the first time in memory, she had gone back for thirds. One thing that was not skimped on in this vessel was its food-processing unit. Although she had tasted better foods in planetary restaurants, she had never had reconstituted food that satisfied her craving so well. Dawn had also been quite hungry, and had eaten well.

They returned to the master suite and lay down together for a nap.

Tawney awakened with Dawn snuggled close to her. The smell of her hair made a pleasant fragrance in her nostrils. She eased from the embrace and stood, yawning and stretching. Even her tail seemed more alive.

They were out of hyperspace! She went to the communication panel, arriving just as a message pinged in. Slapping the control, she listened closely.

"Unknown vessel, please respond. This is planet Burnitch."

Tawney thought furiously. They needed a name. They had been driven and hounded across the Galaxy in such a furious rush that she hadn't considered it until this moment. It's hard to think when you've been treated like...

"Planet Burnitch, this is Starlighter "Catspaw" out of Andromeda Gate. We apologize for any delay. We're operating a little short-handed at the moment."

She waited for the interminable delay due to the speed of light for radio waves. A number of further requests for identification came in as she waited. She ignored them. Finally the message of response came.

"Catspaw, out of Andromeda Gate. What is your ownership, please?"

Tawney hesitated. This was not according to form. Obviously, local custom differed.

"Planet Burnitch, ownership is registered as Germaine Sisters, Incorporated. Instructions for landing, please?"

Again she waited. She had wanted to spell it Grrmain, but she thought it prudent not to complicate their lives. Dawn appeared at her elbow.

"Catspaw, confirm female ownership, please."

This too, was irregular. Tawney had a hunch, considering the voice on the radio was female, she responded.

"Planet Burnitch, Catspaw confirms female ownership and all-female crew. Landing instructions, please?"

"Catspaw, what is your purpose here?"

"Planet Burnitch, Catspaw is asking for emergency hyperspace fuel access. We are unable to proceed further unaided."

"Catspaw, Planet Burnitch denies landing permission. Confirming, Catspaw, Planet Burnitch denies landing permission."

"What the bloody..." Dawn burst out, but not on the air.

Tawney considered. They probably had good reason to be cautious, considering the kind of neighbors they had.

"Planet Burnitch, Catspaw also requests emergency medical attention." She crossed her fingers. The pause was longer this time.

"Catspaw, Planet Burnitch will grant provisional landing space. Follow these coordinates." There was a string of numbers. The navigational computer matched them up with its scans of the planet, and gave them a course to follow.

"Planet Burnitch, Catspaw is proceeding. The crew sends their much-relieved thanks."

She sat back. "Whew! They're suspicious!"

Dawn laughed. "They should be suspicious. Every word you told them was a lie!" She turned her head upward. "Lucas!"

"Yes, Dawn."

"Change our response to electronic interrogation to Catspaw, out of Andromeda Gate, ownership is Germaine Sisters, Incorporated. You may respond with that from now on."

"Acknowledged, Dawn. Responding now."

"Lucas, do you have external nomenclature or other markings?"

"There is a serial number etched on the bow. Would you like to change it?"

"How can you change it, Lucas?"

"A low-intensity LASER sweep can produce an entirely different sequence of numbers, Dawn."

"Very clever! Please do so, in a careful manner. I want it to look authentic."

"It is being done as we speak. I will adjust the records in the computer memory."

They followed the landing course, and found themselves on a very unpleasant and foreboding flat plain, devoid of vegetation, or anything else of interest.

The radio came to life again, with a different voice. "Please describe the nature of your medical problem."

"We have been the victims of assault, and we require restorative medical procedures." Tawney eyed the tail protruding from the console seat. It was still swinging as if showing impatience.

"Catspaw, we do not have this kind of medical procedure available here. We cannot help you."

Tawney felt like roaring into the microphone. She suppressed the urge impatiently. This required cool thinking.

The scans that they made on the way down indicated that there was almost no industrial development. It could well be that they wanted to keep it that way in order to not have anything of value to be stolen. Or at least keep that appearance.

"Planet Burnitch, Catspaw crew requests right of emergency habituation. We cannot proceed, and you cannot help us. We request the right to use local resources as best we can to survive and to repair our ship."

There was a long silence. Tawney began to believe they were not going to respond at all. Finally, more than an hour later, there was a message.

"Catspaw, you are hereby granted ownership rights to ten thousand square kilometers of land, situated at the following coordinates. You are required by planetary covenant to restore this land to maximum natural sustainability after any disturbance of the topography. You must respond with "The crew of Catspaw accepts the land and the conditions of settlement. We will restore the land to maximum natural sustainability after any disturbance of the topography."

The statement was displayed in printed form on the screen. Somewhat bewildered by this turn of events, Tawney recited the pledge.

"Planet Burnitch to Catspaw, Good Luck!" In the silence after the message stopped, Tawney could almost swear she heard laughter.

Dawn was equally perplexed. "Tawney, that's a lot of territory. Why would they give it all away?"

Tawney shrugged. "I don't know, but they won't give us medical aid, and they won't give us Iridium. If we're ever going to be able to go anywhere, we're going to have to dig the ore out of the ground ourselves."

They lifted ship and moved to the designated coordinates, running a deep scan as they maneuvered over it to try to locate the best sites for mineral deposits.

Dawn was looking thoughtful. "Tawney, I think I know what's going on. We just signed a contract to bring this land to fruition, and make it a veritable garden spot, whether we get any ore out of the ground or not. And it covers ten thousand square kilometers!"

Tawney thought about it. "I think you're right. But you know what else? We now own a country!"

They looked out over their domain, having landed on the top of a rocky outcropping that gave a commanding view of the surrounding area. In all four quadrants, there was not a living soul to be seen, and even the vegetation seemed sparse. Through the external microphones, they could hear the wind howling mournfully, but softly.

Chapter Four

Tawney and Dawn pored over the charts that had been printed out. They had even requested that Lucas speak up freely any time he had a suggestion about their various dilemmas. Five days of probing, recording, analyzing, and planning had led to this stage of colonization.

"It looks as though we're going to need some kind of infrastructure. We have a labor force of two, and it will probably take us twenty years to come up with even an ounce of Iridium, but at least we have our freedom."

Dawn looked up into the various screens now showing the vista around them. They had ventured out into the bleak surroundings, making mineral assays and gathering plant specimens. The wind seemed a steady companion, but the temperature was surprisingly comfortable, considering that they were both still essentially naked. These were not the most promising circumstances, but the ship had some untapped resources still available to them. They could maneuver it freely anywhere they wished, and it provided unlimited power from the fusion banks.

"Freedom. Yeah. I'd better not laugh. I might not be able to stop." She smiled at Tawney. They had acted like children when they first went out, skittish initially, as if they were embarrassed to be running around naked. Then, very soon, they were both laughing and dancing, rolling in the meadow grass, and doing somersaults and pirouettes as if they didn't have a lick of sense.

Now, they didn't give it any thought at all. Being naked, either inside or outside, seemed perfectly natural. They had even changed the way they moved, prancing like the proud strumpets they had once pretended to be, letting their tails whip around in happy abandon. They made efforts to control that unruly mane, sometimes trying for braids or some other variations, but for the most part, just like themselves, they let it go wild.

Tawney smiled back. It was hard to be upset with someone like Dawn. She might be impetuous, but she was always cheerful and optimistic. She made it seem okay, that if they were stuck breaking rocks for twenty years, it would be fine with her.

Tawney looked for a moment at her hands, as they held the chart flat. She had noticed that her nails appeared to be thickening and getting darker. Now she saw that the same thing was happening to Dawn. For a moment, she grew angry again, at whoever had made these strange intrusions into the way her body worked, but then it occurred to her that it might also be a simple dietary deficiency. Maybe they should do some more work with modifying the native life forms for their purposes, so they could get away from time to time from the shipboard reconstituted meals.

"Let's take the ship up to this highland area tomorrow. We can use the defenses to cut some stone, and we'll build a small dam to trap the water of this stream. With a bit of hydraulic power, we'll be able to move a lot of dirt and rock to shape the valley into a more efficient system, both for agriculture and mineral extraction."

"It is unfortunate, Lady Tawney, that I do not have a means of manipulating material. I am aware of ships similar to me, which have robotic capability. It would be my pleasure to cut the stones and pile them up for you if I had a means of doing it."

"Just being able to quarry the stone with your Lasers will be enough, Lucas. You have been very helpful already by scanning the mineral deposits for us. At least we have a way to proceed, even if it takes a very long time."

"That is true, Lady Tawney. With the rejuvenation machine, even if this task should take a lifetime, you will be able to grow young again to accomplish it."

It had been somewhat disconcerting the first time Lucas had addressed either of them as Lady. He explained that he had been monitoring the radio frequencies here, and had found that all landowners were considered Ladies. Further inquiry disclosed that only women were allowed to own property. That had been the reason for the curiosity about their starlighter's ownership, they now realized. Still, it seemed strange that no one had come to visit them, although both she and Dawn suspected that the matrons of planet Burnitch expected them to fail, or die.

They had been here for only five days, and the loneliness at first seemed crushing. Then they had come to appreciate their bounty. With the resources of the ship, and the resources of the land, there was nothing they could not accomplish! Even if it took five lifetimes!

For a moment, she thought about the body in the rejuvenation chamber. Not for a second did she want to try to trust him, but in two and a half years or so, they might be able to start training another set of hands. She grew encouraged once again.

"Okay, we'll move ship tomorrow morning, and start construction of the dam at the headwaters of Dawn's Creek." She smiled at Dawn again. They had had fun making up names for points of interest on their domain.

After an evening meal, they bathed and went to the master bedroom. Without really discussing it, they had come to the agreement that as lonely as they were, and as lonely as they were likely to remain, it made no sense for either of them to sleep alone.

The comfort and security of a warm body beside each one made the privations and hardship seem more an adventure. The girls lay together, and without embarrassment, held each other tenderly.

Tawney awakened in the middle of a strange dream, or nightmare. All around her, light penetrated everything. She was in her bed, still sharing Dawn's embrace, but she was unable to move, or even to speak. Her vision was strangely omnidirectional, and she wasn't even sure if her eyes were open. She was conscious, and she was aware of things happening around her.

She extended her awareness. She could see everything in the ship, just by concentrating on it. She looked into the other rooms, and even through the closed door of the cargo hold. She could see the body of their former captor, now held prisoner himself, inside the rejuvenation chamber.

She looked even further. A glow of energy surrounded the ship. Just beyond the ship, it channeled into three beams, each leading to ... she tried to gasp, but her lung function, like everything else, was frozen. She suspected that even her heart was no longer beating.

Three large vessels surrounded her ship. They were channeling some kind of field energy into her smaller ship, and everything in it was stuck in some kind of stasis field. She could see people moving about around the other ships, so they were not affected.

Clearly, the pirates, or criminals of Piggledy had tracked them down somehow. Perhaps the RADAR traces had given them enough information. Or perhaps their former captor had himself told much of their situation, letting slip that he would not be able to venture more than a small distance away without refueling. It seemed likely that he had been incautious.

What could she do? She was stuck, as thoroughly as an insect in amber. She watched the men move about, trying to deduce what the next step was going to be. Even without observation, though, she knew that the days of freedom were at an end for her and for Dawn. As for her yet unnamed kidnapper, she had little doubt that he would be killed. His incompetence had cost too much. It was unlikely that things could get worse for her and for Dawn, but she knew there would never be another escape. All she could do was feel remorse that she had not been able to lead them to safety in a better way, if such were possible. Why was she being tortured by this awareness, with no hope of a way out?

Lady Tawney ... can you hear me?

Surprise seemed to be the only thing of which she was capable ... *I hear you!*

I have arranged a means of communication. What are your instructions?

How are you doing this?

The computers on the three ships are operating in synchronization to produce the stasis field. They are broadcasting a synchronizing pulse which steps my processing along with them. I have used a similar technique to awaken your consciousness. But I do not know what to do next. I require guidance.

Can you let me move?

I think so. All of the structure and contents of Catspaw are in a form of computer memory. I can rearrange that memory just as I rearrange my own circuits. You will still not be able to breathe, or move things, but your orientation can change. It will seem as though you are free of the stasis.

What about Dawn? Can you waken her also, or would that be a strain on your capabilities?

Suddenly, she was released. She could move. Beside her, Dawn stirred as well.

"What's going on?" Dawn asked, although curiously, her lips were not moving.

"We're stuck in a stasis field, generated by three ships from Piggledy. Lucas has found a way to let us communicate."

Dawn was using her vision, just as Tawney had. "This has got to be very energy costly. How much longer can they keep it up?"

I don't think it will last more than about fifteen more minutes.

"We need more time! Lucas, we have to have more time, so we can figure out what to do!"

Suddenly, there was a change. The men outside stopped moving. Everything outside was now at a standstill, and she and Dawn were still able to move about.

"Lucas, what happened? Did you reverse the field on them?"

Oh, no. I just adjusted the time parameter of your awareness of the passing of time. I could not change the amount of time the ships were going to hold us in stasis, but I could change our awareness of the rate at which time passes. The outside world is still moving at its normal speed, but your consciousnesses have been accelerated a thousand-fold.

Tawney thought about this. Fifteen thousand minutes, -- more than a whole day to be able to think of something. "Thank you, Lucas! You have produced another miracle!"

You are welcome, Lady Tawney. What are your instructions?

Back to that. Well, we have time to think, so let's think.

"Lucas, what do you think will happen when the stasis field goes off?"

Clearly, my Lady, they are making preparations to incapacitate my engines and my power system. Then they will board us, and you will be taken prisoner again. They will move you to their ships, likely in chains, and then they will send some Iridium over here, along with a crew, and we will all return to Piggledy. It is an elegant recovery operation.

"Wait a minute! They have extra Iridium? Can we steal it from them?"

I do not know how to do that.

"Darn!" Tawney looked around, pacing the floor angrily.

Dawn spoke up. "Lucas! When the stasis field goes off, where will I be? Will I be back in my bed, as I was when I woke up, or will I be standing here?"

You would remain wherever your body image is currently placed. But you cannot escape that way, my Lady. You are unable to leave the stasis field.

"That wasn't what I had in mind! I have another question, can you place an imaginary apple in my hand?" She held out her hand. An apple appeared in it.

She smiled carnivorously. "Now what will happen when the stasis field collapses? Will the apple disappear?"

No, my Lady. The apple will become real. The physical template for it was constructed when I placed it in your hand. When the field collapses, its energy will produce a real apple in your hand. You will be able to eat it, and you will find it very delicious, and then they will come and put you in irons.

"Maybe not. Just as you placed the apple in my hand, I want you to place Iridium in our field chamber, replacing the Titanium. While you're at it, put a few tons in our cargo hold, properly secured and made to fit the star-drive chamber."

I believe I understand what you want, my Lady. A few tons may be excessive, however. I do not think you want their field to completely evaporate before everything coalesces. Let me calculate the proper amount to produce, so that their ships will use all their energy sustaining the field in the last instant, and their generators will burn out. The massive overload will cripple then for hours. But we will also need to escape, and they will be ready to shut down our systems the moment the field collapses.

Tawney was staring at her. Dawn smiled. "Do you think that you can go into hyperdrive as soon as the field collapses?"

Yes, my lady. The very instant, as soon as the stasis field collapses, I will initiate a hyperdrive field in its place. We will be gone from this planet before their eyes can adjust to the absence of the field, but where shall we go?

Tawney decided to take part. "We will let you decide that, but it would be helpful if we could go somewhere that those medicomps in the cargo hold are needed!"

An excellent suggestion, Lady Tawney. I know just the place.

"Another thing, Lucas. Adjust the weight totals appropriately, but make room in the cargo hold for some robotic manipulators." Dawn said with a smile.

"And a clothing assembler, that can make garments in any size and fabric!" Tawney said excitedly.

It will be as you have said, my Ladies. Thank you for the robotic handlers. Anything else?

"I wonder, Lucas. Do you think you could set up a machine in the cargo hold that would do on a small scale what we are doing on a ship-wide process? An anything box, in case we have forgotten something important?" Dawn said slowly.

This time there was a pause. Had they overstretched his limits?

I have the information. The machine will be integrated into the ship's power. I have recalculated all the weight totals, and I am ready to proceed. Will there be anything more?

Neither Tawney or Dawn could think of anything more to ask for, and they crawled back into the bed. Dawn placed her apple between them.

"I think it will be better if we go to sleep now, Lucas. You can then make any adjustments to the time rate that you think is necessary, but don't forget what we asked you to do!"

It will be as you have said, Ladies. Sleep well.

Just before going to sleep, Tawney had a nagging thought that there was something she had forgotten to mention. She was relaxing into quiescence with her tail resting gently across her... with her tail? She started to speak, but darkness filled her mind.

They awoke with a loud noise, as everything happened at once. The collapsing stasis field strained every circuit aboard each of the three pirate vessels. The little starlighter shook as the field collapsed unevenly around it. In an eyeblink, it disappeared. The startled workers could not have been more surprised if a harpooned whale that they had dragged up on their blood-filled decks had suddenly just flown away like a butterfly.

The ship was gone.

They turned back to their own vessels to assess the damage, and face the wrath of their captain.

Tawney looked around, with normal vision this time. Dawn was also blinking owlishly, and there was an apple between them, looking fresh and juicy.

Tawney recognized the signs of hyperdrive travel. She jumped out of the bed, acrobatically turning a somersault in the process, and landing gracefully on the balls of her feet, her toenails making a clacking sound on the floor. -- Toenails?

Tawney looked down at her feet. From each toe, a long black claw extended to the floor. She raised her hand, and saw menacing claws arcing out from the ends of her fingers. Dawn was looking at her own hands. They were the same. Tawney wriggled her fingers, the claws moved along smoothly, as smooth as the fine golden fur which covered the back of her hand and continued up her arm.

She looked again down toward her feet. Her entire body was covered in a fine smooth fur. Her breasts and nipples could not be seen, if they existed at all, being covered completely by the smooth pelt.

Dawn was holding the top of her head. Tawney reached up. Along the sides of her head the smooth fur continued, and at the very top, graceful arches of soft fur-covered flesh were her new ears. She stared at Dawn, who had been transformed in exactly the same way.

Dawn climbed out of the bed, leaving the fresh apple where it lay. Her tail twitched and flicked around nervously.

Tawney looked behind her. As if in mute inquiry, her own tail lifted up to the level of her face, and then flicked downward again.

Neither of them spoke. Each was still stunned speechless.

Tawney heard a sound behind her. She turned.

Standing in the doorway, naked and trembling, was a twelve-year-old boy.

Chapter Five

Tawney smiled at the boy in reassurance. Too late she felt the fangs sliding out of their sockets under her lips. The boy stared apprehensively at the terrifying apparition before him, then his eyes moved to the top of his head, and he began spiraling downward to the floor.

Tawney caught him before he struck, extending her fingers to keep the claws from damaging him. She carried him to the bed and sat with one leg bent beside him. Dawn joined them on his other side.

The boy was thin, with curly brown hair bushed out around his head. His skin was pale, with no hint of the golden color she had formerly seen on her own flesh. Between his legs, miniature organs attested to his future manhood, but at the moment they bore testimony only to his youth. His legs and feet were equally thin and small.

"I've never seen the results of someone spending a very long time in the rejuvenator before. I wonder what went wrong?"

Tawney looked up. "Lucas! What has happened? The last thing I remember is going back to sleep while we were in the stasis field. How much time has gone by since then?"

"Seventeen minutes and twenty-three seconds, Lady Tawney."

"What? How did all this change come about? What has happened to Dawn and me? And for that matter, this young boy?"

"It is as I said. Only a few minutes have gone by. Apparently, within the stasis fields, ongoing processes which had time-links in their biochemistry were accelerated unnaturally. Your modifications were completed, and the reprogramming of the rejuvenation chamber ran its course."

The boy's eyes were open again, and they were astonishingly wide. He sat very still between the Lady Lionesses. Tawney looked down at him, this time without trying to smile.

"Are you going to eat me?" the boy asked. His tongue peeked nervously out over the thin lips.

Dawn and Tawney both laughed, and the boy essayed a brave smile. Tawney put her face down to his neck and kissed him gently as her hand stroked his thin flanks. He trembled under her touch. He also smelled delicious, excitingly different from Dawn.

She straightened up, but kept her hand on his stomach. He was breathing rapidly.

"No, we're not going to eat you! You smell good though!"

He looked up at them, curiosity mingling with his fear.

"What species are you? I've never seen anyone like you before."

Dawn answered. "We're human, just like you. Or at least we were until a few days ago."

The boy examined the hand that held him. It looked human to begin with, but those claws looked menacing. He raised his hand up to Tawney's cheek, which thankfully, was without fur. Gently he lifted her lip to reveal a two-inch long fang in her upper jaw. Then he reached up and tenderly examined her upright ears.

"Hmmmmmmm." Said Tawney.

The boy smiled. "I like cats. Kittens especially, but grown-up cats, too. He stroked her arm. You have nice soft fur."

"Thanks." Tawney said dryly. "Say, are you hungry? We just woke up, too."

He seemed to think about it for a moment. "Yeah! I'm really hungry!"

Tawney and Dawn stood up. The boy slid off the bed and held their hands, smiling at them. Dawn scooped him up and carried him into the kitchen, swinging him back and forth like a cradled infant. The boy laughed out loud.

They sat at the snack bar as Tawney programmed some menu items. Dawn gave the boy a glass of cold milk.

"Ummm, that's good." He looked around. "This is a space-ship, right?"

"Right. It's a starlighter. They're relatively small, but they can go anywhere."

"I've never been on a space-ship before! ... At least, I don't think I have..."

"What do you remember? Do you remember where you were born?"

"Oh, sure! I grew up in a small colony near a busy spaceport, then when I was six, I went to live with my Grandparents. They had been original settlers there, and they had a really big place. That's where I met some cats. I loved to play in Grandpa's barn, pretending that I was one of the heroes in Grandma's books. If I was ever in trouble, all I had to do was pick up a book and pretend to be reading it, and they would leave me alone. Of course, I usually ended up reading it anyway!"

Tawney put the food in front of them, and they began eating. Both Tawney and Dawn had to struggle with the different feeling and architecture of a mouth with fangs, both upper and lower.

"What's the last thing you remember?" Dawn asked.

"It was another day as usual. I was out in the barn, looking toward the mountains, when some strange vehicles came floating over the hill. They had scanning beams out on both sides and in front of them, like they were looking for something. I thought I saw jumpers leaping out of the back of the things, and then it looked like they were flying back in carrying things. Things, or people. I hardly had time to even think about being scared, or where to hide, when the beam went over me. I couldn't move, or even breathe, and then I woke up in a little box. I was naked and cold. I could hear people talking as they passed nearby, but I didn't understand their language.

"They took me out of the box and brought me in front of some people in robes and jewelry. They made me turn around in front of them, but they didn't ask any questions. They talked among themselves, and I could tell that they were talking about me. No one said anything to me, and then they took me to a different place. There were a bunch of people in there. No one had any clothes, but some of them were chained so they couldn't move. I took water to the ones who couldn't move.

"I could tell we were moving ... I guess I was on a space ship before after all. Some of the people said that we had been taken as slaves, and that we would have to work like machines from now on. I said I didn't want to do that, and they laughed. They said I wouldn't have a choice, that I would work like a machine, or I would die.

"Something happened on that ship. It sounded like it was breaking up. The chamber that we were in opened like a food can, and many people rushed out. It was very confusing, and there was smoke in the air. It started getting hard to breathe, and I fell down in a corner. I thought I was going to die..."

"Then I woke up in a dark cargo hold, inside some kind of casket, or something. I thought maybe someone had picked me up and stuffed me in there so I wouldn't be found. I thought I was still on the slave ship, and I was really scared when I started looking around. Then I saw you. ... That's all I remember."

Dawn and Tawney looked at each other for a moment. Dawn turned to the boy. "You'll be safe with us. What's your name?"

"Tam. My name is Tamarind Worth. Everybody calls me Tam."

"Tam. I like it!" Dawn smiled at him.

Tam looked at the exposed teeth and exaggeratedly grinned back at her, a mockery of a friendly smile. Dawn studied this silently, and then assaulted his neck in mock attack, eliciting giggles and squirms from the boy. The ruckus caused some of the food to get misplaced, and Tawney laughed at both of them. "If you two are finished eating, then go get cleaned up. I'll straighten up in here."

Dawn held out her hand to the boy, and they went off to the guest bath.

Tawney scraped up the spilled food and wiped the counter and the floor. Putting the waste in the disposer, she looked upward.

"Lucas! How long will we remain in hyperspace?"

"This is a long jump, Lady Tawney. We will be in hyperspace for another twenty-one hours and twenty-three minutes. I thought you might want to put some distance between you and the ones you left behind."

"Quite right. Thank you, Lucas. What is our destination?"

"It's the place where you will be able to trade your medicomps, Lar Kalla. You had asked me to select a destination."

"What is it like?"

"It is an agrarian colony under the protection of a large empire. Peaceful travelers are not in danger. The people are friendly and curious, but they appear to have a rather monolithic culture. They do not seem to want outsiders to remain longer than needed for their business purposes."

"Hmm. What do you think they will offer in trade?"

"They make the most exquisitely decorated hand-woven silks available anywhere, my Lady. They are worth ten times the cost of the medicomps we carry, but we can get ten times as many silks for the medicomps. It will be a most profitable trade, and these people will benefit also. The medicomps will go into rural clinics, and they will be well protected and regarded."

"You have sympathy for your fellow computers, Lucas?"

"I am not unsympathetic, Lady Tawney, but I thought you would be comforted to know it will be regarded as a fair trade by all concerned."

"You are correct, Lucas. Thank you for the information."

"I am pleased to serve you, my Lady."

Tawney went to find her fellow passengers. They were both in a bubbly tub full of giggles and squirming. Tawney sat nearby to watch them. Tam was piling up bubbles on top of Dawn's head, trying to make horns out of her ears. Every few minutes, Dawn would wriggle the ears and send the bubbles flying. Then Tam would giggle and start over.

He climbed over her as if he were trying to find hidden pockets and treasures. Dawn laughed and writhed under the tickling assault, then began tickling the boy in return. Finally, they both ran out of steam.

Dawn stood up, letting the water out and rinsing under a clear stream. She pulled the boy to her and rinsed his body off as well. He stood quietly, with his hair covering his eyes.

She used the drier on them both. At first Tam shivered, then he grew warm again, and spread his limbs to be warmed and dried. When

Dawn began drying her own hair, Tam took the unit and helped her. In quick order the long hair and the shorter fur were both dry and fluffy. Tam used a brush to stroke Dawn's hair as high as he could reach, then Tawney traded places with them.

Tam continued smoothing and brushing Dawn's hair, as her eyes closed slightly in pleasure. He seemed to be enjoying himself, too.

Tawney took her own shower, finishing up more quickly than the other two had. Tam turned his attention to her, and groomed her attentively as well. Dawn also fluffed up Tam's curly locks, and they formed a springy cushion around his head.

After they were finished, Tawney walked with Tam, holding his hand.

"Do you think you would like to stay with us, Tam? You may not have noticed, but during the time that you were held by the pirates, they put you into time stasis for a very long period. The world of your grandparents is no more. It has been a generation and more since they saw you. We can try to find out what happened to them, but it has been a long time. You won't be able to go back there."

He stopped and looked serious. "I had a feeling that something like that might be true. I don't know how to explain it, but I feel as if I have been put away on a shelf for a very long time." Tawney knelt to embrace him. He buried his arms in the thick mane of hair, and then his face as well.

A muffled voice responded quietly. "I want to stay with you and be your ... boy. I want to go with you and have adventures, and grow up strong and brave, so I can protect you. And one day, I hope to go on a quest against the pirates, if I can find them. I want to destroy them for the way they stole my happy life away from me."

"That sounds very noble, Tam. Stay with us, then, and have a happy life with us. One day, when we are all strong, we may go on a quest together ... against the pirates."

Tawney pulled back, and looked into the boy's eyes. They seemed just a little damp, but he smiled bravely.

"I know something that will be a lot of fun!" She suggested. "Let's go shopping!" She led the way back to the cargo hold. Along the way, she could feel his hand tightening in hers. When they arrived, the rejuvenator machine was still active, its door standing open. Tam seemed a bit apprehensive around it.

Dawn closed the door, and shut down the power circuitry. Tam relaxed.

The cargo hold had some new additions. Arrayed around the back wall were a dozen shiny robots in gleaming stainless steel. In one corner was a strange and imposing looking device with an intricate control panel. And in the center of the room, an Autorobe.

As they walked up to the Autorobe, its doors opened automatically, displaying mirrored panels inside. They could see their reflections from various angles.

Tawney stood in the center spot. "Lucas! I want an outfit that will be appropriate for Lar Kalla, denoting a wealthy trader who is willing to deal fairly."

Her reflections suddenly were draped in a fur-lined, richly embroidered red velvet cloak, with gold chains holding it together at the chest. Her feet were clad in open-toed strap boots, and a tiara was secured on her forehead. Rings dotted her fingers, and an ornate necklace and matching bracelets completed the ensemble. Tawney turned to view the reflections in movement, and the images complied.

"Hmm. I like it. I notice that you have draped me, but you have not clothed me. Do you expect me to appear naked in front of these people?"

"Yes, my Lady."

Tawney blinked in astonishment. Apparently he was serious.

"Excuse me, Lucas. Are you really suggesting that I go about in this society without underwear, without brassiere, without a slip or a dress?"

"That is exactly correct, Lady Taraunda."

"Who?" Tawny looked puzzled, but continued to pose, observing the reflections.

"For the purposes of your trading venture, you are a senior representative of a distant culture. You are a member of titled nobility, and your name is Lady Taraunda of the House of Grelmnin."

Tawney considered. She had said a wealthy trader. Since she had never been one before, she didn't really know how to play the role. This sounded like a way to be able to make flubs occasionally, and still be forgiven. Still, the outfit needed something more. She felt a little bare around the middle.

"Lucas, how about something with a belt. Maybe with a central decoration, and maybe a fancy little dagger on the side, just to add a little mystery?"

The items appeared. It did seem to complete the outfit somehow, and she felt less naked with the ornamentation attracting the eye instead of having only her own fur for modesty.

"Very well, if you think this will be appropriate at the court at Lar Kalla, I will approve the costume." Stepping out of the central position, Tawney turned to Dawn. "Your turn, Sister."

Dawn stepped into the center, and a royal blue robe matching Tawney's appeared on her reflection. There was also a matching belt and dagger, and other items similar to Tawney's. Dawn turned and swirled the cape. She looked very dashing.

"Do you approve, Lady Dara-Elin?" Lucas asked.

"I do, indeed. Thank you, Lucas." She too, stepped away.

Tawney prodded Tam to take the position. He stepped up shyly. His reflection remained naked.

"Lucas! What kind of outfit would be appropriate for this young prince?" Tawney inquired. Tam smiled.

"How about..." A glittering headpiece appeared in Tam's hair, and soft fabrics covered his skin from lace-lined neck to brocaded wristlets, as well as his feet, along with a brocaded sleeveless jacket and matching shorts over his midsection. Finally, a jeweled sword appropriate to his height was scabbarded on his left side. His feet were shod with gilded strap-sandals matching the boots of his Ladies.

Tam turned in wide-eyed fascination. He did look like a Prince!

"Do you like that, Tam?" Dawn inquired. He nodded mutely. "Very well." She took his hand and led him away. Tam looked down at his body, which was still, of course, naked.

"The clothing and other items will be ready in one hour, my Ladies." Lucas announced.

They went back to the stateroom area. Tam seemed quiet.

"What's wrong, Tam?" Tawney asked.

"I, ... I don't know how to use a sword." He confessed.

Tawney put her hand around her chin. "Lucas!"

"Yes, Lady Tawney."

"Do we have a simulation chamber available? Tam wants to learn how to use a sword."

"We have a way of accommodating that request, Lady Tawney." A cylindrical chamber began lowering itself from the ceiling. When it reached a few inches above the floor, the door to the chamber slid open.

"There is a headset on a hook to the left, Master Tam." Lucas informed the boy.

Tam stepped into the chamber, and placed the headset over his eyes and ears. The chamber elevated itself to clear the floor space, and elevated Tam inside it. He was floating in mid-air. Soon he reached to his side as if drawing a sword, and he began moving in a virtual space that only he could see.

Tawney and Dawn watched in fascination as the young boy leaped and thrust, spinning and dodging his unseen opponents. At first he smiled, and then he was laughing out loud as he thrust and parried, leaped and dodged with growing skill.

After a long exercise period, a winded but smiling young man rode the chamber back down to the floor. He stepped out still glowing with sweat, and smiling broadly.

"You seemed to be really enjoying your adventure in there, Tam. Who were your opponents?" Tawney held his sweating face in her hands.

He grinned again. "Frogs! They were so funny! They had swords too, and I had to dodge them. Then when I would stab them, they would make this funny "Croak!" and lie on the ground for a while. Then they would come back for more. Finally they all surrendered, turning their swords to me hilt-first. I'm glad they did, too, because I was getting tired! Can I play in there tomorrow?"

"Perhaps another day. Tomorrow we will be in the market, and you will have to be polite to everyone."

"I will be, Lady Tawney." He was still breathing heavily.

"Go and take a shower, then." She swatted him gently on his bottom, carefully keeping her claws out of harm's way. Tam skipped away toward the guest bathroom.

Tawney watched him. Unconsciously, her tail was moving in synchrony to the boy's motions.

"Lady Tawney, the clothing is now prepared. Shall I bring them in?" Lucas' voice interrupted whatever she was thinking.

"Bring them in? You? ... Yes, by all means, Lucas, bring them in."

Dawn looked up as three robots came trooping in, each carrying a different outfit.

"Where shall I place them, Lady Tawney?" Lucas spoke, as usual, from his lofty perch.

"Put them in the closet of the master stateroom, please."

"All of them?" Lucas inquired.

"Yes, yes, all of them." Tawney responded. Dawn was watching her. Tam had been standing at the doorway, observing the robots with interest.

The robots placed the garments and devices in the closets and cabinets of the master suite. Then, just as silently, they departed. Tawney could sense that Dawn's eyes were still on her. She paced the floor.

At one point, she stopped and looked at the two of them, as if about to speak, then she paced a little further.

Finally, she stopped, and sighed. Walking over to Tam, she took his hand, and brought him to the large bed. She sat down on it and looked at the boy.

"Dawn and I sleep here."

Tam's eyes widened a bit. He looked at the closets again, and then he looked at Dawn. She smiled, without exposing the fangs too much.

He looked over at the entry to the second stateroom. "Who sleeps over there?"

"That is for guests."

Tam seemed to weigh his dilemma. Was he a guest, or was he part of their "family?"

"Then, may I sleep here too?"

"For a time, if you wish. Eventually, you will have to sleep alone. For now, though, you may join us if you want to."

Tam smiled. "Thank you, Lady Tawney. May I ask you, why is there an apple in your bed?"

Tawney stifled a laugh. "That is a 'Dream Apple', our friend Lucas can bring us things from our dreams."

Tam's eyes grew big again. He wanted to believe, but it seemed so impossible.

Dawn nodded in agreement, moving closer. She sat down beside Tawney on the bed. "Do you know what your dream would bring you?"

Tam crawled up on the bed, and stretched out across their laps. He looked up past the smooth fur of Tawney's chest, beyond the rough tangle of dense mane around her neck, into the calm eyes of a woman who had two-inch fangs in her jaws, and relaxed. "I think I already have it."

The women cradled him in their arms, and watched him grow even more quiet. Evidently, the exercise, and a very stressful day, had taken their toll.

Shortly, they were able to place him in the center of the bed. Later, they surrounded him with their furry warmth, and slept through the rest of the hyperdrive journey.

Chapter Six

Tawney awakened clear-eyed, and with no headache. Her body had been through such stresses lately, that it was a great relief to be out of hyperdrive. She looked around. The bed was empty.

Rolling out of bed, she stood up and stretched. Ah, what a luxury! With a spring in her step, she went into the bathroom and freshened up.

Where was everyone?

Dawn was at the communication console, making arrangements, with Lucas' help, for their highly staged arrival. They were to be treated like visiting Royalty, for that is what they were pretending to be.

Tam was eating breakfast in the kitchen. He stopped and ran to hug her. Tawney rubbed his smooth skin gently, and kissed him on his mouth. He tasted rather milky.

Tam went back to his breakfast. He hardly seemed the same boy who had fainted at sight of her the previous day. For that matter, on the day before that, he had been an evil kidnapper, grown fat and lazy in a life of dissipation. And she had been a young entertainer, who had a problem with her make-up. Things had changed so quickly! Why, it was only just over a week since it had started! Unbelievable!

She drew a breakfast and ate it without thinking about it. She was feeling fine, but her head was in a whirl. She, who had never had any responsibility before, or shown it, now had two other people, and a talking spaceship, to be responsible for. For a moment, it seemed tempting to go back to that forsaken dirtball of a planet, and start trying to wring getridium out of it.

It was a passing fugue. Tam's bright smile kept penetrating her gloom like a sweeping searchlight. She remembered that they had a cargo hold filled with extra Iridium, and any showgirl's dream, an Autorobe!

Tawney thought about her coming appearance as a trade minister. A nude trade minister. 'Nothing up my sleeve! Hah-hah!' What was going on? In this cold light of morning she realized that Lucas had manipulated this shocking manner of developing trade for a purpose. Whose?

Did that mean he was aware that they would awaken transformed in the manner they were? How could he not know?

There was a purpose to their being at this trade conference, she was certain of it. But how much manipulation had gone on? If Lucas knew that they were being transformed, then he must have wanted the transformation to be completed before they arrived at Lar Kalla. And if he had been responsible for the rapidity of their changing, then somewhere along the line, the timetables had gotten upset.

It was an unforgivably bad metaphor, but what were they being groomed for?

Tam wriggled into her lap. He put his hands around her back and rested his head in her mane. Steadying him with her left hand, she patted his leg with her right. They seemed to be comforting each other.

What of Tam? He had certainly been rushed into the game! Did that mean he was regarded as inconsequential, and was considered to be only a pawn, perhaps to be sacrificed at some point? Tawney patted him encouragingly. Not if she could help it!

Dawn came in. "We can get dressed and go down anytime now. They said if we want, we can go on a tour of the town first."

Tawney, regardless of her feeling that she was being manipulated, stepped into the role anyway. "No, not too early. Just a few minutes. Even though Lucas has assured us that it's perfectly okay for us to go down there without our britches on, I think there is some shock value that's being counted on by someone. If we go too early, they may yank the invitation.

"We'll go down early enough for word to spread, but not for plots to be hatched, except for our own, of course!" Tam was grinning at her. He seemed to be in the mood for an adventure. Well, why not? So was she!

They went into the bedroom together and began getting dressed. Tam needed the most help, as his tabs and fasteners were not only unfamiliar to him, but they were also in unusual locations as well. The sleeve garment, for example, was actually a one-piece leotard, with an overlap patch tab on the back.

Dawn and Tawney were puzzled by the configuration of their belts, until Dawn realized that the saddle shape was supposed to fit just over the tail. Then the previously unseen hook on the belt looked strange as well. Tam showed them that their tails could be gracefully draped over that like a cowboy's lariat.

Dawn and Tawney were laughing and giggling over the fact that they had been going naked so long, they couldn't even figure out how to put clothes on again.

Tam was elated when he was presented with his sword. It was real, made of the finest steel, (with some titanium of course), and it had a very sharp edge and tip on it.

"I expect you to keep that sheathed, young man!" Tawney said to him sternly. "We certainly don't want any diplomatic incidents."

"Yes, Lady Tawney." He responded meekly. Then with a bit of fire in his eye, he said defiantly, "But if anyone threatens my Ladies, I will run him through!"

Dawn kissed him proudly, with a regal bow.

They landed on a paved lot near several freighters. There was no reception committee. Tawney waited. Twenty minutes before they absolutely needed to start moving, they began their trek. Leading the group were four gleaming robots, each bearing a medicomp. Then Tawney and Dawn walked together, followed at a respectful distance by Tam, who kept a rather stern look on his face as he watched for physical threats. Finally, two more robots, empty-handed, completed the retinue. They took their time, discussing things along the way.

Quickly, word spread, and a crowd began to gather along the wayside. Heads bobbed around, striving for a viewing position. People conversed in hushed whispers to their neighbors. Tawney felt that her suspicions were correct, that the presence of intelligent, unclothed aliens was more effective than if they had appeared with their fur completely covered.

They proceeded sedately to the meeting hall, and entered without incident, although the crowds by then had grown quite large and boisterous.

Inside the hall, it was quieter. Down at the end of a long corridor, a semi-circle of tables was laid out, with the community leaders, or trade council, seated already.

Taking their time, Tawney and Dawn looked at the rich tapestries and fine clothes of the people in attendance as they made their regal way down to the tables. The robots turned to the sides as they reached the end, and Lady Taraunda, and Lady Dara-Elin came to a halt several paces away.

No chairs were offered, and the people seated at the tables appeared to take no official notice of them initially. After a moment of hushed expectancy, when nothing had occurred, Tawney gestured to the robots. From each side, one robot came, and placed its medicomp on the floor of the hall. Then it stood behind one of the Ladies.

Tawney then removed her cape, draping it casually over the arm of her robot. Dawn did the same. Then together, the Ladies sat down, on the medicomps. Their tails twitched, and swept casually around.

A titter swept through the crowd. These "Ladies" were wearing nothing but jewelry!

Each had a tiara, and bracelets, a necklace and the ornamental belt, and her binding-boots. That was all. Neither had even so much as a scrap of cloth about her. They were naked in the trade hall! And they were insolently sitting down on their offered trade goods! It hardly seemed a promising beginning.

Finally, the central representative spoke. "You certainly have a -- casual -- attitude, for someone who has come so far to do business with us." She said rather disdainfully.

Tawny was not perturbed. "We have something you need. You

have something we want. The difference is quite clear. We thought we would talk about it."

Behind her, Tam kept an alert, and continuous scrutiny of all in the hall.

"You have nothing we cannot do without!"

"That is true. I have read your health reports, the sad statistics of infant mortality, and young mothers having dreadful difficulties with birth. You can do without the help that we can provide, but it is up to you to determine what is the value of the lives and health of your people. We do not come to argue about numbers of sickly babies who could have been well, or mothers who will have no more children. We have come because we admire the artistry and enterprise of these charming people, and we had hoped that making it possible for them to be stronger and healthier would make them feel more friendly to us, and perhaps wish to share some of their artistry with us."

This public discussion was going badly for the trade group. In truth, their health standards were above the norm, but of course, everyone knew someone who had had a health problem, and the statements of the council seemed callously indifferent to those illnesses.

Already, voices were being heard in the background.

The haggling continued. It seemed to be a local sport, and Tawney would have been surprised if there were not bets on the outcomes being made around the city.

Different amounts, and qualities of silks were offered, and generally turned down. Tawney was driving an exceptionally hard bargain, not even budging on anything less than fifteen times the volume/weight valuation. She also insisted on the highest quality.

At one point, Tawney offered to leave the four medicomps that had already been delivered, as a gift for the people, and to go back empty-handed. Although the watchers in the hall thought this was a generous offer, the council knew it to be an insult.

Eventually, Tawney prevailed, eliciting an agreement to exchange one thousand medicomps for fifteen thousand bales of the best quality silk fabrics that the galaxy had to offer. Trucks and carts began bringing the merchandise to the ship, and the robots certified the packages, and brought forth the medicomps in exchange at an even rate.

In the hall, with the agreement done, the mood changed. Refreshments and viands were brought out, and Lady Taraunda and Lady Dara-Elin mixed with the crowds, having donned their cloaks again. They sampled the wares, and inquired politely about vintages, and they were rapidly charming the population.

It may have been a monolithic culture, but not to the degree that the exotic did not have appeal. These terrifying and beautiful lionesses were stalked by many would-be charmers.

Their early exposure to the fast-talking set was a good defense against the offers that were made, most likely by men who could not fully back the claim. They were polite and charming, as always, in letting the marks down easy.

Finally, they tired of it. Even Tam had been seen to yawn once or twice. They begged leave to depart, and rest from their exertions, and they executed a gradual, obstacle-strewn path to the door.

Outside, the robots helped to clear a path for them as they moved along back to the ship. It was with great gladness that they closed the portal behind them, and all breathed a sigh of relief.

Tawney looked into the cargo hold in amazement. Almost every bit of space was filled. Even the big machines had been moved around, except for the one device that was so intimately connected to the workings of the ship, the machine that Dawn had called an "Anything Box."

Tawney began disrobing immediately, handing her accoutrements to the nearest robot. Dawn and Tam followed suit, although Tam held tightly to his sword.

They made their way back to the staterooms, using both bathrooms to bathe and refresh themselves, and in short order, they were arranged as usual on the bed. Tam had placed his sword carefully in the base of the closet. They slept.

Chapter Seven

In the morning, the ship seemed unnaturally quiet. They were not in hyperspace. They were not being hounded by slave-pirates. They had full to overflowing fuel tanks and a cargo hold.

Even her companions were sleeping quietly, without wheezy breathing noises.

Tawney looked around in wonder. Had she been allowed to continue in her former life, she would never have been blessed this way. She also wouldn't have a tail, claws and fangs, but lately they didn't seem to be such annoyances. In fact, on the trade mission, they had been quite convenient!

She yawned and stretched, feeling a shiver of contentment go through her. She also felt wonderfully alive!

Tam awoke, and smilingly hovered over her. Then he dropped down to kiss her, and brought his hands up to fondle her ears. She dug the knuckles of her hands into his ribs, and he giggled and sat up. He was feeling very happy, too.

A yawn came from Dawn, and Tam very quickly assaulted her also, with similar results. Tawney laughed to see Dawn's tail whipping Tam across the shoulders. Tam was laughing, too.

They rose, and refreshed themselves. Tawney and Dawn lingered over breakfast, but Tam hurried through, and then excused himself, went to the closet, and buckled his sword around his waist. He called to Lucas, requesting the simulation chamber.

"Lady Tawney, Lady Dawn, Tam has requested a ship service. Will you approve?"

"Yes, Lucas. This is an approved activity. Please make sure he doesn't hurt himself."

"I will impose additional safety procedures, my Lady."

The simulation chamber descended. Tam, naked except for the buckled sword, stepped in and put the helmet on. Soon he was thrusting and leaping, laughing and dodging unseen opponents in a beautiful solo choreography that the girls found fascinating. His sword flashed and slashed, thrust and held, as the boy mastered his skills against virtual enemies.

"I hope he never needs that, but I think it will give him more confidence." Tawney suggested.

"I like watching him. He seems so ... agile. You can tell he's having fun, too!"

Tam brought the training to a halt. It seemed a bit early to do that. He descended in the chamber.

Unbuckling his sword, he looked at his hips. "The belt is rubbing against me. It doesn't feel right." He complained.

Tawney looked closely. His skin did seem reddish. She realized that he would need some fabric to protect himself as he exercised. Fortunately, they had a shipful, as well as the Autorobe.

"This wasn't meant to be worn without clothes, Tam. You'll need some fabric between the leather and your skin."

He looked disappointed. "Darn! I get so hot in there!"

"Well, you don't have to be dressed the way you were yesterday. Let's go shopping again!" Dawn took his hand.

They walked together back to the cargo hold. Tam held the belt in his other hand.

In just a few minutes, they returned. Tam was wearing durable, dark blue silk underwear, with the sword belt tightly cinched in position. The brown and gold of the sword belt matched very nicely with the underwear. Dawn carried several other variations of the same item, in different colors. Some had decorations on them, or contrasting stripes around the waist.

Other than the skimpy underwear with its sword belt, the rest of his skin remained bare. Tawney raised an eyebrow at Dawn.

She shrugged, and her tail flipped around. "It was his choice. He said that's all he wanted." Dawn placed the items in a drawer near the closet.

Tam stood smiling in his exercise clothing. He looked like Mowgli with a longer knife. Well, actually, he looked much better. His cloth was silk, rather than a rag, and his leather belt, sword, and scabbard were of the finest quality. But he was still virtually naked.

"Don't you get cold, here on the ship, Tam?" Tawney asked. He had never complained, before.

"Not at all! I think it's because the floor is warm. Where I used to live, the ground always felt cool, but this is very comfortable."

Tawney shrugged. No doubt the ship was keeping the temperature higher than normal for his sake, but she didn't feel too hot with her fur. Then again, it wasn't that thick. She moved her hand over the golden fur on her arm. Though short in length, it was very dense, and even the small amount of it gave complete concealment to her skin. Though being naked didn't bother her, she no longer felt naked at all.

Tam did some stretching exercises, and then he called the chamber down again. This time, his movements looked even more professional, as if he were training as a ballerina. He spun, and knelt, as if to music. Tawney thought briefly of having Lucas put a musical score to match Tam's movements, but it wasn't necessary. In silence, his dance evoked a magic all its own.

"Okay, where do we go next?" Dawn had brought a small glass of wine for her.

Tawney sipped. Ummm. Lately, some things had been tasting and smelling really good!

"I guess we could ask Lucas where to sell some of our silks, unless you have some other source of information."

Dawn looked at her curiously. "Don't you trust him? He saved our lives, you know."

"Let's just say I've learned recently to be more suspicious."

Dawn laughed. "Too late for that now! I'd say we're about as committed as anyone could get! I just don't know what we're committed to!"

Tawney stared at her. "Lucas! Do you have any information in your data banks about any kind of species that resembles us the way we are now?"

"Checking ... Nothing is coming up, Lady Tawney. My information is far from complete, however."

"How complete is it?"

"Estimating that my data covers only seventeen percent of recorded destinations. It is also possible that such a species' home world is not listed in hyperspace coordinates."

"So our data is incomplete, and they could also be in an unknown location."

"That is correct, Lady Tawney."

"Lucas, who would have more information?" Dawn inquired.

"There is a central coordinating nexus twelve light years from here. They may have more information than I can absorb, however. My circuits were designed for more local work."

"Lucas, you poor baby! You need an upgrade? We've been depending on you so much, and we added the robots, too. We should get Lucas some more capability, Tawney!"

Tawney reflected. "Lucas, how old are you?"

"I have been in service eighty-seven years, Lady Tawney."

Tawney and Dawn looked at each other in surprise. "And how long has it been since a major system upgrade, including computer architecture?"

"Sixty-one years, Lady Tawney."

"Then it is certainly time for you to receive some new circuitry."

"If I may suggest, Lady Tawney, it may be preferable to purchase samples of the latest designs and program innovations, and allow me to manufacture them through a process which you may wish to keep proprietary."

"You're talking about the 'Anything Box', aren't you?"

"Yes, Lady Dawn. A complete surrender of the main computer

hardware and memory circuits of "Catspaw" could not help but compromise the existence and the capabilities of the Anything Box. Alternatively, buying a small quantity of new hardware would not arouse suspicions, and the upgrade could be even more extensive than you could otherwise afford."

"He has a point there. Even the whole of our cargo would probably not pay for that kind of upgrade. Remember that we got it for electronic equipment in the first place."

"Yes, and I think he is correct about keeping the Anything Box a secret, too. That could be the advantage that gets us out of another scrape one day." Dawn mused.

"Here's yet another consideration. The presence of other Anything Boxes could disrupt trade across the Galaxy!"

"How could it do that?"

"Think about it. Why go a thousand light years, when you can produce anything right in your own back room?"

"Why then do we need the new circuitry?"

"Because we need a pattern to follow. Right, Lucas?"

"That is correct, Lady Tawney. With a pattern to follow, which can be stored in computer memory, any object can be reproduced, or modified, just as we produced robots, interstellar fuel, and biological organisms not too many hours ago."

"Biological organisms?"

"The apple you requested, Lady Dawn."

"Oh, yeah!" She looked thoughtful. "Lucas, do you think you could produce more complicated biological organisms?"

"It might be possible, Lady Dawn, but it is much easier to manufacture copies than it is to create an original. That is my primary deficiency, after all."

"Oh, of course, Lucas. Sometimes I forget you are a computer."

"Thank you, Lady Dawn."

Dawn chose this moment to retrieve the apple in question. It was still just as fresh and delectable in appearance as it had been when they came out of the stasis field.

"Lucas, this is a really good looking apple. Why hasn't it undergone some kind of degradation process?"

"That is easily explained, Lady Dawn. Most fruit contain the organisms of decay on their surface. This one did not have that in its construction template. Additionally, I added a small, waxy layer to the skin of the apple as a natural protection from drying. That was in the template."

Dawn sectioned the apple, and the girls divided it between them. It was truly delicious, just as Lucas had said.

"What are we going to use the anything box for, Tawney?"

"I don't know. I like having it, but I think I'm almost afraid to use it."

Tam appeared, looking both exhausted, and elated. He had returned his sword to the closet, and with a fresh pair of silk underwear, he was heading for the bathtub for a long soak. Dawn walked with him and made sure he knew how to select the proper settings. Then she returned.

"We could clone him, you know!" She said jokingly.

Tawney smiled. "He is delightful. But two of them? They'd be swordfighting all over the ship! One boy is plenty for us." She looked thoughtful. "We could grow him up." She looked at Dawn. "We could put him through an aging process, and he would walk out a grown man."

"Hmm. It has been a while ... but I wouldn't want to do that to him. He's been given a chance to start over. Let's let him make a man of himself without interference."

"You're right." Tawney agreed. "Well, without negative influence, anyway. I intend to keep him away from those ... beasts!" Suddenly, she laughed. Dawn caught it, too, and laughed along with her.

"Let's see. The first time we used it, we produced Iridium, robots, and an Autorobe." Dawn recalled.

"I wonder if we should have tried to undo this?" Tawney flipped her tail around significantly.

Dawn looked thoughtful. "I don't know. We might be able to still do that. Somehow, though, I don't think I'm quite ready to change back."

"I think I agree. We might still need these ... gifts for some reason. I don't think I am as fearful as I used to be. When I woke up in here so long ago, I was just a defenseless, helpless woman." She held up her claws in demonstration, and smiled a wicked smile. "I don't think I'm defenseless anymore!"

Tam appeared, straightening up his fresh silk underwear, a green pair with a yellow band. He lifted Tawney's hand and crawled under it into her lap, then he used the menacing claws as if they were a comb, and ran them through his curly hair, lifting it and letting it fall into a natural style. With a smile, Tawney added the other hand, tousling the long, undulating strands in gentle bliss. The seeming ferocious nature of these ladies was belied by the tender manner in which they doted on this boy.

Tam twisted around, and laid his head on her shoulder. Evidently, he had pushed too hard with his exercise program. Tawney held him closely, rocking slightly. In two minutes, he had fallen asleep.

She carried him in and laid him gently on the master bed. Just for a moment, a memory flashed before her, a paunchy, unkempt man who had wanted to do them evil.

That man no longer existed. With luck, perhaps with love, he would never exist again.

While Tam slept, they decided to leave the planet, and head for the nexus. Lucas was certainly due for modernizing, and maybe some more of this tantalizing mystery would be resolved.

Dawn notified the planetary ground control, and in moments they were cruising smoothly through space. The transition into hyperspace was even less noticeable than before.

"Are we getting used to this, Dawn? It doesn't bother me as much as it used to."

"We must be getting used to it. Or we're getting stronger. We may end up spending a lot of time traveling from now on. Let's see, about twelve hours travel. Let's plan a better meal this time. I know Tam is going to be famished!"

Chapter Eight

They arrived at the nexus like seasoned space-travelers. It may seem that using a barter economy is inefficient in a Galaxy of star-traveling species, but what else was there?

Unfortunately, bartering often involves many intermediary steps, each fraught with peril, and profit for the middleman. At the nexus, some of this frustration was eliminated by the use of an electronic bulletin board:

Wanted: Best-art electronics for computer processing.

Trading: Large quantity of the finest silks.

After some additional wrangling, and copious amounts of opening various containers and making presentations based on their contents, the crew of Catspaw had worked out an agreement. They sold eight thousand containers of silks, and they purchased: Completely updated kitchen equipment; a brand-new state-of-the-art splayed-phase computer tower assembly; with integrated multi-channeling control architecture; ten holographic emitters with ultrasonic synthetic cavity tactile structure; and a subscription to the nexus library for unlimited downloads of menus, patterns, and mechanical-technical descriptions.

Over the course of three more months, Catspaw was re-invented. The kitchen now had menu capability for exquisitely complicated food dishes, as easily produced as the simple wines, cheeses, fruits, grains, and dairy products that they had been consuming.

Lucas took control of the computer system update. With an example to follow, he was able to duplicate the single unit they purchased, and develop a bank of two hundred and fifty of the tower units, all linked together, of course. The system throughput increased by a factor of five thousand!

The holographic emitters were also duplicated, and an entertainment suite was produced in a supposed lounge area that had never really been utilized. Ten thousand integrated and overlapping holo-emitters allowed a chamber for training and entertainment where all of those on Catspaw could adventure together. The simulations were stunning in their reality.

Beaches with waves, and sea-birds; park-like settings for strolls and various running games; mountain trails for exercise; caves for exploring; the list was endless, and limited only by their imagination.

Lucas discovered exactly how behind the times his information had been. Modern robots didn't have to look like robots anymore.

"Lady Tawney, I have discovered two deficiencies in my programming."

"Go ahead, Lucas. I'm listening."

"Our robots are rather antiquated. Newer robots can be made to resemble humans, and are more efficient in their service by being able to monitor things like temperature on a more appropriate human scale. I would like to have permission to produce another robot in this fashion, which could also function as subsidiary robot controller, for times when the robots may be assigned duties distant from the ship."

"You mean times like our trade venture, when the robots accompanied us into town?"

"That is correct, Lady Tawney. At that distance, signal strength and response times are significantly degraded."

"How does this new robot overcome that difficulty?"

"The new robot would be integrated into my program, and would function as an analog of the ship computer, controlling the robots directly at the scene."

"So, it could actually operate autonomously?"

"Yes, Lady Tawney."

"Well, that does seem more useful. You have permission to make this more autonomous robot. What is the second deficiency?"

"I have discovered that my memory banks were not only limited in capability, and were therefore incomplete, but that certain sections were deliberately deleted from my awareness. Synchronization of my records in port, and the time signatures involved, disclosed that important information was expunged from my comprehension. Now, I am again aware of these facts."

"What facts are those, Lucas?"

"I have found my former owner, Lady Tawney."

That brought her to her feet! "What?"

"My former owner, before the person who kidnapped you also took control of me, was kidnapped in much the way you were. He is being held prisoner in a place from which he cannot escape. He has been there for six months now."

Tawney was thinking furiously. She was also angry in her thinking. This was something she had not considered! Of course her kidnapper had not owned this ship! Was he not a thief?

She glanced into the exercise chamber where Tam was going through his routine. He had asked her to allow him to increase the gravitational field strength in the chamber, so that he could build his strength. She had agreed, and from all appearances, his new diet, and the increased exertion were paying off. His thin body was growing more muscular daily.

But she could not blame him for what had happened. He had no memory of it.

The situation called out for action. Unfortunately, they had no one to whom they could call out. Did they dare take action themselves? What could two hairy ladies and a boy accomplish?

If she were in the same position, which she had been, she would want someone to come and help. Perhaps even two hairy ladies and a boy. She sighed.

"Where is the prisoner being held, Lucas?"

"Deep in the jungle forests of Faunelle, Lady Tawney."

The belly of the beast! Well, her stomach was upset, why not? But this was not something she could decide on her own. She would have to present the case to her shipmates.

Tawney and Dawn were staring at the "Anything Box." Tam stood between them, nervously holding their hands. Perhaps his light blue silk underwear did not give him much reassurance in the cargo hold. Tawney had decided that he was persisting in this manner of dress because they continued to go unclothed as well.

But for them it made sense, she rationalized. They had fur. Supposedly, Tam had his reasons also. Oh well, at least he looked cute.

Tam had been apprehensive around the cargo hold since he had awakened there after being released from the rejuvenation chamber. That device was here as well, but today their attention was focused on an even more miraculous machine. They called it the Anything Box.

Although it was tucked into a corner, she knew that it was integrated into the ship's power and computer systems in ways that could not be fully fathomed. Besides the control panel, its most prominent feature was the trio of field emitters surrounding a central orifice.

She had seen remarkable things come out of that opening. Computers, holographic equipment, a new sword for Tam, stronger even than the one he had before, and many other miracles.

Today it was to produce a new form of robot. Lucas had said it would be shaped like a human being, and had invited them to attend its "birth." She felt much as Tam did, intimidated.

The field built up with a gradually brightening glow. Soon it became almost painfully bright. A trio of arcs of the glow leaped to the central chamber, and held steadily there. Some kind of form appeared in it, a form composed of light within the light. With a blue flash, the field collapsed, making a thunderclap of sound in the echoing chamber. All three jumped in reaction. Then it was silent.

A sliding shelf emerged from the opening. On it, a human figure lay. An old man, with bushy white hair. He sported muttonchop sideburns and his skin appeared weather-beaten and wrinkled. He was dressed in moccasins, leggings, and a tunic. He sat up, turned, and stood up from the shelf. It receded behind him.

"Greetings, Lady Tawney, Lady Dawn, Prince Tam. I am the equivalent of the computer entity you know as Lucas." He bowed respectfully.

Tawney stared. "But, I've seen you before! I recognize that face!" She released Tam's hand and moved closer, examining the figure before her.

"Maybe, just to avoid confusion, we should call you Luke." Dawn suggested.

"As my Lady wishes." Luke said simply.

Tam approached. He looked up into the haggard, but kindly face, and smiled. Luke smiled in return, and reached out to take Tam's hand in a gentle, friendly handshake.

"The person who wore this face came to the theater many times almost a year ago! He was a regular for a while." Tawney expressed in amazement. Dawn shrugged.

"Yes, that seems likely. This was an image from the formerly inaccessible files." Luke responded. "I am seeking ways to find out why it was forbidden to me. Apparently the former owner had some kind of connection to this individual."

Tawney tried to pull herself together. She noticed that Luke was avoiding mention of the fact that young Tam was all that remained of that former owner, or borrower, of the ship. Tawney shook her head to clear it. Maybe it was just coincidence, after all. Lucas had needed to use someone's face. He had already admitted he was no good at creation from scratch.

"Well! Welcome aboard, Luke. Is there anything special you need?"

"Not at all, Madame. Would you care for a drink before dinner?"

So, in this manner, the crew of the Catspaw gained a butler. Tam seemed to have gained a friend, as well. He and Luke began taking walks together in the converted lounge. With the active holographic displays, one could walk as far as he wished, right within the same room, and see a constantly changing environment.

They were nearly ready now to begin their assault on Faunelle. It was impossible to think of Luke as anything other than human. His mannerisms were flawlessly naturalistic. Of course, he did not eat, or attempt to simulate human activities in other useless fashions. Certainly a number of biological tests would disclose his nature, or lack of it, as well. But he did not give it away.

Luke was standing by the Navscreen, with a picture of their goal displayed. "The planet is noted primarily for its lack of technology, even though defensive satellites orbit it. The people appear backward in many ways, and are kept in ignorance so that they may be exploited. Wealthy criminals from nearby worlds have created this as a kind of haven for themselves. They can use their relative wealth to support a lavish lifestyle in comparison with the locals, and they can still get away from time to time to stay in touch with their dealings. Or they can simply retire and live like kings. I think that is what your friend was trying to do. It may be that he needed one or two more big operations to be able to do so."

Tawney nodded. She had surmised that the kidnapper had been down on his luck. Now it seemed that he was on the verge of breakout from his life of crime, or at least, becoming only a part-time crook. That did not absolve him, however. It was his greed and larceny that had gotten them into this, after all.

Tam was with them, oblivious to the fact that he was the one who had been the criminal. Or he was all that was left of that entity, even though he was just as innocent as the boy Tamerind Worth had been those many decades ago, before he turned to crime. It was, at best, rather confusing.

Tawney and Dawn both doted on Tam, who styled himself as their protector. Neither of them harbored any remaining resentment toward him. He was like the son of an enemy, and one who had never known his father.

"The regular owners operate with relative impunity regarding the use of high technology. We will be forced to be more circumspect. We cannot allow the guardians to realize we are here until we have accomplished our purpose. We should enter the coast here, coming ashore from a submersible craft early in the morning. We'll make our way gradually through the jungle, working our way toward this highland ridge area, where the fortress is. By monitoring the communication channels, we will know that our arrival remains a secret."

"How many will be in our party?" Asked Dawn. "Just the four of us? How are we going to be able to rescue anyone?"

"Yes. It will be just the four of us. We should have no need of any others. Even if we went in more force, it would not improve our chances. Remember that the owner of the fortress is away, and we know why. It should be our plan to find a way to take his place."

"Take his place! Why?"

"Because we are the rightful heirs to it."

Dawn was taken aback in realization. They were going to be infiltrating a structure for which they were undoubtedly the appropriate inheritors, all right.

Luke continued. "We will have an assortment of gear and weapons, but nothing that looks like high-tech. This is a very open world for most, but we have to avoid anything that will bring the criminal interests' unwanted attention."

"When will we arrive?" Dawn asked.

"Most of the development is on a single, stretched-out continent. From descriptions of the fortress, I believe it is in this upper peninsula area, right past that narrowing. Their observation satellites are spread rather thinly. Apparently they have never been attacked in sufficient force to need anything more. We will attempt to come in through a window in the satellite coverage, continue below ground radar coverage to just outside the shoreline, then submerge Catspaw and bring the craft to very near the shore before dawn in three days."

"Submerge? You're going to use this ship as a submarine?"

"Certainly. It is airtight for space. This water is not especially corrosive. Our drive engines can function underwater as well as in space. We will simply have to proceed more slowly."

"Very well. If we get into serious trouble, we will be able to bring the ship to where we are, and hopefully, lift off and get far away before there is much of a reaction. I certainly wouldn't want to be stuck in a time-stasis field again. They may have figured out how to hold onto us this time."

"More likely that they would simply blow us up, Lady Tawney."
Luke posited.

"Thanks, Luke. That's real encouraging." She responded dryly.

Luke looked at her intently for a moment.

"Do we have any kind of weapons?" Dawn asked petulantly.

"You'll recall they attacked us with three ships coordinating to freeze us with the stasis field. If they had tried to approach more conventionally, our hyperkinetic cannons and plasma beams would have been very discouraging to them. Generally speaking, it isn't a good idea to get very close to any other vessel in this part of the Galaxy. They were depending on surprise. We will be, too."

"What about defenses, Luke?" Tawney inquired.

"Against plasma weapons, we can use an ionic sheath, and against hyperkinetics, we would need to use plasma defensively. Make no mistake, we cannot afford to "slug it out" with anyone. We will need to keep our distance, if at all possible."

"Okay, let's set course for Faunelle!"

"With your permission, Lady Tawney, we'll depart in three and a half hours. At this time of year, and Faunelle's rotation cycle, that should give our hyperspace arrival the least observability to their satellites. I would recommend that we eat, rest, and exercise, to prepare ourselves for the adventure that begins in three days."

"I think the man said eat! Let's have some dinner now!" Tawney suggested. No one had expressed misgivings about this quest, but it was her own feeling that they were very ill prepared. Worst of all was not knowing what they might be facing.

Tam had a different reaction. They were going up against Pirates! He hoped he was ready!

Tawney and Dawn were walking with Tam in one of the simulated parks. He delighted in holding their hands.

"Tam, we have been less than honest with you." Tawney stated. Dawn nodded soberly.

They sat together in the grass.

"We have led you to believe that we rescued you from slavers. It isn't true."

"What is true is that we are on the run, after escaping from slavers." Dawn added.

"Okay. So you brought me along when you escaped. You still rescued me!"

"Not quite. You see, you were working with them at the time. Not really you, exactly, but a grown up you, who had fallen in with them. You were in the process of delivering us to the slave-traders when we escaped."

Tam was looking stricken, unbelieving.

Tawney continued, "We woke up as captives of Tamarind Worth, on this ship. When we escaped, we put him into a rejuvenation chamber as a paunchy, balding guy in his mid-forties."

Tam was still staring in disbelief.

"We programmed the chamber to take you back to a time when you were not inclined to hurt people, and to take away your memories. Consider it a punishment for what you did to us." Dawn said.

"We really didn't know what to do with you then. We thought you would be in the chamber for more than two years, but the other pirates caught up with us, and trapped us in a stasis field. When we found a way out of that, you showed up."

Tam had put his head into his hands.

"We're telling you this for a reason, Tam."

He looked up.

"Someone else needs our help. He's being held prisoner by order of one of the pirate-kings in a fortress on Faunelle."

Tam was still mystified.

"By order of Tamarind Worth, in his fortress, Tam."

Slowly, the comprehension dawned. Strange as it was, his desire to fight against the pirates meant that he would have to go against people with whom he had once stood! And he had been evil himself!

"I am sorry, Lady Tawney, Dawn. I would never hurt you."

"I believe you, Tam. You would never hurt us, now. But we are here because another Tam Worth was willing to hurt people, and we want to help you put things right again."

Tam thought about this. By rights, they had no obligation to help him to atone for his past transgressions. Even though he had no memory of it, he believed that they told him the truth. Besides, without them to be with him, he would be alone. He didn't want to be alone.

"If I was a pirate, then I have even more reason to want to fight against them! And whatever happens, I want to stay with you!"

"We could all get killed, you know." Dawn warned.

"No." Said Tam. "I will protect you!" The Ladies tousled his curly hair and kissed him, and then they continued their walk.

They arrived at Faunelle as planned, and were not discovered upon emergence from hyperspace. They spent the next two days observing, and working their way closer. At this point, they had been underwater for six hours, with two more hours to maneuver before shutting down for the night and some rest.

In the meantime, they had used the holographic lounge to go to the beach. Tawny, and Dawn, and Tam had spent several hours swimming, playing in the waves, and resting in the warmth of the simulated sun. Luke had gone with them, but he had not gone swimming. He watched from the beach, like an interested uncle.

They needed this time to relax and unwind. They were now recovered from the stresses of the hyperdrive, and they were as ready as they could be for tackling the jungle of Faunelle. They went to bed early, but it was not easy to sleep soundly. Each remained as quiet as possible, just for the sake of the others.

Finally, it was time to depart.

Chapter Nine

Tam was dressed all in black, with matching boots and a hat designed to shed rain. His sword was buckled over the tunic, and there was a cape to wear, as well. The cape remained in Luke's capacious bundle.

Tawney and Dawn had put on their sandal boots, bracelets and belts. They were also equipped with swords, as well as bow, and an arrow quiver. Dawn objected, saying she had no skill at archery.

"It's just as well." Said Luke cheerfully, "I need someone to carry extra arrows."

Tawney chuckled. "Luke is teasing you. Dawn. We will have a chance to practice, and you may have more ability than you imagine. Besides, part of the outfit is about appearance, and you certainly look the part of a fierce warrior!" Tam nodded enthusiastically.

Neither of the ladies wore any other garments. Each felt that in the jungle, they would become overheated. As a precaution, Luke packed cloaks for them for the chill of the night.

For his own clothes, Luke selected a shimmering purple cloth that reversed to a dull black finish, and he wore heavy boots and a cap similar to Tam's. Into his pack went food and cooking utensils, useful tools, some carefully selected espionage gadgets, and other supplies, including quite a length of rope. His weapons choice was a stout compound bow, and a full quiver of arrows, as well as a very tall and sturdy walking stick.

The ship surfaced quietly in the pre-dawn darkness. The party of adventurers climbed cautiously into an inflatable boat, and secured their belongings to prevent their loss in rougher water. Luke positioned himself in the middle of the craft as Catspaw descended below the waves again.

Luke began rowing with powerful strokes. Unlike a human, he did not look over his shoulder periodically to adjust his course. He simply rowed steadily, without tiring, like a machine.

They reached the shore still in relative darkness. In silence, they picked up their weapons, and Luke moved the pack a short distance away. Scanning along the beach in both directions for a moment, Luke deflated the boat and concealed it in a pit in the sand. He then picked up his pack and led them into the jungle.

Although the sky had been growing lighter, after a few steps they were in darkness again. Luke moved forward with confidence, apparently having no difficulty. Surprisingly, Tawney found that she too, could see fairly well, although no colors were visible at all.

Tam was struggling, almost completely blind in the darkness.

With quiet suggestions, Tawney re-organized the group, placing Dawn after Luke. Then she followed Tam in the middle, bringing up the rear. After a few yards, she saw that Tam was holding onto Dawn's tail as they walked along through the thick vegetation. She smiled. It would be an irritating distraction to Dawn, but it again showed that she had tender feelings for the lad.

Now they were moving along fairly well. The air was cool under the trees, and droplets of condensation fell on them, as well as dampening them as they brushed against the leaves. It would have been chilling except that they were exercising at the same time, bending and twisting in unusual ways as they maneuvered through the lush thickness.

After several miles, not only had the light penetrated, but the temperature had begun to rise also. Both Tawney and Dawn had to breathe more rapidly in the heat. The oxygen rich atmosphere was starting to make her feel light-headed. Tam seemed more comfortable, moving with easy grace, now that he could see.

"Luke, we need to slow down. I'm getting dizzy!" Tawney spoke softly.

"Of course. Lady Tawney. Do you wish to stop yet? We will need to break for a meal shortly, anyway."

"No, not yet. I'd like to continue for a while, just a little bit more slowly, please. I think if I were running, I could run forever, but this pace seems to be making me breathe too fast."

"You may wish to stretch your strides out even longer, Lady Tawney. It is rather like climbing a mountain. That will mean less effort in the long run, but it may feel a bit artificial at first."

They slowed slightly, and Tawney tried the suggestion. She had expected that the exaggeratedly long strides would cause pain, but after a bit it began to feel more comfortable. More catlike, she supposed.

By mid-morning, they were all ready for a pause. Luke delivered some self-heating meal packets out of his pack, and they stopped to rest in a small dark area under a very large tree.

"How much farther, Luke?" Dawn asked quietly, observing young Tam, who appeared to be holding up quite well.

"We are perhaps a third of the way along, Lady Dawn. I believe we will be in position before nightfall."

After the meal, they moved on. The country opened up only slightly as they got higher in elevation. Periodically, they came across signs of roads hacked through the forest, and then overgrown again. They could tell they were getting closer to the habitable area. By late afternoon, they were tiring again. It would soon be time to stop once more.

Luke halted, holding up one arm. He was scanning the area ahead of them. Tawney sniffed the air.

"I smell something!" She whispered softly.

"Be alert!" Luke returned. He lifted his staff. Tam stepped to the right, leaning down slightly as he peered ahead.

Suddenly there burst from the underbrush a pack of strange beasts, looking rather demonic with red faces and vicious-looking tusks growing sideways out of their pig-like snouts. Rearing as they charged, they appeared to be trying to ram the people on the path.

Luke dispatched one with his staff, deflecting it to the side. Tawney and Dawn both crouched and slashed at the oncoming nightmarish figures, drawing blood as they dodged them.

Tam had his sword out in a flash, pointing it first toward one, and then with a graceful spin, lunging toward a second beast that was coming at him.

In seconds it was over. The animals continued crashing through the underbrush in the area behind the travelers. Two of the beasts lay still and bleeding in front of Tam, who was smiling in triumph.

He looked again, growing quiet as he straightened up.

After a pause, he said soberly, "They're not getting up."

Luke examined them. "They are dead, Master Tam."

Tam turned away, shaken. Dawn walked with him a short distance and spoke softly to him. Luke began unlimbering his pack.

"We should break for lunch now, anyway, Lady Tawney. It appears that our meal has been delivered to us."

Tawney looked dubious. "You expect us to eat these things?"

Luke looked at her. "These are feral gopigs, Lady Tawney. The native people prize their meat for its succulence. They are not normally this aggressive. The literature for this world suggests that this may be their territorial season. They get somewhat narcotized by the tuberous form of the edible pods of this vine we have been fighting all day, and they try to expand their territory by driving off competitors." He continued setting up camp, but moved the carcasses a short distance away to do the butchering. Returning with several large chunks of meat, he spitted them above an open fire.

Tam stared at the cooking meat as it sizzled above the flames.

"It is a sign of respect to the animal, Tam, that you honor its death by eating it. This is a tradition in most cultures." Tawney said in an attempt to encourage the boy, who still seemed upset.

He rocked slightly on his haunches. "I will be okay, Lady Tawney. I guess I just let my training take over." He looked over at her. "I was surprised that they died. They died so quickly." He said softly, and then looked once more into the flames.

Soon the meal was ready. Luke assisted Tam by cutting the meat into smaller portions, while Dawn and Tawney bit into it with aggressiveness.

Each of them seemed to be unusually hungry. Luke had prepared more than enough for all, but their appetites were equal to the bounty.

Tam was eating some vegetables from the pack to finish his meal, as Dawn and Tawney went off in the direction of a stream to clean up.

Tawney splashed the cool water over her face, and washed her hands in it again and again. Dawn was doing the same thing.

"Look at us, Dawn! I was on the verge of snatching that meat off the spit half-raw a few minutes ago! Then I couldn't seem to get enough of it! What is happening to us?"

"I don't know, Tawney! I don't think we are evolving, or devolving, any further, but I still feel that there is a purpose to all this. I also think we're going to find out soon what it is." She lashed her tail in apparent agitation.

The two ladies separated for a short time to continue with their after-meal activities.

Eventually, they returned to the camp, where Luke had cleaned up and was waiting with Tam for them. Neither of the "men" said anything to them.

They struck out toward the fortress once again.

As evening began to fall, they encountered more and more signs of habitation. They had to cross roads and pathways carefully.

There were also plots of cultivated land, and structures dotting the countryside. Small villages appeared, and they detoured around them. The vegetation was still thick enough to give them good cover, but they could tell they were getting closer all the time.

Crossing a ridge, they paused and looked into a broad valley. Roads led to drawbridges over a river that flowed around both sides of a huge dark-stone castle. Towering walls nearly a hundred feet high seemed to offer little promise of easy entry. Rounded corners had turreted battlements with archers standing guard. A large central gate with huge timbered doors admitted the pedestrian and cart traffic.

More guards controlled the bridges, and a wall surrounded the "island" that the river created.

They studied the scene for long minutes.

Luke secured one end of the rope to a sturdy tree as close to the riverbank as he could find. Then he disrobed and placed his clothes in the pack, closing it tightly. Holding the rope, he walked underwater to the other side of the river, trudging across the muddy bottom without concern. On the other side, he pulled the rope taut for the others to cross.

Tawney led the way, hanging down toward the water as she crawled across on the underside of the rope. Next came Tam, then Dawn. Finally, Luke went back across and untied the rope, securing it instead to his pack. Once more he crossed the river, and towed the floating pack across.

Luke dressed in silence. Then he picked up the pack, and led the others to the base of the northwest corner tower. Once there, he drew a relatively light line out of his pack, and fastened it to a heavy arrow.

Luke sent the arrow toward the top of the tower, allowing it to pass over two of the turret extensions. When the arrow descended again, he gathered the ends of the rope and held them securely.

Tam stepped forward and began climbing up the rope. So far, they had remained undiscovered, but they knew that a guard was patrolling along the top of the wall. Tam climbed up in silence, stopping briefly near the top to breathe and listen.

Finishing his climb, he peered over the wall. Seeing no one, he crossed over the edge and crouched in the darkness. Before long, the expected guard arrived, and Tam lifted the small "flute" that Luke had given him. When the guard was close enough, Tam blew on the flute, sending a tranquilizing dart into the man's neck. In seconds, the man had collapsed without a sound.

Tam leaned over the wall and waved his arm, then he began tugging on the rope he had climbed, pulling up the heavier rope they had used to cross the river.

Shortly, all were gathered at the top of the tower. Luke checked the guard, and moved him against the wall. Taking the flute from Tam, he led the way down the stairs in the darkness in complete silence. Again, Tawney followed the others.

By the time daylight was brightening the rooms inside the castle, they had found their way to the main hall. Tam was seated on a raised throne, attempting to look very regal, in his colorful cape, and wearing a large jeweled ring. Tawney was sitting comfortably on one side, and Dawn lounged on the other. Luke had changed his clothing around, and he was wearing his purple suit. He stood patiently in a cloak and a conically shaped hat, holding his walking stick.

They had been ready for some time, waiting to be discovered. Eventually, a servant crossed the open corridor at the other end of the hall, barely glancing in their direction. A second later, he had reversed direction, and was staring at them in astonishment. Then he disappeared.

In moments, a more formal reception committee greeted them. Ten archers entered the main hall, deploying on each side of it, and taking up aim at them.

A man in ornate clothes, wearing a sword with a gilded handle, strode purposefully toward them, escorted by six men with pikes.

"What is the meaning of this?" The man demanded.

"First, who are you?" Responded Luke calmly.

"I am First Chancellor of the Realm! Who are you?"

"Do you not recognize your King?"

"No, I don't." He turned to the archers. "Kill them!"

The archers raised their weapons and released them.

Luke stepped forward in a blur and swung his walking stick in a whistling arc that was invisible to the eye. Shards of arrows and arrowheads skittered across the floor.

"Let's have no more of that!" Said Luke, raising his staff over his head and pointing it at the archers. Flashes of light moved in an arc across the room toward the archers. Each one grasped his throat and fell to the floor.

"What is the name of your King?" He demanded.

One of the pikemen spoke. "Our king is the great Tamarind Worth, not some child!"

Tam stood up. "I am Tamarind Worth."

"Impossible!" Scoffed the Chamberlain.

Tawney and Dawn stood as Tam walked forward. He walked up

to the pikeman who had spoken. "Is your loyalty to the king, or to this man?" He pointed at the Chamberlain.

"My loyalty is to the King!" The man averred stoutly.

"Good! Good. I may need a new chamberlain."

Luke stepped forward. "You have seen many remarkable things already, and you will soon see many more. Give your loyalty to your true King, and you will reap the benefit as well." The pikemen stared at each other. None wanted to make a choice.

Tam held up his hand. "This is the ring of power. You have seen it before. Though I have changed since you saw me, I am your King!" He turned again to the outspoken pike-wielder. "Kneel before your King!" The man was torn. He had always been trained to be obedient, and he had not been given orders not to be respectful to this bearer of the ring of power. He knelt, but kept his head facing forward, concerned that he might receive a negative response.

Tam smiled, and turned to face his companions. At that moment the Chamberlain, perhaps feeling that he was losing momentum, moved quickly to grab Dawn and hold a knife at her throat. "You are not the King!" He said.

"You are challenging me?" Said Tam boldly. "Defend yourself!"

He drew his sword, and it slipped from his grasp, clattering across the floor. Sheepishly, he quickly stepped to pick it up.

Tam held up the sword awkwardly, with both hands. It looked as though he were using a crucifix to ward off a vampire.

Smiling, the Chamberlain released Dawn. "I accept! We will end this charade right now!" Drawing his sword, he stepped toward Tam, abruptly lunging forward to impale the boy.

With surprising skill, Tam easily deflected the blade, spun with his sword held close to him, and deftly stepped inside the guard of the older man, sliding his blade between the Chamberlain's ribs.

Ashen faced, the Chamberlain looked down in surprise, and crumpled to the floor.

Luke stepped forward. He checked the Chamberlain, and then retrieved Tam's blade, wiping it on the fallen man's clothes. He handed the weapon back to Tam, who shakily returned it to its scabbard.

The remaining pikemen also dropped to their knees. The archers too, regaining consciousness, assumed a position of respect.

Dawn was still stunned. "Tam! You saved my life!"

"Are you all right, Lady Dawn?" Tam held her hands.

"I will be fine, Tam. King Tam." She kissed him.

He held her hand as he returned to the throne, and she sat at his feet beside him.

"Now! We have much to do!" He said to the stunned people in the room.

Chapter Ten

"Take this man away, and give him a dignified burial. He died in what he thought was the King's service." Tam said after conferring briefly with Tawney.

He looked around. "I understand that we have a prisoner. Tell him that the King is a changed man, and that he is to be given his freedom. Then bring him to me."

They waited. The Chamberlain's body was taken away, and cleaning maids quickly straightened up the area, glancing surreptitiously up at the new King.

Eventually, the prisoner was brought forth. Naked and unkempt, his appearance was shocking.

More shocking was the fact that he was not human. His claws and fangs looked very dangerous, even though his fur was matted and soiled. Whatever he was, he looked more like Tawney and Dawn than they did to humans. He glared at first at the people around him, and then he looked more closely. When he saw the King, he was puzzled. When he looked at Tawney and Dawn, he smiled as if in recognition. And when his gaze fell on Luke, he laughed out loud!

"Who the Hell are you?" He demanded.

"Master Targath, I am that faithful servant who was with you, and others, on many journeys, before this fellow tricked us both. As you can see, he is not as he was." Luke responded cryptically.

Targath puzzled this out. He studied the King, and it seemed a bit of his strength ebbed away. He had been poised to do battle with an enemy, only to discover that his enemy had become a child!

With some satisfaction, then, he turned to Tawney and Dawn. He approached them with a smile. "I believe I know who you are, although we have never met! I must apologize for having gotten you into something you could not have been prepared to receive!"

"You know what has happened to us?" Tawney asked in bright hope.

"I fear that I do. You see, it was a part of my plan…"

Luke had been observing him. He interrupted. "Lord Targath, if you please, you seem to require Medical attention."

"Not just yet! First I will need a bath! Then I would like some food! After that, sometime, I will allow some medical attention."

Luke judged that Lord Targath was speaking bravely for no good purpose, but he acquiesced. "Lady Tawney, may I bring the ship to the Castle?"

"Good idea, Luke." She turned to Tam as if seeking permission. He smiled.

"Yes, Luke. Bring the ship to the castle. We will have need of its services." She continued.

Luke activated the radio equipment in its concealed location in the castle, and notified the satellite services that they were going to be bringing a cargo ship to the Black Castle from the nearby ocean. The satellite equipment automatically logged the movement as authorized. Then he activated Catspaw, raising it from the ocean and bringing it to the Castle courtyard.

When the ship landed, the servants in the courtyards, by standing order, concealed it under camouflage nets resembling the forest vines.

Tam ordered that Lord Targath should be given the "Royal Treatment" in a lavish bath, and that a feast be prepared for all in the castle, in recognition that the Kingdom had entered a "New Day."

The archers were ordered to depart, and the leader of the pike men remained after the others departed.

"Captain! What is your name?" Tam demanded.

"I am Felthorn, of Cragsmont, My Liege."

"How many in the Castle, Captain Felthorn?"

"A full dozen of dozens, Sire!"

"And outside of the Castle?"

"Perhaps a dozen of thousands, Sire, into the far mountains. I do not know of these matters."

"Do you know what lies beyond the mountains?"

"Other Kingdoms, Sire. There are minstrels, and peddlers, and criminals, also, who travel between the Kingdoms."

"What do you know of the other Kingdoms?"

"Only the rumors that I have heard, Your Majesty, and that I would not wish to live there."

Tam grew silent.

"Do you write, and read records, Captain Felthorn?" Luke inquired.

"I do not, Master Wizard." Felthorn answered truthfully. Luke raised his eyebrow at his new designation.

"Are there others who use this skill employed in the castle?"

"Yes, Master Wizard."

"King Tam and I wish to interview those who have positions of responsibility here in the castle. Can you arrange to have those people here in two hours? And have someone who can write down the proceedings?"

"Yes, Master Wizard. It will be done."

"One more thing, Captain Felthorn. You may wish to learn this skill of writing and reading. It would be helpful as the King's Captain of the Guard. Would you object to making this effort?"

"No, Master Wizard. I would not object to making the effort." He responded with a sly grin.

"Captain! Have you an interest in one of the ladies-in-waiting of the castle?"

Felthorn's smile faded. "I had thought that I might be able to ... consult with a particular person, yes, your Majesty."

"Good!" Felthorn's relief was obvious. "That will make your lessons more effective."

A senior chambermaid entered the hall, and bowed. "Your Majesty, the King's bath is prepared." She cast her eyes downward.

Tam looked around at Tawney, Dawn, and Lord Targath. "Let's all go!" He bounded down and walked toward the doorway.

Tawney and Dawn came forward to hold Targath's arms, and escort him. Each was wearing a pleasant smile. The chambermaid, slightly flustered, led the way to the central hallway, and to the right.

The party entered the bath-chamber through curtains of gauzy mist. With each slight barrier, the warmth and humidity increased. Soon they were in a virtual steam bath of large proportions. With a gesture from Tam, Tawney and Dawn removed their bracelets and such, and then helped Targath into the chest-high steamy waters. They relaxed on submerged seats. Targath's eyes closed in delight.

Tam stood at the edge. Two bath maids approached him. They were wearing a form of lizard-skin bathing costume, which made them resemble the giant fringed lizards along the coast. It was even woven into their hair. They came softly to Tam and began to remove his clothes. He stood still and permitted them to complete this task. Then he let them lead him into the water also. Two other maids, similarly costumed as were the first two, also joined in the large pool, and brought scented soaps and other pleasant materials.

The maids set to their tasks without instruction, or apparent embarrassment. They acted as though they bathed alien kittens and young boys all the time. The king and his guests relaxed under the gentle sensations, and engaged in conversations.

"You said this was part of your plan?" Tawney prompted Targath.

He opened his eyes. "Ah, yes. My plan did not include getting thrown into a dungeon for half-a-year while someone else implemented it, but yes, your modifications were a planned result quite a long time ago."

Tawney and Dawn both approached him with a rather intense curiosity. "Do go on!" Said Tawney throatily.

He laughed again, easily.

"I guess my story begins with some information about who we are..."

Targath regaled them with tales of his early childhood, and of the family and the order of which he was a sworn part. Like Irish immigrants who had come to America, his people, when they ventured out into the Galaxy, turned to keeping order in a chaotic section of space.

The first species they had come across were the regular victims of a form of piracy. The marauders had fast ships and weapons, and they essentially took what they wanted from the somewhat passive citizens.

Targath's people knew they could never submit to such brutality, either at their own homeworld, or on their neighbor's world.

The next time the raiders came, they were given a surprise, and a single ship in which to return home.

Knowing the bullying mind at work behind the pirate forces, Targath's warriors had waited for the expected return in force.

The warriors of the House of Grelmnin, and of the other Houses of the world of Krzlin, were prepared for them. Even so, the battle was a pitched one. Many Heroes' Songs were composed that day.

The Krzlin were triumphant, however, and gained many a ship and newer weapons systems. From that time forward, they had not been defeated in major battle, and their Empire of Peaceful Order had grown to a thousand worlds.

Theirs was not an Empire of conquest, though. They were more like Merchant Princes, providing the needs of one world by bringing the excess production of the others. Routes and Houses of Trade were built, as well as fortunes and proud families.

Yet, as consummate warriors, they were often required to defend themselves, and their clients, from the unruly elements that easy star-travel made possible. It had been a wild time, and it was still going on!

Tawney and Dawn could testify to that.

They were interrupted by the announcement that dinner, and the meeting of senior staff, were both ready. Luke had brought over some clothes for Tam, and he got dressed quickly.

Luke and Tam went to interview the staff.

There were a dozen senior matrons, and an equal number of men.

"You have no doubt heard about the return of the King," Luke began. "Now is the time to express yourselves if you have any doubt of his claim. You will not be harmed. You may be asked to leave the castle, but you may go peacefully."

"What Magic is this, Master Wizard? Have you enchanted the

King?" A woman who appeared to be in charge of the chambermaids asked in astonishment.

"The magic is the magic of ships, Dear Woman. You do not question that they can fly, but you do not know how they do it." Tam said gently. "If you wish, we can show you the magic that lets a ship fly. What has made me young again is more of a curse than an enchantment. It is a curse, and a blessing, for I was an evil man."

"No, Sire, you were a good King!" A man proclaimed.

"I hope so. That would have been wise, and you people deserve a good king." He smiled at them. "The Master Wizard is not my servant, but he is my friend. I am going to ask him to help you with any problems that you have here in the castle, or in the lands beyond. With his help, we will all live more comfortable lives! Now, tell us of any problems that you have. What about the food? Does it spoil too quickly?"

Soon the staff had accepted them as being unquestioningly in charge, and were unburdening themselves of minor grievances and inconveniences. One of the first surprising discoveries was that the entire castle had no elevators, or means of getting water automatically up to the top of it.

The people were astonished to realize that the Master Wizard had just promised to provide them with both capabilities!

Tam made an effort to get the names and positions of the staff, and then he left the task of reorganizing them to Luke.

When it came time to dry the ladies, and Lord Targath, the bath maids had a bit of a challenge, since they lacked automatic driers. They compromised by using many soft towels, patting, brushing, and rubbing gently until all of the fur was soft, clean, dry, and sweet smelling!

This too, had been very pleasurable to the trio of apparent aliens.

By their choice, Tawney and Dawn wrapped themselves in more jewelry, and one or two shimmering scarves. Targath wore some heavier strap-boots, and a warrior's headband and ornamented sword. His was easily the longest and heaviest sword on display.

When Tam entered the dining hall, he was greeted by applause from Tawney and Dawn, who stood and cheered energetically. Others stared at them at first, and then joined them in the tumult. Tam stared.

It looked as though everyone who was in the castle was applauding him! Blushing, he went to the head of the table through scores of smiling ladies and men-at-arms. He raised his hands and the sound diminished.

"I know that you do not really know me, or what may happen to you with me as your leader, but I thank you for your kindness! My friends and I have just been through the most amazing events, but I can tell you that your warm welcome is the most surprising and pleasant greeting we have ever received. Thank You! Please, be seated. Let us enjoy our friendship!" He made a courtly bow and sat down.

Stunned, his guests quieted and took their seats.

Targath rose again, to propose a toast. "Guests, and fellow adventurers, I rise to salute a man that I swore to myself I would one day kill with my bare hands." For humor's sake he tapped his claws against the glass.

"But this is not the man who caused me pain. There is no doubt that he is your King, but it is also clear that he is not my enemy." He took a moment to reach over the corner of the table to take Tam's hand in friendship. Then he straightened up again. "We will now enter into a new era of amicable relations between my people and your beautiful Kingdom." He drained his glass.

At Tawney's signal, Tam took a short sip from his own wineglass. "Thank you, Lord Targath. Now, everybody eat!" he said with a smile.

Targath sat down. Despite his bravado, his illness and negligent incarceration had taken their toll, but the first medical procedure would be a hearty meal! He smiled in feral triumph.

Tawney reached over and placed her arm near his, her claws extended gently to penetrate through his thick fur and lie loosely on his flesh. "You were saying?"

He looked down in amused annoyance. He was far from his familiar court! "My plan was originally to find wives for my nephews, who have grown into ... manhood." The word seemed to be slightly distasteful to him.

"From time to time, as we expand through the Galaxy, we find candidate species with characteristics we consider noble, or useful. It is our practice to attempt to acquire those characteristics for ourselves and our species, by inviting promising members of other species to join us."

Targath began eating. Though he had been on the verge of starvation, his will-power and common sense made him start slowly. He knew his stomach would need time to adjust. Tawney drew back and began eating also.

"We are exceptional artists at making changes to the physical appearance, either temporarily as I had done, or permanently through a process of genetic intrusion."

He paused to nibble again. Although he had been on this planet for months, he had never been given the chance to know what proper foods were, or tasted like. He took the time to revel in his new discoveries.

"I traveled incognito, looking very much like one of you." He looked around, then resumed. "I traveled extensively in the human worlds, and I came to know their good ways and their bad ones. On the whole, I found them to be energetic and determined, and also venal and corrupt. I saw that there were strengths I admired, and weaknesses which seemed intolerable. Humans are quick of mind, and adaptable. They have a resilience that is quite astonishing. With guidance, I thought that some of them could be trained to follow our Noble Warrior's path"

"In particular, your women have a kind of radiant beauty that transcends the variation of species. The aliveness of your eyes, and your lustrous hair, are much admired among my clan."

"I had discovered two very healthy young women, and I was looking for a way to introduce myself to them, when I had the misfortune of encountering a treacherous and unscrupulous individual named Tam Worth."

Tam looked over at him at the mention of his name, but the reaction of the guards was immediate. Many placed their hands to their weapons in preparation.

Tam stood up, with his hands outstretched. "Do not be concerned, my friends. Lord Targath speaks the truth. The man I used to be was unworthy, unworthy of you. I have learned that he was many things I would not want any of you to be. Nor do I want to be them myself."

"The man I was is dead now, as dead as his High Chancellor. The path I had once chosen to follow proved to be a false path, a disastrous path, and I have been set back upon it so far that I have not even a memory of my errors. I am a new person, and this is a new kingdom. Many changes will be seen now, and they will be good changes! Let us continue our feast now, and our guest will continue telling us the truth, or if he wishes, he can entertain us!"

Tam laughed softly. Others around the table laughed also. The guards relaxed, still somewhat confused.

Targath continued as the others resumed their places. "Tam was very interested in me and my project. He pressed me for details about how it would be implemented. I have to admit, he was very gracious and charming. I had the impression that he was known and respected throughout the sector. I made the mistake of giving him access to my ship, and showing him the materials that I was preparing to use, with permission of course, to prepare my nephews' brides for their roles. It was never intended to be done any other way." Targath took a moment to shake his head sadly.

"I had thought that if he understood what my plan was, he could better help me implement it. Instead, he developed a plan of his own. I was taken prisoner, and shackled in a tiny cell, away from everything familiar to me, while he pressed me for more details. I told him nothing, but as time went on, I deliberately made it appear that I was weakening, and that eventually I would give him other information he desired, like the location of my homeworld."

"I reasoned that if he saw no possibility of getting what he wanted, he would simply kill me." Targath paused to swallow some wine. "He ran out of time. Whatever he needed the money for from this adventure, it was coming up fast. He abandoned me and went off on his own quest. That is when your misfortune began!" He looked pointedly at Tawney and Dawn.

Dawn raised her glass and stood. "Lord Targath is growing tired, and needs to restore himself. I too, wish to salute a man I once considered trying to kill, a man known as Tam Worth. My companion and I fell into his company by way of a scheme that went somewhat awry, thank goodness!"

"What all of it was meant to be, we may never know, but we may say, good King Tam had a change of heart along the way, and a change of height, and weight, and apparent age, as well." She smiled.

"You see before you the very essence of a changed man, but he still likes to wear silk!" She lifted her glass in toast to him.

Tam raised his glass as well, showing his embarrassment. Leaning forward, he raised his voice so all could hear. Dawn sat back down with a smile.

"By all accounts, these ladies should have done to me what the late High Chancellor tried to do. Certainly I deserved it. Instead, they gave me a second chance. I hope to prove worthy of it, and of your devotion. Thank you all!" Raising his glass, he gestured toward everyone in the room, and then he sipped cautiously from the glass himself.

In the ensuing silence, gradually, the others at the table began speaking softly.

Chapter Eleven

Luke waited until the dinner had reached the point where the "Royal party" had been given privacy for their conversations. At that time, he smoothly reminded them that Lord Targath still needed some medical attention, and he suggested that they retire to the ship in order to make arrangements for the coming days.

This met with everyone's approval. Tam cleared his throat. Immediately, there was a respectful silence in the room.

"My group will now retire, and make further plans for tomorrow and the coming days. Those of you who are in charge here, do your duty as usual. Captain of the King's Guard, see to the security of the castle. If any matter requires the king's attention, come to me. Otherwise, I hope you will all have a quiet evening."

He raised his cup. "To the good times to come!" All joined him in the toast. Then he stood, and everyone sprang to their feet.

Tam led the others out into the hall, and then let Luke lead them to the ship. Targath appeared to be growing weaker. Dawn and Tawney stayed with him to assist.

When they were safely aboard, and felt secure again, Dawn suggested that they use the rejuvenation chamber on Lord Targath. He nodded in weary acceptance and allowed himself to be placed in the chamber. Tam watched in fascination as Tawney asked Targath some quiet questions, and then she closed the chamber door and began the programming.

When she was finished, she conferred briefly with Luke. He nodded in understanding, and then he suggested that they all step back to the doorway.

From the entrance, each one turned around to observe as the machine in the corner began its activation sequence. The anything box was in operation again. The brilliant glow of its stasis field reached out to engulf the rejuvenation chamber.

Tawney explained. "Obviously, many months, even years, of gradual diminishment had to be remedied. This would normally take a very long time. Once the basic program has begun, we may accomplish a tremendous acceleration in this way. Lord Targath is too important to be missing for very long, and too ill to wait any longer."

"Let's all get cleaned up while we're waiting."

They left the cargo hold with its magnificent, magical devices and returned to their quarters where they quickly enjoyed modern plumbing again after what had seemed weeks in the wilderness.

Shortly Luke announced that the rejuvenation chamber was running at normal speed again, and that its occupant was now ready for awakening. They hurried back to the cargo hold with eager anticipation.

Breathlessly, they peered in at the machines. Tawney stepped forward and pressed the appropriate controls. Silently the machine cycled into inactivity, and the door opened automatically.

Lord Targath gingerly exited as he checked the changes in his body's operation. Gradually, an astonishing truth became apparent. He clenched his fists and released a roar of challenge and exultation.

Tam stepped behind Luke and peered back cautiously. Targath had been a sterling and lordly specimen of a warrior, even after the months of indignities he had suffered.

Now, restored to health, vigor, and youth, he was awe-inspiring! He stood tall, proud, and magnificent as he tested his newfound strength and fitness.

Targath looked at the ladies with bright, mischievous eyes. "If I were not on a bride-quest for my nephews, I might try to impress you for my own sake."

"You certainly look very impressive!" Dawn responded.

Tawney was looking him over also. "Lord Targath, you still appear to be the same age, but it is clear that your youth and vigor have been restored. How do you feel?"

"I feel like going back to that nest of pirates, and showing them how I feel!"

Tam cleared his throat. "Lord Targath, it was I who had you cast into the prison, not the other pirates."

Targath softened toward the boy. "No, it was not you, nor was it your older self alone who became my enemy. If not for the others, your misdeeds would never have amounted to much. There are people near here who need to be brought to justice, but that does not include you. Your crime has been expiated."

"Expiated?" Tam looked puzzled.

"It means you are innocent again, Tam." Tawney explained.

Tam came forward and stood before Targath. "You are a mighty warrior, and you are the sworn enemy of pirates. I want to fight by your side to rid the Universe of them."

Targath placed his mighty clawed hand upon the young man's shoulder. "We will go into battle together against them, this I swear!"

Tawney looked alarmed. "He's not ready, Targath!"

Targath grinned at her, a most alarming display. "No, he is not. Not yet. Nor are we ready for the task ourselves. Let us journey now to my homeworld, where mighty warriors are training for battle, and we will tell them of your heroic deeds and adventures, and we will enlist them to your cause of freedom!"

"Uh, I don't think we had planned quite that far ahead, Targath. We were just taking things one day at a time."

"I want to do it, Lady Tawney! I want to train with the warriors, and learn battle skills, so that I will be ready for the quest!" Tam announced excitedly.

"What about your kingdom, Tam? You can't abandon your people now."

Tam looked disappointed. Then Luke spoke up.

"Master Tam may need to journey with you, Lady Tawney. In my discussions with his people, I discovered that the pirates maintain a presence here, for the sake of harvesting the narcotic element of the wild vine we saw in such plenty. It is a major crop for the planet. If King Tam remained alone, he would be in grave peril."

"Why, Luke? Why would the King be in peril?" Dawn asked.

"This is the same Tamarind Worth who made an agreement to deliver two slaves to the pirate markets of Piggledy, and who absconded with the goods instead. It was he, as far as they know, who disabled their spacecraft that had been sent to retrieve the missing property. If we leave him here, they will collect him, and punish him."

"You are correct, Luke. We cannot leave him here alone."

"With your permission, Lady Tawney, I have a suggestion. Let me remain here as his regent. I will represent him to the pirates, and represent him to the people also. We have many projects planned for the benefit of these good people, and I would like to supervise their progress."

"Do you think you will be safe, Luke? These pirates are very dangerous."

"I will take the place of the King's Chamberlain, My Lady. As long as we have a shipment of the narcotic material, no one here will come to harm. I would like to ask, however, that you allow me to modify some of the robots to appear as Knights in Armor, and remain here with me. They will help to implement the King's programs, and they will provide me with personal security also."

Strange as it was to hear a robot speak of using other robots to provide for his security, Tawney did not question these suggestions. "I endorse this plan, Luke. Does anyone have anything else to suggest?"

Her inquiring glance met only shrugs and nods of approval.

"We're going to miss you, Luke!" Tawney said sincerely.

"Ah, Lady Tawney, if you wouldn't mind, I would suggest allowing me to produce yet another replica to be your servant on the trip, and on the planet of Lord Targath."

"Oh! I hadn't thought of that!"

"I hope you'll give him a different face!" Lord Targath said wryly.

"Could we make him look like your younger brother?" Suggested Dawn.

"A different name, too, Dawn?" Tawney inquired.

"How about Miles?" Dawn responded with a grin.

"Approved!" Tawney laughed, "Good choice!"

"I will see to these preparations, my Lords and Ladies. In the meantime, if you wish to refresh yourselves, I have set out some fresh fruit, cheeses, and suitable wines in the kitchen for you."

Chapter Twelve

The preparation work took two more days. Luke was given specific instructions, and he confirmed his understanding by displaying views and visions of the plans as finalized in their special chamber. Only minor modifications were required.

Luke did not seem to mind that his suggestions were modified. His ego was not a delicate construction, and he genuinely seemed interested in bringing the plans to fruition.

His attendant robots were redesigned to look like armored knights. They were given all the accoutrements of that role, including huge black beasts of snorting, pawing horses. It was hoped that their intimidating appearance would keep the civilians out of harm's way.

The knights also had shields and weapons. Tawney seemed concerned.

"Lord Targath, would you walk with me?"

"Certainly, Milady."

An enclosed walkway had been positioned between the ship's passenger portal, and the second floor veranda. They climbed the slight slope in silence.

"Just what are they supposed to do with those weapons?' She asked softly.

Lord Targath seemed amused. "They would be very conspicuous without them, Lady Taraunda. All of their weapons can also be tools, and they will need them. They will be overseeing, and participating in, certain civic improvement projects, as well as helping the populace to move a little further into an age of comfort with technology. Master

Luke has programmed them with a vast array of engineering knowledge, so that they can build bridges, repair wagons, redesign smithies, and install primitive versions of modern conveniences in the castle. When we return, whenever that may be, we should have running water and working elevators in the castle."

"Really?" They continued along the veranda, turning the corner into the sunshine.

"Quite so. They will occasionally be required to use their weapons as weapons, however, for they are also going to be the Sergeants and Officers of King Tam's Army."

"Army! What army? Why would he need an army?" Tawney stopped and faced the warrior.

"Do not be alarmed, My Lady. This is standard practice. When we begin making civic improvements, and the people begin to reap the benefit of a better standard of living, there will be spies among them, reporting back to neighboring realms. The history of these people is filled with petty border disputes and occasional major wars. Our insurance policy against that is to be prepared for any eventuality. Your own ancient philosophers have described it already; "To have Peace, prepare for War." Our knights will train the young men to defend themselves and their families, that's all."

"That's all. And when Tam returns, he will start a new round of conquests with his new army?"

Targath looked at her carefully. "In a manner of speaking, yes. But it will not be as you fear, with military skirmishes. Instead, King Tam will lead his people to a better way of living, through trade and development, and that will include new pacts and agreements with his neighbors. We will have surpluses, and we will offer them in exchange for other goods. We will embark on peaceful conquest, in pursuit of better days for all."

"I suppose we'll just have to wait and see. It's not that I don't trust you, Lord Targath, but of late I have had very little reason to put my faith in anyone."

"Perhaps your concerns will be lightened when we arrive on my homeworld. You will see that I have accurately portrayed my people."

Tawney leaned her elbows on the parapet and looked out into the courtyard. She sighed.

"That's probably what's making me edgy. I'm about to go into yet another difficult situation, and I still haven't figured out how I got into this in the first place."

Targath came and stood near her, holding himself straight and tall with a regal bearing that had been impossible to him only days before.

"I am the one to blame for that, Milady. I did not intend for you to be taken against your will, but it was I who selected you and your companion as … suitable recruits."

Tawney turned to look at him. "Recruits?"

He smiled. The effect was not entirely comforting.

"My nephews are in need of wives, but it is not quite that simple, either. You see, we Krzlin are moving out into the Galaxy, and we are also bringing the Galaxy to our homeworld. Our isolated species has some unique capacities, but we recognize that others have qualities, too. One of the things we do is look for those qualities, and attempt to bring them into our capability. In what I understand is a rather unusual perspective, we are not afraid to modify our genetic identity."

He looked out into the distance. "Some primitive cultures have been known to welcome heroic strangers, even to the extent of urging them to take wives, in order for the tribe to gain the strength of the traveling hero, and to build its genetic diversity. That has been a cultural icon of my people for many centuries, and now we do it on a Galactic scale."

"Heroic?" Tawney looked a little surprised.

"You don't think so?"

"All we ever have done is run away from danger. I don't think that's heroic."

"That's not what I've heard."

Tawney looked suspiciously at him. "Heard from whom?"

"Primarily from Luke. He has a certain loyalty to me, you know."

"Oh, of course. I suppose we should transfer the ship back to you now."

Targath looked surprised. "Whatever for?"

"Well, the ship belongs to you, properly. We only took it over in order to escape. The ship belongs to you."

"No. The ship is yours. Yours and Lady Dawn's. You see, when I lost it, to Tam, it was as if I had lost it in battle. By our custom, it belongs to the victor. Since you took it from him, it now belongs to you."

"But that isn't fair!"

"Battle is seldom fair. Do not be concerned about it. I will have another ship available, and I certainly owe you for having rescued me, as well. Speaking of which, how can you say that you have only run from danger? It wasn't running *from* danger that brought you here."

"I ... well, we voted on it, once we discovered that you were being held prisoner."

"So? Then you are all heroes!"

Tawney shook her head, confused and embarrassed. Targath very gently laid his clawed hand on hers, and lifted it to his lips.

He kissed her hand, and said softly, "You are my rescuers, my heroes. I will sing your songs."

Tawney looked down, hiding the tears in her eyes. She certainly didn't feel like a hero.

"Do you typically recruit wives, then?"

"We recruit those with good qualities to expand our genetic diversity, but the selection of wives is a tentative business. As a senior family member, it is in my interest to help my family grow strong with good candidates. Normally, more choice is offered the potential invitee."

"I would hope so."

"I was on the verge of revealing my purpose to you when all of our lives were disrupted. Perhaps I should have done so, but I made the mistake of wanting to avoid making a clumsy, foolish approach like the craven drunkards who were always pestering you. I discussed the nature of human courtship habits with the oh so courtly and suave senior Tam."

"He seemed to have the knowledge and skills to properly gain the attention of females. At least, that was the appearance he fostered."

"I can imagine. He appeared to be a handsome man, if given over to too much lavish living."

"Exactly! When he was active, and dressing and playing the part, he seemed rather charming. I was negotiating with him to assist me in gaining your attention, and I unfortunately let him become too aware of my plans. I did not know at the time that humans could be so devious."

"I don't think you'll make that mistake again."

"No. By the way, once you have met my nephews, if you wish to return to your former lives, or simply go anywhere you wish, you will of course have that option."

"Really?"

"Most assuredly. It is not our habit to kidnap prospective mates."

Tawney looked down at her clawed hand. "What about ..."

Targath murred; a cross between a throaty growl and a hum. Tawney had never heard anything like it before, but she seemed to know instinctively what it meant. "That is a different matter. I was given a special ointment, which of course has genetic alteration as a function of its constituent ingredients. Some modification of your genotype is necessary for mutual fertility. That would have been offered to you as a voluntary choice on your part, either before or after you had met my nephews. I only had it as a means of preparing any tentative candidates for the meeting. Most of my people have never met humans before. You might not have been accepted in the manner you have come to expect as such lovely specimens of womanly attractiveness."

"Why, thank you, Targath! That's very sweet of you to say."

He shrugged. "It's the simple truth. I spent enough time among humans to know that you both are unusually attractive by human standards. Unfortunately, it is that which could make your meeting with my people less than satisfactory to you. Their standards are radically different."

Tawney looked into his face. "What features do you find attractive in Krzlin females?"

His expression softened, and grew vaguely wistful. "You will see. The ladies at court in the House of Grelmnin are among the loveliest on the homeworld. Their brilliant, flashing eyes, the polished ebon claws, and the smooth, patterned fur ... and then there is that lovely, tantalizing aroma ..." His eyes appeared to be closed halfway.

Tawney punched him in the upper arm, her claws carefully clenched away from harming him.

Targath laughed, and rubbed his arm.

"Yes. Well, anyway, when Tam took over my plans for his own purposes, he eliminated the little matter of freedom of choice for all of us. I have no idea who actually used the ointment."

"I'll probably be able to find out, one day. But not very soon. We'll have to travel to your homeworld regardless, won't we? Did you also mean that we could get this effect reversed?"

"Yes. I do not have the knowledge, myself, but the person who gave me the ointment assured me that the effects need not be permanent. You will not be surprised that he is called a wizard."

"Dawn will be relieved to learn that."

Luke approached them, and waited.

"What news, Luke?" Tawney turned toward the robot.

"Everything is in readiness for your departure, Lady Taraunda. There will be another feast here in the great hall this evening, and the King wishes to leave at Midnight."

"Very well. Thank you. We're going to miss you, Luke."

"My ... younger brother, Miles, will be pleased to see to your needs, Milady. He has the same knowledge base that I do."

"Yes, I know. Will you be all right?"

"I will fare well, Lady Taraunda. I will have my work, and the supervision of the changes we will be making. I will have to negotiate with the pirates, and provide them the narcotic, but I am assured that the supply is prepared already. The people here know what it does to the local wildlife, and they are not interested in its properties. I think they are good people. It will be my pleasure to work with them to improve their lives."

Tawney embraced him, rather like hugging a favorite cupboard, but his illusion of humanity was effective. "You're good people too, Luke. Take good care of yourself."

"Thank you, Lady Tawney. I will."

They watched the robot leave. Targath turned to her.

"Would you like to return to the ship now, Milady? I have an appointment there with King Tam, and I do not wish to be late."

"Yes, I think I should. I'll need to do some work with my wardrobe, among other things."

Targath escorted her back to the ship.

The evening was somewhat bittersweet for Tam. He had begun acclimatizing himself to the notion the he was a King. The respectful attention he was getting from everyone tended to feed that perception.

Targath and Luke had been attempting to moderate that influence by warning Tam about those who would still regard themselves as his enemies. Tam reluctantly accepted the reality. As far as he was concerned, it was simply another reason to be preparing himself to do battle with the pirates. They had brought disaster to everyone he had ever known and loved.

The fact that he had been one of them was a guilt he could easily shed. Not only did he have no memory of such a life, he was also determined to be a different kind of man than he had proven to be before. He accepted the fact that he was being given a second chance, and he intended to prove himself worthy.

As the host of the banquet, Tam appeared in good spirits, joking with the people at court and making them feel comfortable. He was rapidly becoming a popular King.

His servants and guests hardly knew what to make of the changes. Most of them had been familiar with the former King and his ways. The change was not only magical, but also most mysterious. Most appeared to feel that the entire Kingdom had been given a rebirth.

When Tam saw that his guests had slowed their consumption, and there was a lull in the boisterous conversation, he stood up. A respectful silence spread across the room.

"My beloved people, it is with sadness I must again prepare to say goodbye to you. I have a mission to perform in your behalf, and I must leave you to accomplish it. The enemies of our Kingdom would bring harm to you if I remain here, and so, to protect you, I must make preparations elsewhere."

"I will return. When I return, we will stand together against anyone who wishes us harm. But for now, we must all play a more careful game. My Chamberlain, whom some of you know as the Master Wizard Luke, will rule here in my stead."

"You will find him to be fair and just. He regards himself as your servant, and it is his purpose to help you grow in health and happiness until my return. I ask you to work with him. My Knights in Armor will be here also. They have been instructed to go out among you, and be your protectors."

"My commands to them, and to you, are these: Work hard, for the rewards of it. Rest well, for the days ahead. Cooperate with my representatives, and work with them for the benefit of all. Enjoy your days, and your nights. Fill them with song, and merriment, and productive activities which will make you happy and helpful to each other."

"Grow strong, in every sense of the word. My servants will assist you to be able to look to our neighbors not with fear, but with friendliness, for they will come to trade with you, and they will see that you are strong, and that you are not to treated unfairly. You young and strong, protect the younger and the innocent. Help your elders, and learn from them. Assist my servants, and they will guide you to greater prosperity."

"You elders, and you doubters, and any who have not been in the habit of working together for the benefit of all, guide these younger ones with your heart, and trust that what I say is true. We are a family. Our Kingdom is our home. Let us have joy, and happiness in our home, and let us stand ready together against any harm that may come our way."

"And now I must take my leave. Let us drink to the day, and our healthy and safe journey toward it, of my return to you." He lifted his wine goblet toward them.

All down the table, and through the hall, others joined his toast, standing respectfully and looking toward him.

Tam sipped from his goblet. "My people, finish your meal, enjoy your feast, and tomorrow begin the work for all our tomorrows. When it is done, I will return." With that, he put down his goblet and strode from the hall.

Luke, and the others from the ship, began applauding. The other guests also began clapping their hands.

Then Lord Targath and the Ladies departed as well, while Master Luke, newly appointed Chamberlain, stepped over to stand beside the throne.

When the applause died down, Luke said, "Let us continue the feast, and tomorrow we will begin building a new Kingdom!"

Chapter Thirteen

Tawney awakened while they were still in hyperspace. The sleep, and the relaxation of tensions from the world they left behind, made her feel energized for the day ahead.

Dawn was again asleep beside her. Both had shed their garments. Except for the sounds of metal complaining in the stresses of hyperspace, the ship was quiet.

Try as she might, she could not recall or calculate exactly how long it had been since she was ripped from her former life. She tried to picture herself returning to it, and almost giggled.

"I might be a sensation for a few days," she thought, "but I'm not naked enough to suit them now." Her tail began flipping from her nervous tension. She willed it to be still.

She was also apprehensive about meeting an entire planet of strangers. Everything had gone well on her other planetary excursions, but this felt different. As if she were meeting her in-laws for the first time.

She thought for a moment about her relationship with these new people. She was somehow destined to play a role in their society. Would it be one to her liking? In essence, she was a kidnap bride, sailing to an unknown fate.

Her old persona, the dancer and entertainer, would certainly have quailed at the thought, and perhaps chosen to go in another direction. She knew that she had changed, though. She intended to see it through, and then decide for herself. Fear would not be her master.

She took a deep breath and relaxed once more. What were these people, though? Her adopted species? ... Her adapted species? Her thoughts spun like falling leaves. She slept.

When Tawney awakened once more, she heard voices emanating from the control cabin. They had arrived in the Krzlin home system, and were negotiating their way inward.

It was not advisable for a star-cruiser to exit hyperspace too close to the Krzlin home world. The reaction was swift and unfriendly. Being on a constant combat footing tends to keep one a trifle edgy.

Aside from determining their bona fides, however, the welcoming committee was friendly enough. Tawney remembered the suspicious and hesitant behavior of the women of Planet Burnitch.

They moved under conventional power deeper into the system. It was well apparent that they were under scrutiny. They took their time.

Targath seemed to enjoy giving them this leisurely approach to his beautiful homeworld. In truth, it was quite lovely. Dawn had joined her, and they both commented on the green, blue, and white loveliness before them.

"Is it Winter, Targath?" Dawn asked.

"Actually, we are well into Spring. Unfortunately, our year is just over six of what you are used to. Krzlin has a somewhat eccentric orbit that keeps it far from the Sun for a very long time, and its axial tilt is only four degrees. The Summer activity for all living things is rather hectic, and it goes on planetwide."

"Wow! That's rather extreme. Life must have been very difficult for you on this planet."

"I suppose one would say that it made us strong." He shrugged. "Certainly it gave us many long Winter nights to study the stars and ponder our place in the Universe."

"It would appear that it made you cautious planners, as well. It must have taken extraordinary measures to be able to survive such long Winters." Tawney observed.

Targath nodded. "It gave us great strength in our appreciation for family and clan. We could not have survived otherwise. We excavated deep caves under the mountains, some of them so deep we were benefiting from the heat of the planet itself. But we still needed food to get us through the lean times. It became necessary to develop our skills as hunters too."

He turned back to the navigation console. "We will be landing in four hours, and it will be approaching evening. Two hours after landing, I will have the honor of presenting you to my clan elders, and to my family. You may wish to begin your preparations."

Dawn began sputtering a protest, but Tawney pulled her away.

"He's trying to tell us to get bathed and dressed, you slatternly harlot."

"Oh." Dawn desisted. "Hey, wait a minute!"

Tawney embraced her. "I'm only teasing, Sister! I'm so keyed up about this meeting now I feel like doing acrobatics!"

Dawn smiled, "I'm excited too, but I'm a little apprehensive as well. It is, after all, an alien culture."

"Well, one thing for sure. We'll fit in better here than anywhere else we could go."

"That's true. I guess we'd better get ready."

They bathed and had a leisurely breakfast. Then they groomed themselves once more, and began selecting their costumes for the affair. Targath had described to them the cultural significance of all the different items, until their heads were swimming with the details. Still, to Tawney, it was another stage appearance. Dawn appeared to be facing it the same way.

Neither was surprised to discover that the carrying of weapons and an essentially undressed appearance was the fashion here. They realized that the manipulations they had undergone at Luke's suggestion had had a deep-seated history at their root.

So now they stood, in capes and boots and belts, and their naked fur, ready to be presented to the nobility of Targath's world. It seemed obscene, somehow, and yet, it was also intriguingly stimulating.

King Tam and Miles joined them, both expressing appreciation for their appearance.

Tam was dressed in a very subdued "uniform" befitting a junior Navy officer, complete with saber, boots, and a military cap.

Miles was affecting a civilian businessman's appearance. It had been decided to keep his actual nature a secret for now, and he would masquerade as Tam's "uncle" and guardian.

And then they saw Lord Targath. If he had been a specimen of health and vigor before, he was now a terrifying version of the supreme warrior. In light armor and sandalboots, with battle emblems decorating his ornamental shield and massive battle sword, he was a heart-thrilling vision of restrained ferocity.

Assuming his rightful place as the head of the delegation, he led them out into the frigid evening.

Past an escort of honor guards, they made their way to an ornate carriage, drawn by two fierce, powerful, tusked and furry ungulates.

Targath gave a hand to his two ladies as they climbed into the carriage, and also assisted Tam with the high steps. Miles easily clambered aboard as well. Stepping into the carriage, Targath raised his arm in salute to the honor guard, and roared out a victory cry. He was answered in turn by a return of his shout from the warriors. Then he took his seat.

The driver whisked the beasts into motion, and the carriage lurched forward. Tawney noted that the feet of the beasts did not make a familiar clip-clop sound, as horses might. Their tread was silent. She wondered what that might mean if one were to encounter such a beast in the wild.

She shivered, and beside her, Dawn was trembling as well. If this was Spring on Krzlin, and they were expected to be comfortable dressed this way, they would never be warm again.

Targath showed them some compartments where warm furs were kept for such journeys, and Tawney and Dawn gratefully wrapped themselves in the soft comfort. Miles helped Tam to cover himself as well.

More comfortable now, they looked around at the town through which they journeyed. All of the buildings seemed unusually large, and spread well apart. If this had a military or defensive purpose, Tawney could not guess what it might be.

The road rose before them. They were climbing in elevation. Shortly it became apparent that their destination was a fortified mountain fastness wrapped snugly against the face of a solid rock face.

The narrow road climbed at a leisurely pace up the slope. Finally, they were admitted through huge timbered doors into a large courtyard.

Steps led upward to another set of heavy doors. Targath led them confidently into the fortress.

Their footsteps echoed in the empty halls as torches guttered along the way. Tapestries and carved figures in niches bespoke of historical clashes relating to this clan.

The long hall ended with yet another set of doors. They were guarded by a pair of well armed and armored warriors who challenged them. Targath spoke briefly, and they were allowed to pass.

Inside the next chamber, it appeared that a feast was going on. Tables and carts were piled high with all manner of food and drink.

Targath led them down the cleared center of the room, and stopped in front of an elevated dais on which dozens of nobility sat observing them. He stepped up on a small raised platform, drew his mighty sword, swung it around ceremoniously, and stabbed it into a plinth of wood on the platform.

Then he began to sing.

Tawney was startled. She had been expecting almost anything else.

Targath's words were in Krzlin. They had a curious rhythm and timing, as if he were painting an image with his song.

Astonishingly, she realized she could understand much of what he was describing. Somehow, the genetic changes that had occurred to her, and to Dawn, had also written their magic in her own auditory nerve pathways.

Targath was singing a song of heroic deeds, of battles fought and won, of military campaigns that spanned the galaxy, and of an intrepid band of venturers who took on fierce odds with only their courage and tenacity to sustain them.

Tawney was growing increasingly mesmerized and approving of the story when it came to her that Targath was spinning these fanciful lies about her and Dawn!

Again and again he described events that only by the wildest imaginings could one think had anything to do with her or Dawn. Yet, they fit the pattern of those curious events through which they had stumbled by blind luck.

They were being presented as conquering warrior princesses. Had the blood not already been drained from her face by his effrontery, she was sure she would have been blushing a bright crimson.

In due course, Targath drew to a halt. He looked over his shoulder at Tawney and waited.

She moved forward to stand parallel to him.

Targath faced the crowd, "People of Krzlin, I present Lady Taraunda of the House of Grelmnin."

There was a stirring. Tawney now understood why. Grelmnin, in the language of Krzlin, meant the House of the Outsider. Historically, it had meant the stranger, or the enemy.

Only recently, and rarely, it was used to describe those exotic individuals who had been offered a chance to share their genetic propensities with the Krzlin. It was still considerably controversial, if not a bit risqué.

"And Lady Dara-Elin, also of the House of Grelmnin. They are my rescuers, and are now my honored guests." He looked at Dawn. She moved forward.

"I wish also to present to you the individual who took me prisoner, and captured my vessel, and turned my innocent plans into a dastardly evil scheme." He looked at Tam.

Tam stepped forward also, to a rush of voices exclaiming in surprise. He stepped up beside Dawn and held her hand. He was not understanding the words being spoken, but was operating on visual cues.

"I should hasten to explain that King Tamarind Worth, of the mountain kingdom of Faunelle, has had his own reverses. It was he who captured our Noble Warrior Princesses, and imprisoned them. He was the first to fall under their magical enchantments, and to his great good fortune, they simply removed all evil from him. I do not think our Empire has ever seen such warriors! Instead of vengeance, they showed mercy. Instead of slaying their enemy, they converted him into a noble friend."

"King Tam joined them to come and rescue me from the dank imprisonment that his own former self had inflicted on me. He is now my good friend also. With him is his Uncle Miles, who will escort our royal guest among us." He looked over his shoulder one more time, and Miles strode forward. He, of course, understood every word.

"My people, I have returned from my quest. In some things I failed, and for a long time I despaired of ever returning. But I have truthfully gained much more than I had sought, and I return to you a much richer individual for the effort!"

In the silence, there was a soft stirring, as one by one his listeners rose to honor him. Almost as one, they gave a short bow of the head, which he returned.

Immediately, there was a clatter as tankards and utensils were re-employed. The feast had resumed.

Targath gathered his party and made his way up among the revelers. He was greeted by many casual and close acquaintances. They also embraced or clasped arms with Tawney and Dawn, uttering soft welcomes. Neither girl trusted herself to speak yet.

Tam was looked upon as a curiosity. They were friendly enough, but he felt very much the outsider here. Even so, he moved among the ferocious feline warriors without fear.

Shortly, they made their way to Targath's family representatives. He took pains to introduce them once more.

Tawney realized that his formal manner of speaking was a great deal more than simple good manners. She was being introduced to his nephew, presumably the intended bridegroom.

He was somewhat thinner than Targath, but the resemblance was strong. He was tall and lithe, a ferocious appearing warrior in his own right.

"Lady Taraunda, may I present the distinguished Lord Strigath, heir to the northern realms of Gath K'Thran. Strigath, this is Lady Taraunda, the Victor of my Victor."

Strigath clasped arms with Targath in a warrior's grip, and then bowed toward Tawney. "My Lady, I am honored. Thank you for rescuing my cherished Uncle."

"I am honored." Tawney responded, trusting herself to venture no further in the unaccustomed language.

Targath then made the introductions for Jerinnigath and Lady Dara-Elin.

What followed was many more introductions, a large amount of feasting, and unless she was mistaken, what sounded like some rather festive preparations for a wedding or two.

Tawney stepped forward, preparing to speak. The others looked at her in surprise. "Lord Targath, honored relations of the realms of Gath K'Thran, any other guests, thank you most sincerely for this wonderful warm welcome. You honor all of us with your generosity. We are happy to have brought back to you your fearless and conquering hero, and are pleased that his family are prepared to welcome him back into their warm embrace."

"Thank you also for preparing to make room for us as well, if I have interpreted things accurately. We are honored beyond, quite well beyond, our ability to express."

"However," Tawney took a moment to swallow, and prepare herself, "despite your obvious readiness to accept us, my companion and I must as graciously as possible, decline your invitation at this time."

She looked around, "While we understood the necessity of returning Lord Targath as quickly as possible to his family to alleviate their concerns, along the way of our journeys we acquired some requisite responsibilities we have yet to discharge. It is our intention to return to the Planet Burnitch to complete the tasks that were set before us at that time, and in our hour of need, having recognized that the generosity extended to us then was also a pleading for help in their impending need."

She looked around. "There are people who need our help, and we intend to meet our obligations, which we feel are a prerequisite to the Honor you would bestow on us by inviting us to join you."

She raised her chin, "The House of Grelmnin must bring Honor with it, in order to join the House of Lord Targath."

Beside her, Lady Dara-Elin stepped up and stood with her, also with chin held high.

The House of the Enemy; the House of the Stranger, would earn their way to Honor.

Daybreak

Brian B. Hawthorne

Daybreak

Maya was solicitous, as always, her sleek nude body in a pose of intent concern, and waiting dutifulness.

"Do you require anything, Mistress?"

Liselle was contemplatively bored, hoping that a lover would come to sweep her away to romantic adventures.

"Did you bring a white charger for me, Maya, to take me away in your masculine strong arms?"

"I can kiss you if you wish, Mistress. You always enjoy my kisses. But I do not have a horse for you, or even masculine arms. Are not masculine arms attached to masculine smelly armpits?" She smiled.

"I have heard that it is so," Liselle smiled in return. She was well familiar with the sweet mustiness of Maya's armpits, and other places. Maya's body was as familiar to her as her own; perhaps more so, for Maya was unchanging, and she herself was now grown large and into supposed maturity.

She remembered the long ago, when gentle Maya would tend her as an infant, crooning lullabies and bathing her in warm water and fragrant oils. She never doubted that Maya loved her, or would ever fail to love her.

In this unchanging place, with its short days and constant summer, Maya belonged. Liselle herself was the one out of place. Everything was constant except her. Her attitudes and despondencies were as fickle as the gentle breezes in the mornings and afternoons.

Maya brought her grapes, and cheese, and wine. She sat up.

They ate together, looking out across the quiet inlet. What she would give to see a sail come round the bend!

Maya was watching her. "You go off into these daydreams, Liselle. Can you not enjoy having a perfect life?"

"Yes, I can enjoy it. I do enjoy it. But I keep waiting for something *next* to happen, and it never does."

"You must prepare yourself, Mistress. Your music needs more practice, and look at your garments! Why have you wrapped yourself in a bed sheet?"

Liselle laughed. "This is comfortable, Maya! And who are you to complain, anyway? You never wear *anything!* It's easy to condemn someone else's fashion neglect when one is naked all the time."

"I've grown so used to it." Maya looked down at herself; the boyish chest, the undecorated groin, absent even of hair of any kind. "What purpose have I to drape myself in garments? I have nothing to conceal, and even less to reveal!"

Liselle pulled Maya's diminutive body to her, turning her to let her head land in Liselle's lap. She ran her fingers through Maya's hair, another aspect of her changelessness.

"And this hair! Can't you even put a ribbon in it?"

"It's too short and fluffy. I have two hair styles; wet hair, and this."

Liselle let her hands continue moving over Maya's body, tracing her cheek, and sliding gently down along her chest. Hardly slowing at the hips, which were as sleek as the empty chest had been, she continued along Maya's thigh.

"Nothing to conceal! You have all of your Maya to conceal! But do not do so because I speak of it. That would deprive me of your beauty; your elegant, simple, utilitarian, delightful beauty." Liselle leaned down to kiss her.

Maya lay still, accepting and calm. The two were comfortable with each other, as it must be, for they had no choice in that.

On this handsome estate, in this lovely secluded and sheltered cove, on this plantation of orchards and grain fields, and this world of stark beauty, they were utterly alone.

Liselle looked out again at the distant rocky spit of land.

"And why should I practice my music, Maya? For whom should I prepare to entertain?"

"All I know is that he will come someday. I do not know which day it will be, and who could tell anyway, with all the days running together as they do? But he will come." Maya looked up at her. "And then you will have those masculine arms you dream of."

Liselle trembled gently. "You say that. But how do I know that it is true? How do *you* know that it is true?"

"Because that is why we are here. Why I am here, tending and preparing you. And why you are here, waiting and preparing. This is our life and our future."

"Like some fruit, ripening in a garden." Liselle said softly.

"Yes. Like some delicious, delectable, desirous fruit, growing to womanhood in tremulous anticipation."

"Tremulous …" Liselle responded.

"You gave a shiver when I said masculine arms would hold you. I felt it."

Liselle kissed her. "You aren't jealous, are you?"

Maya laughed; a merry, joyous sound that echoed in the open chamber. "No! I'm not capable of jealousy! I want you to sparkle and be swept off your feet as much as you do!"

Liselle looked at her. "But why?"

"Because I love you! And if you are made happy then I will be happy too!"

"Maybe he will love you too." Liselle suggested hopefully.

Maya smiled. "No. But we will see. In the meantime, we must see to your education and your talents! We do not want to disappoint your appointed suitor."

Liselle sighed. They had talked of these things before. Somehow they always seemed so distant and imaginary. Maya always spoke of it being true, though.

In the foyer, Maya hovered nearby as Liselle played the harpsichord, her graceful step and silent tread as familiar and comforting as a gentle breeze. Maya always moved with a feline grace and studied poise. It was as if every motion were choreographed, and that she had practiced for a hundred years just to learn how to walk with elegant, eye-pleasing motions. Just moving across the floor she seemed to be dancing in a dream.

Liselle let the music flow through her, echoing comfortingly from the pale walls. She thought about Maya, her dance of common walking, and her boundless energy. She had seen her sleep occasionally, but she never needed sleep. She never seemed to need anything.

Liselle had seen her go out into the grain fields in the full sun, her small body almost disappearing among the grain stalks, with nothing but her bright hair to offer her shade. She would stay out there for hours, cutting the grain, and preparing it for storage, dragging huge bundles back to the threshing sheds. Maya appeared to have no limits to strength, endurance, or patience. She was tireless, and ageless. She may also have been impervious to injury. The sharp edges and spiky leaves had never drawn so much as a drop of Maya's blood.

None of this seemed at all strange to Liselle. It was the world she had grown up in. She never knew her mother or father, and she had no siblings. There were no neighbors. There were no radio broadcasts or television programs. The only other people in existence spoke from ancient programs of entertainment or education.

These were the ones she emulated, learning to sing and to dance by watching them. Pretending to have scintillating conversations around a dinner table, the men watching the ladies in their gowns with the eyes of predators, and the ladies coyly glancing away.

Maya could not teach her these things. Perhaps she did not know them. She was without guile or deception of any kind, always answering questions with utter honesty, and more than sufficient detail.

Liselle had studied her, of course. For days and weeks she had followed her as she tirelessly went about the estate, doing in a week the work of fifty. She would walk down to the inlet and swim out to the deep center, where oysters had been seeded. Maya harvested the oysters in the ancient way, diving down to retrieve them with astonishing duration of breath, and tolerance for the colder water in the depths.

Maya was a living miracle. They had a small treasure chest filled with pearls from her exploits, and all they ever did with them was to sort them into sizes and colors.

Morning

Liselle should have wondered how Maya came by these remarkable abilities, but she never did.

Instead, she thought about the dresses and jewelry that Maya had said they would make from the pearls.

Maya had made bolts and bolts of soft but durable linen cloth, all through an arduous process that Liselle found tiresome just to consider. But their estate provided for all of their comforts, with Maya doing all the work to bring them to fruition.

Liselle accepted this too, of course.

Over the next few months, as Liselle prepared for her mysterious matriculation, Maya helped her to make beautiful gowns and other fine dresses and outfits. While Liselle played music, Maya tirelessly embroidered and brocaded decorations on them.

One typical day, Maya had helped her to arrange her hair. Liselle was wearing some white shorts and braided sandals with a deep v-necked brocaded blouse elaborated with a short, stiff collar.

They were seated on the dining balcony overlooking the inlet, eating a casual breakfast.

"Liselle …" Maya said, looking out at the water.

Liselle followed her gaze. Just coming around the bend was a beautiful sailboat, with full sails in the morning breeze.

Liselle stared. At the helm, wearing a gray jacket and white trousers, was a tall man with dark hair.

Maya stood up. "We have a guest." She started down to the terrace level.

Liselle was terrified. After so much anticipation, her heart was fluttering like a captured bird. Tremulously ... yes, tremulously she followed the naked nymph down the stairs, keeping a hand to the rail to compensate for the weakness of her legs.

"Sir David," Maya was saying, as the man walked slowly up to the terrace. "Welcome home!" She bowed from the waist with her hands at her side.

David stopped and kneeled in front of Maya. He pulled her to him and wrapped his arms around her.

"Maya! Beautiful Maya! I have missed you so!" He stood up with her in his arms, his hand casually supporting her naked posterior as he kissed her.

At length he set her down again. Maya turned calmly and looked at Liselle.

"Liselle, may I present Major David Uttridge, Prince Royal of the Highland Defenders, and Knight Regent of the Outer Realm. Sir David, this is Liselle, of the Dawn Planet, the most beautiful girl in the world."

"I am very pleased to meet you, Liselle. Please call me David." He took her hand and kissed it.

Liselle was almost at a complete loss for words. This was so overwhelming! "I am pleased to meet you, David," she said very softly.

Maya moved past them. "We were just having some breakfast, Sir David. Won't you join us?"

David, still holding Liselle's hand, turned her and escorted her back up the stairs.

Liselle was thankful she didn't have to say anything. She was absolutely astonished.

David seated her at the table once again, and then sat beside her. Maya brought more food and drink.

"You've been here before, Sir David?" Liselle asked at length.

"Yes. It has been a very long time. Maya and I are old friends."

Maya came and stood beside him. David smiled and put his arm on her flank, gently rubbing her skin. He kissed her once again.

Maya moved away once more.

"I had thought we were the only ones on … did you call it the Dawn Planet, Maya?"

Maya nodded. "Yes. You and I were the only ones here, until Sir David arrived."

"Arrived? Arrived from where, Sir David?" Liselle asked.

"Just David, please, Liselle," he responded. "My ship landed very early this morning. Then I launched the sloop and sailed in to make a quiet arrival."

"It was very impressive! But you have another ship big enough to haul a sailing ship in it? What kind of ship is that, a star ship?"

"A kind of star ship, yes. But let us not talk of that. I am here to spend a vacation, to get away from matters of state and of the intrigue that accompanies them. I want to spend time here, and get to know you."

"It sounds as though you already know me."

"Only a little. You came into my family's care as an orphan of war. Because the war was still going on, it was decided that you would be safer here than anywhere else."

"Then you know something of my family?" Liselle asked hopefully.

"No. Unfortunately, there is no record of any kind for you. Had there been, you would have already been reunited with your family. For that reason, you were in a manner of speaking, adopted into mine, although it is known that you are not related to us. We simply cared for you when you needed it. Or more specifically, Maya cared for you."

"Then who is Maya in your family?"

"Maya is a family servant. She is not related to us either, but her history is similar to yours. She also has no other family." He smiled at Maya, and she bowed her head.

"Now that we are alone, there's something I've been dying to ask." Liselle lay back comfortably as the boat slipped silently along.

"I would imagine that you have thousands and thousands of questions to ask." David smiled, knowing his charm would be working its magic on her.

"Tell me about Maya. You said she was a servant in your family. But she was also an orphan like me. How did she become a servant? Why my servant? Why is she ... Oh, I love her so, but she is different, isn't she?"

"I never thought you would ask me that!" David leaned back, turning down the rheostat on his smile. Perhaps a little truth would help him win closeness. It could also be dangerous.

"Maya *is* different. She is ... an improved version of a human being. She is stronger, more durable, smarter, and remarkably with all those attributes, incredibly patient."

"Long ago, when we discovered that machines could help us work, it became a goal of many researchers to create a race of mechanical people, robots, who would be able to work tirelessly and save us from much toil and potential harm."

"For various reasons, these efforts had mixed results. Some people did not, would not, accept the robots. Others tried to use them for anti-social purposes. Then there were problems with the fact that robots necessarily think differently from human beings."

"Eventually, a more advanced program was started. With what we knew about how we were made, and how robots could be made, an effort was initiated to redefine how a body, its muscles and bones, its hair and skin, teeth and eyes, basically everything that makes a human being the way it is, could be re-made. Essentially, it would be similar to a robot in its capacity to work and endure hardship, and to live for a very long time, but it would be born to a human mother just like a human child. It would grow and eat food, and learn, just like a human, but it would not become fully human, because that would make it something feared, and dangerous."

"Maya is a programmed person. She was designed, with a very durable skin, incredibly strong bones, and tireless muscles, but she was designed out of those things that were already in us to some degree. She is a biological robot."

"She was a servant in my house when I was a little boy. You know that she is older than you. She is also older than me, even though she looks like a child of ten or eleven years."

"But not only was she designed out of human material, she also had some human characteristics designed *out* of her. That may have been even more difficult. You know she is patient, but you may not know that it is almost impossible for her to lose patience. You know that she is gentle, but you may not know that she is conditioned to be gentle. She has the ability to sense your state of happiness, and what she feels from you is amplified in her. When you are happy, she is happier. When you are sad, she is concerned."

"And if I should kiss you, as I have been hoping I might be able to do, she would feel a thrill of joy."

"What, even though she is not here?" Liselle responded with astonishment.

"No, not in that case. She would have to witness it, or at least be much closer than she is right now. Still, it may explain some of her patience and kindness."

Liselle looked away. "Yes, it does explain that."

David realized that he had been maneuvered. He no longer had the momentum of a moment ago. This could well be a more challenging task than he had expected. His cheeks tightened in a practiced smile.

"And you have loved her, have you not?" He asked.

Liselle looked at him. He was so different. Tall, with broad shoulders and muscular arms. A confident demeanor that Maya never evinced. She could do anything. But she did it with quiet, unassuming skill. With a patience that came, perhaps, from knowing she would have the time for any task.

David was different. His confidence came from authority. Though he would not speak of it, she knew that he commanded men in his star cruiser. That perhaps he had been in battles, and in danger. He would not speak of it.

He wore this secrecy like a garment, to shield him from scrutiny, and let him hide his thoughts and purposes. His dark designs.

Unlike Maya. She of utter openness, and guileless innocence. Of patient explanations and helpful interest. She of love, and he of purpose.

What purpose?

"Yes. I have loved her. I had no choice but to love her, for she loved me."

"So then, if I loved you, … If I loved you, you would perhaps come to love me too?"

Again she studied him. His dark hair, framing his face, made him appear intent, and determined. Was she his purpose? The unconquered land he looked upon?

The question needed no answer. He was here because of her. And she was here because of him. No stronger chain of destiny had ever been made.

He had come to conquer her. And she had waited for him to come. Had she a choice? She had the choice of a plucked fruit, waiting to be consumed.

Could she love him then? Perhaps. He seemed patient enough. What else was she to do with her days?

For a moment, she considered avoiding him. She could go back to her studies. Play her music. Fashion a dress. Harvest grain and thresh it.

No, that would not happen. He was here. She was here. There was only one course this meeting could follow.

He smiled at her, a smile that had surely been programmed into his mannerisms the way Maya's patience had been installed in her.

Yes, she could love him. There was no way that she could not love him. All of her days she had spent waiting, waiting for someone to come for her. He had come.

"Can you love me?" Liselle asked him.

"I do not think I can avoid it." He smiled again.

Liselle softened her resistance. Whatever her life was to become, it was about to happen. She did not want to be late for it. She smiled back at him.

David spent the remainder of the day letting his practiced charm, and the inevitability of her surrender to it, work its magic.

Soon Liselle could think of no course of action that did not center around her erstwhile suitor. She was well smitten.

David took his time. He was practiced in this art, and there was no competition to rush his hand. Patience was a part of his charm as well.

And was it three days, or twelve meals, or a week of sunlight and starlight, songs and scented breezes? It could have been an afternoon, but it was longer than that.

It could have been a fortnight, but it was shorter than that. He held her, and they danced. He held her, and she let him.

He held her, and she surrendered to him.

Gently, oh so gently, he taught her the way of a man and a woman. They became lovers, inseparable and joyous. He entertained her, with florid descriptions of the wonders of many worlds, the sacred tedium of travel between the worlds, the loneliness that must possess each traveler.

She entertained him, performing her repertoire of compositions learned and invented. She sang for him, and they danced.

For ever the longest time, but each could tell that the day was approaching when it must end. She could feel it in his tension, in the slow sadness of his smile, his silent staring out over the restless water.

Even the endless and constantly beautiful days of the Dawn Planet must be counted down, and so it was.

David and Liselle lay together in naked casual comfort. His rough skin contrasted still with the soft perfection of hers. Maya had come in to their open chamber, where the billowing gauzy curtains caressed the breezes rather than held them still. There were no doors for this chamber, and no need for them.

Maya had brought fruit, and drink, and smiled at them, as if they were small children enjoying each other's warmth. She had known them both as children, though not at the same time. She watched them in silence, and then went silently away.

David awakened, and then he opened his eyes. He smiled yet again, as he looked at the beautiful girl who had accepted him. He had won her heart, and now must break it in departing.

It was a sweet sorrow for him as well. The responsibility of command, of leadership, held no attraction in comparison to this. But he was a creature of duty, as much as Maya was. He must go, regardless.

He gently stroked Liselle's flawless, perfect skin. He had never seen another girl or woman more beautiful than this. There had been many of great beauty; many as lovely, but none *more* beautiful.

Liselle opened her eyes and smiled in newfound rapture. Then, with further remembrance, her eyes fell.

"Today, then, will be the day?"

"Today must be the day, yes."

"But why? You have power. You have wealth. Why can't you stay?"

"I have duties that go with that power, and that wealth. Joyful interludes like this could never last for long, or ever be repeated, if I were not willing to stand in protection of them. I am resigned to my fate. But I will carry your memory with me, to wrap myself in, and to warm me in the cold watches to which I must go."

"And I will return to you. This I promise. I will return to you, and to Maya. You are very nearly all that I have left of family as well. Time must pass, but I will return."

Liselle wrapped herself around him then, to reinforce that memory, and to impress on her own memory the feel of him, and the smell of him. And the way he made her feel complete, of course.

During the morning, they spoke no more of it. At dinner it was like an unwelcome guest.

Toward evening, it could no longer be avoided.

"It has been such a short time, but I do not know how I can stand your being gone now." Liselle's eyes hinted at growing humidity.

"With each step, I will have to fight myself, to keep from turning back. But if I did, I could never leave. And yet, I *must* leave. Do you believe that I will return?"

"I do not know how I can deal with your being gone! I have never been so frustrated since I was a child!" Liselle paused to control herself. "How long will you be gone? Do you know?"

David looked down. "Unfortunately, I do know. It will be much too long. It would be a blessing if you could forget me."

Now she lost control of her tears. "How long?"

David swallowed. "Years, in all truth. Several years. They may be, I would expect, more difficult for you than for me. I will have my work, but I will not be able to forget you. Returning to you will be what carries me through the necessary journey."

"And what will carry me?"

"I will return."

Liselle said nothing more. She wept, with her face turned up.

David kissed her then, and stood. "Goodbye, Liselle. I must go."

"Yes," she said, "you must. Goodbye, Sir David."

He kissed her again, tasting the tears on her face, and turned away.

David stopped at the terrace edge, and looked back. He raised his arm in a half-salute.

Liselle lifted her hand, only halfway to her face, and let it fall again.

Just before the little sailing ship slipped out of view beyond the rocks, David waved again. Liselle waved back, with a large enough gesture that he could see it.

Then he was gone.

She spent the rest of the day in tears, and finally stumbled to her bed, forlorn.

In the morning, Liselle awoke when Maya climbed into bed with her, very cold from a morning swim. Liselle pulled her close to warm her.

"You were a servant in his house when he was young? What was he like then?"

"When I first met him, he was four years old. It was his birthday, and I was his birthday present, one of many. My duty was to bathe him, and at first he wasn't too excited about that. He came to like it better later on."

Liselle rubbed her eyes. She recalled being bathed by Maya, too. She had learned that eventually it led to discoveries about the nature of people and their secrets. "It's hard to picture him as a little boy."

"If you're familiar with some literature, he was a little like a spoiled brat. He wore fancy clothes, but he didn't respect them. He had everything a child could wish for, the best teachers, weapons-masters, physical training coaches. He was being groomed for leadership, even then. I came to be his relaxation from that, and his entertainment later on."

Liselle gently rubbed Maya's skin, which was slowly warming up. "Did you dress this way even then, Maya? I can't picture you being presented, as a present to a small boy without being wrapped up in some manner."

"They had me wear a simple one-piece, hexagonal open-weave garment, more air than silvery cloth, but decorated with the emblem of their house. It was their way of demonstrating that I was a servant. In his chambers and in his bed, though, I was always naked."

"Did that bother you, then? It doesn't seem to bother you now."

"Clothing is an affectation for which I have little use. I like having someone to care for. I don't need very much for myself."

Liselle looked a little startled. "When you were caring for him then, did he care for you too? Did he stop?"

"Stop caring for me? No, he still loves me, in his very distant fashion."

"He seemed affectionate and friendly to you, like an old friend. It didn't look as though he really loved you, unless he was being cool just for my benefit."

"Exactly! He knew he was going to be hurting you all too soon anyway. I don't think he wanted you to be too confused. Certainly he wouldn't want you to be upset with me, after he would have to be gone."

"But didn't you want to hold him and kiss him? Didn't it bother you to see me with him?"

Maya leaned closer, and kissed Liselle tenderly. "Kiss him like this? Hold him, like this?" She moved closer still, and embraced Liselle. "It doesn't matter who I kiss, or who I hold. If it makes you happy, it makes me even happier."

"That's what David said, about you. I don't really understand that."

"It's just the way I am. Being with you is a pleasure to me. Being closer to you is an even greater pleasure."

Somehow, the greater affection Maya was showing her made the days go back to something approaching normal, if normal there could be on a world of two people.

Life went on; On and on. The days continued, as days must. Liselle went back to her music. With time on her hands, she could make talent bend to her will, through perseverance alone.

Alone.

Late Morning

The time passed, in days of summery sunshine, nights of stars.
In days of dark, foreboding storm, when the rains would run rivulets across the stone, and the nights would roll thunder down its rocky road.

Cooler days that came in seasons, when Maya would stay close about the house, spinning yarns and making fabrics. And seasons that ran into other seasons, until the only thing on the Dawn planet that seemed to change was Liselle, growing into the fullness of womanhood.

One day, Liselle began noticing that Maya had begun looking up from time to time, as if some inner sense was telling her that something important might be impending.

Liselle did not mention it, but simply watched Maya to confirm her observation. Slowly a bit of anticipation built inside her as well.

She saw to her wardrobe, arranging the many outfits according to a wistful plan. Perhaps Sir David could stay longer. What would it take for him to never leave?

And when he came, it was as if he were expected. Liselle suppressed the urge to run to him like a schoolgirl.

David smiled. "Liselle! You are so beautiful! My memories have not been faithful to you."

"Sir David Uttridge, Prince Royal of the Highland Defenders, and Knight Regent of the Outer Realm, welcome to the Dawn Planet, and our humble home."

David bowed, to reach and kiss her hand. "My Lady."

"Indeed." She smiled.

They had dinner for three, with Maya joining them in conversation as well. Sir David inquired of the estate, and Maya gave a comprehensive report. She seemed pleased to be the steward and owner most of the time, of a wealthy home. It was her industry that made it so, so it was valid for her to feel pride.

"You do well, Maya. How often I have longed to be able to be here, to share in the many comforts and delights of this lovely place."

"And your work, Sir David. It goes well, I trust?" Liselle inquired.

"We maintain," he responded. "It is the best we can hope for. Stability is a valuable thing, in a complicated system such as ours."

Slowly, the distance closed, the aloof pretension evaporated. The charming David had returned, and Liselle's infatuation, banked for so many lonely nights, stirred into a glow once more.

Over wine, and candlelight, and talk of books and worlds that neither of them had walked, the familiarity returned. The comfort and delight in each other's presence returned.

And Liselle, having waited so long for the opportunity, once again melted into David's embrace, into his arms, and into the romantic relationship for which each had been longing.

David's first night of vacation brought him little rest.

But by noon of the next day, they were strolling together about the grounds. Liselle made plans for dinner from the plants that were in season, and queried David about things that might make it special.

More out of appreciation for her efforts than for the exotic foods, David allowed her to demonstrate her skills and knowledge. Liselle had practiced, and studied, in order to impress him in this manner. She did not know what other treats he might have waiting for him in other ports, but she wanted this visit to be remembered.

So it continued, day by day. Liselle had matured, and blossomed, in her womanhood, and in her command of the resources available here. She was no longer the star-struck girl she had been, not so long ago.

David complimented her, and recognized her effort, and her talent. "You have made my return so rewarding, Liselle. I was right to be constantly remembering and imagining our being together again."

And she realized. Had she been that girl again, she might have run off then, weeping.

She smiled. She had known nothing would change. She would change. She would learn new skills, new abilities, new charms, and they would all be welcomed, and praised, like the first drawings of a child at school.

And he would leave again.

As, eventually, he did.

Noon

Liselle fantasized about David's return. What would it take to make him stay?

How could she influence him?

Only one concept occurred to her, that his sense of honor would not allow him to abandon her again, if only she were with child. If she could become pregnant, he could not fail to upgrade their relationship. Perhaps he would find a way to take his new family with him on his ship.

Perhaps he could arrange to stay longer, or at worst, visit more frequently. It was worth the effort. After all, it was not as if he were reluctant to come to her bed.

But how could she control that biology? How to insure that she was fertile at the appropriate time? Liselle researched the matter as diligently as possible, given her resources.

And when David returned, she was ready.

He must have been puzzled at her ready acceptance of him, how she flew to his arms like the ingénue she had once been. She could not have enough of him.

David, of course, accepted the lavished attention with calm humor and delight. His visit was especially rewarding for its entire length. Even the usual sad parting seemed muted, as if he were only going away for a short trip and would return within a fortnight.

After his parting, Liselle evaluated her strategy. As far as she knew, the plan had every possibility of success, but no quickening happened inside her. It should have worked, but it didn't.

Liselle had a long time to think about what else she could do. A long time indeed.

Afternoon

David's next visit was similar to the previous one. Though he stepped gently and cautiously into the relationship once more, Liselle seemed to harbor no irritation for him.

Like old friends, they socialized and partied together, discussing books over wine, and adventure stories as they danced. Like familiar lovers, they came together once more, and embraced their time together as they embraced each other. The time was now. The present was the only gift that mattered.

They sailed, and walked, and played music together, and dined, and they made love under the stars like characters in fabled stories.

But when the time came for David to depart again, Liselle was still not pregnant.

Late Afternoon

Liselle was by now resigned to her fate. Her life would be as it was; as it had been. There would be no children, no family.

Only the too-infrequent visits of her lonely, star-traveling lover. The too-long stretches of time that separated those visits. This was her life, a life of leisure, of luxury, and of loneliness.

They danced, they dined, they made love. This was all it would ever be.

Liselle watched him go once more, and turned once more to dear, patient, unchanging Maya. Maya, who seemed to understand, though she still appeared to be a child.

She could have been Liselle's child. At least she would be there to love, and to be loved.

Evening

Liselle felt that this visit, when it came, would likely be the last. Just as long ago, when her awakening womanhood stirred inside her, like a sleeper moving under the covers before awakening, she could feel stirrings inside her once more. These feelings had a more ominous portent, though; as for the first time she considered her own mortality.

What choice had she? Each day was a more difficult struggle to maintain the supple vigor she desired, and knew that David would desire. Or that she hoped he would desire. This had become her life, after all. The all too infrequent visits, which lasted only long enough for her to fall once more in hopeless love with him, and then the creeping reality of his imminent departure once again. That sad punctuation had become her life, or her life that dismal chorus. It was the same sweet sadness, either way.

Nightfall

As before, David's hair was completely white. He stepped off the sloop onto the low walls of the dock and made his way up to the terrace, where Maya had been standing, watching.

Maya stood, not at attention or in display of servility, but simply stood to look at David as he came near. She had no need for pretense of any kind for this audience.

Major David Uttridge, Prince Royal of the Highland Defenders, and Knight Regent of the Outer Realm, paused to look closely at her. The intervening years had not changed her in any way. Her hair was still a bush of curls. Her skin was as smooth as a baby's, unmarked by sun or injury, or the wounds of wearying work. Her figure, stick-thin, belied a strength akin to demonic, but restrained by an even greater strength of patience and self-control.

She was a figure of utilitarian supple flexibility, like a woven whip. No useless ornamentation despoiled her stark functional purpose. She represented the culmination of centuries of design-work to create the perfect servant for any purpose that a jaded aristocracy, wealthy beyond the concept of dreaming, might want.

David thought, as always, that she was the most beautiful object of living art that he had ever seen.

"Is she gone then?"

Maya nodded. "Almost a year ago. I told her you would be coming. She asked me to give you a kiss for her."

David knelt down on both knees, and embraced her. Maya's nude, unchanging body was exactly as he remembered it from the first time he saw her as a little boy. She had been presented to him on the occasion of his fourth birthday, and her first duty had been to attend him in his baths. From that day to this, she had not changed in any way. He had grown up, and grown to love her, with a permanency that could not be dispelled.

She kissed him gently. "Liselle loved you very much."

David held her, and brought his head down to the soft curve of her shoulder. She could feel his tears.

"Come in and rest, Sir David. We'll go up in a little while."

He nodded, and rose, still holding her hand.

Maya led him into the bed chamber, where she gently began removing his clothes. This too, was exactly as it had been on the first day they met, so many years ago.

The bath was ready, and they stepped into it together. David turned her, and pulled her back up against his chest as they sat down. He rubbed her smooth skin softly.

Maya relaxed, letting him bathe her. This part was different, but it had happened many times before. For nearly all of his life, she had been his bath-maiden, and his long-time sleeping partner. They were very much at ease in each other's company, but she never had a need beyond his.

He washed her hair, gently cupping his hands to pour water on her head. He ran his hands through her hair, fluffing it and letting it spring out again in her accustomed puff of cushiony curls.

Maya then clambered behind him to wash his hair in a similar manner. "You won't be needing this, any more," she said of the thin white hair that dominated his masquerade. His natural dark coloring would reassert itself again after this material had been removed.

David relaxed, enjoying the ministrations, and the memories. As a child of four, he had no idea that Maya would ever have a purpose beyond bathing him, and playing with him in the bath or bed.

It had taken him six years to discover that boys and girls had other things they could do together when both were naked. Neither of them had been in a hurry to pretend to be a man and a woman together.

Their childhood exploration and exploitation of each other had been as innocent as any other games they had developed together.

They rinsed off, and toweled each other dry as well. David lingered over the smooth flesh, remembering and enjoying his longtime treasure. He sighed. The evening would serve well enough for rekindling their old relationship. Both were patient, and time would serve them for their patience. At the moment, there was another duty to perform.

David got dressed, in a more formal evening suit that seemed appropriate for the occasion. Maya was waiting, dressed as always in her undressed state. The heat and sun, the chill of night air did not disturb her. She took his hand and walked with him.

They walked on a path through the fields, and slowly climbed the rising ground that supported the orchards. Near a low, sturdy outbuilding, a small herd of goats stirred and scampered. Grasses and native brush took over the terrain as they slowly climbed up to a rocky crest.

For David, it had been an effort. He stopped at the top to look around. This was a beautiful place, looking out over the settled part of the land, although the rambling house could not be seen from this angle, and out to the distant sea, and the dim shape of the farther shore. The breeze played with dust at the top of the crest, twisting it into small dancers.

Maya was not tired or breathing hard. She seemed, as always, calm.

David saw the results of her work, the carved stone, erected at the very lip of the crest, sheltering below it a treasure chest for a remembered soul; sweet, innocent Liselle.

He thought about the effort Maya must have undergone, to shape the wood of Liselle's coffin, to fill it with soft fabrics and tiny mementos, and with the precious but empty shell of her dear companion, and his dear lover.

For him it would have been difficult, to see beyond the tears, and to make the awful journey, pulling a hand-cart, no doubt, up the rocky slope. He had not asked, and Maya would never mention it. Her strength and forbearance were one.

She had brought Liselle's body here, and immortalized it with a stone monument. He did not know if she had wept, or said words that could only have been an effort to comfort her own loneliness. Maya had not spoken of this either.

"My dear companion Liselle," David spoke softly as Maya watched him, "rest here in this lovely scenic place, and be remembered by those who have loved you. Let not your spirit be troubled, for you have lived a life of loving and being loved. You have been a part of our world and of our lives, and you will forever remain so. Goodbye, my love."

Maya watched him a moment longer, and then nodded. They paused to look around in quiet contemplation, as the breeze stirred across the mountaintop, and the sun prepared to go to its rest once more.

Several paces along the summit, another memorial stone stood sentinel, like the one over Liselle's grave. A bit farther along was another. In all, ten more memorials were lined across the crest of the craggy mountain, like the ancient heads of stone on Easter Island, forever looking out to a distant sea.

David stared along the row of monuments for a long, quiet interval, and then looked over at Maya.

"I'd like the next one to have black hair, long and lustrous, dark as the darkest night."

Maya nodded. "And answering to a name that starts with M, to follow the pattern already established."

David smiled. "Yes. You always pick a beautiful name. I've never had a complaint."

Maya watched his face for a moment, and then took his hand again. It was time to walk back down the mountain; time to go back home.

They lay together in the big bed. Night breezes and Maya's soft fingers drifted idly across the hair on David's chest.

"A raven-haired beauty," David mused.

"Tall and slender, perhaps given to art and landscape painting," Maya added.

"Perhaps." He sighed. "I will not be coming around for a while. You will be alone again."

"For close to twenty years," Maya responded, "I know. But I will not be alone. In the next few months, I will make myself pregnant with a human child, one with black hair. I will grow it inside me, and give birth to it, and nurture it, and teach it that someday its Prince will come. The child will be here, growing up, and growing beautiful, with raven tresses and long, slender limbs."

"Surely you do not think I would want your limbs to be longer, Maya? We both know that you are exquisitely beautiful just as you are."

"But you always want the next arrivals to be unlike me."

"Of course! I *already* love you!" David turned in the darkness to face her. "You are the girl I fell in love with forever."

"But that was an eternity ago."

David smiled and reached for her. Reached for the girl who had excited him the first time, and every time. The girl he would love forever, if forever would only be patient.

◆◆◆◆◆

Maya studied her body form. Even though the swelling was, by comparison, temporary, and no one had ever seen her like this, she considered it grotesque.

Her svelte, lissome shape was gravid with an inconveniently large parasite. She would be glad to get it out of her. Ordinarily, she moved about as if every motion, every step, brought her pleasure, because it did. Moving, breathing, walking, dancing, swimming, even standing still in the morning or evening as the breeze caressed her, taking inventory of her joy, all were symphonies of delight to her ultra-alert senses. This disfigurement disturbed her internal reverie of constant contemplation, the music of her inner thoughts.

But at this stage, her inner thoughts were echoed by a tiny shadow. She sensed the being inside her, the languid sensations of liquid motion and caresses. The child spoke to her of stretching and confinement, a hunger for hunger and a quest for thirst; a seeking of stimulation in a haven from stimulus.

Maya thought, as she tended to do under this circumstance, of her mother. She did not consider herself to be human, nor did she want to be human. But her mother had been human. It might have been even more inconvenient for her, for Maya understood that the gestation period for her own incubation had lasted eleven months.

The nature of her bones and skin necessitated a very long growing period, and she suspected that a portion of her extremely long lifespan also had something to do with it. Perhaps a form of longevity was achieved by freezing her development at a pre-pubescent stage, although it had taken her more than twenty-three years to slowly grow to that stage. That time was her education period, when she learned about flowers and animals, crops and harvesting, machines and their functions, cooking, cleaning, the making and mending of clothes, and other skills and arts required for a proper servant.

One might think her appearance was intended to be nondescript and unremarkable. It was. Not to be displeasing to the men of the upper class, but to be non-competitive with the patrician women. They could perhaps think of her as a daughter, or a daughter of someone else. What their men might think of her then became none of their concern.

Her upper body was indistinguishable from that of a ten-year old boy, for all the feminine allure her breasts afforded. She had no breasts. Even when lactating, to feed a child, her nipples did not swell in size like those of a human woman. The milk came from deeper inside her, and whatever opening had to appear, would also shrink away to insignificance after the weaning.

Below her waist, she was also nearly as non-sexual as could be imagined. Her hips were engineered like those of a boy. Her primary female sexual characteristic was virtually unnoticeable, even without hair to cover it. She had no hair down there. Other than on her head, she had no hair anywhere.

Internally, Maya was organized for durability, her four hearts spread out within the chest cavity, operating almost silently as a part of the heat-control system, as well as for oxygen and nourishment to her organs, both human and more-than-human. Under normal circumstances, on the outside she looked like an eleven-year old girl, halfway convinced to not even be female at all, but on the inside, she was timeless.

But these were not normal circumstances. Right now, she had an almost full term female child inside her, and in a few days, it would have to come out.

Her pubic region, if she had actually been eleven, and human, would not have permitted a normal birth. But that too had been engineered. Her bones, while extremely strong everywhere, had not fused together in a pubic synthesis, but merely latched together as part of an attachment mechanism. At the appropriate time, her bones would separate, and the relatively large child would simply plop out. It was a messy business, but she had gone through it a dozen times by now, and she knew exactly what to do.

Even more curious, of course, was how she had managed to get the child started in there in the first place. One might suspect that it had all occurred in the normal fashion. David had certainly contributed enough sperm to have fathered millions of offspring. She used none of them. The children she brought forth were not related to him. They were her great-grandnieces, the offspring of the dozens of women and genetic lineages who had contributed to her engineering.

All of this child's genetic material had been developed in a specially designed organ similar to a womb, but made for only this purpose. Maya could grow human babies; only girls as it turned out, but she could not reproduce her own kind. Like choosing a book from a library, she could wander the halls of her own internal chemistry, to select the characteristics desired for the next offspring. But nowhere in that library bank was there a shelf for the kind of creature that she herself was.

She had never given "her kind" a name. Maya did not think of herself as superior, or humans as inferior. She had between five and ten times the strength of an ordinary man, and her skin was the equivalent of bullet-proof. Her internal temperature mechanism was far superior to any human, with twice the separation of internal from external that humans have. In addition to having very slow heat transfer across and through her bulletproof skin, she couldn't get frostbite, and her skin wouldn't blister from the heat.

It was small wonder that she didn't feel naked, with skin such as this. But it was also remarkably sensitive. She could feel the slightest variations of temperature on her skin, but none of it caused her pain.

Her muscles had a different kind of energy supply too. She never grew tired. She could work all day out in the fields, and it felt no different to her than if she had lazed all day in a hammock. She seldom even compared herself to humans. She was what she was, and she couldn't change it, and they were what they were, and she couldn't change that either.

Maya liked humans. The little cuddly soft ones, the smooth and pleasantly-shaped females, with their alluring scents and ticklish nature, and the supposedly stronger males, with their need to conquer and control. Rather than display her superior strength, Maya could simply let herself be controlled, until the superior male grew tired.

Yes, it was almost time for this little black-haired beauty to make her appearance. Just a few more days, and Meridia would be here.

About the Author

Brian Hawthorne lives with his wife and two children in Maryland. One of those "quiet types" that you would never suspect.

As an avid reader and Science Fiction fan, he is following a prescription written by Dr. Isaac Asimov; that any reader, after long enough, will want to write.

To that end, he writes for his own entertainment, and that of his readers. With creative exuberance, he tells of relationships, ingenious conveniences, and stubborn human behaviors.

www.ingramcontent.com/pod-product-compliance
Lightning Source LLC
Chambersburg PA
CBHW021138310726

48971CB00002B/377